Alexander Fullerton has been a submarine officer, Russian interpreter, shipping agent, salesman and publisher. Through nearly all those periods, he has also been a writer – he has lived solely on his writing since 1967 and now has several bestsellers to his credit.

Praise for Alexander Fullerton:

'The research is unimpeachable and the scent of battle quite overpowering' *Sunday Times*

'The accuracy and flair of Forester at his best . . . carefully crafted, exciting and full of patiently assembled technical detail that never intrudes on a good narrative line' *Irish Times*

'The most meticulously researched war novels that I have ever read' Len Deighton

'You don't read a novel by Alexander Fullerton. You *live* it' *South Wales Echo*

SIXTY MINUTES FOR ST GEORGE

Alexander Fullerton

WARNER BOOKS

A *Warner* Book

First published in Great Britain in 1977
by Michael Joseph Ltd
Published in 1994 by Little, Brown and Company
This edition published by Warner Books in 1998

A CIP catalogue record for this book
is available from the British Library.

ISBN 0 7515 2366 6

Typeset by Hewer Text Ltd, Edinburgh
Printed and bound in Great Britain by
Mackays of Chatham PLC, Chatham, Kent

Warner Books
A Division of
Little, Brown and Company (UK)
Brettenham House
Lancaster Place
London WC2E 7EN

CONTENTS

AUTHOR'S NOTE

SIXTY MINUTES FOR ST GEORGE is a novel about the Dover Patrol in 1917–18.

The story is built around fictional ships and characters. But the general background – Dover itself, the ships, commanders and operations of the Patrol, and the assault on Zeebrugge – is as close a reflection of historical and technical fact as research has been able to make it.

PART ONE

Christmas to New Year: the Straits

CHAPTER 1

Out of the confusion of ice-cold wind and broken sea Nick Everard caught the yelled report, high and weather-cutting as a seagull's shriek: 'Clear anchor!' He glanced round towards the port fore corner of the bridge where until a moment ago his commanding officer, Lieutenant-Commander Wyatt, had been standing hunched, heavy-shouldered, muttering with impatience while the cable's rhythmic clanking had seemed to be going on and on with no end to it, the destroyer still tethered by her nose to the sand of Dunkirk Roads. The visual memory of an outbreak of gunfire to seaward, westward, six or eight minutes ago tugged at all of them – felt as if it pulled even at *Mackerel* herself – like the most powerful of magnets. Behind Nick now, Wyatt's voice was an explosion of relief: 'Half ahead together! Starboard ten!'

'Starboard ten, sir.' The coxswain, Bellamy, was at the wheel, a shorter, slimmer figure with Wyatt's bulk looming close to it. Bellamy was leaning slightly forward across the wheel's spokes and peering into the dimly-lit binnacle, waiting to be given a course to steer. The engine-room telegraphs double-clinked and the ship began to tremble as her turbines drove her forward, rudder swinging her to port across wind and sea. From the dark triangle of foc's'l at which Nick was looking down across a gull's-eye view of the for'ard four-inch gun he heard the thud of the anchor slamming home into its hawsepipe and Cockcroft's simultaneous shout telling the stoker at the capstan to 'vast heaving. Then a clatter of heavy metal, the cable party working fast to get the slips on the cable and lash them down. They had to finish and clear the foc's'l before the ship gathered much way seaward, because in a matter of minutes there could be green seas bursting on that steel deck and sweeping aft; to be still on it wouldn't be just uncomfortable, it would be almost suicidal, and Wyatt wasn't waiting on anyone's convenience, not with a Hun destroyer raid in progress. There'd be precisely one aim, Nick knew, in his commanding officer's mind, and it matched the urge in his own: to get *Mackerel* out there on the raider's line of retreat, cut them off from their Belgian bases.

Proceed vicinity No. 9 buoy, the signal had ordered. *Rendezvous with Moloch and Musician*. No. 9 buoy was about halfway out along the net barrage that zigzagged between the Goodwins and Gravelines. Admiral Sir Reginald Bacon's pride and joy, that net-line with its electrically-detonated mines; and he was hanging on to it, still patrolling over it with drifters, in spite of the Admiralty committee's view that it wasn't stopping any U-boats.

'What course, pilot?'

Pym, *Mackerel*'s navigator, told the captain, 'West-nor'-west to clear Snow Bank, sir, then north eighty west when Middle Dyck's abeam.'

'Midships.'

'Midships, sir.' The rate of turning slowed; wind

4

came like a whip now, cracking across the bridge. In the Dover straits in December, warmth was hardly a commodity one could look for. You set your teeth, tried not to think about it. Wyatt had told the coxswain, 'Meet her. Steer west-nor'-west.' Compass variation in this year 1917 was slightly more than thirteen degrees west, so their next course of north eighty degrees west would be a true one of just *south* of west. The wheel span through Chief Petty Officer Bellamy's practised hands, and Wyatt snapped – perhaps deciding that if the foc's'l hadn't been cleared by now a wetting might teach the cable party a lesson – 'Six-fifty revolutions!'

He'd make it seven hundred in a minute, when he'd allowed them some time to work her up. At her trials in 1915 *Mackerel* had clocked up thirty-six knots at seven-fifty revolutions per minute of her twin screws; but now, after two years of hard steaming, she'd be straining every nut and bolt to squeeze out thirty-three. Less, even, seeing that she was overdue for a bottom-scrape; and that wouldn't be enough to catch the modern thirty-four-knot German destroyers, whose object in their sneak raids was to create some havoc and get home fast, intact, avoiding action with anything like equal forces. To bring them to action you had to trap them, take them by surprise and then slam into them with everything you had – just as *Broke* and *Swift* had done so sensationally earlier in the year.

'Number One!'

'Sir?'

Nick reached for a handhold as he turned aft. She'd begun to pitch as well as roll, a jolting, corkscrew motion as she gathered speed with wind and sea buffeting her port bow. Wyatt shouted, 'Might be that swine Heinecke out there, eh?'

5

Chat – from Edward Wyatt?

There were a couple of dozen destroyer COs in the Dover Patrol under whom it would have been a pleasure to serve. Nick had had the rotten luck to fall in with this one. And his future – present, for that matter – lay in Wyatt's hands.

'Let's hope it is, sir.'

Captain Heinecke led a flotilla of outsize destroyers which Germany had been building for Argentina and taken over when the war had begun. Intelligence had reported that he was bringing them down from the Bight to base them on Zeebrugge. Not long ago he'd destroyed a Norwegian convoy; he'd also sunk a number of neutral merchantmen and allowed their crews very small chances of escape. On top of which he had the un-endearing habit of crowing about his successes in wireless broadcasts, shouting his own name in tones of Teutonic glee.

Wyatt thumped his gloved hands together. 'God, give me Herr Heinecke!'

Bellamy muttered, 'Amen to that, sir'; and Pym, the navigating lieutenant, chimed in with 'Make a nice Christmas present, I must say!'

Five days to Christmas. In Dover the shops had sprigs of holly in their windows. And *Mackerel*, due for a boiler-clean; might have the luck to be enjoying her three-day stand-off period on the 25th. On the other hand she might have finished it, and be back at sea.

But thinking of Hun raiders: although there'd been no surface attack since *Broke* and *Swift* had carved up that raiding flotilla back in April, an attack hadn't been unexpected in this present dark period. The new floodlit minefields barring the straits from Folkestone through the Varne to Gris Nez had begun to catch and

6

kill U-boats literally within hours of lighting up, and it was only logical to anticipate a reaction from the enemy. They needed to get their submarines through, rather than send them round the top of Scotland wasting time that could otherwise be spent sinking ships in the Atlantic; it would make sense to them now to send a surface force to break up the mob of drifters, trawlers, P-boats and 'oily wads' – old, pre-war destroyers, known also as 'thirty-knotters' – that was providing the illuminations.

Wyatt hadn't increased *Mackerel*'s revolutions beyond six-fifty. Most likely he'd be keeping her a knot or two below her best speed so as not to show flames at the funnel-tops and thus advertise her arrival on the scene. And on a night like this, black as a cow's insides, thirty knots felt fast enough – through the shoals, minefields, unlit and often explosive waters which it was the Dover Patrol's job to hold, use, deny to the enemy.

The Army in France and Belgium was manned, supplied and fed across this neck of water. Every single day transports, hospital ships, leave ships, supply convoys had to be escorted to and fro and the sea swept clear of mines ahead of them. The Front, the trench-line, met the sea at Nieuwpoort, a dozen miles east of Dunkirk, and looking shoreward now, eastward, you could see the sporadic outbursts of artillery fire, the intermittent burst and lingering glow of starshell. Closer still, on the bit of coast *Mackerel* was leaving, an air-raid was developing over Dunkirk.

Nick heard Cockcroft, the sub-lieutenant, arrive on the bridge and report to Wyatt.

'Foc's'l secured for sea, sir!' *Mackerel* plunged, a long slither before she lifted to the swell and began

7

her roll to starboard. There was more of it, as she left the slight shelter provided by the bulge of the Pas de Calais. But this was nothing: only a little icy spray lashed the bridge from time to time, just enough to remind them that tonight the straits were letting them off lightly. Wyatt had his glasses up; he was sweeping the black horizon on the starboard bow. Nick waited, wanting to speak to Cockcroft but making sure the skipper had nothing to say to him first.

Wyatt spoke, but his bark wasn't addressed to Cockcroft.

'Porter!'

'Sir?'

From the after end of the bridge Leading Signalman Porter pitched his voice above the turbines' high whine and the roar of wind. Wyatt bellowed, 'What's the challenge?'

'JE, sir!'

'Reply?'

'HK, sir!'

'Sure, are you?'

'Certain, sir!'

'How far to the Middle Dyck, pilot?'

Pym cleared his throat. 'Mile and a half – bit less, sir.'

'Why can't I see it, then?'

Charlie Pym had his glasses up too, and he'd been searching for the lightship for several minutes. It wasn't lit, of course; but at less than three thousand yards, with high-powered binoculars – and they'd all developed cats' eyes, by this stage . . .

Nick called Cockcroft. 'Sub – here a minute.'

Cockcroft came groping like some great insect along the bridge's starboard side, keeping both hands on the

8

rail to steady his long, awkward – uncoordinated might be the better word for it – frame as he negotiated the eight or nine feet of heaving, jolting platform. Still gripping the rail above the splinter-mattresses that were lashed to the outside of it, he craned like a bent flagpole over his first lieutenant.

'Yes?'

Wyatt interrupted: 'Number One!'

'Sir?'

'Have small-arms been issued?'

'About to have it done, sir.'

'*There!*' Pym had picked up the lightship's meagre silhouette. Nick told Cockcroft, 'Go down and have pistols, cutlasses and rifles passed out. You know the drill.'

It was an idea Wyatt had borrowed from Teddy Evans, late captain of the *Broke* and now Admiral Bacon's chief-of-staff. The object was to have weapons handy for repelling boarders if one's own ship were disabled, or – more hopefully – for boarding a maimed enemy. Loaded rifles with fixed bayonets at each gun, each pair of torpedo tubes and at the after searchlight; revolvers to all petty officers, and two spares – loaded – up here on the bridge. Cutlasses at various points around the upper deck where they could be snatched up quickly. Nick pushed his bunch of keys into the sub-lieutenant's fist. 'Here. And get a move on, eh?'

'Can I borrow Hatcher?'

Hatcher, invisible at the moment at the back of the bridge, was the wardroom steward. His action duty was to operate the Barr and Stroud transmitter by which Nick as gunnery control officer passed settings and orders to the guns.

'No. Take one of your after supply party. Then inspect

all quarters and tell 'em what's going on. D'you *know* what's going on?'

'Well, not quite encyclopaedically, to tell you the absolute truth, but—'

'There are Hun destroyers in the straits and we're steaming to join *Moloch* and *Musician* and head 'em off. Most likely they're having a crack at the lit minefield — but they'll have to come back again . . . Clear?'

'Topping!' Cockcroft had let go of the rail as he pocketed the keys. *Mackerel* leaned hard to port: he swayed, staggered, grabbed for a handhold and just made it. Nick added, 'Tell Mr Gladwish too, will you?'

'Aye aye!' Gladwish was the torpedo gunner. As Cockcroft began to grope towards the ladder – he was a useful and a pleasant fellow, despite his verbosity and a tendency to fall about – the coxswain was bringing *Mackerel* round to her new course. If the lightship was abeam already, Nick thought, it must have been a lot closer than two miles off when Pym spotted it. Well, this was about as dark a night as one could get . . . An odd thing about Cockcroft was that despite his instability, top-heaviness or whatever it was, he could run like a hare. As a midshipman up at Rosyth he'd won the squadron athletics championships over practically every distance. One could imagine him tumbling in a welter of his own tangled limbs each time he breasted the tape . . . Nick heard Wyatt calling down the voice-pipe to the chartroom, which was immediately below this bridge.

'Chartroom!'

'Chartroom, sir!' That was Midshipman William Grant's voice. Wyatt rather bullied young Grant, and he'd accused Nick recently of being too soft with him.

10

'He gets seasick, sir. Half the time we think he's being stupid he's just ill.'

Wyatt's eyebrows knitting as he scowled. 'What are you – his nanny?'

'Sir, I only—'

'He needs toughening-up, not babying! Good God, man, Nelson used to get seasick – and so do I and so do you!'

Nick had refrained from reminding Wyatt that Nelson, in his early days, had been undersized, a bit of a weakling, certainly not regarded as promising material. As to any toughening-up process, the sea would attend to that, and the rigorous day-and-night routines of the Patrol. Nineteen consecutive nights at sea, sometimes: in tin cockleshells and weather which in peacetime would have halted all cross-Channel traffic. They were all tough, hard as seaboots: they had to be, and if Midshipman Grant stayed with them long enough he'd soon become unrecognisable to the mother who *had*, probably, babied him.

'Grant – have there been no signals at all since we weighed?'

The wireless office was immediately abaft the chart-room, with a connecting hatch. It was the midshipman's job to receive whatever messages the telegraphists passed through to him, decode them or otherwise make sense of them in relation to the chart, and pass the results up the voicepipe to the bridge.

'Nothing at all, sir.'

'Are they *awake*, in there?'

'Oh, *yes*—'

Wyatt had straightened from the tube. Grant's voice – scratchy, still in the breaking process – died away, and Wyatt swore as he raised his binoculars again. It

11

was peculiar. If there were German surface forces in the straits, surely by now there'd have been a shout from someone? A sighting report, or a call for help? That gunfire half an hour ago – *someone* had been in action or under attack, but nobody had said a word. . . . Until someone did it was all guesswork, blind man's buff, and all the advantage of the blindness was with the enemy. The Germans knew that any ship they met would be hostile to them: *they* wouldn't waste time challenging . . . Nick, swaying to remain upright while *Mackerel* flung herself about, thought how much easier it must be for the intruder, the fox in the hen-run; and therefore how much more vital it was to see him first. He lifted his own glasses, adding his eyes to others already at work. Above the cloud-cap the last splinter of the old moon would be hanging; down here there was only the gleam of bow-wave spreading, curling away into a black shine streaked and laced with veins of duller white. Farther out the shine faded, the black became smudged, confused; only when a breaking wave gleamed, spread and faded again into the dark background could one tell roughly where the division came between sea and empty, salt-damp night. Empty – or *not* empty suddenly, as the glasses swung their overlapping circles over it: imagination stretched the nerves, and it was a mistake to look at any one spot too hard. The thing was to keep the glasses moving, let the eye drift on. *Mackerel* shuddered, quivering as she smashed her bow through the lifting seas, and mixed with the turbines' whine was the thrumming of her hull, the sound the sea drew from her like fingers on a string, and the rush of wind and throaty intake of the ventilators, the roar of the stokehold fans. Rattlings: sounds that had always been there and could never

12

be identified, and other sounds that could be – like the creaking of the whaler against the griping-spar in that port-side davit. Someone touched Nick's arm: 'Number One?'

Cockcroft . . .

'All done. They seem to be on their toes all right, and I've put the small-arms round.'

'Up here too?'

'Porter's stowed two pistols on the searchlight platform.'

'Good.' Nick put his glasses up again. 'You'd better go down, then.' From the Dyck lightship to No. 9 buoy was only about five miles. At thirty knots – ten minutes. Cockcroft's action station was aft, with the midships and stern guns. 'Yes, go on down.' He heard Charlie Pym call out, 'Float – Carley float with men on it – forty on the bow, sir, about two cables!'

'*Float?*' Wyatt whipping round. 'Where, for—'

'Ships starboard quarter, sir!' Porter was shouting from the searchlight platform. 'Near bow-on, sir – destroyers – *two* destroyers, sir!'

Wyatt shouted, 'Make the challenge!'

Nick reached Hatcher at the Barr and Stroud. 'All guns load, train starboard quarter and stand by.'

Wyatt rapped at the coxswain, as the shutter on the light began to clatter, 'Starboard fifteen!' He raised his voice: 'If we engage, Number One, it'll be to port.'

'Aye aye, sir.' Nick told Hatcher to follow the bearing of the enemy on his transmitter and set range two thousand yards. He went back to the port fore corner of the bridge, the torpedo sight there, and got Gladwish on the navyphone.

'Tubes stand by to port!'

Porter yelled, 'Ships are friendly, sir!'

'Very good.' Wyatt sounded disappointed. 'Ease to ten. Four hundred revolutions.' *Mackerel* rolled harder, with the sea on her beam now. Still turning . . . Wyatt had been taking her round in an almost full circle, starting from near west and turning through south and up to north-east in order finally to pass the strangers on a reciprocal course with guns and tubes all bearing. Nick said to the torpedo gunner, 'Better luck next time, Guns.' He hung up the navyphone. A lamp was flashing from the leader of the two destroyers; you could see their low black silhouette now without any need of glasses, and the froth of white around them. The lamp was saying, *Take station astern, course south-west, speed fifteen.* The leading signalman called it out word by word as it came in bright stabs of light and *Mackerel* still pivoted in a whitened pool of sea. Wyatt told the engine-room, 'Three-sixty revolutions.' Still keeping her under starboard helm, port rudder. 'Pilot, where'll that raft be now?'

'Port quarter, sir, probably about a thousand yards. I can't see it now, but—'

'Signalman. Make to Moloch, *Believe survivors on Carley float half mile south of me. Propose investigating before joining you.*'

Clatter of the lamp . . .

'Midships!'

Nick called down to the midshipman in the chartroom. 'Grant, we may be picking up some survivors in a minute. Go aft, warn the doctor, and make yourself useful.'

The 'doctor' was a young RNVR surgeon-probationer, a Scot named McAllister. If it hadn't been for the war he'd still have been a medical student in Edinburgh. Nick cranked the telephone to the after steering position.

'CPO Swan?'

'Sir?'

Swan, Chief Boatswain's Mate or more colloquially Chief Buffer, came after Bellamy, the coxswain, as the destroyer's second most senior rating.

'We may be picking up some chaps from a Carley float, Swan. Get your gear ready and stand by.'

'Aye aye, sir!'

'Better call away whaler's crew too. But have 'em just stand by the boat, don't turn it out yet.'

Moloch had replied, *Carry on. I will stay with you.*

Wyatt grunted. He said, 'Meet her, cox'n, and steer south.'

'Steer south, sir . . .' Bellamy dragged the wheel over, putting on opposite rudder to 'meet her', check her swing. Back again now, letting the spokes fly against the palms of his hands: 'Course south, sir!'

Nick asked his captain, 'D'you intend to use the whaler, sir?'

'Not unless I have to.' Wyatt, like Pym, was searching for the float. An object so low in the water would be hidden in the troughs except in the brief moments when a wave-top lifted it; it must have been sheer luck that Pym had spotted it in the first place. Wyatt said, 'We'll give 'em a lee and haul 'em up . . . *If* we find 'em.'

'Aye aye, sir.' It would be a quicker job, if it could be done without lowering a boat, and speed was a priority consideration. A lot of ships had been lost already in this way – in these straits – because they'd stopped to save lives and become sitting ducks for U-boats . . . Swan knew the score: down there on the iron deck abreast the funnels he'd be preparing scrambling nets, one each side; his men would be lashing the top-ropes of the nets to ship's-side cleats and leaving them rolled, ready to shove over.

'Sir – gunfire!'

Everyone on the bridge had seen it. Lighting the horizon and the underside of the cloudcap ten or twelve miles southward, where *Mackerel's* short black bow was pointing. Well, south-westward. Yellow-red: more of it now, in the same place exactly, and to the right a glow rising, tinting the horizon yellowish-orange: steady, hanging there quite motionless. A crackling sound: like the vibrations of a thin sheet of tin: and more sparks: all of it so distant, impersonal, but that crackling was gunfire.

Wyatt muttered, 'Ship burning . . . Pilot, come on, where's your Carley float?'

'May we use the searchlight, sir?'

'No!'

'*Moloch* signalling, sir!'

The other two destroyers were on *Mackerel's* starboard quarter, nosing after her, watching, keeping station there, white bow-waves easily visible to the naked eye even at this low speed. But they'd be feeling less patient now; Carley floats didn't rate highly when there were German destroyers making hay down there . . . Porter called out the signal: 'From *Moloch*, sir – *You have five minutes to complete your search and rescue.*'

More gun-flashes in the south-western distance. Remote, mysterious. Now to the left of them – nearer Cape Gris Nez than the Varne – a twin pair of sparks, one red and one white, showed tiny like small gems glimpsed then lost.

'U-boat signal, sir!'

'*Where?*'

Red and white Very lights meant *U-boat in sight*. Destroyers attacking the patrolling drifters and P-boats,

16

Nick surmised, and submarines breaking through simultaneously on the surface. The floodlighting brigade down there on the deep minefield had orders that if they were attacked by surface forces one green Very light would be the order to extinguish all illuminations; there'd been firing, so by now one could reckon the lights would have been put out, and while the attention of the patrol vessels was still occupied by the raiders, U-boats would be pushing through. Nick could only see one answer: that the Hun destroyers ought to have been stopped before they got that far west . . . Something dark lingered in the circle of his vision: he swung the glasses back, and there was the Carley float, tilting on a wave-crest.

'Float, sir, and men in it, fine on the starboard bow!'

He lowered his glasses, checked with the naked eye, narrowing his eyes against the stinging wind. He could see it easily.

'There, sir. Cable and a half off.'

'Slow together!'

'Slow together, sir!'

'Go down and get 'em up like lightning, Number One.'

'Aye aye, sir.' Nick was already at the top of the ladder. He went down it like a sack down a chute, his weight on his hands on the rails – just – and feet skimming the rungs; he hit the foc'sl deck almost as hard as if he'd jumped, and turning aft he rattled down the short flight of steel steps to the iron deck. Here, abreast the twenty-foot motorboat, two sailors crouched beside the long sausage of rolled scrambling-net.

'Chief Bosun's Mate?'

'Here, sir!'

17

Swan appeared ducking round the for'ard davit. A big man, bulkier still in his oilskin, very little except his eyes showing above the 'full set' of his black beard. An impressive, piratical figure of a man. Nick told him, 'Stand by this side. We're almost up to them. Five men, I think.'

'Aye aye, sir! Morgan – 'Oneycutt – starboard side 'ere!' *Mackerel* was losing way, and as she slowed her pitch and roll increased. The drone of her turbines fell away to nothing: you heard the sea now, and the wind, and the creaks and rattles.

'Get the net over.'

He was assuming as a matter of common sense that Wyatt would pick the men up over this starboard side. The raft had been on this bow when he'd spotted it, and since *Mackerel* had been pointing south with wind and sea from the south-west, this was the obvious way to do it. Nick watched the four sailors roll the bulky net over until gravity took charge and it thumped away over the side. Then he saw the Carley float.

'There they are!'

Twenty yards away: and four men, not five, he thought. One was up on his knees, waving both arms above his head, two others were visible in silhouette against the sea and the fourth was a lumpy extension of the float itself. It could even be a *dead* man: surely at the moment of rescue anyone who could move would be upright and taking notice? The float swung upwards on a rising sea, tilted over: the men's hands were grasping the rope beckets that ran round its circumference. Sinking in a trough now, as *Mackerel* soared upwards; with no way on, a lot of the movement was vertical, up and down, a motion to make itself felt in even the most hardened stomach. Nick asked Swan, pitching

18

his voice up above the ship-noises and the weather, 'Heaving line – near enough now?'

'Might be, sir ... 'Oneycutt, get it over 'em!' Nick saw Grant, the midshipman, coming for'ard with the doctor, and two men behind them carrying folded stretchers. *Mackerel* had stopped completely now. From the dark overhead loom of the bridge superstructure Wyatt shouted, 'What are you *waiting* for, down there?' Honeycutt had about a third of the heaving-line coiled in his right hand and the rest of it in his left: he swayed back, paused while the ship began to rise to another sea: then he swung upright, body straightening and right arm swinging over and the line flying out behind its weighted turk's-head knot; forty or fifty feet away it fell neatly across the Carley float and it was the man who was up on his knees who caught it. Everybody cheered. Swan growled out of his beard at Honeycutt, 'Pull 'em in steady now, don't go an' lose 'em.' Behind Nick, Midshipman Grant asked nervously, 'Shall I climb down the net and help them?' Wyatt bawled again, 'Get a *move* on, Number One!' Nick told the snotty, 'No.' He watched the float come rocking in towards the destroyer's side; if it hadn't been for the froth of white around it, one might not have seen it even at twenty feet. But there was less movement on it as it came under *Mackerel*'s lee. *Five* men. The one sprawled on his back wasn't a corpse, but he looked as if he might be wounded; two of the others were supporting him. Swan said, 'You – you, Nye – get down there an' grab a hold of 'em.' What Grant had offered to do: but it was work for a strong man, not a kid who, conscious of his captain's disapproval, contempt even, wanted to justify his existence. Nick remembered only too clearly his own midshipman days,

19

that dreary gunroom up in Scapa, the dog's life snotties had been forced to lead; he had sympathy for Grant, and a corresponding distaste for Wyatt's intolerance of him; but if that wounded man had to be dragged up the vertical and highly mobile ship's side it would take two powerful men on the net and probably two more up top here to do it; the rescue had to be completed and *Mackerel* got under way again quickly, immediately; there wasn't time for boosting the morale of a little midshipman who'd only get in the way. The first of the rescued men came up over the side, with Swan lugging at his arms; Nick asked him, 'Is one of you down there hurt?'

'Ah.' A pale, narrow face turned to nod at him. 'Skipper – got a leg chewed up.'

'What ship, and what happened?'

'Drifter *Lovely Mornin'*. Some murderin' bloody 'Un 's what 'appened, mate.' Swan had gone down on to the net to help Nye with the wounded skipper: another man came up over the side, and the top of a wave came with him, shooting straight up and then collapsing on the destroyer's deck like a suddenly up-turned bathful of ice. Honeycutt swore, as he helped a third man over; behind him the first two were assuring McAllister, the doctor, that they were right as rain. Honeycutt grumbled, 'That last 'un filled me seaboots!' Below him, out of sight and half in the actual sea, Swan gasped, 'Up with ye, lad. Us two'll see to this cove.' Nick shouted down to Swan, 'Don't bother with the float. Let it go.'

'Aye aye, sir . . .' Water surging up, frothing, leaping: Swan roaring 'Grab 'old that arm, Nye! *Grab* it, ye clumsy—' Another sea swept up, engulfing them, swirling to their shoulders before it drained away.

A hoarse voice panted, 'Easy, mates, easy does it . . .' That was the wounded skipper as they hauled him up the side. Behind Nick, McAllister was telling Grant, 'Take these four down to the wardroom, Mid. They can strip and dry off in blankets. I'll be along presently.'

'Right.'

'Off ye go then, gentlemen.' The doctor clapped the nearest of them on his shoulder. 'Find a tot of rum for ye, by and by.' Nick saw Swan and Nye come over the side, manoeuvring the wounded man between them. Grey hair and a surprised-looking, square-shaped face. Nick cupped his hands to his mouth and shouted up towards the bridge, 'All inboard, sir!' Wyatt didn't acknowledge it, but the telegraph bell clanged and in a moment the hum of the turbines and the suck of the ventilators began to rise through the weather sounds. Nick crouched beside the prostrate skipper while McAllister's assistants opened a stretcher on the deck and eased him on to it.

'Can you tell me anything about the ship that sank you?'

'Aye. Bloody 'Un. An' sod 'em all, I say!'

They had him on the stretcher. A stocky, solid man. Nick asked him, 'How many destroyers were there? And heading which way after they'd sunk you?'

'West. Varne, likely. Took a swipe at us wi'out 'ardly so much as slowin' up. Four o' the devils – you say destroyers now, but—' he coughed, and spat out salt water – 'more like cruisers. *Big* . . .' McAllister murmured, 'Fragment, was it . . . In one side an' out the other?' He was nosing at the injured leg. Nick said, straightening, 'Put him in my cabin. Tell Grant to clear my stuff out of the way.' He thought of a question he hadn't asked: 'Skipper, d'you know if they attacked any of the other drifters on the net patrol?'

'Wouldn't 'a seen no other. We're that spread out now, d'ye see.'

The net barrage was only thinly patrolled, now that so many craft were needed on the lit minefield. The Germans had happened on this one drifter, and used it for target-practice on their way by. Quite inconsequentially: the minefield patrol had almost certainly been their real target. And that was where they'd be now: where the shooting was.

'Well done, Swan. You and Nye 'd better shift into dry clothes.'

'Well stow the gear first, sir.'

On the bridge, Nick told Wyatt as much as he knew. *Mackerel* was following astern of *Musician* now, at something like fifteen knots. Wyatt dictated a signal down the voicepipe to the wireless office, addressing it to *Moloch* – whose captain was the senior officer in this division – and repeating it to Dover. It was plain enough that the destruction of the *Lovely Morning* had been shooting which had been seen from *Mackerel*'s bridge while she'd been weighing anchor; and it seemed probable that the four big German boats were Captain Heinecke's.

It looked as if it was indeed a concerted plan: south-westward, another pair of red and white Very lights had just floated up, hovered, vanished. A concerted plan that seemed at the moment to be working well – from the German's point of view. Smash up the minefield patrol: first to put the lights out, for immediate purposes, and in the longer term in the hope of discouraging its continuance. Meanwhile, have the U-boats waiting, ready to slip through – quite

22

likely in both directions, some on their way out to patrol in the Atlantic and some returning to Ostend and/or Zeebrugge and thence up the canals to their inland base at Bruges.

There'd been a plan to capture those ports, and Bruges. Admiral Bacon's 'Great Landing', which was to tie in with the Army's advance towards the Belgian coast. But the Army had bogged down, at Passchendaele, and by the middle of October the scheme had been abandoned, much to Bacon's disappointment.

Wyatt muttered, watching a new outbreak of firing – more like due west, that lot, which would mean from the section of patrolled minefield between the Varne and Folkestone – 'If he comes back *this* way—'

He'd broken off: the hope, the longing to get to grips with the 'Argentinian' flotilla was too intense to be put in words. Every destroyer captain in the Patrol prayed for a meeting with 'Herr Heinecke' . . . It was a fact. Nick realised, visualising the chart – which by this time he could just about have drawn free-hand from memory, with all its buoys and shoals and known minefields, with reasonable accuracy – it was a fact that if the Germans were west of the Varne now and took the direct route homeward to the Belgian coast, this was the way they'd come. *Mackerel*, following in line astern of the other two destroyers, had crossed the net between No. 9 buoy and the Dyck – West Dyck – lightship; there was comparatively deep water under them now. Ahead, *Musician*'s wake was a greyish track ending in a small bank of white under her stern; and *Moloch* was visible to the right of her – a smaller, less clearly defined but otherwise identical shape that changed quickly, lengthening as she altered course, hauling round to starboard. *Musician* began to follow; Wyatt was silent as he watched her through his binoculars and waited for the right moment to put *Mackerel*'s helm over.

'Port ten.' He turned her with her stem cutting into the inside edge of the curve of wake, in order to end up – as she would do, carried by her own momentum – in the centre of it. The new course seemed to be just about due west.

'Midships.'

'Midships, sir.' Bellamy let the wheel centre itself.

'Steady in his wake.'

No firing now. The straits were black, silent, empty of everything except these three destroyers. And at the same time one knew they were *not* empty, not by any means: there were literally dozens of ships down there, and four of them were Germans who'd have to retire eastward while the night was still thick enough to cover them. The German squadron, Nick told himself, could appear *there* – now – or *now*—

Cold . . . Under a duffel-coat and a reefer jacket he had a towel round his neck with its ends tucked inside a flannel shirt. But the wet had got in there, as it always did. The upper half of his body might have had a film of ice on it; a single trickle was extending down his left leg. When there was work to do, you could forget about the cold; but it never forgot *you*, it waited patiently until you had time to acknowledge it again. Wyatt's voice sounded hollow in the engine-room voicepipe: 'Three-forty revolutions.' Nick heard the reduction in speed repeated back. *Mackerel* had been getting too close up on her next ahead; it was possible that the corner of that turn had been cut.

'Bridge!'

Charlie Pym answered the voicepipe from the chartroom.

'Bridge.'

'Signal, sir.' Grant's voice. 'Flag Officer Dover to SO minefield patrol: *Have you anything to report?*'

Wyatt had heard it. He muttered, 'Might well ask.' Pym cleared his throat; 'Does seem to be rather a dearth of information, sir . . . I suppose SO patrol will be the duty monitor.'

The heavyweights of the Dover force, were the monitors. They were also the tortoises: five knots, and less than that into any kind of tide. Admiral Bacon used them for bombarding the enemy-held coast, as cover to inshore operations such as mine-net laying, and now apparently as searchlight platforms. Although a monitor with her twelve-inch guns should have been some deterrent to surface raiders, too. Chief Petty Officer Bellamy reported, 'Next ahead's altering to port, sir.'

Wyatt turned to look at her. He'd been staring out over the port beam, southwards where a moment ago yet another pair of red and white Very lights had soared, hung, disappeared. Bellamy was right: they were about to file round to port again. It was a toss-up for *Moloch*'s captain; he could only cover as much sea as possible, trust to luck. The enemy might be creeping up inshore of them: or he might already have got by: or be over on the Dover side.

'Follow him round, cox'n.'

'Aye aye, sir.'

'Bridge?'

Pym answered it. 'Yes, Mid?'

'SO patrol to Flag Officer, sir: *Drifter at No. 30 buoy reports trawler fired green Very light. Have had no reports about recent firing south-eastward and on bearing of Folkestone.*'

25

'That's all?'

'Yes, sir.'

Pym turned from the voicepipe. 'Did you hear, sir?'

Wyatt grunted. Then he struck the binnacle with his fist, and shouted, 'What the blazes is the *matter* with 'em? God help us, what's wireless *for*?'

'Red and white Very lights, sir, starboard bow!'

Porter, the Leading Signalman, had reported it. The lights dimmed, and vanished; and that was *another* U-boat through. In October – November figures hadn't appeared yet – about 290,000 tons of shipping had been sunk in the Atlantic and another 60,000 in the Channel: those soaring Very lights were like markers to German success in the form of Britain's slow strangulation. Pym was answering Wyatt: 'Some of the patrol vessels don't *have* wireless, do they, sir?'

Pym's smarmy manner with Wyatt could get on Nick's nerves, sometimes . . . Wyatt, in any case, seemed to have been irritated by the observation. He snapped, 'All the thirty-knotters have it, so've the P-boats. Some of the drifters – *most* of the trawlers—'

'Red and white Very's, sir!'

CPO Bellamy reported, 'Steady, sir, on south-west.'

Down-straits, in fact, parallel to the coastline, with Calais about three or four miles on the beam. Nick's suspicion that the night's work was amounting to a fairly thoroughgoing mess was hardening into certainty: and he guessed, from Wyatt's tone to Charlie Pym, that his captain was feeling the same way. He tried to reassure himself: he thought, *We* could *still run into them: they can't just vanish* . . .

Couldn't they?

On a night as dark as this – stealing away cautiously,

at half speed to show no tell-tale bow-waves, dead silent and alert and keeping a stringent lookout: making in fact a burglar's exit?

Herr Heinecke could be halfway home by now. Laughing himself sick.

CHAPTER 2

Dawn was silvering the sky to starboard and putting a polish on the sea as *Mackerel* followed *Musician* and *Moloch* north-eastward at ten knots between the Outer Ratel and East Dyck banks. Against that growing light Nick – leaning on the bridge rail while behind him at the binnacle Midshipman Grant performed the routine duties of an officer of the watch – could see quite clearly the low, black silhouette of the Belgian coast. From La Panne a searchlight poked at the sea like a nervous, probing finger; there'd be a monitor anchored inshore there, a nightly guardship with an attendant destroyer, watching and protecting with her guns the few miles of flat coast that lay immediately behind the Front – in case of a German landing or an attempt at one, a quick strike to turn the British Army's flank. The Huns guarded *their* backyard similarly, but with an armed trawler known to the destroyer men as 'Weary Willie'. Willie came out of Zeebrugge each evening at dusk and pottered the ten miles down-coast to drop his hook three miles off Middelkerke, on the eastern edge of the Nieuwpoort Bank; and just about now, as daylight arrived, he bumbled back again. Ostend would have been a more convenient base for him, but the Germans had abandoned Ostend as a port now, used it only as an entrance and exit for Bruges, the inland base to which like Zeebrugge it was linked by waterways and locks. Ostend had been too hard hit too often, for the Germans' liking, by Admiral Bacon's monitors.

That searchlight had been switched off. Dawn pressed up, streaked the sky: the line of the land was darkening, its edges hardening under a pinkish glow. Starshell still broke intermittently over Nieuwpoort's eastern perimeter. Nieuwpoort itself was only ruins now. Artillery fire was a steady mutter with occasional pauses and crescendos: like, Nick thought, a malfunctioning wireless receiver with erratic volume-control. Directly east, German ack-ack guns were providing a firework display over Ostend, engaging aircraft from naval squadrons which must either be attacking Ostend itself or returning over it from raids elsewhere. St Pol, the main RNAS airfield at Dunkirk, had been badly strafed a month or two ago by Hun bombers and there'd been some dispersal to other airfields and to RFC squadrons; in any case the naval fliers worked a great deal with the RFC. But they were still part of the Dover Patrol. Eight squadrons of fighters – Sopwith Camels had replaced Pups now – and four of Handley Pages and two of daylight bombers; plus odds and ends, including one huge American flying-boat that spent its time on anti-submarine patrols. That ack-ack fire might have been at RNAS fighters on their early-morning Zeppelin hunt: pilots got up there early after pre-dawn take-offs to intercept Zeppelins returning from attacks on London. Nick, watching the little sparks of fire puncturing a still half-dark sky over Belgium, wondered whether Johnny Vereker, who a few months back had bagged a Zeppelin of his own, was with his squadron or on leave again.

When Vereker was in Flanders, Nick and another of Johnny's friends, Tim Rogerson, had the use of his motor-car in Dover, and if *Mackerel* was going to be allowed her boiler-clean and three-day rest period now it might come in handy.

If on the other hand Johnny was on leave, he and his motor – a 1909 Swift, with a two-cylinder water-cooled engine – would be in London. He was going great guns with a girl who called herself Lucy L'Ecstase; she was a dancer in the musical show 'Bric-à-Brac', which was still showing to packed houses at the Palace Theatre.

If Johnny was *not* on leave – might one motor up to Town oneself, take the lovely Lucy out to supper?

Intrigued by the idea – it was already almost a decision – Nick turned from the rail to glance ahead and check that Grant was keeping *Mackerel* in her proper station; at the same moment, Wyatt stepped into the bridge from the port-side ladder.

Wyatt had been down in the chartroom, eating breakfast. But an intake of food and hot coffee hadn't helped his mood. Grant jumped back smartly from the binnacle: just in time, since if he hadn't Wyatt would have walked through him or over him, as if the boy was non-existent or at least invisible.

A quick, testy glance ahead . . .

'You're astern of station, Number One!'

Nick didn't agree, but there was no point disputing it. Wyatt glanced round, small eyes and bull-head swivelling like a rhino suspecting the presence of some enemy on its flank, towards Grant.

'Who has the ship? You or Grant?'

'I have, sir,' Nick said it quickly before the midshipman could answer. He reached the voicepipe: 'Engine-room!'

'Engine-room . . .'

'Two-seven-five revolutions.' He looked at *Musician*'s stern again. The revs would have to be reduced again pretty quickly, he realised, or they'd be running up on her quarterdeck. Wyatt said bitterly. 'More signals have been coming through. Looks as if we lost seven drifters and a trawler sunk, with two drifters and a P-boat damaged. Hardly a shot fired from our side, and not a single report that could've been any use to anyone.'

Nick frowned. Quite a few U-boats must have got through, too, while all that was going on. It was difficult to understand how such a shambles could have come about.

He called the engine-room: 'Two-six-oh revs.'

Wyatt muttered, turning his shoulder to the helmsman, 'And yet I come up here and find you practically laughing your head off.' His voice was low, but his eyes were vicious. 'Something to be *pleased* about?'

'It was – a personal thought, sir. Nothing connected with the Service.'

'Indeed.'

Wyatt's breath smelt of kippers. Mick glanced at *Musician*'s stern and at the compass-card, then back at the small, censorious eyes. Wyatt told him, 'Last night was a damned disgrace. A shame on every man-jack of us. The *Patrol*'s in disgrace – and the Patrol includes this ship. There's no making light of it and no time for *personal thoughts*, Everard. Understood?'

'Yes, sir.'

'I want this ship smartened up. In every way. You've been allowing things to slack off – and I shan't stand for it, d'you hear?'

If one hadn't been at Dartmouth and then in a

31

battleship for a few years, one wouldn't have believed a man could talk such hot air and rubbish. He nodded politely. 'I'm sorry, sir.'

He thought he knew what part of the trouble was. Wyatt had made himself a reputation in the Dardanelles campaign; first as a destroyer captain, and then, after his ship had been sunk under him, commanding a naval landing-party. He'd won himself a DSC leading a bayonet attack on some vital Turkish gun battery. It had left him – Nick thought – with the impression that he was Francis Drake reborn in the hour of his country's need.

He'd brought *Mackerel* down from Harwich about six months ago, at a time when M-class boats were taking over at Dover from the older L-class. This had been partly as a result of America coming into the war in April and, by accepting her share of Atlantic convoy escort work, releasing dozens of British destroyers for other duties. Wyatt's own first lieutenant had been invalided; he'd been going deaf, with flattened eardrums from the effects of gun-blast, and it had reached a stage where he couldn't hide it any longer. Nick, appointed in his place, had moved over from one of the departing L's, where for the previous twelve months he'd been navigator. He'd been delighted to get a No. 1's job so soon – particularly as he'd blotted his copybook somewhat, just after the rather startling success – for him personally – at Jutland.

Jutland had won him promotion to lieutenant. 'Noted for early promotion' had been the official phrase; and promotion had come within weeks. They'd also given him a Mention-in-Despatches, and its oak-leaf emblem was on his shoulder now. If he hadn't fouled things up just afterwards – a piffling business, no more than sending a man on leave when he'd no leave due to him, but it had raised the roof – they'd have awarded him a DSC. So someone at the Admiralty had confided to Nick's uncle, Hugh Everard, who'd also distinguished himself at Jutland and now had his own cruiser squadron in the Grand Fleet . . . But a week *before* Jutland Nick had been in the gunroom of a battleship: bored to distraction, and marked down as a failure, a useless sub-lieutenant who'd almost certainly never be promoted. Loathing just about everything about the Service: sure, by that time, that the Navy he'd dreamt of all through his childhood and adolescence – the Navy which Uncle Hugh had told him about with such pride – didn't exist, even if conceivably it had many years ago.

And then he found it, at Jutland.

But there was another navy too. He could see it in Wyatt's eyes, hear it in his tone of voice. It reminded him of that Scapa gunroom, and of Dartmouth. Pomposity: more than a hint of sadism: and so much *sham* . . .

But one could not afford to fall foul of Wyatt. To be here, second in command of a modern, quite powerful destroyer in what was the most active and hard-worked sector of naval operations – one had, finally, a sense of one's own worth and competence and of a job worth doing. And Wyatt, if he felt so inclined, could destroy all that with one 'adverse report'. He had, naturally, all his officers' Service documents; he knew that Nicholas Everard had been a flop at Dartmouth, a misery as a midshipman and – until Jutland – a dead loss as a sub-lieutenant. One really bad report could make Nick's performance at Jutland look like a flash in the pan, a circumstance where luck had shown him up in an entirely false light. He'd be back to where he'd started, then. A failure. Wyatt knew it, knew *he* knew it. He also knew that nothing was 'slack' in *Mackerel*, that she was run about as smartly as a destroyer in Dover Patrol conditions could be run.

He stumped heavily across the bridge. The wind was astern on this course and the funnel-smoke was acrid in one's eyes and nostrils. He muttered, 'You'd better go down to breakfast, Number One.'

McAllister had wrapped Skipper Barrie's leg like a limb of an Egyptian mummy. He'd also given him Nick's old woollen dressing-gown to wear. Well, someone had.

Barrie was a thickset man of about fifty, with grey hair, grey eyes and a square-shaped, weather-darkened face.

Nick leant against the doorway, inside the hanging curtain. Admiralty-issue, blue ... He nodded at the trussed-up leg. 'How's it feel? Doc done you any good?'

Barrie said, without smiling, 'I'd as soon have a vet to it.'

'What?'

'Pullin' *your* leg, lad ... This your cabin, eh?'

'Not really. According to the builders' plans it's spare, for cases of serious illness. I use it, but I'm supposed to bunk with the others in the wardroom.'

'First lieutenant, eh?'

'Right.' The skipper's thick eyebrows were black, not grey, and hooped; they gave him a permanently enquiring look. The other thing Nick had noticed was that when he spoke his lips hardly opened, hardly seemed to move at all.

'Where you from? Your home, I mean?'

'Yorkshire. West Riding . . . Are your men being looked after all right, skipper?'

'Look after 'emselves, my crew can . . . Yorkshire, eh?'

'Yes.' He didn't want to have to talk about Mullbergh, that great mausoleum of a house with its seven thousand acres of keepered shooting and stables for thirty or forty horses, and more gaunt, freezing-cold rooms than anyone had ever bothered to count. Sarah, Nick's young stepmother, had turned part of it into a hospital; Nick thought it might have been kinder to wounded soldiers to leave them in their Flanders trenches.

He was heir to Mullbergh, now that his elder brother David was dead. David had drowned at Jutland.

He asked Barrie, 'Where are *you* from?'

'Tynemouth. Know it?'

'Afraid not.'

'You'd be afraid, all right. We *eat* Yorkshiremen, up there.'

Nick stared at the deadpan, grey-stubbled face. He nodded. 'That explains why you have vets instead of doctors.'

Barrie chuckled. Nick pushed himself off the bulkhead. 'They given you any breakfast yet?' The grey head shook, briefly. He said, 'I'll see you get some.' He was hungry, suddenly, in need of his own. He added, 'I expect the captain'll be down to see you presently.'

'Oh, aye?' He hesitated: as if he'd been about to add something, and then changed his mind. He asked Nick, 'Know Teddy Evans, do you?'

'*Captain* Evans?'

'Aye, if ye like . . . He's a right 'un, is Teddy.'

Evans of the *Broke*, he was talking about. He added,

'No damn side to him. You could do with more like that one!'

'Yes.' Another Evans, perhaps, and one less Wyatt. But the drifter crews and trawlermen all liked Captain Evans. He always had a word for them, or a joke over the loud-hailer, and his cheery, forthright manner appealed to them. That and his alarming way of bringing a destroyer alongside a jetty at twenty-five knots while he himself made a show of lighting a cigarette before murmuring 'Full astern together . . .' Seamanship: and style . . . The skipper patted the dressing-gown: 'This your'n?'

'What?' Trying to look as if he hadn't noticed. 'You're welcome. Keep it to use in the hospital ship, if you like.'

'Hospital ship, be buggered!'

'Eh?'

'They'll not keep George Barrie laid up, lad!' Nick glanced at the wrapped-up leg: the skipper shook his head. 'I'll hop about, all right . . . Listen – you brought a ship back from Jutland, did you? Everard, is it?'

He nodded. Everyone in Dover knew everything about everyone else, of course. One tended to forget it.

'Yes. Destroyer – *Lanyard*. I had a lot of luck.'

'Know Snargate Street?'

The conversation seemed to leap about, somewhat. But of course he knew Snargate Street; you could hardly be in Dover for half an hour *without* knowing it, and he'd been based there for some eighteen months. He nodded, wondering what might come next.

'Know the Fishermen's Arms?'

'I know where it is.'

The only pub Nick and his friends used much

36

was called The First and Last. It was handy to the naval pier.

Barrie said, 'Back o' the Fishermen's, lad, there's a bit on its own – a bar hid away, you wouldn't see it if you didn't know to look. It's – well, you might say it's us drifter skippers' club.'

'Ah.'

The skipper stared at him. Then he nodded. 'Welcome, any time.'

'Very kind of you. Thanks.'

Barrie rubbed his jaw. 'What's breakfast, then?'

Odd cove . . . Nick went past the foot of the ladder and the door of Wyatt's cabin, and into the wardroom. Charlie Pym glanced up from his kippers, and nodded affably; Mr Watson, the commissioned engineer, raised a butter-knife in salute and muttered a 'good morning'; Percy Gladwish, the torpedo gunner, winked over a tilted coffee-cup.

Cockcroft was on the bridge. The system of bridge watch-keeping in the straits was that Wyatt and Pym took turns at sharing the navigational responsibility, while Nick and Cockcroft did the same for gunnery control. That was the general principle, when *Mackerel* wasn't closed-up for action.

Pym murmured smoothly, with a slight lift of the eyebrows, 'Hardly the most successful night in living memory, h'm?' He touched his lips delicately, fastidiously with his napkin. Nick called the steward as he sat down; then he glanced across the wardroom at the prone figure of McAllister, who was dozing in an upper bunk. The oval table was set centrally; there were bunks like shelves – with curtains that could be drawn across them – against the ship's sides.

'Doc!'

An eye opened, shut again. A hand came out of the blankets to ward off the light.

'God's teeth. What time is it?'

'Time you were up . . . Are the drifter's crew all fit, bar their skipper?'

'Fit as horses. Swan found 'em hammocks or somesuch.' The surgeon-probationer rolled over the other way, and yawned. 'The old man's wound's clean as a whistle too. Marvellous stuff, salt water.'

Gladwish was pouring himself more coffee. He asked Nick, 'Huns havin' it all their own way, weren't they?' A dark, quick-eyed man. He added, 'Made us look silly, I reckon.'

Nick told Hatcher, 'Kippers, please, and I'm in a hurry. Then take breakfast on a tray to Skipper Barrie in my cabin. No short rations, or he might bite you.'

He didn't want to spend too long down here, with Wyatt in his present mood. And he'd have to shave before he went up again. Gladwish seemed to read his mind: 'Skipper suckin' his teeth a bit, is he?'

Nick shrugged. 'He's not *happy*.' He looked at Watson, the engineer. 'All well in your department, Chief?'

Watson was three-quarters bald, and his skin had an engine-room pallor that would have taken years of sunshine to dispel. He mumbled with his mouth full, 'Couple o' weeks in dockyard 'ands, *then* we'd be all right.'

'We'll get our three days, if we're lucky.'

'But not right away, let's hope.' Pym wiped his lips again. 'I want to be on *terra firma*, this Christmas.'

Plump, always clean-looking, with carefully mani-cured fingernails and hair always smoothed down,

Pym was more like some shore-based admiral's flag-lieutenant than a Dover destroyer officer. Nick had no idea how he found time to groom himself so well – or why he bothered, for that matter. The fact that Wyatt always seemed well-disposed towards his navigator and surly with him, Nick Everard, who was his second in command, didn't exactly encourage friendship. He tried to ignore it and treat him equably, but the simple fact was that Pym was not Nick's sort of man. He didn't think much of him as a destroyer officer, either.

Wyatt . . . Nick remembered an interview in the captain's cabin a few days after he'd taken over as first lieutenant. Wyatt had told him, glowering, 'I'll be watching you, Everard. You won't let me down twice, I promise you!'

Incredible . . . He'd been asked down for a chat and a glass of gin!

'I'll do my best not to let you down at all, sir.'

Wyatt had pursed his lips, set down his empty glass and stared at the faintly-pink liquor still in Nick's as if suggesting it was time he drank up and left. He hadn't said another word. That was the whole interview: one drink, one threat.

Had he felt insulted, perhaps, at having so young an officer appointed as his first lieutenant? Possibly tried to have the appointment cancelled, and been obliged to take him?

Nick pushed his kipper plate aside, and buttered a triangle of toast. He'd been down here too long already.

If *Mackerel* was to have her stand-off and boiler-clean now, she'd be ordered to a buoy or to a jetty. Otherwise, she'd be sent alongside the duty oiler to replenish with fuel, and as likely as not straight out again as soon as her tanks were full.

Nick stood by the bridge rail to starboard and watched Dover's cliffs and castle loom up ahead. It was a grey, cold morning, but there was very little wind now. What there was of it was still in the south-west, raking the crests of low, close-ranked waves.

From here, the grass slopes around the castle looked like deep green velvet.

'What's the set, pilot?'

'Very little, sir. Eastward about one knot or less.'

At some stages of the tide, the tidal streams could make for problems. In a real wind it wasn't much of a harbour anyway; a night's 'rest' at a buoy in the destroyer anchorage, for instance, could mean a night of rolling twenty degrees each way. About as restful as being out on patrol. And in a south-westerly gale – well, the distance from the outer edge of the Admiralty breakwater to where the hospital ships berthed inside it was a hundred and fifty feet, but the ships still found solid sea, green sea, crashing down on their decks.

A light was flashing from the end of the naval pier in the main harbour. *Mackerel*'s pendants, her identification signal, already fluttered from the starboard yardarm; now her searchlight's louvred shutter clashed in acknowledgement of each word as it was received. Nick read it for himself: *Berth on west jetty, tidal harbour*.

Wyatt glanced at Pym. 'Boilers, then.' Pym said sourly, 'And back at sea for Christmas, no doubt.' Mick asked Wyatt, 'Close up sea-dutymen, sir?'

'Yes, please.'

Nick glanced over his shoulder. 'Pipe it, bosun's mate!'

40

Wyatt bent to the voicepipe: 'Three hundred revolutions.' As *Mackerel* got inside she'd have to spin round hard to port, under the stern of the western blockship, to enter the commercial harbour between the Admiralty and Prince of Wales' piers. At the top end, half a mile up from the harbour mouth, was the narrow entrance to the small – twelve-acre – tidal harbour. It was a basin for drifters and trawlers mostly, but destroyers in their stand-off periods also used it sometimes, and there was an old steel lighter there fitted as a workshop and with a dynamo that could provide power to ships whose fires were out.

Gladwish called up the voicepipe, 'Permission to withdraw charges?'

'Yes, please.' They were almost in harbour; no need to ask Wyatt's agreement to removing the firing-charges from the torpedo tubes. Nick saw Cockcroft waiting for orders, and Wyatt studiously ignoring him; he beckoned him to come over to his side.

'Probably port side to, Sub. But have springs ready both sides, just in case. And an anchor ready, of course.'

Cockcroft nodded, and went down. Chief Petty Officer Bellamy had the wheel now. Wyatt muttered to him, squinting across the compass-bowl, 'Steer two degrees to port.'

'Two degrees to port, aye aye, sir!'

Wind was over the port quarter on this course; *Mackerel* was hammering the small waves with the starboard side of her short, black stem, flinging up intermittent bursts of spray to infuriate Cockcroft's cable party as they veered the anchor to its slip, a-cockbill from the hawse. If Wyatt got himself into any sort of trouble when he was manoeuvring inside there, one slam of the blacksmith's hammer could knock the slip off and send the cable roaring out. Nick watched the entrance seeming to widen as the destroyer ploughed up into it; then, as she thrust in between the sunken blockships, it seemed to close in on her again. The blockships, at right-angles to the gap in the harbour wall, were two old Atlantic liners, both stripped, cut down to their main decks and fitted with iron supports for the torpedo netting to hang from. The one to starboard as *Mackerel* entered harbour was the former SS *Montrose*; aboard her a passenger by the name of Crippen had been arrested on a charge of murder. Wyatt straightened. 'Two hundred revolutions!'

'Two hundred—'

'Starboard fifteen!'

'Starboard fifteen, sir.' The coxswain span his wheel. 'Fifteen o' starboard wheel on, sir!'

'Stop port.'

'Stop port, sir!' Biddulph, bosun's mate acting as telegraphman, jerked the brass handle forward and back again. *Mackerel* began to fairly spin around, and Wyatt said, 'Slow starboard, one hundred revolutions. Slow ahead port. Midships the wheel.'

Cockcroft had his men fallen-in on the foc's'l, properly at ease. At the back of the bridge the searchlight began to clash again, as a new message came stuttering from the naval pier. Signalman Hughes scrawled it on a pad, at Porter's word-by-word dictation. Then he bawled it out:

'Signal from Captain (D), sir! *You may grant shore-leave this afternoon. Boiler-cleaning party will board you noon tomorrow.*'

A cheer floated up from the waist, the iron deck, where Swan's berthing party must either have picked up the dots and dashes for themselves or heard the signalman yell it. Shore-leave: it was a rare thing, and to be prized. Destroyers got three days like this between twenty-four days of sea duty, and ten days for docking and bottom-scraping once in four months. Between those periods there was no shore-leave at all.

'Port ten.'

'Port ten, sir . . .'

Rounding the end of the Prince of Wales pier. Transports lay on the other side of it. To port, coal hulks rocked at their buoys. Tomorrow would be the 22nd, and a boiler-clean took three whole days; so with luck, they *would* have Christmas Day in harbour.

CHAPTER 3

He heard Petty Officer Clover, the gunner's mate, reporting to Cockcroft that libertymen were ready for inspection, and Cockcroft's breezy 'Ah, right-oh then, GM!'

Cockcroft *should* have said 'Very good' – in a clipped, impersonal tone. Nick had told him a dozen times about this sort of thing – for his own sake, because Wyatt and others of that stamp had deep reverence for the customs and habits of the Service; Wyatt would have just about thrown him over the side if he'd heard that chirpy 'Right-oh'.

The sailors liked Cockcroft. They called him – amongst themselves – 'Cocky-Ollie'.

Wyatt was in London. He'd gone up on the evening of the day they'd docked, two days ago, and he wasn't due back until tomorrow afternoon, the 24th. In his absence, life had been quite enjoyable. Nick had had to forego the pleasure of going up himself, the idea of an evening's dalliance with Lucy L'Ecstase; with Wyatt away, this was where he had to be. And in any case, the luscious Lucy didn't lack admirers, and might not have been available at such short notice.

He'd passed the time pleasantly enough. That first

night alongside he'd appointed himself duty officer, and invited his friends over from the submarine basin. Tim Rogerson, who was first lieutenant of an E-class submarine; Harry Underhill, a CMB – coastal motor-boat – man; and Wally Bell, who commanded an ML, a motor launch. They'd come over to *Mackerel* for dinner, driving themselves round in Johnny Vereker's constantly backfiring little Swift; and on the second night – last night – Nick had dined with them aboard their depot-ship, the old *Arrogant*.

Meanwhile, *Mackerel*'s boilers were being cleaned – by dockyard stokers, to allow the ship's engine-room staff to enjoy their own rest-period – and Nick had been getting her smartened up and cleaned internally. The sailors had caught the Christmas spirit – which was an easier thing to do in Wyatt's absence – and the work had progressed rapidly and cheerfully. The only defaulters had been minor cases of drunken behaviour ashore, which Nick had dealt with swiftly and as leni-ently as regulations allowed, getting them disposed-of before Wyatt should return to make mountains out of molehills.

When they'd docked on the 21st, Wyatt had gone ashore at once to see Captain (D), who commanded this Sixth Flotilla. But he'd come back without having seen him. There'd been meetings going on, strange persons down from London. Bacon himself had been up at the Admiralty, and nobody would see anyone or tell anyone anything. There was an impression that far-reaching decisions were being taken behind locked doors.

Wyatt had told Nick, 'I'm not hanging about down here. I'll be at my club in Town. You can hold the fort, I suppose, while the ship's alongside?'

Nick strolled aft – wondering now, two days later,

what was going on. Dover was alive with rumours. Rogerson and the others over in *Arrogant* thought Admiral Bacon was about to get the order of the boot. The destruction of several U-boats, followed by so positive an enemy reaction against the lit minefield that was catching them, proved how right it had been to light it up. Bacon had fought against it, stone-walled the Admiralty committee's recommendations as long as he could – until, one story went, Sir John Jellicoe (Jellicoe was First Sea Lord now) had finally ordered him to implement the proposals. Bacon had argued that his nets were already barring the straits to U-boats, that none at all were getting through. Now it was plain he'd been wrong: on an issue so vital that the war could be won or lost on it.

Rogerson – long, lean, red-headed – had raised his glass. 'Here's to him, anyway. He's done a thundering good job here, *and* with only half enough ships to do it.' Nodding at Nick. '*Your* sort of ships, I mean.'

Wally Bell agreed. Burly, bearded, brown-eyed: until 1914 he'd been a law student at Cambridge. He put down his glass, leant back, stared up at the white-enamelled deckhead. *Arrogant* had been launched in 1896 as a third-class cruiser, and converted to a depot ship two years before the war. In 1914 they'd brought her round from Portsmouth under tow. Since there were now only two E-class submarines in Dover, she'd become mother-ship to the MLs and CMBs as well. Bell said, 'I doubt if people realise what a complex job the old fellow's got. What – four hundred ships? If you can *call* 'em ships . . . And airfields, dirigibles, shore guns—'

'Isn't it what admirals are for?'

Harry Underhill, the coastal motorboat man, was a former merchant navy mate with a master's ticket; no respecter of persons, he had a direct, incisive way of summing-up either individuals or problems. A craggy, rather savage-looking individual. He added, 'In any case – the higher they fly, eh?'

He was right, Nick thought. But one could still say 'Poor old devil . . .' Rogerson added, 'Even if he *doesn't* know how to use submarines. Frankly, I wonder why they bother to keep us here.'

The CMB people had the same complaint: that they weren't used enough. Whereas the destroyers were, beyond doubt, worked to the very limit. The lightly-built, high-speed motorboats were limited to fine-weather operations, that was the main restriction; they needed moonless nights, too, for their kind of work.

Nick, strolling aft, saw Cockcroft, followed by Petty Officer Clover, completing his inspection of the libertymen.

'Carry on please, Gunner's Mate.'

He'd got *that* right, anyway. He might as easily, if he'd been in true 'Cocky-Ollie' form, have said 'Well, have a spiffing time, you chaps . . .' No – not *quite* . . . Nick smiled to himself; he liked Cockcroft. Clover had saluted, a rigidly correct, Whale Island gunnery-school salute that practically broke his wrist: and now his heels crashed together as he whipped round to face the lines of smartly turned-out, wooden-faced sailors who were about to be turned loose on Dover.

'Libertymen – right – *turn*! Rear rank, quick – *march*!'

The *Mackerels* began to file down the gangway to the jetty. Nick stopped beside the guardrail, and Cockcroft joined him. Cockcroft said, stumbling slightly as he stopped, 'Fine body of men, what?'

47

He was grinning after them as the front rank tailed on behind the others. Nick said, 'See 'em in three or four hours' time, and *then* say that.'

'Well, dash it, I *would*!'

'Yes. As a matter of fact, so'd I.'

He might not have, though, when he'd been Cockcroft's age. Since then he'd seen, at Jutland, how sailors who were paid next to nothing, cooped up in miserably uncomfortable and overcrowded mess-decks, subjected to a continuous, often petty and sometimes ruthless discipline and looked down on as riff-raff by quite a large section of the general public, how men like this could fight like lions, face quite terrifying danger and privation, remain disciplined, cheer themselves hoarse to keep their own spirits up, and die like heroes. He'd seen them doing all those things, at Jutland; and the knowledge, the recognition of the sort of men one led, was one of the things that made the Navy bearable.

He stood with his hands resting on the guardrail, and watched the crowd of destroyer men moving off towards the town. He murmured, 'If anyone ever had a right to get drunk now and then – well, there they go.' Cockcroft was delighted: 'I say! D'you know that's *exactly* what I was thinking when I was inspecting them just now?'

Nick glanced at him sideways. He advised him drily, 'Just remember to keep it to yourself.'

He didn't know what to do, this evening. Except for himself and Cockcroft, all the officers were ashore; and the *Arrogant* lot, his personal friends, were all otherwise engaged.

Rogerson had gone up to London, driving himself there in Vereker's motor; he'd 'found' some petrol for it.

He'd wanted Nick to go with him, to dine at his parents' house in Mayfair, but it had been out of the question to leave the precincts of the port with Wyatt absent. He'd have liked to: Rogerson, who was probably his closest friend these days and perhaps the first real friend of his own age he'd ever had in the Navy, had an extremely pretty sister, Eleanor, who was a VAD at St Thomas' Hospital; she would have been there, this evening.

Wally Bell was at sea, on patrol in the Downs, and Underhill had taken his CMB over to Dunkirk.

It had been a good evening, last night in *Arrogant*. There'd been a fifth member of the party later on, an amusing RNVR friend of Rogerson's named Elkington, who was first lieutenant of *Bravo*, one of the old 'thirty-knotters'. She was so decrepit, Elkington had told him, that they all yelled 'Bravo!' whenever she covered a sea-mile without something falling off . . . Nick remembered snatches of the conversation round that after-dinner table: about Evans of the *Broke*, for instance – how, when in some emergency last year no boat had come inshore to take him off to his ship, he'd sprung into the harbour and swum back – fully uniformed, and in a stiff December blow. Wally Bell had laughed . . . 'A man of action, surely. But not – well, with all respect to him, not exactly brimming with the old grey-matter?'

Underhill had wagged a forefinger: 'Ah. *Certain* to reach the top, then.'

Nobody had argued: it was more of a truism than a joke. Rogerson cast a friendly glance at Nick: 'How does that place *you*, Nick? Are you going to the – er – top?'

Nick had taken the question seriously. 'Doubt if I'll stay on at all, when the war ends.' This had been the opening of a discussion about what any of them might do when the Navy no longer needed them, or they the Navy, and eventually it was agreed they'd team up and start a shipping line. Between them, they had the talents: Underhill from the Merchant Navy, Rogerson's rich family to provide the capital, Wally Bell with his knowledge of the Law, Elkington's father some kind of city merchant. Nick, they decided, could be chairman . . . 'After all, you'll be a blooming baronet by that time, won't you?' They laughed: 'Just what we need, a baronet!'

He'd told them he thought his father might live for ever. Sir John Everard had survived so many battles – from *somewhere* in France. He was still a brigadier, though – which was odd, when one thought of majors who'd become generals by this time. Nick never heard from him. He wondered sometimes what would happen when the fighting stopped; whether Sarah, having enjoyed several years of freedom from that cruel, overbearing bastard, would find it possible to submit to living with him again. In most ways, and for her sake, one hoped she wouldn't. And one saw, day after day, the hospital ships arriving, stretcher-cases flooding into the Marine Station here. One read the casualty lists and the 'Roll of Honour' in *The Times*. In the latter part of this year of 1917 nearly half a million men had died in the 'push' that had been swamped out at Passchendaele. And yet: he frowned, tried to clear the subject from his mind. There were enough things here to fill it with, and it was healthier not to allow that kind of speculation. The matter of inheritance had nothing to do with the way one's thoughts ran: but one was left all the same with a sense of guilt – as if it *did* have.

*　　*　　*

He found some paperwork to clear up; and listed the jobs that had to be seen to tomorrow. Then he and Cockcroft had a rather early supper – served in Hatcher's absence by Leading Steward Warburton, the captain's steward – and after it he decided to go ashore for a walk. He had a vague idea of strolling along the Marine Parade and having a nightcap in the First and Last, the tiny windowless pub quite near the admiral's house and offices. It had no windows because a hundred or two hundred years ago it had been a Revenue Officers' depot for seized contraband, and windows would have added to their security problems.

There was quite a swell running in the harbour; even in this inner basin its effects were noticeable. *Mackerel* was sawing up and down against the timber catamarans which held her off the wall; the gangway lurched with the ship's movements, its foot scraping to and fro across the stones. He stood on the jetty for a minute, watching it; Dover really was a rotten harbour, in anything like rough weather. And he wanted no accidents for Wyatt to come back to. He warned the sentry, 'I think it's likely to get worse, if anything. Make sure you keep the breasts and springs adjusted. If you've any worries on that score, let Sub-lieutenant Cockcroft know at once.'

'Aye aye, sir.'

He set off northwards, to cross the bridged gate of the Granville dock. This was drifter territory: the stubby little craft lay everywhere, singly and in pairs, or in trots of three and four. There'd be another sixty or seventy of them at sea, on barrage duty. From these in harbour, nets and other gear were spread on the jetties for repair and overhaul. And there was a smell of fish: which there should not be, because it was U-boats they were paid to look for nowadays, not plaice! He decided

51

he wouldn't, after all, go along the Marine Parade; he'd turn inland here, to Snargate Street, see if he could find the backroom bar that Skipper Barrie of the *Lovely Morning* had called his club. He was unlikely to be there, unfortunately; McAllister had predicted at least a week in hospital for him.

In hospital *yacht*, actually. There were three of them for naval casualties: Lord Tredegar's *Liberty*, Lord Dunraven's *Grainaigh* – with his lordship still in command of her – and Mr White's *Paulina*. To one of the three Skipper Barrie had been carted off when *Mackerel* had docked two days ago.

Rounding Granville dock, Nick turned left, with the larger Wellington basin now on his right. Following his nose out through Union Street brought him into Snargate Street; and a short way down to the right, where Fishmongers' Lane led off, stood the gaunt pile of the Fishermen's Arms. Sailors were loafing round it and leaning against its dirty walls. Some were already more than cheerful, while others looked as if they'd no money left and were plainly less so. There were no women on the outside, but Nick saw a few inside as he pushed his way into the crowd. A *Mackerel* stoker spotted him, and bawled something to shipmates at the back of the room; a leading seaman came shoving through the throng – grinning, swaying, spilling beer.

It was McKechnie, a Glaswegian who was coxswain of the whaler. Black-haired, ruddy-faced, blue-eyed.

'Will ye tak' a glass wi' me an' my mates, sir?'

'It's a kind suggestion. But I've come here to meet a friend.'

'Och, she'll not fret if ye tak' just *one* first, sir!'

The killick's friends were gathering round. Nick gave in. 'A half-pint, then. Thank you very much.'

McKechnie, fighting his way towards the bar, told a disapproving-looking Petty Officer, 'Yon's m' first lieutenant. Best officer i' the whole Patrol. I'll flatten the face o' any man as says he's not.' Nick, divided between gratification, surprise and embarrassment, heard a hoarse voice shout somewhere behind him, 'Good ol' Lanyard!'

For a moment, he didn't get it. Then it sank in. *Lanyard* had been the destroyer he'd served in at Jutland. Was that what they called him?

'Thanks. Thanks very much indeed.' The beer slopped over his hand as McKechnie thrust it at him. 'Here's a happy Christmas to you all.'

Cheers, applause. Men were trying to jostle their way through, but the *Mackerels* shouldered them away. Nick told them after a minute, 'Look, I do have to go and find this friend of mine . . . No, Carr, as it happens it's a he, not a she – that drifter skipper we picked up . . . Look, d'you mind if I buy – pay for a round of drinks? If I leave this with you?'

He was offering McKechnie a ten-bob note. The Leading Seaman pushed it back into his fist.

'No, sir. God bless you, but—'

'Oh, come on! Carr, *you* take it.'

'Well, sir—'

He fought his way through the throng and round the side of the bar. There was a low doorway: he went through it, and found himself in a stone-floored passage. A choice of doors confronted him, and a smell of cooking: fish . . . The driftermen's stock-in-trade: did they swap fish, perhaps, for their beer? Nick tried the nearest door, and he'd guessed right: the dozen or eighteen men inside could only be either trawlermen or drifter crew. Among them, one girl: he was staring

53

at her through the floating layers of pipe-smoke when a stocky figure reclining at her side turned and stared at *him*.

'So ye found me, lad!'

Skipper Barrie was in an armchair with his leg up on a barstool; a single crutch was propped beside him. He was lying back with his hand on a glass that rested on the raised thigh, and a pipe between his teeth. The girl, blonde and pretty, in her early twenties Nick thought, seemed to be looking after the old man like a nurse. Except she had a glass in her hand too.

'Come on in with ye, my friend!' Other faces, shading from mahogany-brown to brick-red and most of them unshaven, grinned at him ogrishly from out of the clouds of smoke, and the girl, right there in the centre of it all, made him think, *Beauty and the Beasts* . . . Well, she wasn't exactly a beauty, not as one would use the term elsewhere, and they weren't beasts, just sailormen. Barrie announced, in a voice like a shower of rusty scrap-iron, 'This is the feller pulled me out of the drink and had me use his cabin. Let me borrow his clothes, an' all!' Nick was shaking strong, horny hands left, right and centre; they were hands that had spent years grappling with wet nets in ice-cold seas. Barrie told him, 'Now here – meet Annabel. Annabel, she's – why she's my own little girl, my little darlin' . . .' She was smiling up at Nick, putting a hand to Skipper Barrie's mouth to check his flow of words: Nick hadn't found it easy to hear exactly what he'd said, in all this bedlam of talk and laughter – noise came not just from this bar but the other one as well, and men were singing in there now. Nick asked the skipper, 'Your daughter?' He had her hand in his: an incredibly small, soft hand, after the succession of vast fishermen's paws he'd been grasping: it was like holding something warm and living like a mouse or a bird, you didn't want to hold too tight and hurt any more than you wanted to release it and have it fly away. Laughter and guffaws shook the whole room: Barrie was shouting. 'Aye, my little daughter Annabel . . . Listen now, my precious: this is Lieutenant Everard, as won fame and glory at the Jutland battle. Hear me? Brung his destroyer home single-handed, half wrecked and full o' dead an' dyin' men: destroyer by the name o' *Lanyard*, ye'd 've read it in the newspapers . . .'

Nick would have liked to have shut him up, but the skipper was gathering an audience round him, shouting more loudly to gather others too. The girl hadn't said a word: her hand was still in Nick's, oddly enough, and she was smiling into his eyes as he stooped over her. Barrie roared, in the direction of the bar, 'Bring my friend a drink. What'll it be – rum?'

'No – beer, please.'

'Pint o' the horse here, Jack!'

'Aye aye!'

'Holdin' hands wi' him, are ye, darlin'?'

Applause, back-slapping. The girl – he'd let her have her hand back now – turned a chair round with her foot, and patted it. She had very wide-set, pale-blue eyes and a generous, full-lipped mouth; her nose had a slightly rounded end to it, a sort of blob that finished it off, but somehow it suited the rest of her face, the friendly and outgoing nature which he read in it. He didn't see the tot of rum someone poured into the tankard of beer on its way over to him.

'Here's health, a quick recovery, Skipper.' Funny

55

taste, that first mouthful had. He sat down beside the girl. 'You're from Tynemouth, then?'

'If you say so.' She laughed. Barrie leaned across her and hit Nick on his shoulder with a fist like a brick. 'She's a looker, eh?'

'Indeed she is.'

'Well, drink up!'

'How's the leg now?'

'*Told* ye I'd be hoppin' round!'

'Yes, you did.' He drank some more beer. Barrie shouted, 'You're our guest here. Private club, this is. Drink up, an' have another.' The girl asked him, 'What's your first name?'

'Nick. I think Annabel's a *lovely*—'

'Here's to us, Nick.' She raised her glass, and drank, with her eyes on his. Strangely enough, he wasn't in the least embarrassed; he felt he knew her and he knew he liked her, there was an immediate, ready-made *rapport* between them. She was rather, he thought, the 'Brickie' type: only less giggly. Her hand touched his where it rested on the arm of the wooden chair, between them; she leant closer, until her mouth almost touched his ear: she asked him, 'Do you like me?'

It was an extraordinary question to be asked, he thought, right out of the blue like that. But there wasn't any problem answering it. He nodded. 'Yes. Enormously!' Her eyes smiled, and her hand squeezed his; she was still leaning towards him and he wondered if she knew that she was showing rather a lot of bosom. Bosoms, plural. In a place like this, with only men – and not exactly a drawing-room lot, at that – around her . . . He realised that he felt protectively-inclined towards her. She asked him, 'D'you think I'm pretty?'

He nodded. 'Pretty's not the word. You're *lovely*!'

'You're not bad yourself.'

He was astonished. Not exactly embarrassed: no, not at all embarrassed, just surprised . . . She was so – unusual. How and where, he wondered, had Skipper Barrie brought her up, and where was her mother now? He'd emptied his tankard, and Barrie had gestured, pointing, and one of the others had taken it to the bar and brought it back full again. Barrie was telling the story, somewhat exaggerated, of *Lanyard* at Jutland. The girl had been handed a new drink too; Nick asked her what it was.

'Eh?'

Leaning close again, smiling with her lips apart. From behind her shoulder, Skipper Barrie winked at him. Nick repeated his question; she told him, 'Gin. Only to keep the cold out, mind. And that's my ration now, I never have no more than two.'

This beer wasn't bad, when you got used to it. But it was strong stuff; Nick felt quite light-headed. He told Barrie, shouting through the din and narrowing his eyes against the swirls of smoke, 'I can't stay long. Have to go back aboard, in a minute.' He told Annabel, 'Might take a walk first, to clear my head. This beer's got Lyddite or something in it.'

'What's Lyddite?' She'd glanced at some man behind him, then back at Nick. 'What's Lyddite, when it's at home?'

'Explosive. They make it down the coast there, at a place called Lydd.'

She leant forward, waited for him to lean halfway and meet her; she murmured, with her face so close it actually brushed his. 'I could walk with you, if you like.'

'That'd be splendid!'

'Truly? You'd like me to?'

'*Like*? Why, I'd—'

'I could show you where I live, if you'd like that too?' Skipper Barrie broke in: 'Now drink up there, Lieutenant, lad!'

'No more, thanks. Very kind of you, very kind indeed, but—'

Annabel told her father, 'He's taking me for a walk.'

Barrie stared at her, then at him. Stubble-faced, and eyes red-rimmed: one didn't have to guess how he was spending his convalescence. What of the girl, though, did she have to sit with him all the time? The skipper laughed suddenly, and slapped his thigh: 'So *that's* how it goes, when a man's laid up?' He pinched his daughter's ear-lobe; she squawked, slapping at his hand as she wrenched herself away. Nick assured him, 'Don't worry, I'll take great care of her.' That, for some reason, practically brought the house down; Nick realized they were all pretty well half-seas over. There was a glass – a small one – in his hand, in place of the empty tankard; how this one had got there he had no idea, he'd just looked down and there it was. He sniffed at the dark liquid in it: neat rum. Just that one sniff was enough to make his eyes water. Skipper Barrie boomed, 'Don't *smell* it, lad, *drink* it!' Nick would rather have poured it on the floor. He was already muzzy, and it was an effort to keep things in focus. All this smoke didn't help . . . He shook his head.

'Kind of you, but—'

The girl interrupted his refusal. For a moment he'd thought she was going to kiss him, her mouth came so close to his; she urged him, 'Do drink it down. He'll be upset if you don't. Fresh air'll see you right, and when we get to my room I'll make you some nice strong tea.'

Funny sort of evening. Particularly when one had only come ashore for a breath of air in the first place. He waved the little glass at Skipper Barrie: 'Happy Christmas!' The girl was watching him, and smiling at him as if she was pleased with him. He remembered – next morning, as he fought against a combination of physical sickness and mental shock – exactly how she'd looked at that moment; and then he'd been leaving with her: he could recall the vociferous farewells of Skipper Barrie and his mates, and then, on the way out through the other bar, Leading Seaman McKechnie and *his* friends greeting them with cheers and jokes about the differences between 'he-friends' and 'she-friends'; it was all extremely friendly and Annabel was laughing, enjoying it, clinging to his arm, but the whole feel of it was vague, clouded with smoke and the taste of rum and the roar of voices in the low-ceilinged room. He remembered telling McKechnie that Miss Barrie was the daughter of the skipper they'd rescued, and McKechnie's look of surprise; at about that point, when they were halfway across the room with the crowd of sailors opening to let them through, the town's air-raid alarm started up. A familiar sound, by this time, for the shoreside people: four short blasts and one long one, over and over again, from the siren on the Electricity Works; McKechnie told Nick, swaying like a palm-tree in a tornado and with a pint glass clutched in his tattooed fist. 'Ye'll likely lose her, sir. She'll be doon the *women's* shelter!'

The biggest air-raid shelters in the town were here in Snargate Street; the caves at the back of the old Oil Mills had been equipped with benches to hold thousands of people in complete safety from the Gotha bombers, with hundreds of feet of solid chalk above their heads. But it was true: they'd segregated the sexes, there were caves for men and caves for women. A very *proper* place, was Dover, under the eagle eyes of Lady Bacon and Mrs Bickford, wife of the general up at the Castle.

Annabel told McKechnie. 'You're mistaken. We're off to the Girls' Patriotic Club.'

Bellows of amusement . . . Nobody was taking any notice still of that siren as its last scream died away. The Girls' Patriotic Club was run by a Miss Bradley, and its club-room was over Bernards the grocers; its purpose – heartily approved of by Lady Bacon and Mrs Bickford – was to keep young ladies off the streets. Off Snargate Street in particular. Nick had had enough of the crowd and the din, he felt a strong need of air; he cut into the chat with 'We're going to take a walk along the Marine Parade.' He nodded to McKechnie: 'Goodnight.'

'If she's going for any walk – it'll be with *me* she'll go.'

A large man: trawlerman, by the look of him. In a heavy blue serge suit and a seaman's roll-neck sweater. He stood in front of them, between them and the door, and stared at Annabel.

'With *me*, Annie. Eh?'

Nick stepped towards him. The man put one enormous hand out, like a policeman stopping traffic, but he didn't take his eyes off the girl.

'Well, then?'

McKechnie hit him. Annabel screamed. Everyone was shouting, closing in. The big man raised both his fists together and crashed them down like a sledge-hammer on McKechnie's head; at the same time another of the

Mackerels smashed a bottle against the challenger's ear. McKechnie had staggered from that blow, recovered as he swayed forward, stumbling; the trawlerman had clamped a hand on his throat and with the other he was belting him in the stomach. There was fighting all over the room now, trawlermen or driftermen against sailors. A *Mackerel* stoker, O'Leary, had climbed up on the bar; now he jumped, landing on the big man's shoulders and bringing him crashing down; Mick saw a sailor's boot connect against the trawlerman's jaw, and he thought it was probably McKechnie's. All Nick was trying to do was protect Annabel from flying fists: McKechnie yelled in his ear, 'Ye'd best be awa', sir, while the goin's good!'

'Come on!' Annabel tugged at him. Nick agreed: there'd be redcaps here at any minute. Behind the Leading Seaman he saw a bottle raised – a big one, full of liquor – he shouted, and sprang forward: McKechnie swung round, the other man side-stepped and brought the bottle down; Nick saw it coming and he tried to dodge . . .

'There, my pet!'

Something cool was swabbing his forehead. Sarah's voice was gentle, loving, soothing in his ear and brain . . . Sarah?

Sarah was up at Mullbergh. He, Nick, was in Dover, wasn't he? What was—

He opened his eyes. Annabel smiled at him, her full lips only inches above his face, a damp flannel in her hand. They were on a bed: there was a cracked ceiling overhead, brown-and-grey patterned wallpaper. Grey morning light filtered through a dirty dormer window.

Morning light!

He felt his insides convulse with the shock of it. *Morning.* And he was still ashore. Then he remembered: Wyatt was still in London. He thought, *Thank God for small mercies.* He made a slight effort to sit up: Annabel gently pushed him back.

'Easy, easy now, my darling,' She rested on him. Bare, soft arms moved round his neck. Her breasts — full, heavy — pressed their nipples against his chest. He moved a hand down: she was naked, and so was he.

It had to be a dream. He shut his eyes. He'd been dreaming of — Sarah, his stepmother? Annabel asked him, 'Tell me something, as a favour?' He opened his eyes and found her pale-blue ones smiling into his; she asked him, 'Why d'you call me "Sarah" all night long? Who's this Sarah you're in love with?'

'Love?' It hurt, to move his head: he winced. 'No — no, I'm *not*, I . . .'

His own stepmother: his father's wife: how could one — even in a dream . . . It seemed the most dreadful thing of all. He tried to shake his head again, and felt the same sharp stab of pain. He told himself, *My skull's cracked, I'm deranged!*

'Liar. You *must* be.' She kissed him slowly, lingeringly. 'It doesn't matter. Whoever she is, she's a lucky girl.'

Impossible to *think* about, let alone discuss . . . 'How did I get here?'

'Two of your sailors brought you. They wanted to take you to the ship, but I said no, not in *that* state, I'd look after you myself. So—'

'I must get back on board!'

'Now?'

'Yes — my God, I—'

'Pity.' She smiled, stroking him. 'I thought, when

you woke up –' She shook her head. 'Never mind. Shall I see you again?'

He thought, *Sarah* . . . There were more immediate anxieties, but that was the deepest shock in his mind. Annabel was helping him to sit up. He told her, 'Of course. Yes, of *course* we'll –'

'Do you still like me?'

Standing beside the bed, looking down at him. She put her hands up, linking them behind her head. Then she bounced a little on her toes, and laughed at his eyes on her bouncing breasts. 'Well?'

'You're beautiful.'

'Really think so?'

He got off the bed. She touched him: 'Next time, you'll be well.'

Memory came in spasms. Underneath glimpses of last night, the constant thought of Sarah, his father's wife. Young enough to be his father's daughter, certainly, but still – to think of her – or *have thought* of her – like that . . . He told himself, *I don't: it was a dream. That bang on the head: and obviously they put something in the beer* . . . Sarah: distantly he heard her quiet, pleading tone between his father's angry, drunken shouting echoing through Mullbergh's cold stone corridors: waking, hearing that, feeling the racing of one's own heart, the misery for *her* sake, the loathing . . . Then the night she'd screamed: he'd rushed down, found her bedroom door with its top half smashed in and his father in a rage which faded to a sort of baffled shame when he saw Nick: and Sarah's tear-streaked face, her voice telling him 'It's all right now, Nick. Truly. Go on back to bed.'

Cockcroft said, 'Lucky the captain's up in London. But there's bound to be the most frightful fuss, I'm afraid. The Military Police brought about a dozen of our chaps aboard, and they know the names of others who were in it, *and* that there was an officer involved!'

'God . . .' His head was spinning. 'Look here, I've got to sleep, I'm no good like this. If I can get a couple of hours with my head down before—'

'If you'd tell me what's to be done? Or perhaps it's Pym you ought to tell. But—'

'Mr Gladwish wants a signal made about changing one of his torpedoes. If the ready-use lockers are dry – you know we scraped and painted them out – the GM can see to refilling them. But the important thing is stores. I made a list – or started one . . . But see the cox'n, he'll know what—'

'All right.'

'Stores is the important thing. In case we finish the boiler-clean tonight—'

'They say they'll be done before that. They did a night shift – came crashing on board at midnight, and another lot took over about six—'

'*What!* I mean – *why*?'

'Heaven knows. What with one thing and another it's been a fairly hellish twelve hours, I can tell you. You realize I've had to put the defaulters in *your* report?' Cockcroft's long arms flapped hopelessly. 'Anyway, you sleep. I'll see the cox'n.'

'And fresh water. Ask the Chief Stoker—'

'Right. You turn in now. If anyone asks I'll say you've got a touch of 'flu. I'll give you a shake at noon – that do?'

It wasn't Cockcroft, though. It was Wyatt.

'Everard!'

64

There was a constant hammering and clattering overhead. Wyatt's small, furious eyes bored at him across the little cabin. 'Cockcroft informs me that you have influenza. Is that the case?'

Bulky, aggressive, filling the cabin doorway . . . Nick, even before he was fully out of sleep, out of a nightmare in which he was frantically trying to find Sarah while Mullbergh closed in on him, stone walls squeezing in on either hand and the ends of passages turning into dead-ends so that you turned and tried to run the other way with the narrowing passages trapping your feet, holding your ankles and cold terror everywhere – terror for Sarah more than for one's own predicament: the dream's content faded into confusion and in its place he had the certainty that Wyatt knew at least something of last night's riot.

'Well, is it?'

'All Cockcroft knows is I've been sick, sir. He may have assumed it was 'flu.'

'In fact it was – what?'

Nick slid off his bunk.

'I'll be all right now, sir.'

'Oh? Do you *really* think so? That you'll be *all right*?' Nick waited. He thought there was an element of satisfaction as well as anger in his captain's attitude. 'Listen to me, Everard. You remain in this ship and as my first lieutenant for the time being for one reason only – that I'm unable to replace you before we sail. I've tried to, and it's impossible; they've larger matters to attend to, in present circumstances . . .' A hand rose, pointing: 'You *were* in some bar-room last night, brawling over a tart's favours?'

'No, sir!'

'The Provost Marshal's made it up?'

65

'He's been misinformed, sir, by the sound of it. I went to meet Skipper Barrie – the man we picked up from the Carley float – at his invitation. He had his daughter with him. I was in her company when a man – a trawlerman, I think – accosted her. Then—'

'All right, Everard. That'll do.'

Nick stared at him. Wyatt said, 'I don't wish to hear about it.' He turned, hands clasped behind his back, stared out through the starboard-side scuttle. 'It's possible you were too drunk to know what was—' He shrugged, without finishing the sentence. Nick saw light reflected from the harbour's surface flashing in his narrowed eyes. '*Possible*. The matter will be dealt with – ashore – on our return. I should say a court-martial is the likely outcome. In my view it is an extremely squalid business, and I want no part in it . . . What I have to say to you is simply this: that we are coming to immediate notice for sea, and we are in the process –' he glanced upwards, at the upper deck where the noise was coming from – 'of converting for a minelaying operation. We shall fuel, embark our mines and sail as soon as that work is finished. Clear?'

'Yes, sir.'

Wyatt turned from the scuttle.

'Very well. Get shaved and properly dressed, and resume your duties as first lieutenant.'

'Aye aye, sir.' Nick slid off his bunk. Wyatt paused in the doorway, filling its whole width, looking back at him.

'How could you have been such a *damned* fool, Everard?'

He looked as if he was really trying to understand: or as

66

if he wished there could be some hope of understanding.
Then he'd shaken his head, dismissing the effort as futile,
and turned away, and the curtain had fallen back across
the doorway.

CHAPTER 4

Mackerel drove slowly eastward, a mile and a half offshore, approaching Dunkirk Roads. Six forty-five p.m.: seven o'clock was the ordered time for her rendezvous with the rest of the minelaying flotilla. Able Seaman Dwyer hailed again from the foc's'l break, below the bridge to starboard: 'By the mark, five!'

Pym said to Wyatt, 'As it should be, sir.'

Pitch-dark, bitter cold. Last night there'd been a sliver of moon, enough for the Gothas to see Dover and the coastline by; there was none tonight. Very little wind or sea. Christmas Eve: but it didn't feel like it, except for the biting cold, and even that wasn't the snowy-Christmas sort of cold. It was damp and penetrating, utterly un-jolly, Nick thought. They were all muffled up against it: greatcoats or duffels or oilskins, sweaters over more sweaters over flannel shirts; scarves, gloves, Balaclavas – and either Gieves inflatable waistcoats or the issue swimming-collars. Thin men looked fat, fat ones like dirigibles. It didn't feel like Christmas or like anything else that anyone ashore could know about: only like the Dover straits and a black night and twenty tons of mines to plant in the enemy's front garden. The mines were aft there on their rails, with Mr Gladwish nursing them like a tomtit sitting on forty great cuckoo's eggs. Highly sensitive and destructive eggs: their presence and deadweight aft gave one the unpleasant feeling that one was piloting a floating bomb.

Dwyer had hove his lead again. It was far more of an expert job than anyone who'd never tried would have imagined, but he was an expert leadsman. He called now. 'And a quarter, five!' This was a narrow passage of comparatively deep water inside the shoals and minefields and with shallows and the land itself to starboard; one had used it so often in the past eighteen months that one could have told from the soundings as he sang them out if the ship had strayed so much as thirty yards to one side of the channel or the other. There was plenty of water here, for a destroyer drawing no more than sixteen feet – or a bit more than that now, with the extra weight of the mine-load on her – but depth enough, so long as she held her course well inside the channel, which narrowed, as it approached Dunkirk itself, to something like a cable's width. The leadsman hailed again: 'Less a quarter seven, sir!' Wyatt muttered. 'Very good' – as if the man could possibly have heard him . . . Since Nick had reported to him back in Dover that the ship was ready for sea with all hands on board, and Wyatt had curtly acknowledged his salute and told Mr Watson 'Stand by main engines', he and Nick hadn't exchanged a word. The night and the minelaying operation lay ahead of them, and that was all there was to think about now; soon after dawn they'd be back in Dover, and *Mackerel* would go alongside the oiler to top up her tanks, and he, Nick Everard, would presumably hand over to some new first lieutenant.

Where would he be sent – to a battleship, as a junior watch-keeping officer?

Much better *not* to think about it.

He'd been stupid. He could see that now. He'd played into Wyatt's hands. If you had a captain who'd speak up for you and fight to hang on to you, you could weather a scrape or two. When you hadn't – and your record hung on one single incident where you'd come out well instead of badly . . .

'And a half eight, sir!'

This was the deepest patch that they were passing over now. The sea hissed like a great cauldron of soda-water along *Mackerel*'s black sides as she slid up the channel at six or seven knots. About as dark as ever it could be. Dwyer wouldn't be seeing the marks on his line where it cut the water's surface; he'd be allowing for the two and a quarter fathoms between his hand and the waterline – the 'drift' was the technical term for it – and as the ship passed the lead's position on the bottom and the line came vertical he'd subtract that distance from the amount of line he had out.

'And a half, seven!'

Pym said, 'One thousand yards to go, sir.'

Converting for mines had taken five and a half hours. It wasn't a difficult evolution. *Mackerel* was one of a handful of destroyers fitted for it, with bolts and brackets all there in the right places, and her ship's company had done it often enough before. First the stern gun and the after tubes mounting had to be unbolted, lifted on a crane and slung ashore. Then the crane picked up the mine rails and put them aboard, and they were bolted down like tram-lines to both sides of the quarterdeck and iron deck, with an extended chute from each set of rails over the stern, so that the mines would drop well clear of the propellers. A winch was fitted at the stern and another for'ard, respectively for hauling the mines aft and forward; the release gear at the chutes was operated by a single hand-lever.

It had taken another hour to load the forty mines, each weighing half a ton, and secure them properly. Each mine rested on its sinker, which was like a low trolley with wheels to run on the rails. These were the latest magnetically-fired mines, called M-Sinkers; they'd replaced the useless Elias.

Dwyer called out, 'By the mark, five!'

Wyatt said, 'Starboard ten.'

'Starboard ten, sir.' *Mackerel* heeled slightly to the turn. Such breeze as there was crept up from astern, grew for'ard, blew in over the port side as she swung seawards under starboard helm, port rudder.

The old moon – in fact its last quarter had hardly been glimpsed by human eye – was dead, and the new one as yet unborn. A perfect night, therefore, for laying mines. Or, for that matter, for another German destroyer raid; and the purpose of this new minefield would be to catch any raiders on their return to base. The rest of the Patrol's destroyers – about two dozen, if you excluded the thirty-knotters and the ten or twelve M-class and Tribals on stand-off or under repair – would be at sea and hoping to catch them *before* they made for home. Dover harbour had been emptying fast by the time *Mackerel* had sailed.

The mines were to be planted between Zeebrugge and Ostend. The field's eastern end would be five thousand yards off Blankenberg, and the western end seven thousand – three and a half miles – off de Haan. The approach was to be made from the north after a wide detour up around the outside of Bacon's summer

71

netting area, his Belgian coast barrage from behind which he launched the monitor bombardments. The detour would take the flotilla clear of known minefields and shoals, avoid too close a proximity to the German coastal batteries, and take them clear, too, of Weary Willie, the trawler guardship off Middelkerke.

Wyatt said, 'Midships.'

'Midships, sir.'

Slow speed, and a black, quiet sea. A sharp awareness of the need to *keep* it quiet. Burglars embarking on a night's thievery might feel like this.

'Meet her, and steer north.'

'Steer north, sir . . .' The coxswain's small silhouette bobbed as he flung the wheel around. Wyatt must dislike this situation, Nick thought. His yearning to come to grips with Heinecke, who might well be at sea tonight with his 'Argentinians', would make the need to avoid any kind of action highly frustrating. Destroyers carrying mines were forbidden to engage an enemy unless that enemy fired first: then they'd be permitted to defend themselves. But one bullet, let alone a shell, would be enough to explode that cargo aft.

You had to shut your mind to everything except the simple object of the operation: sneak, in, lay the mines, sneak away again.

'Course north, sir.'

'Should come up with 'em soon, pilot, shouldn't we?'

'We should, sir.'

Everyone was looking out, using binoculars, as *Mackerel* approached Hill's Pocket, the anchorage between the shoals where she'd been ordered to rendezvous with *Moloch, Musician* and two French destroyers, all of them carrying mines.

The leadsman's hail came up through the darkness: 'By the mark, ten!'

At ten fathoms the mark was a piece of leather with a hole in it. Dwyer must have had two fathoms in hand; so he'd have the mark for thirteen – a strip of blue bunting – in the slack of his line.

'Ship eighty on the starboard bow, sir!'

Charlie Pym sounded pleased with himself. Wyatt said, 'Slow together.'

'Flashing, sir!'

Porter was on to it. It was the challenge for the night, and he was already sending the reply on his hand-lamp. Wyatt told the coxswain, 'Port ten.'

'Port ten . . . Ten o' port wheel on, sir!'

The ship that had challenged was flashing something else now: Nick read, and Porter called out for Wyatt's information, *Take station astern of* Musician. *She is now four cables on your port bow. Course will be east-north-east speed ten. Subsequent alterations of course and speed without signal according to operation orders.*

'Midships – meet her!'

'Meet her, sir.'

'Steady!'

Pym said, 'I can see *Musician*, sir. More like three cables than four.'

'Good.' Wyatt told Leading Signalman Porter, 'Make to *Moloch, Ready to proceed.*' Porter's lamp began to spurt its dots and dashes; Wyatt ordered, 'Starboard five, half ahead together, two-five-oh revolutions.' Bellamy repeated the helm order, the telegraph bell clanged, and Pym was passing the speed order to the engine-room; out of the darkness to starboard came an acknowledging 'K' from *Moloch*. Wyatt told the coxswain, 'Midships, and steady on north-east.' *Moloch* was moving off; you could see the froth of white under her counter as she put on speed to give the Frenchmen room to drop into station astern of her. After them would come *Musician*, and *Mackerel* would bring up the rear; which meant that when they reached the laying position in three hours' time, *Mackerel* would be the first to get rid of her mines.

Nick wondered whether they'd allow him to volunteer for the RNAS. Learning to fly couldn't be all that difficult. Vereker and his friends were a splendid bunch, but they weren't particularly brainy. And flying would be a lot better than being sent back to big-ship life – with Wyatts lurking round every corner.

'*Musician*'s signalling, sir.'

Pym getting in first again. Charlie Pym the blue-eyed boy. Now *there* was someone who'd be right for a battleship appointment – with half a dozen snotties to do his work for him, and plenty of senior officers to suck up to . . . Pym knew, of course, what had happened ashore last night and what Nick's position was now; everyone in the ship must know it, by this time. It was more than likely that Charlie Pym would be nursing hopes of stepping into the first lieutenant's job.

If Wyatt allowed that, he'd be showing rotten judgement. Pym was lazy, and he had no understanding of, or level of contact with, the lower deck. The impression you got of Pym was that what mattered to him was his own position instead of what he could make of that position as a contribution to the ship's efficiency and happiness. The senior ratings – Chief Petty Officers Bellamy and Swan, for instance – disliked him; naturally they wouldn't say so or consciously show signs of it, but when you knew them and lived among them, worked with them, you could sense it; and it was

74

virtually certain, Nick considered, that if Pym became first lieutenant *Mackerel* would go to pot.

Perhaps Wyatt knew it? He might. Wyatt was no fool, behind that bullish stare and aggressive manner. *Professionally* he wasn't, anyway. Might he be, in terms of personal judgement? Nick knew he didn't understand his captain. And could half the trouble be that they were simply different kinds of animal? The Navy's answer to that would be clear and blunt enough – and reasonably so – but perhaps for oneself it was something to give some thought to. Faced with authority in a form that seemed hostile or critical, did one tend towards a hedgehog attitude?

Nick had dim, approaching destroyer-shapes in the overlapping circles of his binoculars. The French destroyers. No need to report them: Wyatt had picked them up himself, and muttered something to Pym about them. Nick thought of himself as a boy at home at Mullbergh, and his father's dislike of him, the long years of mutual hostility, with David the heir as favourite and himself as the unwanted lout: that was how he'd felt. And curled up, inside the defensive spines?

Musician had signalled, *Let's go. Follow father.* Wyatt told Porter gruffly, 'No reply.' *Moloch's* wake was a pale smudge in a black haze; the lean grey shapes of the French destroyers, closing in from eastward, shortened as they swung round to follow her. *Musician* was coming in from the opposite direction to take her place in the flotilla, but *Mackerel* was already where she had to be: *Musician* was therefore sliding into a gap in a formed line, as opposed to *Mackerel* tagging on astern of her. So much for 'follow father': that signal had been unnecessary in the first place, and Wyatt, without saying a word, had let *Musician's* captain know it.

75

Able Seaman Dwyer's singsong tones cut upwards through the dark: 'And a quarter, ten!' *Mackerel* must be passing over the deepish patch inside the Breedt bank. Nick asked Wyatt, 'May we secure the lead, sir?'

'Yes please.'

He leant over the rail: 'Dwyer! Secure the lead!'

'Aye aye, sir!'

Wyatt said tersely as Nick turned inboard, 'We'll remain at Action stations, Number One.'

In the chartroom, Midshipman Grant was preparing to keep a running check on *Mackerel*'s position, course and speed in relation to the operation orders, partly so as to be ready to give a dead-reckoning position quickly if Pym or the captain wanted one and also so as to be able to pass a warning up the voicepipe to the bridge when alterations of course or speed were to be expected.

The orders, in a heavily-sealed buff envelope, had arrived after they'd converted and oiled and embarked the mines – great red-painted eggs as high as a man's shoulder as they sat on their wheeled, rectangular sinkers. Forty of them, twenty a side, brought in over the stern and hauled forward by winch, and each one then chocked on the rails before the next was run up against it. It was rather scary, to imagine them as they would be in a few hours' time, under water, tethered down in the cold and secret sea by the wire cables now coiled inside the sinkers: one could think of those great harmless-looking red things as monsters, evil, trying now to appear bland and stupid but ready at short notice to change into lurking, death-dealing horrors – which they would do within – what was it, half an hour? – when the soluble plugs on their firing-mechanisms melted in the water. Very different from the earlier British mines, the sort invented by the Italian Commander Elia. The Elias had had a mechanical firing device, a hinged lever that had to be tripped. As often as not, it struck, and failed to do its job. The Board of Admiralty had distrusted such new-fangled ideas as electric detonation, so they'd opted for the mechanical system; whereas the Germans had had mines that worked, right from the beginning of the war, and it had given them a considerable advantage.

Those days were fading into history now. Jellicoe had pressed hard for hugely increased supplies of the M-sinker type, a year ago, and they'd recently been coming through in thousands. (It was the same sort of thing in the Air Service; a year ago, naval pilots had taken their rations of bombs to bed with them, to prevent brother-pilots pinching them while they slept.) Supplies of all these things had been greatly helped by America's joining in the war, this last April. But in any case this was a new Navy now, re-born out of war experience, and William Grant was extremely proud to have a place in it.

He put his face to the voicepipe.

'Bridge?'

'Bridge.' Pym's voice. Grant told him, 'We should alter to north twenty-one degrees east in two minutes, sir, and increase to twenty knots.'

'Very good.'

Grant lit a cigarette, taking it from a silver case that had his family's crest on it. It had at one time been a cravat-pin case, the property of his great-grandfather, who'd served at sea under Nelson. Grant's grandfather had been an admiral, following in the same tradition; but his father had been in the Army in India, and had died of typhus when his son had been only three. One of the greatest puzzles in William's mind, and one which he knew he'd never be able to solve, was what could possibly have induced his father to become a soldier – in India or anywhere else.

Perhaps he'd blotted his copybook, or the Navy for some reason hadn't wanted him.

He heard, through the voicepipe from the bridge, Wyatt ordering the change of course and increase in revolutions. One could visualize the dark, slim shapes of the destroyers ahead already filing round to port, lengthening as they turned, the white churn of foam piling as they put on power ... Expelling smoke, he looked down at the chart again, where the track stipulated in the orders had been laid-off in pencil, with distances and compass courses pencilled in beside it. He called the bridge again, and told Charlie Pym, 'Forty-five minutes on this leg, sir.'

'All right, Mid.'

There'd been a period, when Grant had been fourteen and fifteen years old, when he'd been terrified that the war might end before he could get to sea. In 1914, Dartmouth had been emptied of its cadets, boys of thirteen upwards all sent straight to ships; but subsequent terms, new arrivals from the prep schools, had been held back, tied to school desks and the parade-ground, while the sands of war had seemed to be running out. All those 'big pushes' that had been so certain to end the war: how they'd been dreaded, at Dartmouth! But they'd fizzled out, one after another, and now one wondered whether it would *ever* end. Certainly the Americans were in now which should help; but to counter-balance their weight had come the Russian collapse and the transfer of thousands

78

of seasoned German troops from east to west. Some newspaper articles had suggested that it could go on for years yet.

Anyway, he'd made it. If he hadn't, he'd have felt all through his life that he'd missed the greatest opportunity a man could ever have. And when one thought that some of one's friends, contemporaries, were actually still at school . . .

'Midshipman Grant, sir!'

The Leading Telegraphist, Wolstenholme, was peering at him through the hatch from the wireless office. A normally placid, quiet man, a Yorkshireman, Wolstenholme looked agitated.

'Signal, sir – urgent!'

Grant leant over, and took the sheet of signal-pad on which the message had been scrawled in blue indelible.

It was from Flag Officer Dover to all ships and shore-stations in his command, and repeated for information to various other authorities; it said *Enemy wireless activity suggests attack on straits by surface forces is to be expected.*

Grant moved back quickly to the voicepipe. Wolstenholme was still craning through the hatch. He was a well-fed man, with small brown eyes set in a pale, roundish face. He said, nodding towards the signal, 'An' us wi' *mines* aboard!' Grant yelled into the voicepipe, 'Bridge!'

Able Seaman Dwyer stowed his leadline and canvas apron in the appropriate locker on the upper deck, just abaft the foremost funnel, and then began to pick his way aft. You had to go carefully in the darkness, and an old hand like Dwyer went *very* carefully; all there was to see by was the faint glow of phosphorescence from the broken water from the destroyer's black steel sides, and it wasn't much.

Cockcroft, at the midships four-inch – which was between the second and third funnels – was in the process of detailing two men to take round cutlasses, rifles and revolvers. He looked up, and saw Dwyer's grey head going by.

'Who's that? Dwyer?'

Dwyer admitted it. He explained. 'Been in the chains, sir – now I'm goin' aft to me action station.'

'Good.' Cockcroft handed him a .45 revolver on a webbing belt; a pouch on the belt held ammunition. 'Give this to Chief Petty Officer Swan, would you, and wish him a happy Christmas?'

'Aye aye, sir. An' all the best for 1918 to you, sir.' Dwyer went on aft. His station was in the emergency steering position, with Swan.

From the twenty-inch searchlight platform, where he was sitting with his boots dangling over his only remaining pair of torpedo tubes, Mr Gladwish watched him pass.

'Oh, Dwyer!'

Easily recognizable, that grey head. Most of the *Mackerels* were youngsters; most destroyer men were young, these days. There were still some old sailors about, of course, but since the outbreak of war one destroyer had been lost every twenty-three days, on average, while hundreds had been built; it thinned out the old hands, rather. Dwyer had stopped, and he was staring up at the gunner (T) on the searchlight platform.

'Sir?'

'Issuing small-arms, are we now?'

'I've a pistol 'ere for the Chief Buffer, sir, that's all.'

'Well, aft with it, and smartish, d'ye hear?'

'Aye aye, sir.' He shrugged to himself as he went on aft past the space where the other lot of tubes should have been. He knew what was agitating the gunner: Mr Gladwish didn't like firearms near his mines. Couldn't blame him, really; you only need to have one pistol dropped, and going off by accident. And you'd only to see Mr Gladwish and CPO Hobson, his torpedo gunner's mate, when they'd been priming the things, just before the ship sailed from Dover. The gingerly way they'd handled the cylindrical primers, carrying them like babies then lowering them as gently as if they were objects of the finest crystal glass into the primer-cavities in the mines. The signal from shore *Prime mines* was always the last to come, when everything else had been seen to and the ship was ready to sail. Then Gladwish and the TI, trusting none of the other torpedomen to handle so delicate a job, would each unscrew twenty cover-plates, fit twenty primers, tighten forty retaining screws . . . Dwyer sympathized. It was bad enough having the mines aboard, let alone messing about with them. The sooner the last one clanked down the rails and out of the stern trap into the sea, the sooner Dwyer – and about ninety other men – would feel safe again.

Squatting on the deck of the stern superstructure were the crew of the after four-inch, the gun which had been landed. They were the mine-handling party now, they and the torpedomen who would normally man the after tubes. Dwyer stopped, and stirred the gunlayer with his foot.

'Treat them 'orrors gently now, Archie lad!'

81

Archie Trew, who was also an AB but young enough to be Dwyer's son, pulled his legs back out of the way.

'Give each of 'em a good kick before we lets it go, don't we, boys?' Trotter, his sightsetter, commented, ' 'ighly disintegratin', that might be.' Dwyer went in through the screen door and down the ladder to the wardroom flat. Ammunition-supply ratings greeted him with a demand for news, information as to what was going on; he told them, 'Windin' up them mines, that's what . . . Course, if you *over*-winds 'em – well . . .' He gestured, rolling his eyes.

'*Bloody* things!'

The young stoker who'd muttered that sounded as if he'd meant it. He looked it, too: over-wrought, or ill . . . Dwyer told him, 'Keep your wool on, Sunny Jim. Steady does it . . .' He went aft again at this lower level, past the wardroom pantry and store and through two more stores to the steering-compartment, right by the rudder-head.

CPO Swan, extraordinarily, was shaving. He'd used scissors first to remove the bulk of his 'set', and now he was scraping his lathered chin with a bone-handled cut-throat razor. A bucket of water steamed gently between his spread feet. In this aftermost compartment of the ship there was quite a lot of motion on her, but it seemed not to occur to Swan – any more than it did to Dwyer, who'd been at sea at least as long as the Chief Buffer had – that using a cut-throat while standing on a deck that rose and fell six feet or more five times a minute might involve some hazard. In fact his hand's sureness seemed totally unaffected by the pitching.

Dwyer asked him, 'Shavin' off, then?'

An eyebrow rose. Swan said, without moving his lips, 'Sick of 'aving me soup strained.'

Dwyer smiled. 'You mean *she's* sick of it?'

The eyebrow flickered again. Swan took soap off the blade with his forefinger, and started on the other cheek. You could see already how different he was going to look. Dwyer sat down on the casing of the steering motor, and delved in his oilskin pocket.

'Brung me 'omework. They reckon we'll be three or four hours closed up, on this lark.' His homework was the final binding of a new tobacco prick. Leaf tobacco, Admiralty-issue and of course duty-free: you spread the leaves, sprinkled them with rum every day for a couple of weeks or so – a few drops from the daily tot wasn't much to spare – and then you rolled the leaves tightly into a hard-packed, rum-flavoured cylinder, which had then to be bound in a wrapping of tarry spunyarn. When it was finished and in its owner's expert view fit for smoking, he'd shave his daily requirement from the end of it, slicing the cross-section of the prick with his seaman's knife. He didn't call it a seaman's knife, though; he called it a pusser's dirk.

Swan drew the razor rasping down his throat, and flicked lather off the blade again. Dwyer asked him, without looking up from his work, 'True about Jimmy, is it?'

By 'Jimmy' he meant 'the first lieutenant'. Swan murmured. 'McKechnie's the Scotch idiot as caused it, cox'n reckons. Wasn't no need at all.'

'Ah.' Dwyer wrenched the yarn tighter, and snatched another turn. 'Lose 'im, though, will we? Lose Jimmy, I mean?' Swan didn't answer. Dwyer went on, after a minute's silence, 'Always did seem daft, to me. If you got a good 'and aboard at sea, real *good* 'and, like –

well, why bother 'im when 'e's ashore?' He gritted his teeth as he put more strain on the yarn. 'I never *did* see the sense in that.'

Swan put his razor on a ledge, and squatted down to sluice his face. He told Dwyer, with water streaming off it, 'That's why you never made more 'n Able Seaman, Dwye ol' lad.'

Pym answered a new call from the voicepipe. *Mackerel* was lifting slightly to the sea now, a short rocking-horse type motion that barely wet the foc's'l deck. Down there, the bow gun's crew were none the less crowded into the shelter of the gunshield; you didn't need to be wet to be freezing cold, in the Channel in December.

It wasn't Christmas Day yet. Not *quite* yet, Nick thought. *What do we do at eight bells, though – sing Old Lang Syne?*

No. That was for Hogmanay. And where might he be, by that time? In Scapa Flow? New Year horseplay in a battleship? Pym said, into the voicepipe, 'Bridge.'

'In about three minutes we should alter to east-north-east and stay on that for fifteen miles, sir. No change of speed.'

'Very good.'

Wyatt said, 'All right. I heard.' He had his glasses on *Musician*'s stern, that heap of white that you could see even when you couldn't see the ship herself.

A quarter of an hour ago they'd had the signal about Hun wireless activity. Wyatt had thought it out in silence; then he'd commented, 'Precautionary, one might suppose. Huns may be sending Christmas messages, for all we know.'

The thing was, Nick realized, that there was nothing they could do about it, except carry on with the operation and hope that if the enemy was at sea they didn't meet him. Not in this vulnerable, explosive state.

Pym failed to understand. He laughed, as if Wyatt's remark had been just a pleasantry. Wyatt cut into the false sound of it.

'Have small-arms been distributed, Number One?'

'Yes, sir.' Cockcroft had reported five minutes ago that he'd seen to it. Cockcroft's action station was aft, in charge of the midships and stern guns; but he had only one, tonight, to look after. The for'ard four-inch had Clover, the gunner's mate, as its officer of the quarters, and besides this Nick could easily control it himself over the forefront of the bridge.

He wondered about the whisper of some 'special operation', the rumour he'd heard them talking about the other night in *Arrogant*. It had been connected, or seemed to have been, with the gossip about a new admiral taking over. Nothing more than that, really, had been said, and it seemed to grow from a belief that if Bacon was being relieved it would basically be for not having pursued a sufficiently aggressive policy against the U-boats. So it could be just wishful thinking: or a harking-back to Bacon's own dreamchild, his plan for a 'Great Landing' which had now been abandoned. Its object would have been to land a force that would have linked up with the Army's advance – the one that had stopped at Passchendaele – and captured the Belgian ports. There'd been a mass of yarns about the plan: how it had involved using 600-foot floating pontoons, a kind of pre-constructed harbour jetty which monitors would push into position against the sea-wall at Middlekerke, four or five miles behind the German line. The pontoons had been designed by an engineer called Mr Lillicrap – which may have been partly why they'd been talked about so much. But that scheme had been abandoned, and this rumour might well be just wishful thinking: by the CMB men, for instance, who felt starved of action. Harry Underhill had said that several of the CMB officers had gone off on some mysterious course: and Elkington – Rogerson's guest, from the thirty-knotter *Bravo* – had a story that a friend of his just down from Scapa had told him privately that Admiral Keyes, who headed the Admiralty committee that had been putting pressure of one kind or another – this was gossip again, of course – on Bacon, and who was also director of the Plans Division at the Admiralty, had been up at Scapa having private talks with Beatty. That certainly did sound as if something was in the wind; and if it involved the whole Fleet, not just this Patrol, it would have to be something fairly big.

Keyes had been the commodore commanding submarines, at the beginning of the war. Rogerson had said he was a live wire, *he'd* give them something to do. And he'd been in the Dardanelles, as Chief-of-Staff to Admiral de Robeck. A man of action . . .

That was how rumours started, of course, and were built up. Adding to the structure, item by item, and probably none of them in any way connected with each other. It could be nothing – simply the expression of a *desire* for action. But – could one, all the same, volunteer?

Pym blurted suddenly, 'Sir, they're altering—'

'Damn it, pilot, I've got eyes!'

Wyatt had snapped Charlie's head off . . . Now he told CPO Bellamy, 'Port ten, cox'n.'

'Port ten, sir.' Following *Musician* round. This was the start of the second fifteen-mile leg of the roundabout route. It would bring them to No. 8 buoy, a fixed marker in 51° 30′ north, 2° 50′ east. From there they'd edge down south-eastward towards the Belgian coast. In fact, almost directly towards Zeebrugge; towards – conceivably – a head-on encounter with any German destroyers that might be coming out of Zeebrugge. But it would be no less surprising or unlikely to meet them here, now, or in half a minute's time: *there*, in that sea that looked empty, like an enormity of black ice crackling down the ships' sides as they pushed steadily, watchfully north-eastward. Air like ice too: and outside a radius of a few hundred yards it looked as solid as the water under it, as impenetrable and as good a cover to an enemy as it was to these minelayers. If you met raiding Germans the meeting would be at close quarters: sudden, savage, shattering.

There'd be no time to think. Not a spare second.

Nick got Cockcroft on the navyphone to the midships four-inch.

'Sub, make sure the guns' crews are on their toes, wide awake all the time. Go and tell the GM the same. There may be Huns about, and if we run into them we'll be alongside 'em before we know it. Understand me?'

'Absolutely!'

'But we do *not* fire unless we're fired at. Drive that home to Clover too. All right?'

'I'll have a chin-wag with him right away – I mean—'

Nick put the 'phone quickly on its hook. Cockcroft's manner and habits of speech would have been understandable if he'd been RNVR instead of RN. Somehow he'd survived the Dartmouth conditioning without letting any of it get inside his skin or skull. One might have thought that to achieve such a feat a man would have to be either incredibly strong-minded or thoroughly obtuse; but Cockcroft combined an easy-going lightheartedness with a brain that was in full working order. It was phenomenal.

Nick had his glasses at his eyes, adding his contribution to the general effort of looking out. *Mackerel* and the ships ahead of her were thrusting into the night at twenty knots, and if one reckoned on an enemy flotilla approaching at the same speed the gap between them would be reduced at a rate of almost one land-mile per minute. With a range of visibility of something like five hundred yards, there'd be no room for late sightings or slow reactions. He wondered, as he tried to distinguish where sea ended and sky began – but you couldn't, they were as black as each other – about that rumoured special operation. And about his own motives for wanting to volunteer for it. As an escape? But it wouldn't be: there'd be an inquiry into that pub row in any case, and nothing would save him from having to face it . . . But – well, if the worst came to the worst, to be allowed to volunteer for something of that sort would be quite a different matter from being simply kicked out of one's ship. Was that it: a question of how his leaving *Mackerel* would look to other people?

And by other people – Sarah?

There was no one else to consider. Uncle Hugh would know precisely what had happened.

The dream he'd had: calling her name, talking to her in his sleep, dreaming that he and she were – that Sarah, and not Annabel, had been in his arms . . . One had to face it, and – displace it. Otherwise it nagged on in one's thoughts. But the mind had a life of its own; this had nothing, surely, to do with will, intention, desire, any waking thought of her. To think of the dream wasn't to think as one had thought *in* the dream.

He'd thought he'd glimpsed something: something more solid than the empty night. In that split second he'd jerked the glasses back, holding his breath for steadiness and to keep the lenses from fogging-up.

Nothing. So easy to imagine . . .

Sarah – as close as Annabel had been?

CHAPTER 5

The inshore marker had been laid last night, probably by a CMB from Dunkirk. It was a small moored buoy with a black flag on it, ten miles east-south-east of No. 8 buoy, where at 8.45 the minelaying flotilla had altered course and reduced speed to twelve knots.

Wyatt watched the destroyers ahead swing away to starboard. He knew they'd be turning round the buoy, but it wasn't yet visible from *Mackerel* here at the tail-end of the procession. *Musician* had put her helm over: you could see the swirl of white, like a pool of spilt milk spreading as the rudder dragged her stern round. Wyatt, with his glasses up, muttered to himself, 'There it is.' He meant the marker buoy. It was very small and so was the flag on it, and nobody who wasn't looking for it in this spot would have seen it except by purest chance.

'Port fifteen.'

'Port fifteen, sir!' Bellamy span his wheel, putting on starboard rudder. Wyatt bent to the voicepipe and told the engine-room, 'Three hundred revolutions.' Acknowledgement floated hoarsely from the tube, and the coxswain reported, 'Fifteen o' port wheel on, sir.' Everyone spoke rather more quietly than usual, as they turned down towards the enemy-held coast. But it wasn't the nearness of Germans doing that, it was the load they carried aft. *Mackerel* swung round across a half-acre patch of ploughed-up sea, and as she went round it the marked buoy was bobbing like a float with some great fish nibbling at the hook below it. They swept round it, heeling, and Pym called down to the midshipman in the chartroom, 'Six miles from *now*!'

'Aye aye, sir!'

It was nine-eighteen. Not that timing was strictly necessary at this point; the next turn, like the others, would be a matter of following when *Moloch* turned. After that it would be stopwatch timing while the mines were laid. Meanwhile six miles at twelve knots meant another half-hour before they could begin to shed the explosive load.

'Midships.'

'Midships, sir.'

The brass caps on the wheel's spokes flickered dully in the binnacle's faint radiance as they circled. 'Wheel's amidships, sir.'

'Meet her—'

'Meet her, sir!'

'—and follow *Musician*, cox'n.' Wyatt left Pym at the binnacle, and moved into the starboard fore corner of the bridge. Nick transferred himself to the port side and further aft. Wyatt called to Pym, 'Come down to two-nine-oh revs, pilot.'

Wind and sea – about enough to make the snotty and the ship's cat seasick – were on the starboard bow now, on this course just west of south, and the ship was rolling as well as pitching. She'd get livelier when she'd lost the weight of the mines; and if the breeze had risen this much in the last half-hour there was no telling how it might be by midnight. Poor little Grant, he thought. There weren't many things worse than chronic seasickness. He had his glasses up and he was sweeping the darkness on the port side, starting at the bow and sweeping back across the black frozen emptiness towards the stern. The glasses were trained out at about seventy on the bow when the German destroyer-shapes swam into them.

Just suddenly – like that – there they were.

And only himself seeing them. For half a second perhaps they were his private, as well as hardly believable, enemy. Staring at them; and conscious of the mines . . .

'Enemy destroyers seventy on the port bow, moving right to left – three – no, *four*—'

'Very good.'

Very *good*?

It wasn't real enough to be a nightmare. One had thought of it, envisaged it: here it was, and it was as if it *wasn't*. Wyatt said, 'Yes, I'm on 'em! Pilot, keep *your* eyes on the next ahead.' Nick was telling Hatcher, 'Bearing red ninety degrees, range oh-one-oh.' Hatcher was setting it on his transmitter dial. Nick snatched up the navyphone. 'One and two guns, follow pointers, load and stand by!' He said into the torpedo-sight navyphone, 'Mr Gladwish – train your tubes port beam. Enemy destroyers passing on opposite course, fifteen knots, range one thousand. Do *not* engage, just stand by.' His voice had been little more than a whisper, he realised. But *Mackerel* sounded like a brass band, felt like a cruise ship – floodlit, impossible not to see from miles away, let alone that bare five cables . . . He had his glasses on them again now; he heard Wyatt mutter, 'They're big destroyers. Almost certainly

92

it's . . .' His voice faded out. For a small ship moving at only twelve knots, *Mackerel* seemed to be throwing an enormous wake. Were the Huns blind? Or still so near their base – Zeebrugge – that they weren't bothering to keep a proper lookout yet?

No. It would start, at any second. There'd be the blinding flashes of their guns: Nick had his eyes narrowed, actually ready for it. At this range, they wouldn't miss.

Bellamy's voice broke the silence.

'It's the schnapps they put away. Rots the eyeball, I been told.'

Nick was holding his breath. He thought, *Why don't we slow down and cut that bloody wash?* He answered his own question: if they did, they'd lose contact with *Musician*. And this was the run-in to the minelaying area, it would have botched the whole operation.

Might the Germans think these British and French ships, so close to Zeebrugge and steaming towards it, were Huns like themselves? If that was the case it would mean there were even more of them about, and at sea, in this area . . . But all four had passed the beam, which was the closest point. From now on the range would be opening, and the chance of some Hun opening his eyes or considering the possible rewards of turning his square head to the left were being steadily reduced.

Did Germans have square *eyes*, too?

He didn't think those were Heinecke's ships. They'd looked big at first, but—

Using the past tense, he realized. It was incredible: they'd passed, a whole flotilla of Germans had passed at no more than five cables' lengths and just – gone on . . .

93

Wyatt roared suddenly, 'Herr Heinecke! Damn sure of it! Of all the filthy luck!'

He was wrong. Nick was certain those hadn't been the 'Argentinians'. Ship recognition was something he was good at, and he'd have sworn they were either *Schichaus* or Krupp 'G' class. He also felt that there was luck *and* luck, and that *Mackerel* had just had her share of it. Touch wood . . . The enemy ships were still in sight: not separate shapes now, only a smear on the quarter drawing aft and growing fainter, merging into the surrounding dark. He heard Wyatt ask Pym, 'How long before we're there?'

No relief in his tone: only a touch of impatience. One could guess the intention in his mind: to get rid of the mines and then go after those destroyers. But it would be necessary to contact *Moloch* by lamp first, and to use a lamp when they were as close inshore as they would be when the laying started – it simply wasn't possible. Any more than one could have sent an enemy report by wireless, giving German shore-stations a chance to take cross-bearings on the transmissions.

Pym had told Wyatt, 'Twelve minutes, sir.' And the Huns had disappeared north-westward. An enemy report would have been of enormous value to Admiral Bacon in his Dover headquarters, and to the other divisions of the Sixth Flotilla. But at least they'd been warned, with that signal about German wireless activity – which looked now as if it might have been well founded. Intelligence was pretty hot these days, under Admiral Hall. Nick heard Wyatt say to Pym, 'All right, I've got her.' He meant he'd taken over the conning of the ship again. Nick told Hatcher, 'All guns train fore and aft.' He went to the navyphone at the torpedo sight and spoke to Mr Gladwish.

'We were lucky, that time. Train fore and aft, please.'

Gladwish said, 'I lost a stone, that's all ... Aye aye.'

Everyone knew how Gladwish felt about mines. He hated them. It happened that mines came into the scope of the torpedo department. Wyatt asked Pym, 'How long now?'

Pym got the answer from Grant, up the voicepipe, 'Seven minutes, sir.' Wyatt raised his voice above the ship-noise, wind-and-sea racket. 'Number One! Have 'em stand by aft!'

'Aye aye, sir,' He got Gladwish again. 'Stand by to lay mines. I'll use the voicepipe now. First one at my order when we finish the turn in about five minutes, then intervals of seven seconds.'

The explosive eggs had to be laid one hundred and fifty feet apart. At twelve knots the intervals between dropping them should therefore be seven and a half seconds, but to make sure of getting rid of them inside the distance it was better to ignore that half second and call it seven. The first twenty would be laid in one half-mile line, and then the ship would be turned four points, forty-five degrees, to starboard, to drop the second twenty in a line at that angle to the first lot. As the last mine, number 40, splashed into the wake, a flash on a shaded blue lamp would tell *Musician* to start laying hers. She'd spread her first twenty along the original straight course and then turn four points to port, not starboard as *Mackerel* had done, for the others. Ahead of her, as she finished laying, the rearmost Frenchman would put down the same right-handed dog-leg pattern as *Mackerel* had done; and so on, alternately one way and the other,

95

so that the end result would be two hundred mines planted in a sort of fishbone pattern, much harder to locate and sweep than they would have been in straight lines.

Grant called up, 'One minute to the turn, sir!' Nick used the voicepipe to what was normally the stern four-inch gun. 'Stand by, Mr Gladwish. Less than one minute.'

The gunner would have a stopwatch in his hand. His right-hand man, CPO Hobson, would be operating the release-gear of the trap while CPO Swan supervised the business of winching the mines aft, one from each side alternately so the ship wouldn't take on a list. It was always tricky work, in total darkness on a slippery, pitching deck dotted about with gear and fittings to trip a man and send him skidding overboard. And it had to be kept moving smoothly: no jamming-up, no trolleys coming off the rails.

Wyatt said suddenly, 'There he goes.' He meant *Moloch*, turning hard a-starboard. Grant squawked in the copper tube, 'Should turn now, sir!'

The leading French destroyer was under helm. And now the second one . . . Just after 9.50: a few minutes ahead of schedule. Wyatt ordered, 'Port fifteen. Stand by to lay mines.'

'Port fifteen, sir!'

'Stand by aft!'

'Stand by!' Gladwish in one shout acknowledged the order and passed it to his minions. Even more faintly up the voicepipe came CPO Hobson's 'Ready, sir!' to Gladwish.

'Midships.'

Musician had steadied on the laying course, due west.

The flotilla was now less than three miles off a coast bristling with Germans and heavy guns.

'Meet her!'

'Meet her, sir!' Wheel flying round . . . Wyatt shouted, 'Steady! Start laying!'

'*Go!*'

A bellow from Gladwish: a clanking sound echoing in the voicepipe: then Gladwish counted the first one as it went off the chute: 'One!'

Craning out over the bridge rail, looking aft, Nick saw the splash expanding in a white circle from the wake, and then the mine itself bobbing astern like some great toy before the sinker took charge of it, dragged it down to its set depth, which would allow for the rise and fall of tide. It was just about low water now: it had been half-tide when they'd groped their way past Dunkirk. Each time a mine dropped off the chutes Mr Gladwish called its number: 'Five . . . six . . . seven . . .'

Bellamy said, 'Steady, sir, course west.'

Gladwish's voice up the tube: 'Eleven . . . twelve . . . thirteen . . .' Lucky number: time for one of the rollers to jam in the rails, or the winch to break down, a wire to snap . . . 'eighteen . . . nineteen . . . *twenty*, sir!'

'Port fifteen!'

Bellamy's growl acknowledged it as he flung the wheel around. Gladwish's team continued sending mines over as the destroyer began her turn to starboard. 'Twenty-one . . .'

'Midships!'

'Midships, sir.' And from that after voicepipe, 'Twenty-two . . . twenty-three . . . twenty-four . . .'

'Meet her, cox'n, and steer north-west.'

'Steer north-west, sir!'

'Twenty-eight . . .'

'Course nor'-west, sir.'

'Very good.' Wyatt was staring aft through his glasses, seeing the mines bob and sway away and vanish into the grim cover of the sea. Leading Signalman Porter, with the signal lamp resting in the crook of his left arm, was using binoculars one-handed to keep track of *Musician*, so he could aim his lamp accurately when the moment came. Wyatt asked gruffly, 'Ready, Porter?'

'Ready, sir.' Gladwish shouted, 'Thirty-two!' Eight to go. Less than a minute's work. *Then* what? Nick asked himself what he'd do, in Wyatt's shoes. Chase that enemy flotilla? Or obey the orders, go to No. 8 buoy and wait for the other four to rendezvous there when they'd finished turning this strip of sea into a new death trap . . . He knew what he'd have done, all right. Now Gladwish's final yell was triumphant: 'Forty!' Porter's lamp clicked, emitting its bright-blue wink: *Musician* would have seen it and by this time her first mine would be trundling off its chute. Wyatt roared into the engine-room voicepipe, 'Seven-five-oh revolutions! I want all we've got now, Chief, full power!'

Full power . . .

Going hunting!

Racing north-westward, wind and sea on her port bow, *Mackerel* plunged and rolled and shook, the high whine of her turbines and the throaty roar of ventilators competing with the sounds of weather. On the bridge you had to scream if you wanted to be heard, pitching the voice high to cut across the cacophony of steel and sea and engines and the howl of wind, wind mostly of the ship's own making as she tore into it through the dark. Seas burst crashing against her bow, flinging spray that lashed like hail across the forefront of the bridge, ringing on the thin steel plating and drumming on the canvas splinter-mattresses; the spray streamed overhead, slashed at icy, numbed hands and faces, more like chips of ice than wind-driven water. Wyatt yelled into the funnel-shaped opening of the engine-room voicepipe, 'Seven hundred revolutions!' Reckoning that if they were going to cut off those Germans at all they'd be within a few miles of them by now, and that glowing funnel-tops wouldn't help *Mackerel* to get in close: even Germans as blind as that lot must have eyes for flames coming at them out of the night. Wyatt had shouted, a minute ago, 'They can't see, so perhaps they can't *fight*, either!' Guns' and tubes' crews were standing by: there was a chance, no more than that, and if it came they weren't going to miss it. Not a *bad* chance, more than the usual needle in a haystack; the enemy ships had been steering a northerly course and it was virtually certain they'd turn westward at some point, that by now they *would have* turned; and they'd been doing roughly fifteen knots. *Mackerel* was thundering north-westward at twice that speed, cutting the corner; if it had been daylight she could have expected to run into them, she'd have had a lookout up on the searchlight platform to expand her range of vision and she'd have quite likely had them in sight by now: by *now*, Nick thought, knowing they could at this moment be a mile away, no more than a couple of thousand yards and still invisible. There wasn't time to think about the odds of four to one, or of having only two guns and one pair of tubes. If it did cross one's mind one could also think of the four other ships, two British and two French, just a few miles to the south'ard there; if *Mackerel* managed to bring the enemy to action, gunflashes would very soon bring up reinforcements. But that was something to consider later, if at all: one thing mattered, one thing was to be prayed for, and that was to find those four—

They found *Mackerel* . . .

An explosion of light: a searchlight: its beam burst in their faces. A great bayonet of light, bomb-like in its suddenness, blinding, mind-stabbing. Guns firing ahead, scarlet spurts in an arc across the bow, funnelling-in on the blinded ship as she rushed towards them.

'*Hit that bloody light!*'

Wyatt's bellow: men blinded, shielding their eyes. Nick was already telling Clover over the navyphone, 'Target that searchlight, rapid independent, *commence*!' It must have been three, four seconds since the light had first stabbed at them and transfixed them. Wyatt roared, 'Open *fire*, Number One!' The foc's'l gun fired before he'd finished the sentence, and *Mackerel* was already being hit repeatedly by the broadsides of the four Germans as they raced westward across her bow. All she could do for the moment was take punishment and use her one gun that could bear. Shellbursts flamed: the reek of cordite swept over and away in the wind: there was a shoot of livid flame on the port side for'ard and a clang as another hit skipped off the foc's'l and ricocheted away without exploding. You could hear shrapnel tearing into the splinter mattresses, battering the superstructure: another crash for'ard, and Nick saw the great spray of the explosion, orange and yellow with expanding points like shooting stars – that one had burst near the capstan, on the centreline. Wyatt was shouting above the din of gunfire and bursting shells and the roar of wind and sea, 'Tubes stand by starboard – I'm turning to port, Number One!'

'Aye aye, sir!' He got on the line to the torpedo gunner. 'We're altering to port. Train tubes starboard and stand by!'

Shells scrunched overhead: *Mackerel* bow-on was a small target, and more were missing than hitting. Then a section of one funnel flared orange, burnt crackling for a moment until the paint had scorched off it, died to a glow of red-hot, wind-fanned metal. Nick had Cockcroft on the gun-control navyphone; he told him, 'We'll be turning to port now and your gun will bear. Rapid independent and pick your own targets, right?' He heard the foc's'l four-inch bang off about its eighth or ninth shot, and at the same moment a tearing crash just below the bridge to port told of another hit. Stink of burning: the back of the bridge seemed to be all flames. Racket tremendous, deafening, shots and explosions and other noise merging into one continuous roar of sound; on the port bow, flames sprang up, danced long enough to silhouette black figures of German sailors rushing aft along a destroyer's deck. Clover's gun was scoring, then. Nick yelled even louder into the navyphone, 'Sub, are you there, d'you understand?' Cockcroft said yes, he was and he did; he didn't sound as if he was shouting, just chatting rather more loudly than usual; Nick heard cheering, and that torturing light went out, as abruptly as if someone had pulled a fuse. The for'ard gun had hit the searchlight: he found himself waiting for another to take its place. Cockcroft added, 'Couple of chaps 've been hit by splinters, here.' Nick heard Wyatt shout to Bellamy, 'Hard a-starboard, cox'n!' He told Cockcroft, 'Helm's going over *now*.' He banged the 'phone down on its hook and half slid across an already tilting deck

101

to the starboard torpedo sight. The searchlight beam and most of the gunfire had been coming from clear out on the port bow in the last – oh, minutes, seconds, you couldn't reckon time once all this started – so it would probably be the tail-end ships they'd fire their fish at. He lined his binoculars up with the pointers of the sight as *Mackerel* tightened her turn to port; the night was all flying, whistling, scrunching shells and blossoms of flame, thuds and crashes as shells burst and the sharper snapping crashes of *Mackerel*'s own guns firing: Cockcroft's was in it now, and getting hits. Nick had the torpedo sight set – giving the enemy twenty knots and a course of west. It was a matter of waiting for the turn, for the ship to get round through ninety degrees and the aiming pointers to come on their target, and the hope was that the torpedo would streak out and find a meeting-point with the enemy destroyer. The third in the line of four, he was going for. All she'd have to do, to meet the torpedo which he'd be sending out ahead of her, was continue at her present course and speed. And now most conveniently one of *Mackerel*'s guns scored a hit on that German's stern and started a blaze going . . . But they were pumping shells over this way fast as *Mackerel* swung and exposed her length to them; there'd been a number of hits aft and there was at least one fire burning. Nick shut his mind to it: all that mattered was to get the torpedo on its way. You had to ignore distractions, concentrate on the fighting and cope later with the damage. There'd be plenty, he knew. An explosion just behind and above him threw him forward against the sight, and he thought he'd cut his face open: no time for anything but *Mackerel* swinging and not far to go now, no need for binoculars with the target lit up by her fires: the first one had taken hold and spread. He watched her along the pointers of the torpedo sight while *Mackerel* leaned hard over under helm and the sea crashed against her bow: both guns firing rapidly, using the enemy's blazing stern as an aiming point. *Mackerel* herself still being punished. Men would be dying back there where the German's shells were bursting, and more would be killed and maimed before they got that fish away and turned back out of this storm of high explosive. He was pleading through clenched teeth, *Come on, come on!* He heard Wyatt's shout to the cox'n, 'Midships!' and crouched intently behind the sight, narrowing his eyes against the gun- and shell-flashes; he knew that the after end of the bridge was wrecked and that there'd be frightful damage as well as loss of life and more surgical work than McAllister would be competent to handle; but both guns still fired and the sight came up passing the rearmost enemy: range what, three cables? – and touching now the stern of the target ship, moving on up – flames almost covering her, now – where *Mackerel*'s shells were driving in and bursting. He called Gladwish with the navyphone in his left hand, 'Stand by!' Then the sight touched the German's for'ard funnel, which was part of the black mass of his bridge; in the second after he'd yelled 'Fire!' he realized that she was slowing and that the fourth ship was closing up on her quite fast. So the torpedo would miss: he'd had the sight set for an enemy speed of twenty, and she wasn't doing twelve now. A shell burst in the side of the bridge just below him: a white sheet of flame shot up vertically, with a thrust and roar of heat that pushed him back and scorched the skin of his face, momentarily blinding him. There was a smell like shoeing horses, and it was his own hair or eyebrows singeing off, but he was at the sight again hearing Wyatt ordering 'Port fifteen!' Somewhere in very recent memory Gladwish had reported 'Torpedo fired . . .' *Mackerel* was swinging back northwards again; it had all been for nothing, for one torpedo that would run out its range and then sink. Another hit close by sent the same whitish-yellow flashing upwards, scorching heat and blast. Slightly aft, to his right; he glanced that way half expecting to see Wyatt dead, the steering gone; but Wyatt was there, rock-like, silhouetted against the fires in the ship's waist and afterpart, and Bellamy sang out in his calm but strident, noise-beating tone, 'Fifteen o' port wheel on, sir . . .'

Turning for what, Nick wondered – to reduce their size as a target for the Hun gunners, or to pass under the last German's stern? There'd been two hits for'ard and now three enemy ships were on the port bow as *Mackerel* swung her stem past them; they were continuing westward while their guns still fired on the after bearing, over their port quarters. The other, the fourth of the line – no, the third, those two had changed places – the destroyer that was on fire was almost right ahead, just fine on the starboard bow; Wyatt yelled at Bellamy, 'Midships, and meet her!' Nick saw it suddenly: *he was going to ram* . . . The foc'sl four-inch was still banging away fast at the already hard-hit enemy, while Cockcroft's gun admidships was lobbing shells after the other three; Nick, wondering if they were getting any hits, had just raised his glasses for a look when the nearest of them – the ship that had originally been number four – blew up in a great gush of flame.

Mackerel's torpedo had missed one, hit another. Wyatt shouted, 'Every shot a coconut! Well done, Number One!' Guns' crews were cheering. Orange flame edged and patterned with black, oily smoke lit the night: the German had been struck abaft the bridge and almost certainly in a fuel tank. She was a torch – no, two torches, two burning halves drifting apart. A roaring sound ripped across the sea: then the sound died with the flames as both halves sank and the water snuffed out everything except oil floating on its surface. Wyatt bawled, 'Stand by to ram!'

The for'ard gun was still banging away and hitting the burning enemy ahead, but it wasn't deterring him from shooting back. But *Mackerel* had some advantage: she was a narrow, bow-on shape, and the German was broadside-on and already much worse hit. One cable's length away now, or even less. Nick leant over the front of the bridge and shouted to the gun's crew, 'Stand by to ram! Lie flat and hold on!' A shellburst drove him back, and at that moment he thought he'd seen Clover, the GM, fall. *Mackerel* was lurching, plunging forward, Bellamy handling the wheel with strength as well as skill, holding her against the thrust of wind and sea, grinning slit-eyed into the wind, his weight to the left to keep weather helm on her and Wyatt shouting in his ear, 'Make sure of it, now, cox'n!' Nick called Cockcroft – the after gun had ceased fire, lacking any target it could bear on – and told him, 'Stand by to ram – pass the word to hold on!' It was the last thing Cockcroft would ever hear from him. The German destroyer lay right ahead, lit by her own fires and with men running for'ard along her upper deck and two guns still firing. She was trying to turn away to starboard but she'd begun the attempt too late: *Mackerel* was rushing at her – a black, battered, flaming missile tearing across broken sea. Just before she struck she seemed to launch herself upward – as if the ship knew what she was doing and wanted to do the job as effectively as possible;

then her stem with its underwater ram smashed like an axe-head into the German's side.

As if the world had been jolted off its bearings and stopped dead, and the sky had fallen in, blackness smothering, crushing, and light then springing through the wreckage, yellow leaping light of flames from the burning German with the British ship embedded in her. Some time had passed: moments, or a minute? Moments, probably. He heard, as he scrambled up, Wyatt shouting down to them to stop both engines. Shouts, screaming, and shots – small-arms – and suddenly the crash of the foc'sl four-inch: it had fired at maximum depression but its shell had passed over the German without touching him: he was ridden-down, still going over, under *Mackerel's* forefoot. Rifle or revolver shots, and something whirred past very close. Looking for its source, Nick saw the flash of another shot, from the German's bridge: then Wyatt had lurched up against him at the front rail, and he was shouting to the gun's crew below them, 'Cutlasses! Cutlasses and bayonets, you men down there! Repel boarders, damn you, don't stand and *watch* 'em!' He'd swung round: 'Bosun's Mate!' The German destroyer was right over, practically on her beam ends and nearly cut in two; men were trying to scramble from her port side to *Mackerel's* foc'sl. Boarders? Nick looked back over his shoulder for the bosun's mate, Biddulph; but there was no back to the bridge, only a tangle of twisted steel, torn plating, the mainmast's paint smouldering and the foremost funnel riddled, shot through like a colander, hardly enough of it left to hold up; in the remains of the bridge's afterpart Nick saw a foot in a boot with some shinbone sticking out of it, and what might have been the same man's (or

106

another's) shoulder, and a pulpy mess in a Balaclava helmet dangling from something impaled on ribbons of black metal. Biddulph wouldn't be piping 'Hands to repel boarders', or anything else. And Porter, the leading signalman: he'd been at the rear of the bridge, and so must Hatcher have been: they too must be part of that horror-fantasy. Wyatt, leaning over the front of the bridge, was shouting '*Stop* them! *Stop* them!' He was sighting down the barrel of a pistol. Nick saw the coxswain, Bellamy, with his right hand on the wheel still but his left round Pym's shoulders; his face was all blood and you could see the bone of his skull. Pym looked dazed. Wyatt roared. '*At* them! Shoot 'em! Drive 'em back where they belong!' Nick looked down there, saw a group of Germans and some of *Mackerel*'s men rushing at them, and another German sailor coming over the side, climbing over laboriously with his mouth wide open, either screaming something continuously or his face distorted like that by fear: he was right up now, beside the clump cathead, with his hands up; Wyatt took aim, and shot him. Nick saw the man collapse and fall backwards into his own ship's flames. Wyatt was chuckling as he pointed the revolver at some other German, and bellowing encouragement to the men down there to clear the ship of boarders. Nick heard him shout, 'That's the way, young Grant! At 'em, seek 'em out, go *at* 'em!' Grant, that kid? Wyatt had fired again; he shouted, 'You *would*, would you, you damned Hun!' He turned to Nick, grinning happily: 'Here, Number One, want a shot?' Offering him the revolver. Nick didn't want it: Wyatt insisted, 'Here, take it, I've had *my* fun!' Nick, looking down at the mêlée on the foc's'l, saw that the bow seemed to have been forced upwards, out of line: there'd be plates strained and buckled and quite likely underwater damage. He opened his hand, let the revolver drop, turned to see Pym easing Bellamy down on to the deck with his back against the binnacle; Wyatt shouted, 'Pilot, get the Leading Tel up here, and a position from young Grant.' Then he remembered that Grant wasn't in the chartroom, and corrected, 'No – go down and work out a position, and have Wolstenholme send this: *To Moloch, repeated FO Dover and Captain (D) Six, from Mackerel: Have sunk one German destroyer by torpedo and rammed another. My position so-and-so. Two regrettably surviving Huns last seen proceeding westward twenty knots.* Got that?'

'Aye aye, sir!'

'Where are you going, Number One?'

'Below, sir, to inspect the damage for'ard.'

'Damage? What damage?' He'd been preoccupied with his 'fun'. Now he was gazing down at the bow itself, ignoring the few surviving Germans on it. They were being permitted to surrender, apparently. Nick didn't wait. The starboard side of the bridge was smoking, smouldering hot, and the ladder had been shot away; he crossed to the other side and went down the port ladder. There was a jagged-edged rip in the starboard side of the chartroom; inside, everything was smashed. He was looking in through smaller perforations in this near side. It was a miracle that Grant had survived. The wireless office seemed to be intact. Pym grasped Nick's arm: he was staring at what had been a chart-table, charts, instruments: 'How – how *can* I work out a position?'

'Tell them "vicinity No. 8 buoy". That's near enough. *Moloch* will have seen the shooting anyway.'

Pym nodded, as relieved-looking as if Nick had saved his life. Nick thought, *Bloody fool!* He turned aft, found that the ladder down to the iron deck was distorted but useable. The whaler's planks were still burning in the davits: on the other side the 20-foot motorboat was matchwood piled round a charred engine. He was wrenching at the buckled screen door, wanting to get in past the galley and down to the for'ard messdecks; a sailor stopped to help.

McKechnie. Last night they'd been in a different kind of fight together. It might have been a year ago . . . McKechnie added his weight to Nick's and they forced the door back; he asked Nick, 'Did ye know the sub-lieutenant's killed, sir?'

It sank in.

Cockcroft, dead. McKechnie added, 'There's a dozen or more, sir, and a lot wounded too. Back aft it's terrible.' Nick told him, 'Find the doctor, tell him the cox'n's on the bridge with a bad head-wound. Then go up there yourself and tell the captain I've sent you as relief helmsman.'

'Aye aye, sir.'

Memory was to come in fragments: like snapshots, impressions printed on the brain that would probably never leave it. Images, bursts of recorded sound that you heard again afterwards and thought about, glimpses of detail in a broad area of confusion. Important things and utterly unimportant ones – like Chief Petty Officer Swan, when Nick stared at him for a moment hardly knowing who he was, telling him 'I shaved off, sir.'

'I think we've some flooding for'ard. Come on down.' Then a hideous grinding sound, and the nightmarish impression that it was the bow breaking away from the rest of her; but it was the German destroyer rolling over, turning turtle, scraping against *Mackerel*'s stem as she slid away and sank, the sea hissing, smacking its lips as it engulfed her and drowned her fires. Nick and Swan and the men on the bridge and foc'sl saw her go, a boil of foam and steam grey through the darkness, and light from that distant oil-slick flickering across the water. Then – suddenly – *Mackerel* lurched: as if she'd been relying on her beaten enemy's support . . . As Nick flung himself up the twisted ladder to the foc'sl he heard Wyatt bellow over the bridge rail, 'Collision mat, there! Get a mat over, *jump* to it now!'

The bow had changed shape: the foc'sl deck from just for'ard of the gun had folded downwards, so that it wasn't a deck anyone could have walked on now, only a sag of steel that groaned and creaked as the ship moved to the sea. Nick told Swan, 'Take charge here. I'm going below.' He saw Grant, and called to him, 'Mid, you come with me.' The snotty said, 'Two of the gun's crew are dead, and the GM's wounded in the stomach.' Nick thought, *Cockcroft's dead, too* . . . Someone had told him so – an hour ago? Cockcroft, with his small eccentricities and his amusing, pleasant manner . . . Grant asked him, pointing, 'What about *them?*' The German survivors: they stood in a close group, some of them frightened-looking and some hostile: two sailors with fixed bayonets faced them. Nick told one, a leading stoker, 'Take 'em below, and keep a guard on them.' He thought as he hurried down the ladder that with any luck the bulkheads down there might hold for a while, so long as Wyatt didn't try to use the engines. He thought, *They've got to, that's all! We've a lot of wounded, and no boats.*

110

CHAPTER 6

The collision bulkhead was bulging with the pressure of water on the other side of it. This seamen's messdeck with its ranks of scrubbed tables was at the best of times a cramped, gloomy cavern; now, sparsely lit by emergency lamps and with the deck-head crushed downwards and water seeping, it was a trap, coffin-like, echoing to the noise the sea made hurling itself against the thin steel plating, and the frightening racket from the damaged bow. You could imagine the compartment being crushed: the bulkhead splitting, a rush of sea . . . He said, 'Paint locker's flooded. Presumably all for'ard of this point is.' Watson, the commissioned engineer, nodded. 'Dunno about down below. Cable locker, an'—'

'We'll have a look, in a minute. Meanwhile –' Nick looked back at the cluster of tense faces behind him and the engineer – 'we'll get this shored. Allbright?'

'Sir?'

Leading Seaman Allbright squeezed forward, between two seamen. He was thin, young-looking for his leading hand's rate; now he could demonstrate his right to it. Nick told him, 'Get the bulkhead shored. Tables, mess-stools. Send to the Chief Buffer if you want spars or planks. He's on the foc's'l. Right?'

Allbright nodded, running his eye over the job and the men at his disposal. The ship's motion seemed more pronounced down here, and the noise – particularly the clatter and scrape of the ripped stem – added to the sense of danger. Imagination was half the trouble: better if one were bone-headed, solid. White-enamelled bulkheads glistened, ran with condensation; there were leaks from the perimeters of scuttles, dribbles from loose rivets. In bad weather, the for'ard messdecks were never dry. Dirty water, vomit, swept rubbish and gear to and fro across the corticene-covered deck: a shoe, a battered cap, empty cigarette packets, a half-written letter. Stench: and men *lived* in this hole! Watson, his round face almost as white and as shiny as the bulkheads, pushed his cap back with a black-nailed thumb and ran the other oily palm across a dome of forehead. 'See what's what below, then?'

'Yes.' Nick, pushing aft through the crowd of men and with the engineer behind him, heard Allbright starting briskly, cheerfully: 'Right then – clear all this muck aft! Then let's 'ave them two tables flat ag'in the bulk'ead: mess-stools to 'old 'em ... Jarvie, fetch us 'alf a dozen 'ammicks out o' the nettin' ... Slap it abaht now, lads!'

Eyes wandering to that for'ard bulkhead. Shoring might strengthen it enough to make it hold. But if it didn't—

If it didn't, the compartment would have to be surrendered to the sea; the next bulkhead that could be shored, after that, would be this one through which they were passing now, leaving the big messdeck and going aft into the leading hands' space. From here a hatchway and steel ladder led down to the stokers' and ERAs' messes.

'Mid.' Nick stopped on the ladder. 'Tell the captain there's flooding for'ard, I'm still checking and I'll report soon as I can. Tell him I'm shoring the collision bulkhead and for the time being will he for God's sake not use the engines. Then come back.'

'Aye aye, sir.' Grant shot away. Nick, followed by the hard-breathing engineer, went on down. At the bottom, he turned for'ard, through the bulkhead door.

This stokers' messdeck was smaller than the seamen's mess above it; at its for'ard end, ten feet short of the collision bulkhead which now one could hear them working at overhead, was an engineer's store. Watson opened its steel door. Dark, wet-smelling, echoing like the inside of a drum; Prior, the stoker PO, peered in over Watson's shoulder. Nick passed him a lamp; they all went inside, and Watson held it up against the suspect bulkhead. He whistled, shook his head, glanced at Nick.

'We're in trouble, all right. An' all the way down, I'd say, would you?'

It was worse here than on the higher deck. The bulge was so pronounced that it looked as if the steel had actually stretched. It wouldn't do that, though; when the strain reached a certain limit, it would split.

Watson banged his heel on the rectangular hatch that led down to a lower store. 'Try it, shall us?'

Nick hesitated. He suggested, 'Leave one clip on, and just crack it.'

'Aye aye.' The engineer knelt down. *Mackerel* was rolling harder than she had been, and erratically; Nick realised she must be beam-on to the south-wester, which in any case was obviously blowing up still. He hoped Wyatt wouldn't be tempted to use the engines to keep her head into it. Watson had freed one of the two butterfly clips; now, squatting, he was using his heel to start the other one.

'God almighty!'

Fighting to screw it down again, with water spurting in a thin, hard sheet . . . 'Purchase-bar!' Watson looked round for help. 'Prior—' A savage lurch of the ship flung him back: Stoker O'Leary pushed in past Prior, jammed a section of steel tubing on one arm of the butterfly clip, wrenched it round; Prior stood on the hatch, and Watson, cursing fluently, joined him. Eventually they had it tight again and the spray of icy, dirty water stopped. Watson was dripping wet; he told Prior, 'Shore this bulkhead and the deck too while you're at it. *Some* bloody 'ow . . . But solid, make it rock 'ard top to bottom, can do?'

'Do me best, sir.' O'Leary, whom Nick remembered seeing in that pub brawl last night, muttered as he got off his knees, 'An' a very *very* happy Christmas to us all.' He got a laugh, for that. Nick went back into the messdeck and asked Grant. 'Did you tell the captain?'

'Yes, sir. He said will you be as quick as you can, please.'

No – I'm trying to give her time to sink . . . 'Chief –' he pointed downwards, as Watson came through and joined him – 'No. 1 oil-fuel's down there, right?' The engineer nodded. 'Well, if there's any leakage to it from the store that's flooded—'

'Wouldn't say it's likely.'

'If there is, there'll be an upward pressure here, this deck we're standing on. Isn't that so?'

114

'Could be, but—'

'We'll shore it, then.' He staggered, half fell across a mess table as *Mackerel* flung over. Watson, as if he was talking to a horse, 'Whoa-*up*!' He was holding himself upright on the open door. 'Fine time to blow up a force eight, ain't it though . . . 'Ere. Spo –' Prior, he was talking to – 'when you got that done, shore this deck down, right?' He looked around: 'Only joking, lads, it's no force eight.' Nick said, 'Let's check the magazine now.'

Aft through the bulkhead door, and down through the four-inch ammunition hatch to the lobby with shell-room to port and cordite-room to starboard. All dry: and there was no indication of any straining of the bulkhead. On the way up again he said, 'We'll get her back all right, Chief . . . Now what's *this*?'

They were bringing the Germans down. Lister, one of the crew of the foc'sl four-inch, asked him, 'Where'll we keep 'em, sir?' Nick looked at Watson, who suggested, 'Fore peak?' Men laughed: the fore peak was flooded. Nick said, 'ERAs' mess.' Watching them troop aft, Watson answered Nick's remark about getting back: 'Aye. Be all right if he keeps her slow an' steady, and the weather 'olds.'

'It *is* blowing up a bit.'

'Oh aye?' Rubbing his bald head. He'd got it well blackened; all it needed was a polish. 'How far 're we from 'ome, then?'

'About – sixty miles.'

'*That* much?'

Watson looked unhappy. 'Three, four knots is all that bulkhead's goin' to stand. Shored or not shored.' He pushed his cap on again. 'Fifteen, twenty hours – an' blowin' up, you say?'

*   *   *

115

Wyatt, feet wide apart for stability and an arm crooked round the binnacle, was using binoculars one-handed, whenever the ship was on a more or less even keel, to sweep the black seascape that surrounded them. Beside him McKechnie, feet similarly straddled, clutched the wheel although she was only drifting without steerage way. It was her beam-on angle to wind and sea that was making her this lively; so far it was only quite a moderate blow.

Enough to make that smashed-in stem sound like a busy smithy's shop, though.

'How long?'

'Perhaps another ten minutes, sir.'

He'd left Grant down there, with instructions to keep him and the captain informed, in particular to report when Allbright and Prior were satisfied with their areas of shoring, so that *Mackerel* could go ahead – or try to. Coming up from below a few minutes ago Nick had been disappointed not to find other destroyers standing by; he'd expected that *Moloch* and *Musician* would have found them by this time.

Dark all round: only white foam and wave-crests, close-to, broke up the blackness. The oil-patch must have burnt itself out.

'No signals, sir?'

'Wolstenholme's uncertain of the receiver. Transmitter's all right – so he *says*.'

Not so marvellous, Nick realized. He'd been quite confident they'd have had help close by. What if the transmitter was *not* working – if that signal hadn't in fact gone out, and nobody knew anything of what had happened?

'Do you know if he's checked the aerial, sir?'

'Yes.' Wyatt muttered furiously, under his breath, 'Come on, come *on* . . .' He twisted round: 'Reeves?'

'Sir!'

Reeves was the next senior signals rating after Porter. Porter was dead. So were a dozen other men, according to McAllister's preliminary count, and there were more than twenty wounded. Wyatt asked Reeves, 'Have you got a lamp there, and do you know the challenge and reply?'

'Yes, sir, I do.'

'H'm . . .' Studying the compass card, glancing up to check the wind's direction and the ship's head. 'Coming up stiffer, Number One.'

'I'm afraid so.'

He'd left out the 'sir'. He didn't give a damn for Wyatt, he realised, or for Wyatt's opinion of him. The only thing that mattered was to get this ship back to Dover; for the sake of the men in her, particularly the wounded, and because it was a natural instinct to fight to keep one's ship afloat. Not to please Wyatt, though; *nothing* to please Wyatt.

'Can't they get a damn *move* on, down there?'

'They *are* trying to.' He added, 'Sir.' Wyatt was staring at him across the black, swaying, rackety bridge. 'You said the paint store's flooded?'

'Yes, sir.'

'Then the cable locker—'

'The bulge seems worse at that lower level.'

The collision mat was in place, over the outside of the crumpled bow. Swan had secured it there with steel-wire rope, and it would help, so long as it stayed in place; but with the motion of the sea increasing steadily, and when *Mackerel* went ahead—

The wireless office voicepipe: Nick answered it. Pym

117

reported, 'Signal received from *Moloch*, saying *Use your searchlight to guide me to you*. Leading tel says it was a very faint transmission.'

Nick told Wyatt. It was a relief to know they could receive at all; and that the other signal had gone out. He added, 'Have to be the after searchlight.' This one over the back end of the bridge was part of a tangle of junk which must still have parts of men in it. Daylight would be welcome, if *Mackerel* was still afloat to see it; but it would have its horrors to offer too.

'Have the light switched on, Number One. Point it upwards.'

'Aye aye, sir.' Nick got Gladwish on the voicepipe, and told him what was wanted; the gunner (T) answered flatly, 'Not a chance. Cables are shot away, and we can't rig jury connections until we've some light to work by.'

Nick wondered if he was trying to be funny. The situation seemed to be singularly unamusing. Except for the fact that *Moloch* and others knew *Mackerel* was in trouble and were looking for her . . . Wyatt was calling down to Pym, who seemed to have established himself in the wireless office, 'Pilot, take this down and send it off to *Moloch* repeated Captain (D) and FO Dover: *Have no searchlight working. Am hove-to while shoring collision bulkhead. Intend proceeding south-westward at slow speed shortly*. Got that?'

'Yes, sir . . . Captain, sir?'

'Well?'

'Barometer's falling fast, sir.'

Wyatt snorted angrily as he straightened up. As if it had annoyed him to be given information of that kind. His manner, Nick thought, suggested that he regarded the shoring of the bulkhead as a mere formality, a

ritual drill he had to allow before he shrugged it off
and shaped a course for Dover. As if he didn't realise
that without the support of shores – and well-placed,
evenly distributed ones at that – the bulkhead could
rip open like a sheet of cardboard: might do so even
when it *was* shored . . . But Wyatt perhaps felt superior
to this kind of detail: his prayers had been answered,
he'd met the raiders and sunk two of them – on his
own, with no senior officer present to claim a share
of the glory. He'd be expecting a DSO and a brass
hat; he'd have liked now to be steaming proudly into
Dover – not drifting, crippled, in a rising sea.

'Everard.'

'Sir?'

'Go down and see what's happening. Tell 'em I'm
giving 'em five more minutes and not a second
longer!'

Nick hesitated.

'Do you mean that, sir?'

A bull-roar: '*What?*'

'If the shoring's not done, would you risk carrying-
away the bulkhead?'

Wyatt was a black mass hunched, head forward over
massive shoulders, eyes gleaming in the binnacle's small
light. McKechnie's head was turned towards him too.
The questioning of orders was not an everyday occur-
rence. Nick added, 'We've only the Carley floats, and
two dozen wounded men. If the bulkhead goes—'

'Everard!'

'Sir.'

'Do what I told you. Go down and tell 'em to get
a damn wriggle on!'

'Aye aye, sir.'

Climb-down. Nick thought, *He won't love me for it.*

But what difference, for God's sake, did that make . . .
'Everard.'

'Yes, sir?' He stopped at the top of the ladder, clung to the rail as *Mackerel* rolled and shipped green water that swamped across her gun'l and exploded against the bridge's battered side, swirled, came pouring out of the holed chartroom and over the side again as she hung for a moment and then flung herself the other way. You didn't need a barometer to tell you what was happening with the weather. Wyatt said, 'By daylight we may have a full gale on our hands. In the state we're in, we couldn't stand it. So we have no option but to make port at our best speed and as soon as possible. Understand?'

Best speed?

How much warning would one get of the bulkhead bursting? Time enough to evacuate the messdeck and the lower – stokers' – deck? He didn't think so. If it went there'd be a split and a sudden rush of sea . . . Might the answer be to finish this shoring operation and then clear everyone out from between the two bulkheads, shore up the second one as well?

He thought about it on his way below, weighing pros and cons. Grant met him in the leading hands' mess. 'Just about done, sir, except for the deck down there.' The midshipman was pale, ill-looking. Nick thought, *Poor little bastard* . . . He put a hand on his shoulder: 'Let's take a look.'

Wyatt staggered, caught off-balance as he moved to answer the wireless office voicepipe; he fetched-up in the corner of the bridge like a drunk colliding with a fence. 'Bridge!'

Pym reported, 'There's been a signal from the West

Barrage patrol, sir. They met two enemy destroyers and damaged one by gunfire, both last seen retiring north-eastward at high speed.'

'What ships are on West Barrage?'

'*Swift* and *Marksman*, sir – but *Attentive, Murray, Nugent* and *Crusader* are close by in the Downs.'

It was surprising that the Germans had pressed through that far, after losing half their force up here. The Hun raids were aimed at quick and easy killings with no losses to themselves, the 'fox in the hen-run' technique. This time, the foxes had got bloody noses.

Nick hauled himself off the ladder into the bridge. His seaboots were heavy, full of water; he'd timed his sortie from the screen door up on to the foc's'l badly, and a sea had caught him in the open, on that lower ladder.

He saw Wyatt at the voicepipe. Pym's voice was a faint gabble in the tube; Wyatt yelled, 'What's that?' The navigator told him, 'Signal just coming through from *Moloch*, sir, addressed to us.' Wyatt, holding himself at the voicepipe with an arm hooked round its top, the other hand grasping the bridge rail, shuffled his bulk around and stared towards Nick: 'Number One?'

'Yes, sir. The shoring's complete, as good as we can make it. Mr Watson's view is the bulkhead should stand up to a speed of three or even four knots, sir.'

He'd thought that to quote the engineer would be the best way to make the point about low speed. Wyatt wouldn't want *his* opinion.

'That's his *view*, is it . . . Yes, pilot?'

'From *Moloch*, sir: *I will continue to search for you. Are you under way yet?* That's the signal, sir.'

'Make to him: *Proceeding now course west-sou'-west.*' Wyatt straightened. 'How's her head, McKechnie?'

'North sixty west, sir!'

'Starboard ten, then.'

'Starboard ten, sir.' How she'd steer, with her bow askew as it was, remained to be seen. Wyatt, back at the binnacle now, called down to the engine-room, 'Mr Watson?'

'Sir?'

'I'm about to go ahead, Chief. I'll start at one hundred revolutions and work up to two-fifty.'

Ten knots?

'Sir –' hearing the engineer's instant reaction, Nick could imagine the alarm on his pallid, oil-smeared face – 'sir, that collision bulkhead—'

'Chief, I'm sick to *death* of being told about that bloody bulkhead! Slow ahead, one hundred revolutions!'

'One hundred revs, sir, aye aye!'

Wyatt might reconsider that intention, Nick thought, when he saw the sea's force on the damaged area for'ard. The man wasn't mad, he couldn't *want* to sink her . . . The turbine's low drone was a welcome sound, a stirring of life and purpose; the last hour's helpless wallowing had been far from pleasant.

'One hundred and twenty revs!'

'One-two-oh revolutions, sir!' Watson's acknowledgement came as a wail, a cry of despair from the ship's steel guts. Nick told himself *Imagination* . . . He raised his glasses, watched the movement of her stem against the background of white breaking sea; she seemed to be answering her helm quite normally, swinging steadily round to port. But the turning motion involved pushing that damaged bow against the resistance of the sea, adding the ship's own movement to the weather's force. He watched closely;

122

he could *feel* the impact, the thudding jars crashing against split plating – and worse, forcing *in*, into the already flooded 'watertight' spaces and the cable-locker and paint store: already the pressure on the shored bulkhead would have increased considerably.

Wyatt too was angling his binoculars downward, watching the ship's stem. Nick heard him ask McKechnie, 'How's her head?'

'Just passing west, sir.'

'Ease to five.'

'Ease to five, sir ... Five of starboard wheel on, sir.'

'Still swinging?'

McKechnie checked the lubber's line's movement round the card. 'Aye, a little, sir.'

'Bring the wheel amidships when you've ten degrees to go. And steady on south-sou'-west.'

'Aye aye, sir.'

The point being that she was turning so readily to port, and she might need compensating helm for the distortion for'ard, starboard rudder to keep her on a straight course. She was rolling less and pitching more as she came round closer to wind and sea. It wasn't good at all, that pitching. Wind, Nick estimated, about force four, rising five. *Rising* ... If you had a huge net – say a single section of mine-net as the drifters handled it, which would be a hundred yards long and thirty feet deep – and filled it with scrap-iron and then swung it from a crane against a solid wall time and time again, that would be something like the noise the sea was making against *Mackerel*'s bow. So what would it be *doing* to the bow, he wondered, and what must it be sounding like to the men who were watching the shores down there?

123

'Captain, sir.'

'Well?' Wyatt kept his glasses at his eyes. Nick said, 'I'd like to go down and see how the shoring's holding up.'

'Go on, then.' Wyatt bent to the voicepipe. 'One hundred and fifty revolutions!'

They'd brought some of the tables aft, out of the for'ard messdeck, to use them as bases for the shores on this second line of defence. They were working on it now, here in the leading seamen's mess and, at the foot of the steel ladder one deck down, the leading stokers'. CPO Swan had taken charge; the faces of the bulkheads were lined with upended mess tables, and hammocks placed to cushion the butt-ends of benches and spars which, with their other ends jammed against angle-bars and centre-line stanchions, held the tables firmly against the flat steel surface. Not too hard, because there was no pressure yet – hopefully never would be – on the other side of it . . . Planks had been criss-crossed where space didn't allow for tables. Swan shouted, over the fantastic volume of sound, 'That's all me timber, sir. The lot.' In the confined, below-deck spaces, the Chief Buffer looked bigger than ever; and without his beard, quite a different character.

Nick went into the stokers' messdeck. It looked something like a shaft of a coal-mine, only with more pit-props than any mine would have; Prior had hammered wedges in at deckhead level to jam spars down on to upturned tables that covered practically every square foot of deck. Now he was squatting on the sill of the door to the engineer's store at the compartment's for'ard end. He stood up, as Nick joined him.

'How are things here?'

He meant the shoring inside the store. Prior ushered him in to see for himself.

'Needs watchin' all the time, sir. You'd think nothing 'd shift it, wouldn't you, but – well, it's this pitchin' does it, the ends of the shores seem to keep slidin', sort o' – look, see there?' He used his mallet to knock it back. 'Wouldn't 've thought it, would you, sir. See it slide, did you?'

'Could you brace the feet from below?'

'If we 'ad more spars, I could,' Prior shook his close-cropped greying head. He had a reddish face, black-stubbled now, and very calm, steady eyes. The noise here in the store was appalling, to most people it would have been almost unendurable, but it didn't seem to bother him. He shouted, 'Chief Buffer's brought out all 'e's got, 'e *says*.' One eye winked. 'Not my part o' ship, sir, I can't tell.' He turned away, watching the shores again, mallet ready, as *Mackerel* plunged and shook. 'Be all right, sir, long as I'm 'ere wi' this.' He meant the mallet. And he was alone here, with the shored-up messdeck a dark and uninhabited cavern behind him; if the bulkhead gave way, the odds were he'd never reach the one aft, the one they were shoring now.

Nick said, pitching his voice up high, 'I'll ask for someone to relieve you presently. Every half-hour, say, watch and watch?'

Prior smiled. 'I'm quite 'appy, sir. We done a right good job on 'er, sir, don't you worry.'

Nick doubted whether it was a job to make anyone 'happy', hammering in shores as the ship's jolting shifted them, watching that bulkhead that had a whole sea's force only needing a bit of elbow-room on the other side of it – and the noise, the deafening metallic crashing,

125

crashing . . . He was on his way aft and up to the other messdeck, and he found it much the same except that it was only the for'ard bulkhead, not the deck, that was shored; in spite of being stove-in at its for'ard end where the deckhead caved downward it seemed less gloomy, less of the trap-feeling about it. Grant had come into the messdeck behind him; he shouted, thin-voiced, 'Seems to be holding up, sir.'

Grant seemed to be holding up, too. Perhaps he'd just been sick; one always felt better, for a while. He was up close to the bulkhead now and he could see where a spar or two had shifted; by this time Prior would have knocked them back into position, but Allbright didn't seem to have noticed the change. Nick asked him, shouting above the din. 'Those need tightening, don't they?'

'What's that, sir?'

Allbright looked dead tired. Dark rings under hollow, dull eyes, and face thinner, paler than ever. Nick shouted in his ear, 'Time you had a rest, Allbright.'

'*Rest*, sir?'

The killick smiled. He seemed drugged, stunned – by the noise, perhaps – and puzzled at the suggestion that he might take a breather from this job of keeping sentry-go against the sea. Grant made an offer: 'I'll take over, for a spell.'

He took the mallet out of the leading seaman's hands, and began to knock the shores back into their original positions. Nick yelled, 'I'll send someone along, in a minute.' Allbright objected, 'Look, sir, *I* can—' Grant shouted, with his eyes fixed on the shore he was about to belt, 'Leave me to it, I'm perfectly all right.'

Nick took Allbright aft. He told Swan, 'Midshipman

126

Grant wants a turn at the bulkhead. Give him half an hour, then have someone relieve him.'

'Aye aye, sir.' Swan peered for'ard through the shadowed messdeck. He glanced at Nick. 'Not the most salubrious of spots, sir.'

'You looked better with your beard, Buffer.' *Mackerel* was rising, rising: it was time she stopped and came down the other side. Here in the half-light, enclosed, ears ringing with the noise and mind full of what could happen at any moment and what could or could not be done to counter it, surrounded by men whose eyes were either alarmed or carefully controlled into showing *no* alarm as they watched the bulkheads and the props they'd placed – props which, in comparison with the weight and power of the sea out there, were really matchsticks – you could visualize the ship suspended on a wave-crest, hanging, tilting ready for the great rushing plunge: and then the feel of her moving, the downward slide, accelerating, falling almost as if through air not sea, and as suddenly brought-up hard, her bow deep in the next oncoming wave, sea rolling white and green, high, right over her, drowning the foc'sl gun and exploding in a mountain of foam against the foreside of the bridge superstructure: you heard it, felt it, knew that it had been the first big one of the night and that before long they'd be coming bigger.

Swan asked him, 'Don't really say so, do you, sir?'

Nick yelled back, 'I'd grow it again, if I were you.'

The flurry of sea ahead as *Mackerel* ploughed into it was all the wilder because of her misshapen bow; instead of a stem slicing knife-like into the waves it was a partly flattened, unwieldy mess of steel that smashed instead of cut, bludgeoned instead of lanced. From the

127

bridge one looked down on a mass of white, a huge lathering that surrounded, smothered and moved with the ship, rose up around her as she wallowed into the troughs and fell away again as she climbed the slopes. Through the froth solid seas, piles of black water, rolled like battering-rams, racing aft and bursting against the gun and superstructure, cannoning by and cascading aft on to the iron deck, boiling around the torpedo-tubes, ventilators and the bases of the funnels. Down below, one had been conscious mostly of the pitching, because that was the greatest danger to the shoring, with water hurling itself to and fro inside the flooded area; up here one realized that the weather was on the bow and she'd got into her familiar corkscrew action: bow up, roll port, bow down, roll starboard . . . You could look down on that seesawing, foam-covered foc's'l and mentally see right into it, see the timber reinforcements to the bulkheads, the messdecks like narrow, ringing tunnels, and the men waiting, trying not to eye the bulging steel too often . . . Wyatt moved, as if he'd suddenly become aware of his first lieutenant's presence.

'Satisfied with your shores, Number One?'

'Holding all right at the moment, sir.' He added, 'But the motion's tending to dislodge them, we're having to keep a close eye on it.'

'Naturally. But so long as it *is* holding—'

He was leaning towards the voicepipe, the tube to the engine-room. Nick, seeing the movement blurred by darkness, said quickly, 'With respect, sir, it might be premature to—'

'You're like an old woman, Number One!' Wyatt shouted, 'Engine-room!'

'Engine-room!'

'Two hundred revs, Chief!'

Wyatt straightened. He told Nick, 'That's revs for six or seven knots, Number One.' Pointing at the sea. 'We'll be making good – what, three?' He nodded. 'We'll do better, by and by. I'm going to berth this ship in Dover on Christmas Day – we'll have our evening meal alongside, d'you hear?'

What one heard was the rise in the turbines' note as they came up to the ordered speed. From one-fifty to two hundred revolutions per minute meant a third more thrust, a third more pressure on the bulkhead. Christmas Day? It *was* Christmas Day, it had been for the past hour. What did that have to do with seamanship and common sense? Wyatt shouted, 'Your fears, Number One – or Mr Watson's – are unjustified. I've been at sea in destroyers a great deal longer than you have. You might remember that, eh?'

'Yes, sir.' He wondered, as he watched the sea battering her stem, whether it would be practicable and helpful to lighten her for'ard, so the bow would float higher and take less punishment. But there was really only the ammunition that one could shift. One might empty the for'ard shellroom and magazine, move the stuff aft or ditch it? The only other movable heavy weight was the cable, and that was inaccessible. Wyatt bellowed, 'Watch your steering, helmsman!'

'Aye aye, sir, but she's—'

'Pilot!'

He'd lurched over to the wireless-office voicepipe. Pym answered, and he told him, 'Make this signal to *Moloch: Happy Christmas. Am steering sou'-sou'-west at revs for seven knots. Owing to weather conditions regret may be late for turkey and plum pudding.* Got it?'

'Yes, sir!'

129

'Send it, then. Repeated Captain (D) and FO Dover.'

'Aye aye, sir. And a happy Christmas to you, sir!'

Wyatt groped back, chuckling, to the binnacle. Good humour faded abruptly as he checked the compass card.

'McKechnie, d'you want to lose your rate? I said *watch your steering!*'

'Aye aye, sir. Sorry, sir. Only she's been gettin' a wee bit cranky. There's a change, sir, she's—'

'Rubbish, man! Just watch what you're doing!'

'Aye aye, sir!'

Then the bulkhead went.

CHAPTER 7

It went with a thump, heavy like a big gun firing, and a jolt that shuddered through the fabric of the ship. For about a second as he cannoned into Wyatt, Nick thought *Mackerel* had struck a sandbank. Then he realized.

Wyatt had been flung against the binnacle. He'd recovered and he was yelling hoarsely into the voicepipe, 'Stop both engines!'

Nick had a vision of the bursting bulkhead as he threw himself down the port-side ladder and a sea broke on him, round him – it was thunderous, shoulder-deep . . . He had to stop, cling to the side rails of the ladder, wondering if they'd hold and if his arms would; he couldn't feel his hands, and the sea was over his head for a moment then dragging at him, like a live creature sucking at his body with its mouth, clawing tentacles of ice. Then the ship rolled hard to starboard, the sea let go of him and he was down, diving for the head of the next ladder, clambering down it, blind from cold and the sting of salt and the wind's black cutting edge, but the impulse to get down there making all of this trivial and inconsequential. He found the screen-door and blundered in, slipping on wet, slimy corticene, hurrying for'ard while *Mackerel* flung herself sideways and shot up, up . . . Tilting, now, bow-down: a crowd of men surged round him.

'We goin' to stay afloat, sir?'

'Of course. And by daylight there'll be other ships standing by us.' The words, the reassurance, came almost without thought as he pushed for'ard and the men let him through: he heard a cheer. Through the chiefs' and petty officers' messes, and the leading seamen's: the bulkhead door ahead of him was shut and in the process of being shored, all the other shores were in place and wedges were being driven in to brace them harder. Midshipman Grant said desperately, 'CPO Swan, sir – he's – he took over in there and—'

Mackerel plunged, digging her stricken forepart into the sea and at the same time sliding to port, a sideways slither with a rapid accompanying roll to starboard. Doing circus tricks, now; the men on the shores were having to stop work, cling to anything nearby and solid for support: one was vomiting. Grant had stopped whatever he'd been saying because he'd been hurled sideways and lost his footing: an OD, Jarvie, was hauling him up again.

'Chief Buffer was up the fore end, sir.' Trew, Able Seaman, layer of the stern four-inch, jerked a thumb towards the bulkhead. Little Grant's face was the colour of watered milk, it had that faintly blueish look; he gabbled, 'He'd just come along and said I'd – "done my spell", he said, *he'd* take a turn at it . . . I'd just got back here, literally *just*—'

'All right, Mid, all right.' Swan's death was a tragedy in ordinary human terms; in more practical ones the loss of a highly experienced and able seaman and NCO was as great a blow. Swan was – had been – a linchpin in the ship's strength and capability; to cope now, without him, would be just that much more difficult. Nick was studying the shoring. 'Looks solid enough here, Trew.'

'So did the other, sir.'

Nick scowled at him. *Mackerel* was climbing up another sea-mountain. He said, 'We're hove-to, now. There'll be much less pressure. Just keep your eyes on it; and if anything shifts or looks like shifting – well—'

Dropping: tilting over and rolling to starboard, like a barrel in a mill-race, and the thunder of big seas smashing down overhead. Trew nodded: 'Aye aye, sir.' He was a good hand, but unimaginative. Nick dropped down the ladder to the stokers' deck. It was the same scene here: door shut and being shored, the other shores being strengthened. Stoker Petty Officer Prior was in charge.

'You all right, Prior?'

'Not like up top, sir. It begun there, so we got warnin'. I was up for'ard, in the store there, I 'eard 'er goin' an' I run like 'ell.'

'Well done ... Sure it is flooded, though, at this level?'

Prior rubbed his jaw. 'Care to go in an' see, sir?'

Men chuckled. Nick said, 'You mean it *is*.'

'It bloody *chased* me, sir!' More laughter; he added, 'She split right down.'

'Magazine?'

Prior glanced down at the hatch, right at their feet with its clamps screwed down tight. He shook his head. 'Don't like to open up, sir, not really. But there's the oil for'ard; I reckon that might sort of cushion it, sir, I mean the bulkhead, 'old it firm d'you think?'

'Have you tried pumping?'

'On the – magazine . . .' Prior banged his forehead with a fist. 'I'm goin' *stupid* . . .' Glancing round: 'O'Leary! Where's that Irish—'

'Here, Spo . . .'

Nick left them to it, and went up again. To say he was glad he'd decided to shore this second bulkhead would have been to put it mildly. If he hadn't, *Mackerel* would be on the seabed now, and most of these men would be dead. Perhaps they all would; not only because she'd have gone instantaneously as the sea burst through her, but because in water close to freezing-point you couldn't hope to stay alive for longer than a quick Lord's Prayer.

He saw Grant, and considered sending him up to Wyatt with a report on the situation. But Wyatt might try to go ahead again, once he knew the flooding had been contained. Only a lunatic would try it; but Wyatt had, Nick thought, been showing signs of lunacy. He was obstinate, and basically – incredibly, for a comparatively young and well-thought-of destroyer captain – basically *stupid*. He'd want to prove his point: or something . . . And little Grant couldn't argue with him. Besides which he, Nick, couldn't stay down here, out of touch with what was going on; and it was as well that an officer of sorts should be here . . . He wondered what Gladwish was doing: he couldn't surely be on the tubes still, with the upper deck almost continuously under water.

Prior heaved himself up the ladder, hung on to the top of it through a savage roll . . .

'She's dry, sir. The magazine and shell-room – dry as a bone!'

'Thank God for small mercies . . . But now keep the hatch shut tight, eh?'

To have shifted the ammunition aft would make so

little difference, now, in comparison with the hundreds of tons of water in the forepart of the ship, that it wouldn't be worth the work involved. Whereas keeping that space battened-down would maintain it as a pocket of air-pressure against any thrust from the oil-fuel tank for'ard of it. And it had the support, aft, of the second fuel tank, the after end of which was the for'ard bulkhead of No. 1 boiler-room. You couldn't shore that one, first because there was such a huge area of it and virtually no shoring materials left to work with, second because the for'ard pair of boilers were only about eighteen inches clear of it. There'd be no room either for shoring or for men to work there.

In other words, *this* bulkhead had to hold. If it didn't *Mackerel* would go to the bottom.

Trew said, 'Never knew a ship could roll so. Never . . .' He was flattened against the destroyer's port side, the curved steel of her hull, which for the moment had swapped places with the deck. Now she was whipping back the other way . . . Nick wondered whether it would be possible, by going slow astern on both screws, to hold her stern to the sea. It might be, he thought, if the rudder could hold her, if the force of the sea didn't constantly drive her off. But the waves would break right on her, they'd pile clear over her low stern and crash down on to the quarterdeck and iron deck, and they'd leave nothing there, everything would be swept away or flattened: but the hell with that, if it kept her afloat, at least until some other ship was standing by . . . He was thinking, he realized, as if he was *Mackerel*'s captain rather than her first lieutenant. The decisions weren't his to make. And it was high time now to be getting back up there and telling her real captain what had been happening down here.

'Grant – I'm going up to the bridge. I'll be back later, I expect.'

'Right, sir.'

He looked round. *Mackerel* was standing on her stern end, wallowing for a moment before the weight of the bow took charge and brought it crashing down like a great hammer . . . He told them, as that motion checked and she began to sway to port and rise again, 'We'll be all right now. We'll have our Christmas in a day or two. We'll have a devil of a good one to make up for all this, right?'

They cheered him, or the thought of Christmas. He was staring at the bulkhead. Swan was somewhere on the other side of it. Drowned. Washing to and fro.

Wyatt shouted, clutching the bridge rail with Nick beside him, 'When did you shore the second bulkhead?'

'Soon after the first, sir.'

After you'd said something about 'making our best speed' . . .

He waited, but Wyatt had no further questions or comments, apparently. He'd already concurred with the proposal to try her stern-on to the sea with engines slow astern, or as slow astern as might do the trick; they were waiting for Mr Gladwish and his torpedo gunner's mate to reach the bridge.

Wyatt leant sideways, to the wireless office voicepipe. Nick moved, to give him elbow room, but he made sure of not letting go. One slip, and a man could be over the rail and nobody'd even see him go: this bridge was something like a soaped saddle on a crazy horse. Wyatt shouted, 'Pilot!'

'Sir?'

'Take down a signal—'

He'd lifted his head from the tube as *Mackerel* wallowed over almost on her beam-end: she was hanging there as if she hadn't quite made up her mind whether to finish the whole thing off, go right over and be done with it. It was almost a surprise when she recovered and started to roll back. Wyatt dictated to Pym, 'To *Moloch*, repeated usual authorities: *I am hove-to and unable to proceed owing to extensive flooding forward. Request assistance at first light. Have twenty men wounded and both boats were destroyed earlier*. Send that off, right away.'

'Aye aye, sir!'

So now they'd know, Nick thought. It was as if Wyatt had only just begun to appreciate their predicament! Well, better late than never: and at the price of one life, Swan's . . . He saw Gladwish arriving in the bridge, with the lanky shape of CPO Hobson behind him. They'd been on the searchlight platform all this time; so far as Gladwish was concerned, the ship was at action stations, and nobody had told him until now to leave his.

Wyatt shouted, 'Hobson, you're acting cox'n.'

'Aye aye, sir.' A tall man, slow-moving and heavy-jawed, Hobson clawed his way in a bent position across the wet, gyrating bridge to take over the steering from McKechnie. At the moment, with the ship lying stopped, there was no steering to be done. Nick told McKechnie, 'And you're acting buffer. If anyone's kind enough to offer us a tow, at daylight, you'll have your work cut out.'

'Aye, sir.' The Glaswegian laughed as he fetched-up against the rail and clung to it. 'Be a lark, gettin' a line out in *this!*'

He was right, Nick thought, it would be. But you could only deal with one situation at a time; and in any case someone would have to find them first – find them still afloat . . . He heard Wyatt calling down to the engine-room, 'Is that you, Mr Watson?'

'Aye, sir!'

'I'm going to try her slow astern on both engines, Chief, and see if we can hold her stern to the weather.'

'Ready when you are, sir!'

'All right, then. Slow astern together!'

Leaning across Hobson, peering at the compass card . . . 'Port fifteen, TI.'

'Port fifteen, sir.' The voicepipe squawked, 'Both engines going slow astern, sir!' Hobson said, 'Fifteen o' port wheel on, sir.'

It meant the rudder was angled fifteen degrees to starboard of the centre-line. As the ship had stern-way on, or would have at any moment, her bow should swing to port. Wyatt and Hobson both craned over the binnacle, watching the card and the lubber's line.

'She's not answering, sir.' The TIs voice was deep, gravelly, rather like Skipper Barrie's. Wyatt called down the pipe to the engine-room, '*Half* astern port!'

'Half astern port, sir!'

You could hear it now, the hum of the turbines through the louder but irregular buffeting of wind, the crash of seas . . . 'Port engine half astern, sir, starboard *slow* astern!'

McKechnie, staggering sideways as the ship rolled, crashed into Reeves, the signalman . . . 'Sorry, Bunts!'

'She's coming round, sir.' Relief in Hobson's tone. *Mackerel* wasn't only turning, though, she was climbing, pointing her broken snout at the sky. Nick asked Reeves, 'Still got your lamp?' He had. Wyatt shouted at the TI, 'I want her steadied on north-east, so her stern's into

138

the south-wester. Understand?' Hobson checked the compass, and acknowledged, 'Aye aye, sir, steady on north-east, sir . . .' She was level-keeled for one long moment, balanced along a crest of white: then her bow was falling as she went into a long headlong rush ending in the fast, hard roll to starboard. She was halfway round now, with wind and sea driving at her starboard quarter; Wyatt told the engine-room, 'Slow astern both engines!'

'Slow astern both, sir!'

Hobson was still holding all the helm on, though . . . Nick proposed to Gladwish, 'Like to pay them a visit down below, at the shored bulkhead?' A sea came hurtling from astern, rose mountainous, black with white edging, white feathers streaming from it: it loomed higher as it caught the ship up, gathered size and weight, threatening anything that floated, anything in its way: then it crashed down, the size of a house, exploded where the stern gun would have been. *Mackerel* was floundering with her stern buried in black sea and leaping foam, and Nick was thinking of the men aft, the wounded in McAllister's care in the wardroom and his own cabin and the captain's; it wouldn't take many seas like that one to smash the after superstructure and sweep it overboard, and then there'd be only the hatchway with its lid of not-so-heavy steel covering the top of the wardroom ladderway.

And if *that* went . . .

Gladwish yelled, 'Won't long be dry aft!'

It wasn't dryness or wetness, mere discomfort, that Nick was thinking of. It was flooding, swamping. If *Mackerel* was going to get pooped like that every other minute – or several times a minute—

'Say you want me down for'ard?'

139

Nick nodded, put his mouth closer to the gunner's ear. 'And you might send young Grant up for a breather. Tell him I want to hear from him how it's going.'

'Aye aye—'

'Mind how you go!'

Gladwish growled as he moved to the ladder, scuttling crablike across the tilting bridge, 'Teach y' grannie . . .'

It would help that both screws were at slow astern now. If she could be held like this, with the lowest possible revs, just enough so she'd answer her helm and lie stern-on . . . Wyatt was of the same mind, Nick realised thankfully; he'd just called down, as Hobson was easing his helm, 'Stop starboard!' The less resistance the ship offered to the sea, the less thrust of her own, the easier she'd ride, the fewer missiles like that last one would smash down on her stern . . . He heard CPO Hobson report, 'Course north-east, sir!'

It would be surprising if just one screw would hold her. And thinking ahead – if they were taken in tow eventually, it would have to be stern-first: and *then* there'd be some seas pounding over that low counter.

He was thinking ahead too far, perhaps. The weather might have eased, by then . . . Nick delved through layers of wet protective clothing, found a handkerchief and used it to clean the lenses of his binoculars. Hobson was being hard-worked at the wheel, fighting hard with the rudder first one way and then the other to hold her as she lay; the fact that she was down by the bows meant that her stern rode higher, was more exposed to wind and waves trying to push her round. Wyatt was watching the compass, his wet face glistening bluish as he leant over in its pale light. Now he was moving to the voicepipe.

'Slow astern *both* engines!'

Nick began to study the bow through his binoculars. There was no visible change . . . Except that the water seemed calmer ahead. There was less of it breaking, less white showing than elsewhere; the calmer area seemed to be spreading out ahead of the ship, a broadening 'V' leading from her bow and fading outside the range of visibility.

The reason for it struck him suddenly. Oil – from the for'ard tank.

'Looks as if we're leaking oil, sir.' He pointed. Wyatt put his glasses on it. Now he'd gone back to the engine-room voicepipe.

'Chief – No. 1 fuel tank's leaking to the sea. You'd better shut it off.'

Nick heard Watson tell him it *was* shut off, that he'd done it as a precaution some time ago. His tone wasn't complacent, only reporting fact.

'Very good, Chief.'

But it wasn't good *at all* . . . It meant that, whether oil was leaking directly outboard or through the other flooded compartments in the bow, sea-pressure, wave-pressure, would be acting on the oil still inside the tank. So the bulkhead's lower section, to the magazine and shellroom which it had not seemed possible – or necessary – to shore, had the same force on it now from for'ard as the higher, shored part had. Nick felt a sudden tightening in his gut as this truth hit him and he realized there was a weak point in the defences he'd established, a back door left unguarded. The ammunition space had been dry when they'd put the pump to work, and he'd thought no more about it; now it might be flooded, or even if it wasn't it could become so at any moment – and it was *on the wrong side of the shored bulkhead.*

The next break could be upwards into the stokers'
accommodation space – where not one but twenty
men would be trapped – or aft to No. 2 oil-fuel and
the boiler-room . . .

'Number One, sir?'

Grant's pale face peered up at him.

'All right, Mid?'

'Yessir. Shores are all holding, and there don't seem
to be any problems.'

'Has Petty Officer Prior been watching the magazine?'

'Not particularly that I *know* of—'

Grabbing for support, as she rolled . . . And now she
was digging her bow deep into the sea and wriggling,
shaking like an up-ended duck. One thought of those
flooded compartments, of the way the sea would surge
through them, the pressures . . . Nick moved up the
side-rail of the bridge until he was level with Wyatt
at the binnacle.

'Captain, sir. Grant's here, if you need him. He says
all's well below, but I'd like to go down and take
a look.'

Wyatt had his glasses up. He didn't lower them; he
yelled, 'Go on, then!'

'I though I'd go aft, too, and see how McAllister's
managing.'

'Very good . . . We must be losing the devil of a lot
of oil there, Number One.'

He hurried, falling over himself to get down there
quickly, rushing past Gladwish and down to the lower
level. Prior seemed surprised by the urgency with which
he put the question.

'Still dry, sir. I 'ad the pump runnin' not five minutes
ago, and there's not a spoonful in there. I reckon she'll
'old up now, sir.'

The sense of relief was enormous; but it didn't last. There was a decision to be made now: to open up the magazine and try to shore it with such bits and pieces as were left to them, or keep the hatch shut tight and trust to providence.

Did one have any right to trust to anything except what one knew *should* be done? He asked Prior, 'If we got all the shells and cordite out and ditched it, could you make the timber of the racks into shores?'

'No, sir, I don't think so.' Prior shook his head. In the last couple of hours his stubble had developed into what was almost a beard; and while the first sprouting had seemed black, it had now turned out to be grey, to match his head. He said, 'All short sections, ain't it. An' too light, sir, any road. If you was askin' me, sir, I'd say leave well alone.'

The trouble was that with a fuel tank abaft it – No. 2 – if you didn't shore the magazine you couldn't shore at all. Nick felt the right way to go about this, the *thorough* way, would be to get down inside there and shore it up solid. Against that, however, was the fact they hadn't any materials; they'd lined and strutted two whole bulkheads and there was hardly a stick of timber or a mess-stool left.

'All right. We'll leave it.'

'I'll watch 'er, sir.'

Fat lot of good *watching* it would do.

'Don't run the pump more than you have to.' One wanted pressure in there, not a vacuum. He didn't feel at all easy about it, as he went up the ladder to the killicks' mess. Trew said cheerfully, 'Feels better, sir. Weather easing, is it?'

Nick shook his head. 'Just that we're riding stern-to, for the moment.' Men were sprawled about on the deck dozing, propped against bulkheads chatting, playing card-games. Unshaven, dirty-looking, a crowd of thugs . . . He felt his own jaw, heavily stubbled too, and he knew there was caked blood on his face from that collision he'd had, heaven knew how many hours ago, with the torpedo sight. He realized he must look as rough as any of them. Gladwish's eyes were red-rimmed, probably from his long ordeal on the searchlight platform; he had the look of a mad dog, Nick thought. He said, 'I sent three 'ands to the galley to knock up bully sandwiches an' tea. We'll let you 'ave some on the bridge, if you're p'lite to us.'

'How about aft, the wounded?'

'Well, they got the wardroom galley!'

'Not much in it for all that crowd.' Nick shrugged. 'Shouldn't think so. I'll let you know, anyway.'

He hoped they might be self-sufficient aft there, because it wouldn't be easy to get food and drink to them, carrying it over a deck that was behaving as *Mackerel's* was now, rising and falling thirty feet at a time and pitching, rolling while seas broke on it and over it, and only lifelines to hold on to. If your hands were full of mess-traps, what did you hang on *with*? With nerve – and the balance of a trapeze artiste, a tightrope walker. It was something to face even now, this trip aft; it was time someone visited the wounded, and the only way to get to them was over the top, running the gauntlet of the seas right aft as far as the superstructure where iron deck met quarterdeck. There was no way through the ship, since the two boiler-rooms and the engine-room were three individually watertight compartments, divided by solid bulkheads without doors in them. For damage-control reasons, it had to be so; the compartments were so large, potential flooding area so great – from a torpedo hit, for instance, or ramming ... From the screen-door by the galley Nick peered out into noisy, spray-lashed darkness. Holed, shot-battered funnels glistening to his left; the whaler's davits empty and the paint charred away. His eye marked the positions of the ventilators, charting a clear route aft: clear if you could call it clear, over that sliding, tilting, heaving deck that was constantly being washed-down by breaking seas. But the sea helped, in one way: the phosphorescent effect of foam racing alongside and leaping and sliding along the whole cavorting length of her did to an extent outline the limits of the area through which one would have to pass. And by swirling round the obstructions it showed them up. The second funnel, he saw as he passed it, was almost untouched; the third, in steel tatters, made up for that, and a loose flap of it banging to and fro as the ship rolled rang like a great dinner-gong. He passed the tubes, which were trained fore-and-aft and seemed to be intact; a wave landed aft, crashing down around the mine-winch and the release gear, and water rushed for'ard knee-deep, but he was ready for it, in against the searchlight platform and holding tight to the rail that ran around it. The further aft one got, the greater was the pitch, the rise and fall, the dizzy roller-coaster swing of it. He stayed where he was until a new one poured down on her stern and spread in sheets and cataracts of foam: then he moved quickly, bent double against the wind and with the object of lowering his centre of gravity, crabbing his way across the space where the after tubes were normally, and heading for the lee of the quarterdeck superstructure. Just as he reached it, *Mackerel*'s stern was going down and on either side of her the sea was heaving, piling upwards: astern, too, it was hunching itself up menacingly as her bow angled skyward, and at any second now these piled tons of water would collapse across her afterpart, boil across her as much as six or ten feet deep. He finished a long, desperate slide down the wet slope of deck by crashing into the superstructure's vertical steel side; then he was around its corner and into the screen-door like a rabbit going to ground. He heard it happening out there: like big guns at close quarters, and the steel structure shuddering, booming from the water's impact: might *this* be the moment for the tin chicken-house to be flattened, flung overboard? A rush of invading sea burst through the screen-door just as he forced it shut. Knee-high: well, his boots had been full already, he'd have to empty them before he began the trip back for'ard. Full seaboots seemed to weigh half a ton. They'd shut the hatch-lid above the wardroom ladder, and secured it with one clip. The clips were operable from either side, of course; and he was glad they were having the sense to take precautions . . . He got down far enough on the ladder to reach up and pull it shut again above him. Then, at the bottom of the ladder, he found himself confronted by Warburton, the captain's steward.

Warburton grinned at him.

'Come for a spot o' breakfast, sir?'

McAllister had transformed the wardroom precincts into a sickbay and operating theatre. One that swung, rocked, slanted, soared and swooped, while the sea's crashing hammer-blows boomed and pounded at it. But the conscious wounded seemed in surprisingly good spirits, and McAllister seemed to be on top of things and to have their confidence. They had everything they needed. Nick had drunk a mug of cocoa while he chatted to them, and now he was back on the bridge, reporting to Wyatt.

'Nineteen seriously wounded, sir. Three have died since the action – Nye, Woolland, Keightley. The GM's a doubtful case, but McAllister's happy about all the others.'

Pym, back on the bridge now, asked how was Bellamy, the coxswain.

'He'll be all right.'

CPO Bellamy was in one of the wardroom bunks, turbanned like a Sikh. He'd asked Nick, 'Is it right you're leavin' us, sir? Leavin' *Mackerel*?' An odd time to ask, Nick thought; *everyone* might be leaving her, at any moment. No one was listening; he told him, 'I should think you can count on it.'

'Then I'll be puttin' in for a draft chit too, sir.'

Nick, looking down at the stubbly, weather-beaten face, shook his head. 'Better you stayed, cox'n. We can't all leave her at once. I'd hang on, if I were you.'

There would have, in any case, to be a ship to leave: she had to be kept afloat, and got home. It really did seem premature, trivial, to natter about draft chits. The magazine and shell-room was like a needle in his brain, a ticking bomb under all their feet, a bomb he could have de-fused and hadn't. He heard Wyatt call to Pym, 'I believe it's getting lighter, pilot!'

Wyatt was sweeping the sea ahead with his binoculars; and Nick thought he was right. In the east, on *Mackerel*'s starboard bow, there was a suggestion of greyness, a faint gleam like polish on the surface of the sea. The sea itself might be down a little, too . . . No. Studying it, he realized it was only that there was less broken water now. And working it out – from a year's experience as a navigator in the Patrol – well, about ten o'clock last night when they'd laid their mines it had been near enough low water; so for the last five or six hours there'd have been a south-running stream: and a southerly tide competing with a wind out of the south-west was a combination that invariably kicked up a breaking sea. Now, it would be roughly high water, so the tide would be north-running – for about four hours.

It made things *look* quieter, that was all. It didn't reduce the wind's strength or the size of the seas or *Mackerel*'s motion in them.

They'd had Mr Gladwish's tea and sandwiches up here. It had made everyone feel less exhausted, for the moment . . . Grant squawked suddenly, excitedly, 'Ship forty degrees on the starboard bow, sir!'

'Porter!'

Porter didn't answer. Only wind, sea, ship-noises . . . Porter couldn't have answered; not unless he was in those sounds. Porter had died, here on this bridge, last night. Nick prompted, 'Reeves—'

'*Signalman!*'

Wyatt had realized his blunder. But Reeves was already doing his job, and the signal-lamp was stuttering, piercing the gloom and illuminating the wrecked bridge with its staccato burst of flashes. It was the challenge he was sending, aiming his lamp out on the bearing Grant had named; Wyatt shouted, 'What should the reply be?'

'Baker Charlie, sir!'

That was what came back to them: by searchlight probing from the eastward.

'Ship's friendly, sir!'

Just as well, Nick thought. *Mackerel* was hardly in a state to cope with anything *un*friendly. Reeves was

148

flashing her identity to the newcomer: and he'd got an answer from her . . . 'It's *Moloch*, sir!' The searchlight began to call again: he gave it the go-ahead with his lamp, and then called the message out word by word, although everyone on the bridge read it at the same time for themselves: *Good morning. Happy Christmas. Shall we wait for daylight before we pass the tow?*

CHAPTER 8

A final volley of rifle-fire crackled into the grey sky roofing Dover. Nick, standing to attention with half the ship's company behind him and the rest facing him behind Wyatt, was aware that the last of the coffins, draped in its Union flag, was being lowered into the chalky soil, and that Wyatt was staring at it – stern, granite-faced. Enjoying, Nick wondered, this parade? Would he feel gratified by the big turnout of townspeople who'd watched the slow march through the streets and then trailed along behind?

The *Last Post*'s bitter-sweet, lonely wailing had begun. Its notes soared, floated in cold December air, and Nick, looking up at the castle with its flag fluttering at half-mast, thought of Cockcroft, and of Swan; of Swan particularly, who'd been sacrificed to nothing but one man's obstinacy.

One should try, perhaps, not to entertain such thoughts? Shouldn't one simply grieve and glory over the passing of brave men? Accept the praise, honour, acclamation?

There'd been a lot of it. Cheers, to start with; then signals, telegrams and headlines. After the recent enemy successes in the straits it had come as a timely victory.

Out of four German raiders, two had been sunk and one sent home badly damaged. This time, there'd been no German broadcast. And Wyatt, of course, was the nation's hero.

A crowd many yards deep encircled the naval funeral party. Children craned their necks for a better view. Women wept: men stood with bowed heads, with black arm-bands on their sleeves. Nick stared at his commanding officer across the damp strip of turf: he saw him looking down his pistol's sights, chuckling with delight; offering *him*, Nick, the pistol . . . Urging him to take it: 'I've had *my* fun!' Grant stuttered, 'CPO Swan, sir, he's—'

Swan was still inside the flooded bow, unless the sea had extricated him. *Mackerel* would be going in tow to the London dockyards for repairs. Tomorrow, probably: there was a need of calm weather for the tow, and the forecast was hopeful.

They'd buried twenty men. The twentieth, Clover the gunner's mate, had died of his stomach wound during the transfer from *Mackerel* to the hospital yacht.

Nick had an appointment ashore, this afternoon, and before that he had to see Wyatt. He dreaded it: routine contact with him was irksome enough, and the idea of a tête-à-tête was anathema. Formal correctness was one thing: to show personal politeness very much another: and knowing one had to hold one's tongue . . . He'd felt like an accessory, at first, and when the German prisoners had been marched ashore – a crowd of men on the jetty staring at them in frigid, hostile silence – he'd taken care to be out of the way, not to have to meet any of their eyes. Facing them, he'd have felt like Wyatt, as if *he* were a form of Wyatt: and he'd have seen it in their eyes, the dark figures struggling up

151

against the flames of their own ship burning, spurts of small-arms fire and a rush of cutlass-swinging sailors, while Wyatt roared 'Shoot 'em! Drive 'em back where they belong!'

Into the sea, or the flames, he'd meant.

That German with his hands up: and the bark of Wyatt's gun . . . But *had* he had his hands up, in the sense of surrendering?

When you thought too hard about a thing, you confused the recollection of it. Then you found yourself faced with a question you couldn't answer positively, and suddenly what had been clear-cut wasn't so any longer. Last night in *Arrogant*, the old depot ship, drinking whisky round a table with Tim Rogerson, Harry Underhill and Wally Bell, he'd put it to them as a theoretical problem, a sort of 'what-would-you-do-if' exercise; but that hadn't fooled them. They'd glanced at each other quickly, understanding why he'd been quiet and thoughtful, gloomy, when he'd been supposed to be the guest of honour and chief celebrant. Bell, the former Law student, tried to change Nick's perspective of the incident.

'There's no accepted method of surrender for a ship other than by hauling down her ensign. And at night that's no use anyway, since no one sees it . . . But the Huns never actually did surrender their ship, did they?'

'Oh, she was done for!'

'*Did* they, though?'

'No.' And even 'done for', one or more Huns had still been shooting from their bridge or somewhere with a rifle.

Bell pontificated, 'Nobody's ever accepted the idea of individuals surrendering, at sea. If a ship sinks, or strikes her colours, you have survivors or prisoners – and that's clear, beyond argument. But suppose at Jutland when Jellicoe was lambasting some German dreadnought, if a couple of Huns on its signal-bridge had semaphored "Kamerad!"? D'you think the Grand Fleet would've ceased fire?'

Nick interrupted the other two's amusement. 'I'm talking about a man with his hands up and another with a pistol; not Jutland, or—'

'*Sure* he had his hands up?'

'Yes, of course I'm sure!'

'Like this?' Wally Bell had raised his hands in the 'Kamerad' position: 'or like *this*?' Hands forward: hauling himself aboard, or warding off attack, or reaching *at* someone ... Wally added, 'You were looking down at an angle, so—'

'He was scared stiff. He had his mouth wide open, screaming or—'

'Or shouting "Charge!"' ... *Which* way were his hands out, did you say?' He only gave Nick a moment to find an answer; then he banged the table, making empty glasses jump. 'Can't be certain, can you. And that's hardly surprising – considering the distance from bridge-rail to stem-head, and the angle, and flames and smoke and the fact you weren't ever exactly an admirer of the man we're talking about – or –' he glanced round, lowering his voice – 'or *not* talking about ... Tim, Harry, what d'you say?'

Rogerson shook his head. 'You *couldn't* tell. And you're right – in a mix-up like that, a few men shouting "I give in" doesn't stop the action.'

'Harry?'

Bell was asking Underhill for comment. The CMB man turned his deepset eyes on Nick. He growled, 'They

153

shouldn't 've been there in the first place . . . Raiding –
raiding the drifters on the minefield? A drifter's almost
helpless – well, it *is*, it's a sitting duck to a destroyer, less
use even than that clumsy thing Wally drives . . . Well –
what'd those Huns've done if they'd got through to the
drifter patrols? Filled the lads' Christmas stockings? If
a drifter skipper shouted "I surrender" and waved both
hands at 'em – not that you could imagine any such
thing – what d'you think, a Hun destroyer captain 'd
cease fire?'

It was puzzling, and confusing. They were talking a
certain kind of sense, and they were honest, decent men,
his friends. Bell told him, while Tim Rogerson was calling
to the steward for another round of drinks, 'We're on
your side, Nick. Telling you not to be a mug!'

Admiral Bacon had issued a Press announcement
about some action a year or so ago, and he'd included
in it a statement that 'fortunately' many German sailors'
lives had been saved. That word 'fortunately' had let
him in for a barrage of newspaper criticism, and his
mail for days afterwards had been full of vituperative
letters from the public. The Germans were 'baby-killers'
– because bombardments of East Coast towns, and
Zeppelin bombs, had killed some children; and they'd
sunk the *Lusitania*, torpedoed hospital ships. It was
true, they had; hospital ships sailed unmarked now,
for their own safety. And yet not long ago a German
aeroplane had swooped low over the RNAS aerodrome
at Dunkirk and dropped a parcel; it had contained
the personal effects of a naval pilot whom they'd
shot down, and a piece of ribbon from the German
wreath on his grave, and a photograph of the guard
of honour firing a salute over it at the military funeral
they'd given him.

Nick asked the other three, 'Is it necessary to hate them, d'you think?'

Bell only raised his eyebrows and his glass. Underhill rubbed his cleft chin thoughtfully. Rogerson suggested, 'I suppose it does make the whole thing *simpler*?'

There was a dream-quality now about it all, a jumbling of recollections and detail. What had come first or last, what in between: fear of that unshored section of the bulkhead merged into a battle with the sea in which the weapons had been wires, lines, cables, men's strength and courage . . . Nick forced his mind away from it, back into the present: at least, he tried to: he saw Wyatt at attention, wooden-faced, staring straight at him, and behind Wyatt half the ship's company motionless, immaculate, parade-ground bluejackets: this was how the crowd saw them, the civilians packed tightly around this rectangle of ritual grief; but for one's own part one saw through to the dark foul-smelling crowded caverns of the messdecks and a threatened bulkhead, and tired, hungry, haggard men playing cards, joking, even singing . . . Cockcroft said suddenly, as clearly as if he'd been standing there at his elbow, '*Fine body of men, what?*' But nobody had spoken, and Cockcroft had said it – what, four days ago? Only *four days*? Wyatt was still staring at him. Mr Gladwish was on Wyatt's right, while Grant and Watson were on either side of Nick. The bugle's last note blossomed, quavered, died. In the utter silence that followed it, he heard a man sob, somewhere close behind him. He nearly did the same himself: he could have, he could have let go completely, sunk to his knees and cried like a child. But it was over now, all over, and they were marching back through the town, through quiet, sympathetic crowds, grey streets and a bitter December noon.

*　　*　　*

'Sit down, Everard.' Wyatt pointed. 'Help yourself to a glass of that stuff.'

'No thank you, sir.' He sat down, though. Just a few days ago, this cabin had been an operating theatre: it seemed strange that it was now once again a place where one might be invited to sip pink gin. Wyatt looked surprised that he didn't want one: he stared at him for a moment, then he shrugged. He said, 'I wanted a word with you before you go to this – interview, or investigation, whatever it's going to be.'

It was to do with the trouble in the Fishermen's Arms, the brawl and the military police report on it. Nick had to report himself at an office in the secretariat at 2.30 p.m.; that was all he knew.

'Yes, sir.'

Wyatt stood up, and placed himself at the scuttle, staring out. Stooping slightly, and with his hands clasped behind his back. He cleared his throat.

'As you know, I washed my hands of the whole affair. I felt you'd not only behaved in – in an unseemly manner, but that you'd very badly let me down. Let this *ship* down. I –' he turned, glanced at Nick briefly and away again – 'I think in my position you'd have felt the same.'

Nick waited, through another interval of throat-clearing.

'But as I mentioned to you the other day –' Wyatt gestured towards the harbour entrance – 'when we were being brought in – as I said then, I've acquired a very high opinion of your professional abilities . . .'

Nick remembered, rather vaguely: but Wyatt had expressed it in terms of – *gratitude*? Emotionally disturbed, perhaps, by the reception which Dover was giving *Mackerel*. They'd been cheering her into harbour:

ships and jetties lined with shouting, cap-waving sailors, and a bedlam of sirens shrieking from destroyers, trawlers, drifters ... Dockyard maties, driftermen, trawlermen, and crowds of civilians all along the Marine Parade, cheering themselves hoarse. Christmas evening . . . Dusk had been seeping down over the inland hills, and the wind had dropped; it had been quite easy transferring the tow from *Moloch* to the two big tugs who'd brought her in and berthed her. Totally different to the struggle to get the tow connected in the first place – at dawn, working on a heaving, slippery deck with the sea breaking right over her and knocking men off their feet. *One hand for the ship and one for yourself* was the old sailors' phrase for it: but a man needed *five* hands, and preferably feet with suckers on them too. Nick had worked with his men, and the battle had gone on for hours: he still dreamt of it, of enormous seas mounting, hanging over the heads of sailors who couldn't see them coming, who were caught, trapped in loops of wire-rope, doomed: he'd be trying to shout, to warn them, and his jaw locked so he couldn't make a sound, only watch the sea break and boil . . . There'd been a light line to get over first – and heaving lines weren't easy to manage in a high wind from a tilting deck and when ships couldn't approach each other too closely for fear of being swept into collision – and then the grass, the coir rope that floated, had to be attached to the first line and hauled across; then, on the end of the grass rope came the 3½-inch steel-wire hawser. The mine-winch had proved useless, and the after capstan had been smashed in the action, so everything had to be done by man-power, muscle-power. When the ships were linked and *Moloch* moved cautiously ahead, dragging at *Mackerel*'s stern to get her round on course for Dover, the wire had sprung bar-taut and snapped as easily as a banjo-string: two minutes, it had lasted, after two hours' backbreaking work – which had now to begin all over again. This time *Moloch* started by shifting two shackles of anchor-cable aft, and the wire was linked to it so that the chain-cable's weight acted as a spring and prevented further snappings under sudden strain. A pity they hadn't done it in the first place; it wasn't so unusual an evolution. It had worked, finally; but to get the wire inboard and secure it, with the cable's weight dragging at it and the ship flinging herself in all directions, had needed practically every fit seaman in the ship, like a tug-of-war team strung out along her upper deck – slipping, sliding, cursing. A dozen times he saw men slip or be knocked off their feet: seconds and inches more than once saved lives. In the end, hardly knowing how they'd done it, they had the two ships linked, and *Mackerel* was on her way to Dover.

They'd been entering the port, surrounded by the enthusiastic welcome, when Wyatt had called Nick to him at the front rail of the bridge. With the ship in the tugs' charge, there was nothing for anyone to do. Wyatt had said, 'If you hadn't shored that bulkhead, Number One, we wouldn't be here now. I'm very much aware of that. And your conduct generally has been of the highest order. I'm – grateful to you.'

'Thank you, sir.'

It hadn't meant anything to him. Nor had the cheering, hooting, waving. One knew what it was all about, and understood the meaning of Wyatt's words, but there'd been a numbness, a feeling of remoteness. And there were so many things that needed seeing to, to be getting on with as soon as the ship was berthed: even inside the harbour, until that bulkhead's lower part was shored one was aware of the weakness, one's own neglect . . . But now, forty-eight hours later, Wyatt was saying roughly the same thing again, and Nick's immediate reaction was a feeling of embarrassment, that he was sailing under false colours. What his captain was saying to him was *You're forgiven: you can stay with me, now* . . . And he didn't want to. It should have been possible to say so, and to say why: but he couldn't, they'd been right last night in *Arrogant*, it would have been the action of a mug – achieving nothing except damage to oneself.

All the same, this keeping quiet, letting Wyatt assume he'd want to stay with him, felt less like common sense or diplomacy than subterfuge.

Wyatt told him, 'I can't undo what's been said and done already, and I can't predict what sort of view they'll take. Un-officer-like behaviour ashore is not, even in wartime, something to be treated as of no account, or condoned.' He scowled, and cleared his throat. 'However, I've done my best to give you some support.'

He picked up a sheet of foolscap from the desk-top near him.

'I've sent a copy of this – an extract from my Report of Proceedings – with a covering letter expressing my wish to retain you as my first lieutenant, to Captain (D). He'll have passed it on to this chap Reaper, the man you'll be seeing. Whoever *he* may be.'

Wyatt sat down.

'There are – don't discuss this with anyone else, please – there are – new faces about the place. Sir Reginald Bacon is leaving Dover, and Admiral Keyes is relieving him. With, I believe, more or less immediate effect. And naturally this will bring other changes at lower levels.'

It wasn't much of a surprise. There'd been talk of it for some while; and only last night Tim Rogerson had told Nick he'd heard it was imminent.

Poor old Bacon. He'd foundered, finally, on the floodlit minefield. And the Admiralty committee who'd forced that issue had been headed by Keyes, who'd now displaced him ... Wyatt said, 'Here is what I said in my report, Everard.' He coughed, and read: *'I wish to draw their Lordships' attention to the high standard of leadership and initiative displayed by my second-in-command, Lieutenant Nicholas Everard, Royal Navy. First, as already stated, this officer aimed and fired the torpedo which sank one enemy destroyer. Subsequently throughout the hours following the action his personal energy, zeal and professional ability provided an example to the entire ship's company. Finally the passing of the tow, of which he took charge on deck under extremely adverse weather conditions, was a triumph of seamanship and good discipline.'*

Wyatt slid the document on to his desk, and asked Nick, 'Fair comment?'

'More than generous, sir.'

And neat. Commending Nick, it avoided – as no doubt it would in the main body of the report as well – any mention of it having been his decision, not Wyatt's, to shore the bulkhead – or that he'd felt it was necessary after Wyatt had talked of going at *Mackerel*'s 'best speed', against Nick's and the engineer's advice. Obviously, Wyatt wouldn't have filled in such details. *He* was no 'mug', either.

Nick looked down at his clasped hands, and thought. *But Swan's still in there* ...

He glanced up, and met Wyatt's stare.

'I suppose you'll be putting in recommendations –

160

with the report on the action – for honours and awards?'

Surprise: suspicion . . . Wyatt thought he might be about to propose some decoration for himself! He went on, 'Chief Petty Officer Swan, sir. Perhaps you'll have included him already. But in case not – well, he was at that bulkhead in full awareness of the danger of it bursting. Even *because* of that.'

'I'll – consider your suggestion.'

'Thank you, sir.'

Mr Gladwish, reclining in an armchair, looked up over his *Daily Mail* as Nick entered the wardroom.

'There's some mail for you, Number One.'

'Good.'

The gunner winked. 'How was –' He jerked his head, towards the skipper's cabin. Nick shrugged.

'Much as one might have expected.'

He was only just realizing what Wyatt had done: that he'd offered him a trade. Nick should keep his mouth shut about bulkheads and speed and so on, and in return for that he'd have Wyatt's support and commendation.

The mail was on the table, and there were three letters for him. One was a bill, from Gieves. Needn't even open that one. On another he recognised his stepmother's writing, and the third was from his uncle. His spirits rose immediately; those were the two people he liked to hear from.

'Sherry please, Warburton.' He sat down at the table, and ripped open his uncle's letter first. 'How about you, Guns?'

'I don't mind.' Gladwish nodded. 'Very civil of you . . . Plymouth an' bitters, steward.'

'Aye aye, sir.'

Rear-Admiral Hugh Everard had written from his cruiser flagship in Scapa Flow, *I cannot tell you how pleased we have all been, and how delighted I am personally, by the news of your recent success in the Dover straits. Well done! Most refreshing, at a time when affairs seemed to be going less well down there. How splendid that it should have been your* Mackerel *that has – let us hope – turned the tide. I congratulate you most heartily and look forward to your account of the action.*

From this northern fastness I have no excitements to report. Our weather has been some of the worst in living memory, and very trying for all concerned, particularly of course for the small fry. But we keep the seas, and our powder dry, and live in hopes that the Hun may one day poke his snout out of his earth again.

I have been south only once since I saw you on leave at Mullbergh, and this time I did not visit the old place. Sarah has her hands full enough as it is, with her convalescents, and in any case I was obliged to spend some time in the vicinity of the Admiralty. I have had no word from, or news of, your father . . .

When he'd finished reading it, he folded it and stuffed it in his pocket. He had a great affection and respect for his uncle – whose tales of the Navy, all through Nick's childhood, had fired him with the ambition to go to sea. Admittedly there'd been a period, of some years' duration, at Dartmouth as a cadet and later as a midshipman with the Grand Fleet when he'd been thoroughly disillusioned: his feeling had been that the Navy his uncle spoke of with such enthusiasm – Hugh Everard had never ceased to, in spite of the fact that it had once rejected him, virtually thrown him out – that

162

this great Service he loved so deeply was the Navy of past years, changed now into something entirely different, while Hugh clung to his own image of it. Until Jutland, Nick had detested it. The Navy had seemed to be – well, all Wyatts, little ones and big ones; all pomp and humbug, dreary routine and self-importance, silly ritual. That described Dartmouth, all right, and it described a dreadnought's gunroom too if you added a generous measure of sadistic bullying. But the other side of the coin, which Nick had first glimpsed at Jutland, was there as well. If the Wyatts and other distractions could be cleared away, leaving the view of the purer concept, what might be thought of as an updated Nelsonian view . . . Perhaps it could happen. Meanwhile one needed to keep it in mind and see *past* the Wyatts . . . Returning to Hugh Everard's letter now: it was odd that he'd stayed away from Mullbergh. He and Sarah, Nick's young stepmother, got on so well, so obviously liked each other. Nick, adoring Sarah and admiring his uncle, had always been happy to see their friendship. Because Sarah needed support, and because he was ashamed of his father's treatment of her and glad Uncle Hugh existed as proof that not all Everards were brutes.

Sarah had once said to him, 'You're *so* like your uncle!' and he'd thought it was probably the nicest thing anyone had ever said to him.

He sipped his sherry, and read her letter eagerly.

My dearest Nick. Such wonderful, exciting news of you and your magnificent Mackerels! I must hear all about it – write now, at once, if you have been so churlish as not to have done so by the time this reaches you. Better still – take some leave. COME HERE and thrill me with the details! I have absolutely no doubt that you yourself will have

been wildly brave and dashing again; please PLEASE
send or bring me news as soon as you are able!

Life continues to be hectic here, now that we are
a hospital-cum-convalescent home. I have an excuse,
moreover – in fact dozens of them, some laid up and
some hobbling about on crutches – to keep big fires
blazing and warming this cold old place. It's so good to
feel it's serving a useful purpose instead of just rotting
away. Meanwhile I have heard from your father for the
first time in two months; he tells me that he is well,
has a new address and is commanding some training
establishment which is also a remount depot. Alastair
Kinloch-Stuart, whom you may remember meeting here
and who is by chance in the district again – staying with
the Ormsbys as it happens – tells me that it must be a
riding school. Apparently officers are being commissioned
now who do not know how to ride! One finds it difficult to
imagine your father in such company – and one would
certainly not wish to be one of his pupils!

Nick skimmed through the rest of it: with the name
and face of Captain (or was it Major?) Kinloch-Stuart
sticking in his mind like grit. He'd arrived at Mullbergh
for luncheon, one day when Nick had last been there
on leave; he'd been supposed to be staying with friends
nearby then too, and Sarah had introduced him as 'an
old friend from years ago' . . . A bit later, lunching with
Uncle Hugh in London and short of news or subjects for
conversation, he'd mentioned him, and Hugh Everard
had bristled like a dog catching a whiff of cat: and then
denied having even heard the man's name before.

Nick pushed Sarah's letter into his pocket. Her
phrases 'by chance' and 'as it happens' were mistakes,
he thought. She'd overdone it. And she needn't have
mentioned the man at all: she must have *wanted* to,

wanted to put it before his, Nick's, eyes, to *tell* him something . . .

He pulled the letter out, re-read that part of it. It was not, he told himself, any of his business. Nor were his assumptions necessarily correct. He was almost certainly doing Sarah a great injustice. Not that anyone could have blamed her, if she *had*—

One knew nothing, so what was the point of brooding and conjecturing? Kinloch-Stuart was a Cameron Highlander, so far as he could remember. Might his hanging around Mullbergh explain Uncle Hugh's staying away from the place? And what sort of appointment might the man hold that seemed to keep him almost permanently on leave, sponging on everyone in turn?

Forget it. It was fantasy and guesswork building on – on what? On jealousy?

Annabel's voice like honey in his skull: *Why d'you call me 'Sarah' all night long?*

Such nonsense, all of this. The mind played tricks – if one allowed it to . . . He got up, walked to the scuttle, stared out over the harbour and the stone breakwater to the sea's grey-green swell. He made himself think about his father . . . Out of the fighting now, in a safe job. But still a command, of sorts; and to do with horses, so he'd consider it honourable enough . . . Might he have wangled it – or been shunted into it, out of the way? What it boiled down to was he'd survive, he'd return eventually to Mullbergh and to Sarah.

Gladwish raised his glass. 'Your 'ealth, Number One!'

He nodded. 'And yours, Mr Gladwish.'

'Good news from 'ome, I trust?'

'Oh – yes . . .'

*   *   *

He walked eastward along Marine Parade. It was cuttingly cold still, but there was hardly any wind. This morning the flag on the castle had fluttered strongly: now it drooped, hardly stirring, and the clouds were high and static. So *Mackerel* should be on her way soon, as intended; the thing was, would he go with her?

She'd have only a skeleton crew for the tow round. A third of the ship's company had gone off on home-leave this morning; and more would be left in hospital beds . . . He saw motor-cars drawn up outside the Admiral's headquarters, and officers were hurrying in and out of the main door in the centre, where a sentry was constantly springing to attention and then standing at ease again. It was between the three adjoining buildings that the to-ing and fro-ing was taking place; the first house contained offices, the middle one – called Fleet House – was the Admiral's official residence, and the third held the secretariat. Including, apparently, this man Reaper, to whom Nick had been summoned. Room 14 . . . But he had time in hand; he walked on past, on the sea side of the road, looking the place over. Sandbags round the doors and windows stopped one seeing much. He wondered *which* great man would be in there at the moment – the usurper, or the evacuee?

He thought again, *Poor old Bacon* . . . 'Fred Karno' was his nickname amongst the destroyer men, on account of the ragbag collection of ships, establishments, aircraft and so on that comprised the Patrol. 'Fred Karno's Navy' . . . With, behind the scenes, such backroom wizards as the redoubtable Lillicrap; and Wing-Commander Brock, of the famous firework family, who was in charge of flares – the flares that lit the minefield at the Varne, for instance. Brock had a lot to do with Bacon's smoke-laying experiments, too; and a column of smoke rising now from the end of the naval pier showed that experiments were still going on. Testing the new burners that Bacon was so keen on, probably. The difficulty with the existing type, which were used in MLs, motor-launches – it was from Wally Bell that Nick had heard all this – was that at night the flames from the burning white phosphorous showed up through the smoke. They were trying out various kinds of baffle in metal funnels, trying to find a way of baffling flame without baffling smoke as well; and Bacon's inventiveness had devised a way of water-cooling the troughs in which the burners rested, thus thickening the smoke with steam. Cooling was desirable in any case; at a bombardment of the enemy coast during the summer the great man had had smoke-burners placed in rowing boats that were towed by the MLs, and two men in each rowing boat to ignite the burners and keep them burning properly, but the machines had become red-hot, and their attendants had had to swim for it as an alternative to roasting. Now there was a new plan, to hang burners from kites, to blind enemy spotter-aircraft ... One wondered whether Admiral Keyes might yet appreciate the full scope of his inheritance!

But it was time to turn back, face his *own* problems.

He doubted whether Wyatt's new report on him would make much odds. At the time of the pub riot he'd stood aside and washed his hands like Pontius Pilate; and it was that incident, in its own context and circumstances, that was to be considered now. The fact that one had carried out one's duties at sea

in a satisfactory way needn't come into this at all –
any more than the fortuitous success at Jutland had
lessened official rancour over that other, comparatively
trifling misdemeanour. This one was not trifling. For
an officer to become involved in a public brawl, and
with members of his own ship's company – and at
that, fighting (as *they'd* see it) over a woman who—

Who *what*?

In retrospect, he didn't know what to make of
Annabel. There were certain possible conclusions from
which he ran away when he thought about her. He
liked to see her in his mind as she'd seemed to him
in the early part of the evening, at first sight: and in
any case she'd been kind, sweet to him. He *liked* her.
Then there was another image of her in his memory:
she leant over him, soothing his injured head, sponging
it; she was naked and so was he, and her breasts swung,
nipples brushing his chest. There was this enormously
appealing warmth – and the concern, the anxiety in her
eyes. It was a sexually stimulating memory but there was
innocence in it too, a balancing degree of affection, of –
using the word plainly, not in a hearts-and-roses sense
– of love.

And he'd called her – dreamt of her as – *Sarah?*

He pulled his thoughts together. He was about to be
hauled over the coals: and with good reason. He might,
or might not if he was very lucky, face a court-martial
after this, and be formally dismissed his ship.

Wyatt had been looking after his own interests, not
Nick's. He'd tried to ensure that Nick wouldn't speak
out of turn and upset his apple-cart, but at the same
time his commendation of Nick over his usefulness at
sea didn't in any way imply that he'd condoned or
would want to condone *this* sort of behaviour.

A sentry shouldered arms, slapped the butt of his rifle. Nick returned the salute as he walked up the steps of what had been – and would one day be again – a seaside lodging-house.

In Room 14 a young paymaster with a rather supercilious expression stared at him from behind a desk. A coal-fire smouldered in a grate close to his chair, but here, ten feet away, the room was icy.

'May I help you?'

'Everard. *Mackerel*.'

'Everard?' He was checking in an appointment book. 'Oh, yes.' He didn't smile. 'I'll tell Commander Reaper you're here.'

'Hang on a moment.' Nick stepped closer. 'Tell me first – who is he, or *what* is he?'

The 'paybob' raised his eyebrows. It seemed he didn't much like the question. Or perhaps he didn't like any questions, from an officer who was on the carpet. He had a handkerchief tucked into his left sleeve, Nick noticed – a flag lieutenant's affectation. Was that how the fellow saw himself?

It looked as if he wasn't going to satisfy Nick's curiosity about the mysterious Commander Reaper. He was glancing downwards, now, at an elegant half-hunter that had materialized in his palm.

'I'll see if he's ready for you.'

He was getting to his feet, coming out from behind the desk. Nick moved, placing himself between the smooth young man and the door. 'I asked you a question. I'd like an answer, please.'

The paymaster's eyebrows practically vanished into the roots of his hair.

'Commander Reaper is seconded temporarily from

the Plans Division at the Admiralty.' He frowned. 'Would you be good enough to step aside?'

'Of course.'

'Thank you.'

'Not at all.'

Reaper was a man of medium size; he had a narrow head, a beak of a nose, deep-set eyes and a quiet, pleasant tone of voice.

Nick sat facing him across a littered trestle-table. On the far side of the room was a desk which presumably belonged to its more permanent occupant, and from that unoccupied swivel chair whoever it was would have a view down on to the harbour with the destroyer moorings in the foreground. He found that by turning his head and leaning back in his chair he had part of the same view. He could see several destroyers at their buoys; some were doubled-up, moored in pairs. The ship just entering now, with her whaler pulling like mad for the buoy to get there before the destroyer herself nosed up to it, was *Zubian*. She'd been put together from the bows of *Zulu* and the stern half of *Nubian*, after each of the two tribals had suffered appropriate damage. It had been Bacon's idea, to make one new ship out of the remains of two.

Reaper muttered, 'I shan't be long.' He was studying a file, frowning as he turned its pages. The invitation to sit down had surprised Nick; he'd expected to have to stand to attention, the accepted attitude for a junior officer being verbally flayed by a senior one. He waited; the whaler's bowman was on the buoy now, shackling *Zubian's* cable to its ring.

'Well, then.' Reaper's eyes were on him. 'Everard . . .' He nodded. 'The name is not unfamiliar to me.'

170

He'd paused, and seemed to be inviting comment. Nick asked him, 'You know my uncle, sir?'

Reaper nodded. 'But it is *highly* unfamiliar in terms of any possible connection with fisticuffs in back-street bars.'

'Yes, sir. I'm very sorry it happened, sir.'

'Such behaviour, Everard, does not become an officer of the Royal Navy. It does not become a gentleman. It does not become *anyone* you, I imagine, would wish to be taken for.'

'No, sir.'

'And it is particularly, *totally* unbecoming –' Reaper pushed some papers about, then located and held up what looked like the original of the report Wyatt had read out to him – '*totally* so to the officer whose abilities and qualities are referred to in this statement.'

'Yes, sir.'

Reaper leant back in his chair, but his eyes still rested hawkishly on Nick's.

'I have no disciplinary responsibilities here, Everard. And permit me to add that I *thank God* for that circumstance –' he leant forward, and his voice rose slightly as he tapped the file he'd been reading – 'since this kind of squalid time-wasting is utterly beyond my comprehension!'

'Yes, sir.'

'It is also beyond my capacity to tolerate!'

'Sir . . .'

For the last few seconds, he'd been feeling hopeful, but this last remark produced the reverse effect. There was a silence now; he raised his eyes, endured again that unrelenting scrutiny. He was at a loss to understand Reaper's position, attitude or purpose, and he suspected that this was precisely the effect the man was aiming at.

'Well. I presume, Everard, that there were circumstances which might throw a less harsh light on your conduct than the one which – er – shines from the report?'

'Only that I had no intention of getting into any sort of scrap, sir. I was there, and it sort of blew up all around me, and while I was –' he paused, searching for the word – 'while I was withdrawing, sir, I got knocked on the head.'

'Were you drunk?'

'I – well, not knowingly or intentionally, sir. But I think someone spiked my beer with rum.'

Reaper hit the table with the flat of his hand.

'Then you're a *colossal* fool, boy!' Nick frowned, watching him. Reaper blew out his cheeks. 'You enter the lowest drinking den in Dover, and don't keep your eye on your own glass of beer?'

'I hadn't imagined driftermen would be so keen to chuck their rum about, sir.'

'A chance to make a prize idiot out of a young pup with gold braid on his sleeve and the King's commission?'

'Oh.' He nodded, still frowning. Skipper Barrie, he wondered: would it have been *his* idea of a joke? 'Yes. I see, sir.'

Reaper took a deep breath, and let it out again. He asked him, 'You left the place with a girl. Is that correct? One of the town's—'

'Girl, sir?'

Reaper stared at him thoughtfully. Then he tapped the file again. 'According to the military police report—'

'My memory's none too clear on some points, sir. I suppose the rum in my beer . . .' He stopped talking.

172

He could see that Reaper didn't believe him. But Reaper, extraordinarily, smiled.

'Quite.' He looked down, taking his eyes off Nick's face for the first time since he'd started the interview. 'Quite . . .' The smile faded as he glanced quickly through Wyatt's letter. Nodding slowly as he read. Now he looked up again.

'I have a certain function to perform here in Dover, Everard. So far as your own case is concerned, it so happened that this – this –' he poked at the file – 'degrading and time-wasting affair came up when your name was mentioned in another quarter – came up as something which had to be dealt with, decided somehow – and it fell to me to – er – kill several birds with one stone. *This* one is now – dead.'

He saw Nick's joy. He added quickly, 'Except to point out to you that your – your lack of wisdom, shall we say – has let down yourself, your uniform and a distinguished name. It has also wasted the time of quite a number of busy men. You'll see to it in the future, Everard, that you do not become associated with incidents of such a kind: and understand *this*, too: we are busy here, we are *extremely* busy and we have important, *very* important matters in our minds; we have an enormous amount to think about and to get on with. We *cannot*, cannot *possibly*, have our time wasted on such squalid trivialities. Were we *less* busy, and had the matter been referred to some different quarter for decision, you might very easily have found yourself facing a court-martial. Do you understand?'

'Yes, sir. Completely, sir.'

'You'd better not see that girl again.'

Nick stared at him. He hadn't admitted there'd been a girl, or anyway that he remembered one.

Besides . . .

'Very well, we can regard that unpleasant episode as concluded, I think.'

'I'm extremely grateful, sir.'

'What you mean, Everard, is you're extremely *relieved*.' Reaper nodded. 'Understandably. In your place, so'd I be . . . However – in all the circumstances, I hardly think we could leave you in *Mackerel* now.'

Nick waited.

'She'll be months in dockyard hands, in any case. You won't be missing anything worthwhile. D'you mind leaving her?'

'No, sir, I—'

'No . . .' He murmured as much to himself as to his visitor, 'And if you stayed in her, you might miss a great deal.'

'Sir?'

Reaper shook his head. 'It happens there's a job of work we want done. It's suggested you could be the man to do it.' The hawk's eyes were fixed on him. 'Know much about CMBs?'

'I've been out in one on engine trials, sir, and handled her a bit.' Harry Underhill's boat, that had been, on an occasion when *Mackerel* had been boiler-cleaning. He added, 'An RNR called Underhill has told me most of what I know about them.'

'That's the fellow you'll work with. Only –' Reaper pointed at him with a pencil – 'only for a short while, just this one – er – errand.' He got up, walked over to the window. Nick stood up too. Reaper said, staring out at the destroyers at their moorings, 'CMB officers are rather thin on the ground, at this moment. Experienced chaps, that is. Some are down at *Vernon* being told about the new mines we're getting, and the rest are up at Osea Island, the new base that's being built there. So there it is. I want you to take command of one of the forty-footers – I'm told CMB 11 is available and operational and suitable. Your second-in-command is an RNR midshipman by the name of –' he put his hand to his eyes, concentrating – 'Selby.' Turning from the window now. 'Have your gear sent over to *Arrogant*. I'll make a signal immediately, appointing you to her for special duties. It'll only be for a few days, though.'

'What after that, sir?'

'I don't command the Sixth Flotilla, Everard.'

'You mean it'll be decided by Captain (D), sir, after I do this – well, whatever this –'

'As it happens, a Captain Tomkinson will be arriving shortly to take over the destroyer command.' Reaper shook his head. 'Look, I've no time for chit-chat . . . I want you to spend as much time as you can in that CMB. Get the feel of her, and to know her crew, and Underhill can exercise his boat with you. There's still a swell running, but we're promised a period of calm. You've got two days to prepare yourself. Night after next should be right for our purposes, from the weather point of view; there'll be a moon, and that might be the one thing that stops us; but with any luck we'll have cloud to cover it.' He'd spoken fast, disjointedly; now he went to his table, picked up some papers, dropped them, turned to Nick again. 'My reasons for offering you this, Everard, are that you've been in the straits for some while now, and as a navigator – so you know your way about. With the high speed of the CMBs, plus the fact you'll be carrying out the operation on a low-water spring tide, that's vital. Second, your ship's out of action, so you're available immediately. Third, you've shown you know how to keep your head in

175

action. I need these qualities, and the CMB officers who have 'em aren't here, and it's not a thing that can wait. So – you'll command the operation.'

'Command it, sir?'

Reaper nodded.

'But Underhill's an experienced CMB officer, sir – and he can certainly navigate – and I'm coming in as an outsider—'

'He hasn't your experience of action.' Reaper was impatient suddenly. 'Look here, Everard – the nursery days are finished, you're *fledged* now, you can expect to be given quite considerable responsibility at any time . . . If you shirk your opportunities, you'll never amount to anything!'

He'd seemed more genuinely angry, in that outburst, than he'd been during the discussion of the Fisherman's Arms affair. Now he shrugged.

'I know it's – unorthodox. The job has to be done, that's all. And you're damn lucky to get the chance of it!'

'Sir.'

'You'll have an ML with you as well as the two CMBs. A launch will be allocated by Captain Edwards, and her CO will be told to report to you. Tonight, probably. I'll brief you and the other officers tomorrow evening aboard *Arrogant*, and that'll leave you part of the following day to decide how to set about it.'

How to set about *what*, for God's sake . . . He nodded.

'Aye aye, sir.'

Reaper said, 'Better get moving, then.'

CHAPTER 9

He eased down on the throttle. CMB 11's engine-noise dropped from its aeroplane-like roar to a quieter but deep-throated grumble, her bow dropped abruptly as the speed fell off and she levelled in the water, and her own wash came up from astern in a series of humps that lifted, rocked her, carried her bodily along. Then all that was over, and she was motoring quietly but powerfully across the swell.

Off to starboard, inshore, Nick saw Harry Underhill's boat curve hard to port, coming out this way to join him. He said to Selby, 'We'll go in, now.'

'Right!'

Selby laughed. He laughed at nothing: or rather, at everything. Nick found it irritating, and he wondered how Weatherhead could stand having him around on a permanent basis and at such close quarters. In a cockpit ten feet by six, which was roughly this one's dimensions, you couldn't get far from your companions. Midshipman Selby had yellow hair and a bright-red face pitted and scarred by acne; he was about nineteen. Nick had noticed how ERA Ross, the boat's mechanic and the third and last member of her crew, went deadpan at the sound of Selby's laugh: as if he'd have liked to have snatched up a spanner and hit him with it, and feared that one day he might.

Nick said, 'Flash *Let's go home* to him.'

'What?' Selby cackled. 'What—'

'Oh, Christ . . .' Nick pointed. 'Give me the lamp.'

Selby managed to hear that; he snatched it up and passed it over. Nick said, shouting in his ear, 'Now stand still!' He kept his left hand on the wheel and used the other one, balancing the lamp on Selby's shoulder, to call CMB 14, Underhill, and tell him it was time to pack up. Harry acknowledged it. Nick pushed the lamp into Selby's hands; he bent down, peered in at Ross through the small doorless hatchway in the centre of the cockpit's for'ard bulkhead.

'All right?'

Ross, squatting on his wooden seat on the engine's starboard side, grinned and raised a thumb. He was a long-boned man, and the seat was built against the inside curve of the boat's hull: it curved *him*, in conformity with her shape, and in that squatting position his knees stuck up like posts. Nick shouted to him, 'We're going in, now!' Then he straightened, opened the throttle to about one third, and pointed the boat's long, tapering bow at the eastern entrance.

They hadn't been over three-quarters speed this afternoon, on account of this swell that was still running. CMBs were fine-weather boats; in any sort of sea, at speed, they tended to leap from crest to crest, not only trying to knock their bottoms out but also tending to plunge *into* oncoming waves instead of over them. The larger boats – fifty-five-footers – managed a little better, but even they were too lightly built to stand up to the pounding a sea would give them at speed.

Underhill had swung his boat in astern of Nick's, and was following him towards the harbour. The light was going now, and it had been only a short outing, but Nick felt it had been worthwhile. He was happy with her; he could do anything with her, he thought, that anyone else could do. Leaving the jetty he'd been a bit clumsy – he'd forgotten how a boat's stern kicked off to starboard when a large single screw was put ahead and the deeper blade or blades of it, revolving in a greater density of water, had more effect than the upper ones – but he'd got it all under control now, he understood her and knew within reasonable limits what you could do and what you couldn't. At high speed, for instance, you couldn't safely slam on too much wheel; not unless you wanted to turn her right over. And she had no reversing gear: you couldn't go astern, so to come alongside you had to stop in time to get the way off her before she bumped.

The gap in the eastern breakwater wasn't far ahead, and he eased the throttle down. Keeping well to starboard, and being careful not to come in fast with an accompanying wash that would certainly infuriate and possibly damage ships alongside jetties or other ships, who'd be rocked and ground against each other . . . Inside he turned her to starboard, turning just short of three squat monitors at buoys. A Trinity House tender lay at anchor ahead; he turned the CMB close under her stern, then swung the other way to clear an anchored dredger. Now it would be a straight course and about five hundred yards to the camber, the inner basin. To starboard the sea heaved and boomed, lopping against the harbour wall; to port, the destroyer lines were almost empty. *Zubian* was still there, and beyond her lay a tribal, and near the centre of the harbour were two 'oily wads' and one of the big flotilla leaders; but all the rest were at sea – protecting the fishing-craft on the mine barrage, guarding Folkestone and the shipping in the Downs, watching the Dunkirk and Boulogne approaches, or patrolling in other set areas. Destroyers' daytime duties were more varied: escorting transports and leave ships between Folkestone and Boulogne, and hospital and store-ships between Dunkirk and Calais and Dover; escorting allied and neutral shipping through the swept channel that hugged the coast from Dungeness to North Foreland; protecting the sweepers who every single day swept all those routes clear of mines. Under Bacon, the Patrol had certainly earned its living.

But gossip had said that a change of admiral would be linked to a more aggressive policy: and gossip had connected Keyes, who was taking over now, with this rumoured attack or 'special operation'.

And Commander Reaper was from the Plans Division, which up till now Keyes had directed!

Nick thought, *Two and two makes nine, at that rate* . . .

He took the CMB in very gently, her engine barely mumbling to itself, and berthed her under the torpedo-loading derrick in the basin's north-west corner. There were three little jetties here, the spaces between them forming small docks about the same length as the CMB, and the shore-based gunner (T) with his working party was there standing by.

'Lieutenant Everard?'

'Yes.' The gunner looked at his pocket-watch as Nick joined him on the jetty. A small, grey-faced man. Nick said, 'Sorry if I've kept you waiting.' There was a torpedo ready on its trolley, and it had the distinctive orange-painted head that meant it was a practice one,

180

a 'blowing head'. When it came to the end of its run, compressed air would be released to blow water out of it and make it buoyant, so it would bob upright on the surface with its orange nose easy to spot from the recovery-vessel. The gunner asked Nick, 'Want us to load 'er now? Morning won't do?'

He'd have a wife ashore, Nick guessed, a home to go to. Well, hard luck!

'Now, please. We'll be making an early start, tomorrow.'

CMB 11 had no torpedo on board at the moment. The trough that one would go in was a channel that extended, open-topped, from the after end of the cockpit to the boat's fantail-shaped stern. The torpedo – an eighteen-inch side-lug RGF – Royal Gun Factory, the Woolwich arsenal – would be lowered now and slid in from astern, under the steel arches that bridged the channel. It would be slid in nose-first, so that the head would lie pointing into the cockpit. Firing was by means of a hydraulic ram: its shaft passed centrally through the cockpit, and the white-painted, cup-shaped ram-head fitted over the curved nose of the fish. So it would lie there pointing the same way as the boat, and when it was fired the ram would discharge it tail-first over the boat's stern. The CMB would then be doing a few knots less than the torpedo's standard running speed of forty, so as the torpedo's own engine fired and its propellers drove it forward in the boat's wake and on exactly the same course, the driver would swing the wheel over and turn her aside, allowing the missile to travel on. Until the moment of firing he'd have been aiming the boat as if she herself were a torpedo – holding her on what would have become a collision-course with the enemy.

181

To anyone accustomed to more orthodox methods of firing torpedoes, it seemed an odd procedure. Nick thought it might take quite a bit of mastering. He told the gunner, 'I'll need you and your team standing-by tomorrow. We'll be practising all day, I expect. Can you muster three or four practice fish, so we don't have to wait long between runs?'

The motor-launch that was to join him for this mysterious expedition could make itself useful recovering the torpedoes and carting them in. And Underhill in CMB 14 could act as target ship.

Harry Underhill seemed a bit 'reserved' . . . He was a very direct, down-to-earth sort of man, and he disliked the present lack of information. He obviously thought Nick knew more than he was telling him; and under his skin he'd naturally resent an outsider bursting in and taking charge – all the more so, probably, when it happened to be a personal friend who was doing it. He wasn't unfriendly or uncooperative: just guarded, watching points.

It was still quite early, but already pitch dark, by the time he walked out over the floating brow and up *Arrogant*'s gangway. He'd seen the torpedo loaded, and discussed the firing procedure and the ram's mechanism with the gunner from the shore base; then, by lamplight, he'd been over the boat's engine with Ross the artificer, and young Selby. It was necessary to know its quirks and foibles, what could go wrong with it, and so on, in case the mechanic got knocked out in action and one had to cope without him. Nick was surprised to find that the midshipman was about as ignorant as he was himself; it seemed logical to him that with only a three-man crew each of them must know the others' business. He mentioned to Selby a catch-phrase which had been familiar in training days: *knowledge is the basis of initiative*. Selby only sniggered, as if he thought Nick was a bit of a card.

He went into *Arrogant*'s wardroom for a drink before he changed. He asked Underhill, 'Does *your* snotty know how your boat works?'

'Soon be over the side if he didn't.'

'Mine – Weatherhead's – doesn't know his arse from his elbow.'

Underhill nodded. 'Runt of the litter. Wethy's been trying to shed him, I think.'

'Is there one I could swap him for, temporarily?'

'Yes. Lad called Brown's kicking his heels, at the moment. If you've the wherewithal to swing it.'

He hadn't smiled at all. Beside him, Tim Rogerson looked just as serious. Nick thought, *He can't resent me, I'm not pinching his submarine* . . . 'What's up, Tim?'

'Johnny Vereker's dead.'

'Oh, no . . .'

'Shot down. Witnessed – 'plane exploded when it hit the ground. Two other pilots saw it. I've been talking to one of 'em on the blower – he was on his way through, on leave.'

Underhill sighed as he took two glasses from the steward's salver. He asked Nick, 'Gin?'

'Thank you. Of all the *rotten* things. Damn sorry, Tim.'

Rogerson nodded. He and Vereker had been in the same term at Dartmouth, and close friends all through. Nick sat down, and the steward brought him his drink. Tim Rogerson said, flaking his long frame into an armchair, 'I'll have to trundle his old motor over to his people's place in Hampshire,

183

I suppose ... Fine night to pick for a party, isn't it.'

'Are you having a party?'

'Oh, not really. Asked Bruce Elkington over, that's all. But you'll join us, won't you? Apart from the pleasure of your company, I'd like to hear what all this CMB business is about.'

'If *I could* tell you, I doubt if I'd be allowed to.'

'Nothing to do with the big thing, is it?'

Nick stared at him. 'What big thing?'

'For God's sake, *I* don't know.' His glance went past Nick's shoulder. 'Here's Wally. Now I'm afraid it *is* going to be a party.'

Wally Bell had a stranger with him, an RNVR lieutenant like himself. Half his height, though, and rotund. They came over.

'Thought you were at sea tonight, Wally. Shirking?'

'Donkey's giving trouble.' He meant his engine, his ML's. 'Look here, this is Sam Treglown. One of the élite.' By that he meant that Treglown was an ML man too. He pointed at Nick. 'Sam, that's the bird you're looking for.'

'Oh, are you Everard?'

Nick admitted it. Treglown smiled as he shook his hand. 'I've been told to report to you. Something special on?'

'Something. This time tomorrow we may find out what. Meanwhile you'd better have a drink.' He called the steward. Wally Bell was complaining. 'There's too much sea-time in this racket. Of *course* the damn thing breaks down occasionally!'

Treglown said, 'Yours is one of the Yank boats, isn't she. One of the Great Lakes products?'

'So what if she is?'

'Those engines are knocked together in some motor-cycle factory!'

'No bearing on the subject whatsoever. In fact with *normal* usage she'd chug along for ever . . . But you know, what we ought to have is the Channel tunnel they've always talked about and never started. Think of the sea-time it'd save us all! No transports, no hospital ships, no escorts, no mine-sweeping – Lord, *think* of it!'

'And think also,' Rogerson added drily, 'of the Huns capturing the other end of it.'

Rogerson looked ill, Nick thought. Being red-headed he had a pale skin anyway, but tonight he looked like a tall, thin ghost.

'You'd have a damn great plug in it.' Wally stroked his beard. 'About halfway over. You'd have a cable attached to the plug and taken up to a buoy on permanent moorings. If the Huns got there, you'd just give the cable a jerk, and – *whoosh*!'

Treglown nodded. Frog-faced, podgy. He said, 'Glug glug.' Underhill commented, 'Be a hell of a job to pump the thing dry again.'

'Ah!' Bell shook his head, wagged a forefinger. 'The losing side – which means the Huns, naturally – would have the job of baling it out. In buckets. *Small* ones . . . Why, even Kaiser Willy'd think twice about going to war if he had *that* job in prospect!' He turned to Nick. 'What's this you're up to now? Left *Mackerel*, do I hear?'

'Over here, Elkington!'

Rogerson's guest had arrived. He waved, beckoning to him. He asked the new man, Treglown, 'You'll join us for dinner, won't you? We're celebrating the death of an old friend.'

*   *   *

He said later, after dinner, quietly to Nick, 'It's about the worst thing that ever happened, d'you know that? I still can't quite believe it. I tell you, Nick, I –' his hand fastened on Nick's arm – 'I could *cry*, I.'

'I know. I know *precisely*.'

Swan – Cockcroft – and so *many* of them . . . Like the ticking of a roomful of clocks, and every tick a life. One should weep, perhaps, not for individuals and friends so much as for England, for England's blood and strength that were draining out of her.

Elkington had left early; his ship was sailing at daybreak for patrol duty in the Downs. Nick had said to Rogerson, 'Pleasant fellow, that', and Rogerson had nodded. 'He's engaged to marry a girl I know.' He smiled now: it looked like a conscious effort to change his own mood. 'What's this I've heard whispered about some *fracas* at a local hostelry, involving a certain officer and a – er – young lady of the town?'

'I've no idea.'

It had surprised him that there'd been no gossip, so far as he'd known. But there'd had to be, of course, eventually. Rogerson said, still smiling, 'I might tell Eleanor, if you don't come clean.' He meant his sister, the pretty one who was a VAD. Nick said, 'You'd tell her if I *did* come clean.'

'Never!'

He sighed . . . 'Nick, would you say goodnight to the others for me? Being jolly's rather difficult, tonight.'

Nick told Treglown, 'We'll rendezvous with you three miles south-east of South Foreland at 9 a.m. All right?'

The ML captain nodded. 'Right. But I wish it'd only take *me* ten minutes to get there!'

He'd have to leave harbour a lot earlier than the CMBs would. Nick explained that they'd have to be in from sea fairly early in the evening, in order to attend the briefing. So to get a full day's practice in, he needed an early start. He said goodnight to them.

'I'm off now. Going round to my old ship to make a few farewells.'

Mackerel was away at the other end of the port, in the tidal harbour where she'd boiler-cleaned, and the walk of about a mile and a half each way would do him good. He'd had no time for goodbyes this afternoon after the interview with Reaper. Wyatt had been waiting for him, though, and had accepted without much surprise or sorrow the information that Nick was being taken from him. Nick told him nothing except that he was being sent temporarily to *Arrogant*: which sounded, certainly, like an appointment for a man nobody had a job for. Wyatt had muttered, 'Well, I did try . . . I'm sorry, Everard', and on an afterthought he'd gone so far as to shake hands. Nick had arranged for his gear to be sent over, and left, intent on getting to grips with CMB 11 as soon as possible. Now he went down to his cabin on *Arrogant*'s main deck, to get his greatcoat. His stuff was all here, but he wasn't unpacking anything except immediate essentials. Might that be tempting Fate? After this one 'errand' – Reaper had used that term to describe the CMB operation – he'd no idea what they'd have for him to do next. It was distinctly possible that Reaper didn't know either. Reaper, for his purposes or the Plans Division's, wanted a job done, and they'd given him a man to do it. Someone they had no better use for. When Reaper had got whatever it was he wanted, he wouldn't give two farthings for Nicholas Everard's next appointment!

It wasn't a happy thought. He worried about it as he made his way out through the big old ship and down her gangway. Then he told himself not to think about it any more: he was tired, and depressed by the news about Johnny Vereker.

Get the CMB job done first. Then *start worrying.*

He'd turned the top corner and he was walking westward in the direction of the Marine Parade, with the submarine basin and the rest of the harbour shining like silver on his left, when it struck him suddenly that what was making it shine was the moon. The new one, just an infant moon, and only visible now because there was a great rift in the clouds: but it was there – and it might just as easily, therefore, be there again in two nights' time. Reaper had said something like *Moon may turn out to be a nuisance, but with luck there'll be cloud to cover it . . .*

With an absence of luck, there might not be?

CMBs needed dark nights to work in. Being so small and low in the water, hard to see except when they moved at speed, when they kicked up so much wash that they could be spotted as easily as battleships – they could lie stopped and be just about invisible. Being of shallow draught, they could sneak over shoals, too. Ideal for ambush, a quick torpedoing and escape. But a moon was as bad for them as daylight. They were no faster than the modern German destroyers, and they were made of wood and carried only one torpedo and the revolvers on their officers' belts, while the Hun destroyers were steel bristling with four-inch guns and quick-firing two-pounders.

Have your outing now, he thought, addressing the moon's sharp, fang-like shape. *And tomorrow night, if you like. But after that – please . . .*

Passing the naval headquarters buildings now, where this thing had been sprung on him this afternoon. A ray of light shone from one sandbagged doorway, glinted on a sentry's bayonet; otherwise it was all quiet, dark, either deserted or very well blacked out. He walked on, wondering if that bit of moon might bring the Gothas. They'd come without any moon at all, last time. But on recent visits they'd been getting a hot reception, and all because Lloyd George had been in the town on an official visit in September and bombs had been dropped in his vicinity – at least, close enough for him to have been aware of them. Anti-aircraft guns for which General Bickford had been pressing since last year had been delivered within days! Nick thought, with his eyes on *Zubian's* black shape outlined against silvered water, *By this time tomorrow night I'll know where we're going, and what for* . . . He would not, he thought, swap Midshipman Selby for the other one. He'd make the best of Selby – who might, for all one knew, be worth his salt when it came to action. It was remembering Underhill's contemptuous expression 'runt of the litter' that had changed his mind. Hadn't *he* been that, in some people's eyes? If he dropped Selby he'd be doing him a thoroughly bad turn. If one knew for certain he wasn't up to scratch, it would be justified, but on such small knowledge of him he didn't believe it was.

The Prince of Wales pier was on his left, a long black finger poking south-eastward. He walked on, passing it, to where *Mackerel* lay in the angle between the eastern wall of the tidal harbour and the small jetty that protected it. He hardly expected to find much life in her; but at least he'd have been aboard, tried to say goodbye to his former shipmates. By the time he finished the torpedo-firings tomorrow, she should have sailed.

189

The gangway sentry peered at him as he approached. Then, recognizing him, saluted.

'Evening, Jarvie. All well?'

'Yessir, evenin' sir!'

'Anyone still about, d'you know?' He started up the gangway. Jarvie told him, 'They're all in the wardroom, sir. Bit of a do on, I believe sir.'

Nick could hear it. *Mackerel*'s wardroom, evidently, were entertaining. Loud voices, laughter, party sounds . . . He stepped off the gangway and turned aft, went in through the blackout flap, painted canvas covering the doorway in the superstructure, and started down the ladderway. A voice from down there in the wardroom rose above the din: 'Speech! Speech!'

Nick stopped, wondering what was going on. He heard Charlie Pym's voice rise out of a sudden quiet.

'Gentlemen . . . Unaccustomed as I am—'

'Means 'e's a virgin!'

'Don' in'errupt y' first lieutenant!'

'—I should like to say how touched, how deeply moved I am by the enthusiasm with which you have welcomed my replacing one who – who—'

Laughter . . . Gladwish's voice cut through it: 'One who's come a cropper, that's—'

'One who's come to say goodbye to you.' Nick stepped through the doorway. He saw Gladwish, Grant, Watson; and Pym up on a chair, red-faced and with his mouth open. There were a couple of other men he didn't know, a warrant officer and a sub-lieutenant. They all looked quite shocked at seeing him. Grant was blushing scarlet as he jumped to his feet, and Gladwish stammered, 'Why, it's – why—'

'My word, you *have* surprised us.' Pym climbed off the chair. 'A little impromptu celebration of my

190

elevation to first lieutenant. I'm sorry, it probably seems – well—'

'It seems –' Nick looked at him calmly – 'exactly what it *is*.' He saw Warburton, the leading steward, slip away. Pym offered, 'Well, good heavens, you must have a drink!'

'No thanks.' Watson, the engineer, was trying to claim his attention. He nodded to him. 'Hello, Chief.'

'Wanna say – it's a bloody rotten thing they done to you, it's more'n a bloody shame, it's—'

'What are you talking about, for God's sake?'

Gladwish nodded owlishly. 'He'sh right. They should 'a given y'a medal, not—'

'I wish I knew what any of you was talking about.' Nick looked at Pym. 'Can you tell me?'

'Well.' Pym shrugged. An exaggerated movement, but compared to Gladwish and Watson he seemed fairly sober. 'I've mixed feelings, naturally. I mean, I've got your job, I can't pretend I *mind* that . . . On the personal level though, of course, one's sorry—'

'I'm *extremely* sorry, sir.' Midshipman Grant, who evidently had not been allowed anything or much to drink, was still pink with embarrassment. Nick asked him, 'Sorry about what, Mid?'

'Well – you being pushed out—'

'Pushed out?'

He glanced round. They were all staring at him, doing their best to look sympathetic, on his side. He asked Pym, 'Do *you* think I've been *pushed out*?'

'Well.' Pym half smirked at Gladwish, then looked back at him. 'I'm afraid we *know* you have. That business ashore – the captain told me—'

'What, that I'd been dismissed the ship?'

'Nothing as definite as that, but—'

'I'll be damned.' He shook his head. It had been a long day, one way and another. 'Well, I won't try to convince you you're all jumping to wrong conclusions. You are, but it doesn't matter all that much . . . I only came along to say goodbye. I'll be at sea tomorrow before you sail, so—'

'At sea?' Grant had asked the question. What did they think, that he was confined to barracks? Nick looked back at Pym. 'I wish you luck. I hope you turn into a first-class number one.'

'Well, I'll certainly do my—'

'You won't, though. You're too soft with yourself and too damned idle . . . Goodbye.'

He went out and up the ladder, stepped out, pushing the canvas aside, on to the quarterdeck. Moving quickly, trying to master anger and disquiet, and wanting to be away from them. He turned for'ard, towards the gangway.

'Lieutenant Everard, sir?'

It was Leading Seaman McKechnie. There were quite a few other members of the ship's company behind him. 'Warby come an' tol' us you was aboard, sir.' Warburton, he meant, the captain's steward. 'Come to say goodbye, sir?'

'Yes, that's about it.'

'Sir – we want to say – well, the lads is sorry ye're awa', sir . . .' A murmur of agreement came from the others with him. 'Ship won't be the same, sir, not now.'

'Well – thank you.'

It was hard to know what to say. He certainly couldn't tell them the truth, that *they* were the people he should have come to say goodbye to, the only ones he regretted leaving.

192

'All I can say is I hope we may meet again.' It was a crowd, now, filling this port side of the iron deck. He raised his voice, and called out, 'Goodbye, and good luck to you all. You deserve it!' He put out his hand: 'We'll meet again, I hope, McKechnie.' Then he found that he was shaking *all* their hands, and they were singing all around him, *For He's a Jolly Good Fellow* . . . The Glasgow killick shouted in his ear, 'I seen the wee lass tonight, sir, she said tae gie ye her love!'

He got away. In the wardroom they'd have had an earful of that singing; and Wyatt, if he'd been asleep in his cabin, might well have been woken by it. It would annoy Wyatt – and mortify Charlie Pym!

She said tae gie ye her love . . .

McKechnie must have seen her in that pub. And the pubs were all shut now. But he remembered where she lived: at least, he was fairly sure he'd be able to retrace the hurried, rather painful steps he'd taken on that fateful, rum-flavoured morning.

Not only rum-flavoured though: there'd been the taste of Annabel. And her touch, and her gentle voice, the affection in her eyes . . .

Reaper's clipped tones echoed in his brain: *You'd better not see the girl again.*

Well, he'd given no such undertaking.

Left, here. Over the bridge at the end of Wellington dock. Now through there, the alley, and then right into Snargate Street. There was a side street forty yards farther down. He saw Pym's sneer, and stopped. Why give people like Pym what they wanted, why oblige the Charlie Pyms, for God's sake? And a thought on the heels of that one: wouldn't she have someone with her, by this time of night?

Reaper's voice again: *Nursery days are over, Everard. You're fledged, now!*

He turned about, went back across the bridge. Thinking of the man who might be with her now, this moment, making love to her, hearing that soft voice in his ear, seeing those wide eyes in the moonlight flooding in. But he was seeing a man with a ruddy-complexioned face and a black military moustache: not Annabel's client, but Sarah's lover.

The moon had slid behind a bank of cloud. Nursery days *might* have been over, and he *might* have been 'fledged'; but he felt cut off, rootless.

CHAPTER 10

He held CMB 11 on the course for Dunkirk. The
weather forecast had proved accurate: only a light
breeze ruffled the straits, and the swell was long,
leisurely; the boat skimmed it, swooping in long
shallow dives and climbs, a rhythmic, waltz-time
motion accompanied by her engine's steady roar and
the thudding of her bottom-boards against the sea's
solidity. Harry Underhill in CMB 14 was in station
one cable's length astern; there were thirty miles to
go, two-thirds of the distance still to cover. Since these
shallow-draught boats had seldom to bother about such
nuisances as shoals, their route to enter Dunkirk Roads
was 'as-the-crow-flies'.

Nick jerked his head to Selby.

'Here, you can have her. South seventy-three east.'

'Aye aye, sir.'

No snigger. Nick had asked him yesterday, during the torpedo firing practice, 'Why d'you giggle
whenever anyone says any damn thing at all, Mid?';
and he hadn't done it since. It was surprising what
a difference it made; when you separated Selby
from his laugh, he became quite likeable. And
yesterday afternoon Nick had made him take over

for one of the torpedo shots, and he'd handled it perfectly.

Reaper had said to them in his quiet, matter-of-fact tone, 'I want you to go over to the Belgian coast and bring back Weary Willie. That armed trawler the Huns anchor every night off Middelkerke, you know?'

He'd looked round at them – at Nick, Underhill and Treglown, and they'd all nodded. He'd added, 'Intact.'

A cutting-out operation, in fact. Boarding-party in the ML, and the two CMBs to ward off interference. Very simple, really. Nick had been thinking about it ever since Reaper had given them the briefing, and he was still thinking about it now as he moved over to the cockpit's starboard side, leaving Selby to drive the boat. On the way across he stooped to look in at Ross. The ERA was on his little wooden seat, peering intently between tall, bony knees at dials that told him about such things as revs, oil-pressure, temperature. She was a good'un, CMB 11 was, he'd told Nick. Some of the others had to be nursed like babies and *still* gave trouble. He was nursing this one, Nick thought, very much like a baby.

The action torpedo rested where yesterday a succession of practice ones had lain. This one wore a warhead, though, three hundredweight of explosive. He stroked the ice-cold curve of silver steel, and wondered if there'd be a use for it tonight. He hoped not. What was wanted was speed and silence and no trouble, no Huns seeing or hearing or even suspecting anything. The cutting-out had to take place within spitting distance of the coast at Middelkerke and only about five miles from Ostend. Thirty years ago it would have been done with cutlasses and muffled oars.

196

CMB 14 was a dark blob bouncing in a welter of foam two hundred yards astern, in this boat's wake. They were travelling at twenty knots, a fairly economical speed that would get them to Dunkirk in plenty of time to refuel, have a snack and be on their way again. Treglown had set off in his ML much earlier in the day, and he'd have left Dunkirk before the CMBs got there. He had a PO, a stoker PO, three seamen, and one stoker as passengers; his own sub-lieutenant would be taking charge of them as a boarding party.

He moved to the for'ard starboard corner, leant with his arms folded on the coaming and his chin resting on his arms, watched the craft's long grey bow rising to the swells and carving a path across them. After each swoop up there was a fall and a thudding jar as her forepart smacked down again and her 340 horsepower flung her at the next one. Not difficult to imagine how uncomfortable she'd be in anything like rough weather.

Cloud-cover was thick, unbroken. It had to remain so. Provided the night stayed dark, and they had a modicum of luck: or at least an absence of *bad* luck . . . Such as meeting a destroyer or torpedo-boat coming out of Ostend. They had a habit of prowling round old Willie, snooping up between the Ostend Bank and Nieuwpoort Bank, then turning back into the port again or up-coast. The CMBs' function tonight would be to guard against any such interference, watch the approaches while the ML carried out her boarding and cutting-out, and then hang around to cover the joint retirement of the ML and her captive. If a torpedo-boat showed up, they'd try to lead it away and, if necessary, torpedo it. But only if it *was* necessary. So close to Ostend – and to Zeebrugge, for that matter – the important thing was not to attract attention. A Hun destroyer flotilla could be whistled up within minutes. Ideally, the trawler's crew – although she was armed they weren't trained, fighting seamen, apparently – would wake up to find revolvers at their heads; and the Huns ashore would wake to find Willie gone.

'What the devil do they want us to pinch a trawler for?' Underhill had been puzzled, after last night's briefing. 'We've got – what, eighty here already?'

Nick had been thinking about it too, and he had a theory that explained it and pointed to a much bigger issue than this little jaunt. But he gave the CMB man the same vague reason that Reaper had offered: this was the beginning of a switch to the offensive, a policy of keeping the Hun hopping and spoiling his sleep.

'We want 'em on the *de*fensive,' Reaper had told them. 'We've still got to guard the straits, but we want to go out and hit 'em too. As you know, Vice-Admiral Keyes is in command now – and he's never been a man to sit back and let the enemy come to *him*.'

'Right we are, then.' Reaper had begun to roll up his chart. 'Any other questions?'

There weren't. He told Nick. 'Work out your own detailed orders and carry on from here. It's in your hands. Let's have a tidy and successful operation. You're not getting anything on paper – just go and do it . . . Perhaps you'll see me to the gangway, Everard.' He said to him privately, on the way down, 'I said I want this Hun intact. That will include, of course, her crew.'

Nick thought about it for a moment. Then he asked, 'Is that the priority, sir? Prisoners?'

Reaper frowned at him. 'Is there any reason we can't have the whole caboodle?'

'No, sir. Just a matter of priorities, if anything should go wrong.'

'I very much hope it won't . . . You're right to the extent that we haven't any great *need* of another trawler . . .' He'd said it vaguely, as if it didn't really matter either way. The fact was, it had been said.

Nick nodded. 'I understand, sir.' But Reaper had been at pains not to be too precise. 'The object is to take the trawler, crew and all.' He hesitated, near the gangway's head now. 'Look here – we wouldn't want the Hun to think we'd just gone after prisoners. The object is to let him know we're pushing him, that the straits belong to *us* . . . Makes sense, doesn't it?'

Nick saluted. 'Goodnight, sir.'

'Goodnight, Everard. And good luck.'

He'd thought, watching the gold-peaked cap disappear down the depot ship's gangway, that it was pretty obvious what was wanted, and what for, and why Reaper had been so mealy-mouthed about it. It was surprising Underhill hadn't caught on too. But he and Treglown might not have known where Weary Willie came from, where she and her crew spent their daylight hours.

They didn't ask, so he didn't need to tell them.

After supper he'd gone up to the chartroom, alone, to work out the orders he'd give them in the morning. To start with, for his own benefit, he jotted down the essentials of the situation they'd be facing. For instance, that the operation had been planned not only for a calm spell of weather but also for an exceptionally low low-water. The Huns might be thinking themselves safe behind the Belgian shoals; they were shoal-conscious, they'd left the channels un-dredged in order to keep the Royal Navy off their coast. They might not think

199

of CMBs and MLs, which drew so little water they practically walked on it ... Second, there were to be two Dover destroyers patrolling near the pillar buoy at the Hinder, twelve miles north-west of Willie; when the trawler had been taken, she and the ML were to head straight for their protection. While any destroyers – Germans – which the CMBs managed to entice away were to be led east-nor'-eastward, into the minefield which *Mackerel* and her friends had laid a few nights ago.

The emergency situations most likely to arise were (a) a breakdown, engine failure, of one of the three boats of the cutting-out flotilla, (b) encounter with enemy destroyer/s, (c) change of cloud/moon conditions. Nick's orders as he finally produced them dealt almost entirely with reaction to these contingencies.

Everyone knew exactly what to do, now.

He looked across at Selby. 'All right, Mid?'

The pink face turned to him; and this time, Selby laughed. He shouted, 'Bloody *marvellous*, sir!'

Treglown, they learnt, had arrived in Dunkirk and sailed again on schedule. The CMBs refuelled and were clear of the harbour by 9 p.m. The route Nick had planned would take them about three miles offshore most of the way, after an initial zigzag to seaward to clear the silted east side of Dunkirk Roads and the Hills bank. They'd finish up only two miles off Middelkerke; they'd be just inshore of Weary Willie then, and over the top of a shallow patch which the Germans might well consider impassable and therefore an approach not worth watching very closely.

There was a danger that it *might* be impassable, places so shallow at this lowest of low tides that even

CMBs and MLs couldn't scrape over them. The lack of dredging and the removal of navigational marks, all part of a deliberate enemy policy, created that uncertainty. There'd have been sifting into channels, and some of the shoals would have extended this way or that, even moved bodily to new positions.

The distance to cover was about twenty miles. The CMBs could have raced there in not much more than half an hour, but Nick had set a speed of twelve knots – which would leave virtually no wash or broken water to catch a German eye, and allowing for the tides would give a speed-made-good of ten and get them to the rendezvous position by the zero-hour of 11 p.m. Twelve knots was also about the slowest speed a CMB could manage; their engines couldn't put up with low revs for any length of time.

By eleven-ten the trawler should be captured and the flotilla – now of four instead of three – on its way seaward.

He looked to his right, at Selby. The midshipman had his glasses up and he was keeping a fairly constant watch on CMB 14, who was tucked-in close now, only fifty yards astern. Each snotty had the job of keeping track of the other boat; and since at this distance they were within hearing distance of each others' klaxons, a system of emergency sound signals had been established.

The monitor and its attendant destroyer off La Panne had been warned that they'd be passing. And it was a halfway point, a way of checking their position accurately for the last time before they found Weary Willie. The squat, black shape of the monitor loomed up ahead, and Nick moved the wheel gently, easing the CMB over to pass close to seaward of her. Ahead and to starboard a glow hung in the sky over Nieuwpoort, and the small sparks of distant starshell drifted downwards, flickered out to be replaced by others; Nick thought, *No starshell to seaward, please* . . . They'd be worse than searchlights, even; and the searchlight crews along this section of the coast had been warned of the boats' schedule. The rumble of gunfire from the Front was remote, impersonal. He saw the destroyer now: an 'M', lying at anchor beyond the monitor. Both ships were dark, dead-looking, silent; but there'd be more than a few pairs of eyes watching the CMBs slide out of the night and into it again. At Nieuwpoort they'd pass within two miles, four thousand yards, of the point where the trench-lines met the sea. Nick wondered if his father had even been that close to the firing line, or whether his previous appointment had been of a similar kind to this riding-school job he had now. Something to do with horses, most likely. He'd never made any comprehensible statement about what he did. He'd implied, or allowed others to imagine, that he'd been actively involved in the various 'pushes', and talked about the fighting as though he'd been in it; but if it turned out eventually that he hadn't, nothing he'd said would prove him a liar.

He wished his elder brother David was still alive. They'd never got on; but David had been the heir to the baronetcy and Mullbergh, and now he was dead he, Nick, was in his place; he'd have preferred to have been detached, disinterested altogether in the inheritance, in whether his father lived or died.

Underhill was passing the destroyer. From this boat the monitor, well astern now, was just fading out of sight.

'What's the time, Mid?'

'Nine fifty-seven, sir.'

202

Three minutes inside schedule. A rocket soared, burst over Nieuwpoort, a greenish-yellow colour. He wondered what it meant. The land to starboard now was Belgium; France had ended just before La Panne – where, astern, a searchlight beam had just sprung out, lancing the darkness with its silver blade, sweeping the sea to the westward of the guardships. *Their* timing wasn't far out either, he thought; they'd been told to stay switched-off until ten.

'Selby – see if Ross is happy, will you?'

Selby ducked down for a quick chat with the ERA. He told Nick a minute later, 'It's all fine at the moment, sir. Except for the usual worry about oiling-up.'

It was a risk that had to be accepted. Gunfire was louder as they drew closer to the front line. You could see the flashes low down, sometimes, and bits of walls or broken buildings silhouetted for split seconds in their light; but no individual sounds, it was all one continuous background rumble. Inland searchlights wavered, fingering the clouds, searching for aeroplanes or Zeppelins; but those were too far east, he realized, to be anything but German. They'd be watching for the RNAS squadrons, Johnny Vereker's friends. A flare hung, the brilliant magnesium-white illuminating a black spread of land, the horror-ground of Europe.

Selby shouted, 'I think fourteen's in trouble, sir!'

Nieuwpoort was well astern. They'd been in what might be called enemy water for almost half an hour.

'*Think* – or *is* she?'

He heard the letter 'A' on Underhill's klaxon. In their code it meant 'am aground' . . .

With target almost in touching distance, and German batteries a bare two miles to starboard.

There was a quick remedy and a slow one; they'd practised both. This was a time for the faster, riskier method. He was turning the CMB to port, seaward, holding full rudder on her; at twelve knots no amount of helm would turn her over.

'Tell Ross I'll be opening right up in a minute!' He had her on the opposite course now, heading back the way they'd just come. He asked Selby, as the snotty came up from shouting in Ross's ear, 'Was she dead astern of us?'

'Bit out on the quarter.'

'You should've told me.'

Spilt milk . . . Underhill had let his boat swing off to starboard and he'd hit the mud and there he was . . . Nick swung the boat around to port again, taking her in two cables' lengths astern of the stranded CMB and holding on until he was inshore of her. Then hard a-port, right round quickly, aiming her at Underhill's boat, on a course of about east-by-north. When she was pointing the right way and he'd steadied her and centred the wheel, he pushed the throttle wide open. CMB 11's stern went down hard and she surged forward under full power. You could feel the thrust, the sea trying to hold her back and then its resistance lessening as she lifted in the water and began to skim it, bounce it, engine-noise a deafening roar now and sea flying past, wind ripping, whining, wash piling upwards and outwards, flinging high and white from her quarters as she drove forward. Underhill would be ready for the wash that – hopefully – would lift his boat off the sand and give him a chance to clear it. Nick moved the wheel a little, easing her to port and aiming to pass about ten yards clear of fourteen's stern. This boat was right up on the plane now, rocketing along, the sea crashing under her as she hurtled over it: and passing fourteen – *now* . . .

As soon as he'd passed, muttering thanks to God that he hadn't hit the ground himself – in fact with the boat up and skimming she was a foot or two further from that danger – he cut the power. There was an immediate sensation of drag: as if an anchor had been thrown out to pull them back: like brakes slammed on and as if she was stopping dead, and her own wash rushed past and under, lifting and then dropping her several times, making it difficult to hold glasses steady enough to see what had happened to Underhill.

'I think she's off, sir.' Selby was propped with an elbow over the torpedo warhead and glasses at his eyes. Nick was bringing the boat round to starboard, swinging her across the rolling ridges that still followed from that short, sharp rush. Rocking in towards the land again, dead slow. Now he had his glasses on the other boat: and he heard her hooter bleat the letter 'P', which meant 'ready to proceed'.

'See how Ross is, and tell him I want the revs for twelve knots again.' He'd control it by the throttle, but Ross down there could watch the revs minutely and keep them adjusted. That burst of speed should have cleared his worries over oiling-up; and fourteen had been got out of trouble without the delay of passing a line and trying to drag her off. The risks had been of grounding oneself, and of making such a display of wash. He'd been shown aerial photos of CMBs going fast in poor visibility, and the wash and wake was all you could see. Navigationally too it was a nuisance that it had happened; he'd been on the track he'd worked out and needed to be on, and now he couldn't be sure of it any more. If he went too far to starboard he'd do what Underhill had done, whereas if he came too far to port they might run straight into Weary Willie before linking up with Treglown. There was a strong element of chance in it, anyway, with so much uncertainty about what changes had or hadn't occurred in the shoals and channels. For that matter, Treglown could have run into trouble, could be stuck on some inshore bank; or been too cautious and stayed farther out, passed the luckless Willie and now be groping in the darkness, lost . . .

He decided to take Underhill's present position as being fifty yards too close inshore: and turn here, now, on to the old course.

'Tell me when he's back in station.' He waited, searching the sea ahead. It was all black, quiet, empty. The deep growl of the engine emphasized that surrounding emptiness. There was a special feeling, state of mind, when you were in enemy waters, close to his coasts and bases, a distinctly enjoyable sensation of loneliness and danger: a sharp consciousness of being there, armed and secret. You'd have to experience it, he thought, to know it, it wasn't something you could put into words. No sign of Treglown. Selby reported, 'Fourteen's in station astern, sir.'

'Good. Now look out ahead and both sides, help me find the ML.'

'Some way to go yet, sir, isn't there?'

The fireworks over the trenches were well abaft the beam. But perhaps Selby was right, perhaps they weren't yet far enough back. He checked: first that the boat's head was on the course – north 65° east – and then the relative bearing of the pyrotechnics. 130° on the bow: and he had the bearings in his head, memorized, as you had to when you couldn't use a chart: Nieuwpoort would have to be 150° on the bow when they were inshore of Weary Willie's regular anchorage. Selby was right: there was about a mile, or slightly more than that, to go. Say five minutes, then: and expect to meet Treglown in three?

'Time, Mid?'

'Ten-fifty, sir.'

Nicely up to schedule. His sense of timing had been thrown out by the emergency of Underhill's grounding. An excess of anxiety had given him the impression they were late and in danger of messing the thing up. In fact the incident with Underhill's boat had only so to speak taken up the slack.

Lesson to be learnt: to keep on the ball you don't have to *worry* . . . Command was a new experience, and one had to be careful not to allow it to distort one's judgement.

He told Selby, 'You're right. About a mile to go.'

Silence all around them, soaking up the engines' rumble. The sea's blank, dimpled surface hid its secrets. Shoal water: at times there was probably no more than a foot or even a few inches under the boats' keels. And any channels that were still deep enough for navigation might well have been mined. Two miles on the beam there, German gunners would be peering seaward. There was a sudden stench of petrol exhaust as a breeze swept up from astern. Wind rising? Wind didn't only make calm seas rough, it blew cloud-cover off the moon . . . He told himself, *It's moving according to plan, there's no point dreaming up problems that aren't here*. Selby was cleaning the lenses of his binoculars. The sea hissed as it swept along the CMB's wooden sides and the engine grumbled deep in its throat as it drove her steadily through the night. The midshipman had his glasses up again, now. Nick's own last spoken words, *a mile to go* hung in his brain as if he'd memorized them; he wasn't sure if it might be one minute or five since he'd spoken them. It was like a dream when something nonsensical or totally unimportant keeps running through your mind.

He checked the bearing again. Nieuwpoort was slightly more than 140° on the bow now. Almost there. The ML might appear at any—

'There she is, sir!'

Too good to be true . . .

But that odd, cuttlefish shape was too distinctive to confuse with anything else. He looked back, saw Underhill close astern, and put the wheel over, headed to close Treglown. Close up to him, he throttled right down and stopped, de-clutched. The CMB lay rocking on the swell, so close that if Treglown had come out of his little box of a wheelhouse and waved, he'd have seen him. Underhill had stopped too, after getting in much closer; the object was to let Treglown see them and identify them, without the need for exchanges of signals.

He *had* seen them. The ML was gathering way, on a northwards course. Half a mile in that direction, Weary Willie should be nuzzling sleepily at his anchor.

'Time now?'

'Eleven o'clock, sir.'

He checked the Nieuwpoort bearing. South 35° west.

Bang on. The main worry had been a variability of the tidal streams on this coast, but the allowances he'd made for them seemed to have been right . . . He told himself not to count his chickens, that things could still go wrong. He was edging CMB 11 out to a position one cable's length, two hundred yards, on Treglown's port quarter, and Underhill was opening out the other way to put himself on Nick's beam, the ML's other quarter. He could see both the other craft, he realized suddenly, with the naked eye . . . The clouds hadn't broken up, but they'd thinned, enough to let a suffused radiance filter through. Now, of all moments! White froth under the ML's counter suddenly: she'd speeded up.

'They must have the trawler in sight.'

'I have too, sir. Just to starboard of her.'

'Yes . . . Well done.' He pushed the throttle shut, and the engine-sound fell away to a harsh stuttering. Clutch out . . . He kept his glasses on Treglown's craft as it slid up towards the German trawler's tall black shape. It was Willie's funnel that gave him that high look. No light showing: no movement: only the ML sliding across the dark sea like a ghost-ship.

'What's fourteen doing?'

'Stopped, sir, level with us – abeam, I mean.'

Good . . . Except for the moon. Any moment now the ML would be spotted and there'd be shooting, or a rocket soaring . . . The two shapes merged into one as the ML crept up to the trawler. One solid black smudge now, shapeless except for its height on the left edge: Willie's chimney. They could have been just in line from this angle, but they'd been united for so long that it was safe to assume they were alongside each other: Treglown's boarding-party would be aboard the German: if no alarm was raised *now*, why—

'Ship, sir! Starboard there, a—'

A searchlight beam sprang out, swept the sea in a short arc and settled on the ML and the trawler locked together. A German voice boomed gibberish over a loud-hailer. Selby had his glasses on her, and began shouting in a high, choked voice, 'Destroyer, sir, it's a dest—'

She'd opened fire. A gun on her foc's'l: a scarlet spurt of flame and now the sound of it, a sort of cracking thud: four-pounder probably. Moonlight brightening the whole scene now, but nothing like as bright as the searchlight still holding the ML in its hard steel clamp. That side was Underhill's. The ML had left the trawler's side, you could see a gap widening between them as she moved ahead and *towards* the German – whose shell hit her low down and for'ard, a shattering upwards disintegration of timber lit in its own shoot of orange flame. That was all it needed: she was built of half-inch planking, and ML 713 was finished, but the destroyer had fired again to make sure of her. Nick swung his glasses to CMB 14 and saw her gathering way, moving towards the enemy destroyer and rising in the water as she picked up speed, white sea boiling, piling from her stern, spreading as she slammed on power. The destroyer was stopped, or as near as dammit stopped. Harry had a sitting duck ahead of him. But the searchlight swung and picked him up, held him: the Huns would be staring down that beam at a welter of foam with a black dart cleaving through it, racing at them. Nick muttered under his breath 'Fire! Fire *now!*' If he didn't he'd lose his chance. The German was moving ahead, in the direction of the burning ML: no, he was turning, you could see his length shortening as he turned to put his bow towards his new enemy. Harry must have fired, because he was going over to starboard now, listing hard over as he swung away: the fish must be on its way, but the German would be bow-on to it, and unless there was a hit about . . . *now?* Nothing had happened: except that CMB

210

14's white wash was a brilliant fish-hook track across the sea to starboard, and the Hun was continuing his turn and putting on speed himself, still under helm: you could see his bow-wave lengthening, its white curve rising, extending now the full length of that rather high, level-topped foc'sl: a short, high foc'sl, probably turtle-backed, with a gun on its after edge and then a deckhouse in the well before the bridge: a 'V', he thought, built for thirty-five knots but getting a bit old now, probably do 30 at most flat out: a CMB should have the legs of him. Harry would *have* to have the legs of him, he'd nothing left to hit him with. The ML's flames were lower, almost extinguished as she settled in the water; she was only afloat now because she was made of wood. The Hun destroyer captain would be thinking he was on top of things: he was driving the CMB away and he'd smashed the ML, he'd think he'd saved Weary Willie from the English swine-hounds; he hadn't seen CMB 11, thanks to an extra couple of hundred yards and the fact that lying stopped like this there wasn't much to see.

Nick slipped the clutch in, and put the throttle to slow ahead. He told Selby, 'Watch the Hun and fourteen and tell me if anything develops.'

'They're chasing off, sir, that's all!'

'Keep an eye out that way.'

Harry would be heading for the new minefield. Nick steered CMB 11 for the ML. If the German had come from the west instead of the east matters would have been reversed, *he'd* have attacked it and CMB 14 would have lain doggo. He took her up towards the wrecked ML slowly: wouldn't help anyone if he flung up a lot of white water and attracted some Hun's attention. There could easily be another in the offing: or that first one

211

might give up the chase and come back to see if there were any prisoners to be fished out. But most likely he'd be leaving that job to Willie.

There were two men standing on the ML's stern, and she was only just afloat, with her forepart buried in the sea. He shut the throttle and told Selby, 'Get up for'ard, help those two aboard.'

There were raised hand-hold strakes the whole length of the CMB's curved wooden topsides, and a bit lower another raised one was well placed for toe-holds. The top of the engine-space, immediately for'ard of the cockpit, was flat, but everywhere else you needed something to hang on to. Selby crawled for'ard past the round engine-access hatch at the for'ard end of the engine-space and halfway between the cockpit and the stem; Nick gave her another touch ahead, then shut down again: the CMB's stem-post nudged the ML's stern, and Selby was holding on to the bull-ring while he helped the two survivors climb up. Nick shouted to them to get down through the engine hatch, and saw them doing it as he edged her away from the wreckage; it wouldn't be floating for much longer. Weary Willie was off on his port beam: black, quiet, and still at anchor. Then he saw men on her bow and heard a clank of cable-gear; those had to be British, because any Germans at liberty would have been blazing away with her four-pounder. Someone came out of this end of the engine-space and clambered up beside him.

'Glad you were around.'

Sam Treglown.

'Casualties?'

'None. There was only me and my leading hand – that's Eastman here – left on board. I'd decided the rest would be more use in Willie. She was

212

ours without a shot before I shoved off, by the way.'

Too soon to express joy or even satisfaction. There was the question of what was happening to CMB 14. The leading seaman was in the cockpit now, and Selby was coming out of the engine-space behind him. Nick, with the CMB swinging to point her bow at the German trawler, was thinking about the likelihood of that destroyer coming back, and about the low speed of the trawler and the steadily increasing moonlight. That last factor was the clincher that was pushing him towards a variation of the plans made earlier. Treglown asked him, 'Will Underhill be all right?' He couldn't have put the question at a better – or worse – moment: gunfire crackled in the north-east, perhaps a couple of miles away: Nick was looking in that direction when he saw red sparks near the horizon, heard more shouting; then there was a whitish flash and the deep boom of an explosion. He answered Treglown: 'I wouldn't count on it.' He'd arrived at that decision. 'Selby – raise the firing-lever stop.'

'Raise it, sir?'

'Do it!'

'Aye aye, sir!'

If the stop was down, when the torpedo was fired it would knock back the firing-lever, starting the missile's engine so that as it dropped into the water its two concentric propellers would be whirring at full speed. If the stop was raised clear, there'd be nothing to hit the firing-lever, so the engine wouldn't fire and the torpedo wouldn't run. It would simply be pushed out astern and sink.

Selby came back into the cockpit. 'It's raised, sir.'

Nick moved the lever to withdraw the retaining-stops;

213

they would have held the fish in its trough even against the ram's thrust. He put his hand on the firing-lever, and jerked it over, heard the thud of the cordite cartridge firing to create sudden pressure inside the hydraulic cylinder. The boat jerked with the force of it as the ram slammed back: the torpedo was a silver streak that sprang away over her low stern. They heard the splash that represented about twelve hundred pounds of taxpayers' money thrown away; then there was a long, sharp hiss of excess pressure leaking from the cylinder.

'Stand by to go alongside the trawler. Selby, Eastman – hold us alongside when we're there . . . Treglown – I want everyone out of her and into this boat. There's plenty of space where the fish was. I want the Germans – here, Selby – get one of these panels out. *That* one.' He kicked at the cockpit's after bulkhead, on the starboard side. 'We'll put the Huns in there, inside the stern.'

The panel could be removed, and there was room inside, between the heavy timbers that supported the torpedo channel, for several men to crouch or sit. They could be watched and guarded from the cockpit, and there was no equipment in there that they could do any harm to.

He told Treglown, 'Everyone into the boat, then have your stoker PO open Willie's seacocks.'

'Aye aye, sir!'

Selby had forced the plywood bulkhead panel out, and CMB 11 was sliding up to berth on the trawler's starboard side. As she loomed up closer, Willie looked surprisingly big. That tall funnel: and the high, square bridge with sandbags piled around it. Must make her top-heavy, he thought: and every little would help her down, presently. The moonlight was even brighter now.

Treglown's sub-lieutenant, Marriot, appeared on deck and reported that everything was under control, they'd only to get the hook up: then they bumped alongside and Treglown sprang over and started passing out Nick's orders. There was a momentary hush of surprise, then a rush to obey. Nick was searching the sea to starboard, east and north-east: you could see quite a distance now and he knew he couldn't help Harry Underhill, to try to would be like throwing a chestnut into the fire in the hope of dislodging one already in it. And with this moon beginning to break right through now it was simply not possible to remain so close inshore . . . There was nothing to be seen, out there. Since those two spasms of gunfire and the explosion there'd been no sound, either. The explosion *could* have been the German hitting a mine. Otherwise . . .

'Get a move on!'

Four German prisoners were being hustled aboard. Nick told a seaman, 'Inside there. They'll have to crawl in.'

'Aye aye, sir . . . Giddahn, Fritz, giddahn there . . .'

Otherwise: well a CMB wouldn't strike a mine, because they were moored too deep, those M-sinkers. But there'd been gunfire first: and the petrol tank was right under the cockpit floor. It was the only place they could have put it, he supposed. It would be well enclosed, reasonably protected; but still, a four-pounder shell . . .

If the destroyer came back, with this moonlight there'd be no escape from her. Not for a trawler that couldn't make more than about twelve knots. That was why there wasn't going to be a trawler for the destroyer to find if she *did* come back. Men were climbing over from her now. Treglown called, 'Stoker

215

PO's below, sir, opening the seacocks. Only him and your midshipman and myself to come.'

'Very good.'

He waited. That calm 'very good' hung in his ears. Had it been *his* voice?

'She's filling, sir!'

'Come aboard, then.'

'Aye aye, sir!'

The stoker PO sounded like a Devonport man. Nick shouted, 'Treglown, Selby, come on!' They all three tumbled over. He called down to Ross, 'We're overloaded but we need some speed – all right?'

'She won't let you down, sir.'

The CMB was swinging round to point seaward. And Weary Willie was settling, lowering himself sedately but quite rapidly into the sea. When the Germans came back – or when any other German came – they'd think their Willie had been taken. Reaper had said, *We wouldn't want the Hun to think we'd just gone after prisoners.* There was no reason why the Hun should think anything of the sort.

Glancing round, a final look towards the east, Nick thought that if that explosion had been the destroyer going up on a mine, CMB 14 would have been back by now. But there was nothing in sight except the long, flat swells and the increasing moonlight. Reaper had said something about responsibility, and not shirking it. Here it was. Responsibility was here and now and this throttle his hand was resting on.

216

CHAPTER 11

Edward Wyatt, staring out of the carriage window at the familiar features of Dover's Marine Station, waited until the train had stopped before he stood up and beat at the skirts of his greatcoat to knock the dust off. The South East and Chatham Railway Company was a splendidly efficient organization, and there had been times when its officials had worked miracles – at the time of the Somme offensive, for instance, they'd run twenty special hospital trains a day, on top of routine services – but it hadn't the staff to keep its trains as sparkling clean as they'd been before the war.

Wyatt wondered what the admiral was going to say to him. He'd hardly put *Mackerel* into the dockyard's hands, up in the Thames, before he'd had the telegram saying that Admiral Keyes wished to see him personally and as soon as possible.

To give him a new ship, perhaps. And just possibly, promotion! If they were giving him a brass hat, they might give him a flotilla-leader to go with it?

He stepped down on to the platform. It was about one mile to the headquarters houses, and the walk would be good for him. He hadn't seen Keyes since the Dardanelles, two years ago. Keyes had been a commodore then. Now he was an acting vice-admiral, promoted from rear-admiral in order to rank higher than Dampier, who was the admiral commanding the Dover dockyard, the engineering side of things. Last time Wyatt had met Keyes had been when Admiral de Robeck, Keyes's chief at that time, had sent for him to congratulate him on the taking of that Turkish battery, the landing party he'd led.

This time – what? Promotion, and a new ship, and a bar to his DSC? Even – possibly – a DSO?

Tim Rogerson had also just stepped out of a train, but at Portsmouth. He was here to have luncheon at Blockhouse, the submarine headquarters, with an old shipmate, 'Baldy' Sandford. He hadn't the least idea what for: or why one of Baldy's older brothers, who was a lieutenant-commander with a DSO and had apparently just arrived at Dover to join the new admiral's staff, should have sent for him and given him this cross between an order and an invitation.

On the part of the older Sandford it had seemed to be an order, but from the younger, Baldy, an invitation. One might hope to discover, over the meal perhaps, what the devil it was all about.

Rogerson walked out of the station precincts and down to the wooden harbour jetty. A twenty-foot motorboat lay alongside, and its coxswain was a leading seaman with an 'HM Submarines' cap-ribbon.

'Lieutenant Rogerson, sir?'

He returned the salute, and stepped into the boat's sternsheets.

Baldy Sandford was an archdeacon's son, he remembered. And one of a large brood: he was the *seventh* son, in fact. Which made one ponder on how archdeacons

218

spent their leisure hours: and one could marvel, too, at such a churchly man having so un-pious a son. Not a respecter of persons, old Baldy: a very humorous, jolly fellow, a terrific messmate. Determined as a character could be, in spite of that. The iron-jawed type. If Baldy wanted something done, it *was* done.

Even if he had to do it himself.

He greeted Rogerson on the Blockhouse jetty with a warm, bone-cracking handshake.

'How splendid you could manage it!'

'Oh, they don't exactly keep us on the hop, you know, in Dover.'

'They don't?'

'Not the submarines.'

'What *do* you get up to?'

'This and that. We've moored ourselves to anti-submarine barrage nets, pretending to be buoys and hoping Hun submarines might come and put themselves in front of our tubes. And we've done a lot of research on tidal ranges off the Hun ports – graphs of rise and fall, all that ... I suppose it might come in useful, one day.'

Sandford nodded. 'Indeed it might.' His expression changed back to one of amusement. 'But you're bored stiff, eh?'

'Pretty well.'

'I can offer you something so un-boring it might make your ginger thatch stand on end.'

He was a bit conscious of other men's 'thatch'. Rogerson nodded. 'I'll take it, sight unseen.'

'Third hand of an old "C"?'

'Now you're having me on.'

The C-class submarines were old, virtually useless, reserved for coastal-defence – and soon the breakers' yard. As they strolled up the jetty, he could see a couple of them anchored in the mud of Haslar Creek. Here, alongside, were two K-boats and an E. Sandford pointed at the two anchored boats.

'There they are . . . Listen to this, now. What about a C-class boat with a crew of six or seven picked men and her bow packed with five tons of Amatol?'

Rogerson rubbed his chin. He murmured, 'Sounds – explosive.'

'Oh, very.'

'What would we do with it?'

'I can't quite tell you that. What I mean is, I'm not allowed to. But you know that brother of mine who got in touch with you is now working for Roger Keyes?'

'One hears Keyes is collecting quite a large staff.' Rogerson nodded. 'Well?'

'This thing I'm on is part of some great stratagem of our former commodore's. Some kind of mad attack or other.'

'I'm in.'

Sandford glanced at him, surprised by the snap decision. Tim said, 'I'm *in*. Don't try to keep me out of it.'

'Well, there's a spot of preamble I'm bound to give you. It'll be more than ordinarily hazardous. The question of whether or not any of us will get away, or end up prisoners-of-war or blown to smithereens or – well, the point is, it's probably about as near to committing suicide as you could get without endangering your immortal soul. Are you sure you want to do it?'

'Never been more sure of anything.'

'Well, good for you!' Sandford held out his hand. 'I'm *so* glad.'

'Nothing to what I am.' Rogerson told him sincerely, 'I'm tickled pink. Damn nice of you to let me in on it.'

Wally Bell saw Captain Edwards, who was in overall command of the Patrol's MLs, striding towards him down the jetty. Wally stepped ashore to meet him.

'Morning, sir.' He saluted.

'Morning, Bell. Your boat likely to be fit for sea soon?'

'They're putting her together again now, sir. She'll be as good as new, the plumbers say.'

'Better be.' Graham Edwards stared with some disfavour at the litter of engine-room junk on the ML's deck. 'You've a lot of hard work ahead of you.'

Bell jerked his head towards his boat. He said, 'It wasn't just lying around doing nothing that cracked her up in the first place, sir.'

'Work of a particular kind, Bell.' Edwards told him, 'I'm taking you and a few others off routine patrol work, and giving you to Wing-Commander Brock for his programme of experiments. It'll be inshore smoke-laying, mostly.'

'Oh.'

Those bloody burners. Black mess everywhere . . .

'He's got a new system he wants to perfect. None of that messing about with burners. It involves using chlor-sulphonic acid in your boat's exhaust. Much more effective, apparently, as well as neater all round.'

'Chlor-sulphonic, sir?'

'Used in the manufacture of saxin. The sugar-substitute, you know? But that's to be stopped now. All the chlor-sulphonic they can make – or grow, whatever the hell they do – will be sent here, to Brock.'

221

'Sounds as if we're expecting to lay an awful lot of inshore smoke-screens!'

'Does rather, doesn't it.'

Reaper told Nick, 'You did well, Everard. Very well indeed.'

'Thank you, sir.'

'I'm sorry about Underhill.'

'Yes.' Nobody knew yet what had happened to CMB 14. The most likely theory was that the German destroyer had sunk her, or rather blown her up, and then hung around looking for survivors or trying to fish out wreckage for their intelligence people.

'In the circumstances, you took the best possible decision.'

'Are the prisoners proving useful, sir?'

Reaper's eyebrows rose.

'I beg your pardon?'

'I wondered if the prisoners I brought back were worth their salt, sir.'

'Why should you imagine there was any – any *usefulness* about them?'

'Well, sir, they're all I did bring back. And you've expressed satisfaction at the outcome of the operation. And before we set out I did rather understand you to say – well, to *indicate*—'

'You lost one CMB and her crew. Considering you'd had the bad luck to run up against a destroyer, and to find yourself having to cope with moonlight instead of total darkness, I can quite properly congratulate you on having made the best of a tricky situation. And since it was your first experience of command—'

'No, sir.'

He'd brought *Lanyard* back from Jutland.

222

Reaper raised one hand, and let it fall again. 'The first time you'd been *appointed* in command, then. In that consideration, it's considered that your conduct of the affair was – impressive.'

'Thank you, sir.'

'Not only in *my* view, I may add.'

He glanced at his watch, frowned as he replaced it in his pocket. 'So *late* . . . What did you mean about those prisoners, Everard?'

'Weary Willie was based on Zeebrugge, sir. I believe – with respect, sir – I think prisoners are what we were really after. The Germans weren't to *think* so, so it was better if we didn't realize it . . .' Reaper was just sitting there and staring at him, listening. He went on, 'There've been rumours of an offensive. And – well, it would make sense from the anti-U-boat angle to attack Zeebrugge, blow it up or capture it or block the canal? Ostend as well, I suppose. But if—'

'It's a nice idea. And of course it's been mooted more than once, in the last two years.' A moment ago Reaper had looked sharply alert; now he'd relaxed. He smiled. 'You've a powerful imagination. But – don't broadcast your ideas, please.'

Nick felt fairly certain he'd hit the nail on the head. An operation against Zeebrugge and Ostend: block seaways out of Bruges and eliminate it as a base. Reaper murmured, 'Wide of the mark. But we don't want rumours flying.' He was looking at his watch again. Nick, worried that he might jump up and rush away, began: 'About what my next appointment's to be, sir . . .'

Reaper looked surprised: as if he thought it was an odd subject to bring up. Nick thought dismally that he'd guessed right in this area too: he'd done the Weary

Willie job, and that was the end of this man's interest in him.

'Am I to remain in *Arrogant*?'

A shake of the narrow head ... 'I've something else to tell you – and on which to convey to you Admiral Keyes's congratulations. As a result of *Mackerel*'s action on Christmas Eve, you'll be getting a DSC.'

He was astonished. Delighted, as it sank in, but as much surprised as pleased. He said, 'Very generous of – of the admiral.'

Might Keyes really have sent congratulations? Would he even have heard of Nicholas Everard?

'Lieutenant-Commander Wyatt gets a DSO.'

'Is there a full list available, sir?'

Thinking about Swan. About all of them, but particularly Swan. Reaper shook his head. 'Not yet.' Another glance at his watch. 'Have to cut this short, I'm afraid.' He closed his eyes, as if to concentrate his thoughts: then opened them again and reached for the telephone. 'Crosby. Telephone to *Arrogant*'s first lieutenant. Ask him with my compliments to have Lieutenant Everard's gear packed and sent immediately to *Bravo*.'

Nick stared at him. He couldn't surely have said *Bravo*? Reaper seemed deliberately to avoid his eyes.

'If you can't reach the first lieutenant, the officer of the day would do.' He put the 'phone down. Nick couldn't believe this. A 'thirty-knotter' – fit for nothing but defensive patrol work? and *Bravo* already had a first lieutenant – Elkington, Tim Rogerson's pal! Unless they'd moved Elkington elsewhere; that must be the answer ... But – patrolling over the Varne minefield, or hanging around the Downs: no hope of any action or excitement. If you had enormous luck

224

you *might* get a crack at a U-boat: but then, so might a drifter!

Reaper was on his feet. Nick stood up too. He felt sick with the let-down of it. They praised you, gave you a medal, then kicked you down the stairs!

'You'll be glad to be in a sea-going appointment, I'm sure. If you'd stayed in *Mackerel* you'd have been in a London dockyard for months on end.'

Sugaring the pill . . . Reaper added, 'But if in the future some offensive operation should be contemplated, I imagine you'd like a part in it?'

'Yes, sir. I should.'

What was he saying – that *Bravo* would be only a temporary billet? Until the attack on the Belgian ports? Or might she take part in it? Hardly . . . His mind was snapping at guesses like a fish at flies . . . And hard reality remained: *Minefield patrol. This is Wyatt's doing* . . . Reaper said, 'Look, I really must cut along.' Pausing, he looked quizzically at Nick. 'You're not a very *trusting* fellow, Everard.'

'I – don't think I understand—'

'Obviously not.' Reaper smiled. 'Never mind.' Offering his hand: 'Thank you again, for a job well done. And – happy New Year!'

New Year's Eve . . .

It didn't feel like it. It hadn't felt like Christmas, either. He shook Reaper's hand.

'Sit down, Wyatt.' The admiral drew his own chair closer to the desk. 'Last time you and I met was also an occasion for congratulation, as I recall.' He nodded at the ribbon on Wyatt's shoulder. 'That DSC, of course. But hadn't you been nicked by a Turk's bayonet?'

'A pinprick, sir.'

'H'm . . . Great days while they lasted, eh?'

'Damn shame we were obliged to withdraw, sir.'

'As you say.'

Nodding. Thoughts reaching back to the Dardanelles and to his own conviction that the Navy could have forced the Narrows, *should* have done. His commodore's rank then hadn't cut much ice.

'But it's the present and future we must think about, Wyatt. Not the games we've lost.' Fingers drummed briefly on the desk. 'Your ship's out of commission, you face a period of inactivity, and that's hardly to your taste. Am I right?'

Wyatt nodded. The admiral continued, 'Your talents in command afloat are undoubted. But you made a useful soldier of yourself, out there, too.' He wasn't just making conversation; he was watching his visitor closely, to assess reaction. 'How would you like to do something of the sort again?'

Wyatt started carefully, 'If you have some such employment for me, sir—'

'I'm planning a – a certain enterprise, Wyatt.' Keyes slid a drawer open, took out a folded sheet of paper, passed it across the desk. 'Read that, would you.'

It was a letter to him from Admiral Wemyss, who had now taken over from Sir John Jellicoe as First Sea Lord. Wyatt read,

In view of the possibility of the enemy breaking through the line on the North Coast of France, and attacking Calais and Dunkirk, a special battalion of Marines and a company of bluejackets will be placed at your disposal for reinforcements, and to act as demolition parties, etc., to destroy guns and stores. You are to make every preparation for blocking Calais and Dunkirk harbours at the last possible moment, with the ships whose names have been given to you verbally, so as to deny the use of these ports to the enemy if necessary.

Wyatt looked up. 'I see, sir.' He passed the letter back. Keyes contradicted him, with a smile. 'No, you don't. This is a great secret which we'll allow to leak out. It will explain to the overcurious why certain ships are having peculiar modifications made to them, and why we should be training a lot of sailors in various offensive and destructive arts which are more usually left to men in khaki. But I can trust you, I'm sure, to keep your own counsel. No need to burden you now with the details: suffice it to say that my operation will be not *def*ensive, but *off*ensive.'

'I'm pleased to hear it, sir.'

'But it will be an extremely hazardous undertaking. If you elected to join me, I'd be glad to place a section of the landing force under your command. You are, of course, exactly the sort of chap I need for it. But before you give me your answer, I must tell you that the chances of your returning alive from the assault would be – slender. One might say non-existent.'

Wyatt was looking as delighted as if he'd been offered the Crown jewels.

'Where shall I go, sir, and when, to study these esoteric arts?'

Crosby, the paymaster in the other office, was falling over himself in efforts to be helpful. Before, Nick had found him moderately insufferable. He took the long, buff envelope, containing his appointment to *Bravo*, from him; it bore the seal of Captain (D)'s office, and

227

was addressed to Lieutenant Nicholas Everard, DSC, RN. The paybob said, 'Captain Tomkinson's only just in the process of taking over—'

'Tomkinson?'

'The new Captain (D).'

He remembered: Reaper had mentioned him. He was pushing the buff envelope into his pocket; Crosby asked him, 'Excuse me, but – shouldn't you read it?'

As if an appointment to an oily wad was something to drool over . . . Crosby said, 'I do think you *should*—'

'Yes. Later on.' He nodded at the fussy little man. Some of these office people lived for their bits of paper, records, memoranda . . . As for Tomkinson, it seemed Dover was filling rapidly with four-stripe captains, as Keyes built up his staff. God help Dover, Nick thought; and God help Nicholas Everard, too. He told Crosby, 'I'll give it some undivided attention later. But now I think I'll go on down. You say there's a boat already waiting?'

'Should be.' Crosby nodded. He still looked worried. 'Or on its way in. By the time you get down there—'

'Right. Thank you.'

The boat *was* there, waiting for him – if that motorboat out at the naval pier steps was *Bravo*'s. He could see it as he crossed the Marine Parade. He could see *Bravo* herself too, in the centre of the destroyer moorings, rolling and tugging at her buoy. The wind was rising, high clouds scudding over; the usual south-wester was blowing up, and as usual there was ice in it. He pushed his hands deep into the pockets of his greatcoat and set off down the pier.

There was an RNR midshipman in charge of the boat. A skinny, dark-haired lad who looked as if he thought Nick might bite him.

He stepped into the sternsheets. 'Carry on, please.'
'Shove off for'ard! Shove off aft!'

Quite choppy in the harbour. The destroyer berths
were in shallow water; tides ripped in from both
entrances and met here in the middle, to the discomfort
of destroyer men seeking a rare night's rest in port . . .
He gazed at *Bravo* as the boat bounced out towards
her. Strange-looking craft, the thirty-knotters. This one,
a D-class boat of 1897 or '98, had two funnels instead of
the more usual three. They were low, stunted-looking,
and there was an absolute litter of ventilators all over
her upper deck. A turtle-back foc'sl led to a bridge
that was only about half the height of *Mackerel*'s and
two-thirds of which was occupied by a twelve-pounder
gun. There was a six-pounder aft, and two more on
each side between bridge and after funnel. The pair
of torpedo tubes just for'ard of the stern gun would
be eighteen-inch. The general effect was of clutter, bits
and pieces everywhere.

But she was clean, well kept. That would have
been Elkington's responsibility, and it was obvious
he'd been a very conscientious first lieutenant. The
motorboat curved in towards the port-side gangway.
Nick wondered what sort of CO he'd be getting now; he
couldn't remember Elkington having mentioned him.

The midshipman had cut the boat's engine. Almost
at the gangway's foot. Now he'd put her astern and he'd
reversed the helm: and stopped again. It had been quite
neatly done, and Nick told him so. The boat's coxswain,
a leading seaman, looked as pleased as the snotty did.
Bowman and sternsheetman had their boathooks out
and hooked to the boat-rope. Nick stepped on to the
gangway.

Above his head, he heard the quiet order, 'Pipe!'

Pipe?

Only commanding officers – and foreign naval officers, and the King and members of his family, and certain other categories of visitor such as the officer of the guard and four-stripers and above – were entitled to be piped over the side of a Royal Navy ship. He didn't fit anywhere in that list. Someone, obviously, had blundered. He began to climb the gangway: the note of the pipe had risen, dropped, cut off. As he reached the top it began again. He saw Bruce Elkington standing stiffly at the salute, and a colossally broad CPO – it would be *Bravo*'s coxswain, probably – beside him, and two seamen, one of whom was the bosun's mate and doing the piping. Behind Elkington a sub-lieutenant and a warrant officer were also standing at attention. Finally, as he paused on the top platform of the gangway, he saw a long line of sailors fallen-in on the iron deck abreast the funnels, and a similar rank on the other side.

His hand snapped up to the salute, and he stepped aboard. The pipe's note fell, held for a few seconds, died. Elkington stepped forward.

'Welcome aboard, sir. On behalf of all hands may I say how delighted . . .'

His head span. This was – it was happening, it was real, and yet—

His fingers touched the unopened envelope in his pocket. He could visualize one startling, glowing phrase in it: . . . *appointed in command* . . . Reaper's voice grated in his brain: *You're not a very trusting fellow, Everard* . . . Elkington said, 'Ship's company is ready for your inspection, sir. May I first present Sub-Lieutenant York – and Mr Raikes, torpedo gunner . . . This is Chief Petty Officer Garfield, our cox'n.'

Shaking hands . . . Still dizzy. *I'm dreaming this, I*

must be . . . A destroyer command, at twenty-two? Oh
– only an oily wad, but still a—

'Will you inspect the ship's company, sir?'

Walking slowly for'ard, past the tubes and then a
dinghy in its davits. He glanced up at the masthead,
saw the ensign fairly crackling in the rising breeze.

Not just *the* ensign. *His!*

PART TWO

St George's Day: Zeebrugge

CHAPTER 12

'Stop both.'

'Stop both, sir.'

Engine-noise, the thrum of vibrating steel, ceased. *Bravo*, in her station near the van of the assault force, rolled more heavily as she lost steerage-way and the northerly breeze slapped a choppy sea against her port side. More of a sea than there'd been when they'd sailed; but thank heaven the visibility had closed in at last. Cloud obscured the moon, and drizzle was an enclosing curtain.

Admiral Keyes's armada of seventy-six assorted craft lay stopped while MLs embarked surplus crews from the blockships. Stokers, mostly, who'd been needed for the cross-Channel passage but had to be removed before the actual assault. The fewer men on board the blockships when they were run into the canal mouth and sunk, the fewer there'd be to rescue.

To *attempt* to rescue. Nobody was in much doubt as to how the odds lay. And yet there was gossip – *Bravo*'s chief stoker had mentioned it to Elkington – that a lot of those engine-room ratings weren't intending to disembark at this point. Determined to be in on the attack itself, they were planning to lie low until the ships got under way again.

Nick moved out to the port wing of the twelve-pounder platform, which was a forward extension of the bridge, and trained his glasses aft. The CMB they'd been towing should slip now, and York, the sub-lieutenant, should be seeing to it. Elkington murmured at Nick's elbow, 'Slipping her now, sir. Starboard quarter.' As he spoke, the cough and spluttering roar of the CMB's engine proved he was right. And all through the mass of silent, rolling ships other CMBs would be casting off and getting away under their own power. They'd been brought this far under tow so as to conserve fuel. He could see a few of them now, in the lanes and gaps between bigger ships' dark outlines, slinking off like wolves to gather in their various packs.

They'd be the first craft in, laying smoke in the Hun defenders' faces to cover the attacking force's approach. Then MLs, plugging up more slowly – Bell's and Treglown's among them – would take over most of the smoke-laying work.

'Signal to proceed, sir!'

Leading Signalman Tremlett had been watching for it. Nick said, 'Half ahead together.'

'Half ahead together, sir!' Clark, bosun's mate, slammed the brass telegraphs over. There was a lot of brasswork in and on *Bravo*, and every bit of it gleamed like gold. Elkington and his chief buffer, PO Russell, made up for the ship's antiquity by keeping her so spick-and-span anyone might think she'd been prepared for an admiral's inspection, not for war. Every ventilator, for instance – and her upper deck was fairly dotted with them – had a brass rim which in sunlight was blinding to look at. *Bravo* was gathering way, responding to her helm again, and Chief Petty Officer Horace Garfield held her precisely in the centre of her next-ahead's wake. Garfield's cap was, as usual, slanted to the right, while his left eyebrow – also as usual – was cocked up. Whether he wore his cap at that angle to make room for the habitually raised eyebrow, or pushed the eyebrow up to fill some of the space left by the invariably askew cap, probably not even he himself knew.

Grebe, the thirty-knotter ahead of *Bravo*, was to be her partner in the inshore patrol. By way of contrast to these two relics, ahead of them steamed *North Star* and *Phoebe*, two new destroyers who were to patrol the area off the mole's end; and ahead of *Phoebe*, Roger Keyes's vast silk vice-admiral's flag flaunted its St George's Cross over the flotilla-leader *Warwick*.

Marker buoys had been laid with great accuracy to guide the attacking force and mark the stages of its approach. Where they'd just been stopped had been position 'D', and now they were steering for 'G', just a few miles farther east.

Astern of this group of ships – Unit 'L' in Keyes's operational orders – Unit 'M' consisted of two more destroyers towing the submarines C1 and C3. Seen bow-on – from here now, of course, they were quite invisible in the dark, and anyway hidden by the towing ships – seen end-on, they looked like nothing that anyone had even seen before. Spars had been mounted across the tops of their conning-towers, and motor-dinghies slung on each side from the spars. Rather like panniers slung on a donkey's back. The boats were for the submarines' crews to escape in, after they'd done their job of blowing the viaduct sky-high. But only an optimist could have believed they'd have much chance of launching those dinghies, let alone motoring away to safety in them.

Tim Rogerson was in C3.

The dark assembly of ships ploughed steadily, silently eastward. *Bravo* rattled, groaned, hummed and moaned to herself as she thrust across the waves; the wind sang in her rigging overhead. She was entitled, Nick thought, at her age, to talk and mutter to herself. He was used to her now, and loved her. As others had before him; and he wondered suddenly, the thought springing out of the darkness and the tension, the knowledge that before long the night would turn to flame and thunder, whether anyone else would after him.

Idle, dangerous speculation. He dismissed it. He had his glasses on *Greve*'s stern, and he thought *Bravo* was creeping up a bit, inside her station.

'Come down ten revolutions, Bailey.'

'Down ten, aye aye, sir!'

Astern of Unit 'M' steamed another pair of destroyers, one of them towing a picket-boat whose function would be to rescue the submariners after they'd transferred to their dinghies. Rogerson's captain in C3 was a lieutenant named Sandford, and it was this Sandford's elder brother, who was on Keyes's staff, who'd brought the picket-boat along.

The centre column, the line of heavyweights, was led by *Vindictive*. She was an old cruiser – the same class originally as *Arrogant* – but she'd been substantially modified now for her role of assault ship. She was carrying the main body of the landing force, sailors and marines who were going to storm the mole and neutralize the gun-batteries on it – particularly on its end part, what was referred to in the orders as the mole extension – so that the blockships could get past it and on across the harbour into the canal mouth. The rest of the bayonet-and-bomb brigade were in *Iris* and *Daffodil*, two old Mersey ferry-steamers. Not well suited to long journeys in the open sea, they were being towed now by *Vindictive*.

Behind that assault group came the Zeebrugge blockships, the old cruisers *Thetis, Intrepid* and *Iphigenia*. They'd been fitted out during the last few months at Chatham. All their control equipment had been duplicated, with alternative conning and steering positions protected by steel plating and splinter-mats. Concrete had been built in to protect their boilers and machinery and steering equipment, and charges fitted for blowing the ships' bottoms out, with firing keys in both conning positions. Their masts had been taken out of them, as had all their guns except those right for'ard, which they'd be able to use on their way through and in. Twenty rounds of ammunition for each gun were stowed in shot-ready racks. Every piece of unnecessary equipment had been removed, and so had all items of copper and brass, since the Hun was known to be short of both. Only just enough coal for the journey was carried in their bunkers; and finally all accessible and suitable below-decks spaces had been filled with cement blocks and cement in bags, and rubble and concrete.

All the blockship and submarine crews were volunteers – and there'd been hot competition for places in the ships. Command of *Iphigenia* had been given to a lieutenant of Nick's own age, twenty-two, a man named Billyard-Leake: Keyes had approved the appointment for the same reason he'd approved Nick's: Lieutenants Billyard-Leake and Everard had both acquired reputations for coolness, judgement and leadership in action. He'd said so. As a commanding officer, one actually met and talked with admirals!

Sarah had written, *Are you all puffed-up and important, with your medal and your ship, my famous stepson? If you are not, I shall be for you! I am! While your dear uncle – who so far forgot himself as to condescend to pay us a visit here last week – is so proud of his nephew that he can barely speak of him coherently!*

She'd had other cause than that for writing, though. The main content of her letter had been news of her own, and sadness and thoughtfulness, and a need to tell him about it. It had left him no less thoughtful, but perhaps – wrongly, he thought – less sad. *Much* less sad? No point trying to hide it from oneself: her letter had made him happy.

Not for a man's death, he tried to convince himself. By the fact she'd turned to him to confide in. And yet – one stranger, amongst the thousands dying . . .

Astern of the three Zeebrugge blockships steamed the pair that would be going to Ostend – *Brilliant* and *Sirius*.

'Coming up to position "G", sir!'

Bailey, *Bravo*'s RNR midshipman who'd seemed so timorous, was becoming a useful navigator. The previous captain – an RNVR lieutenant-commander, and he'd developed heart trouble – had handled all the pilotage himself, but it had seemed a better idea to let the snotty earn his keep and gain experience.

'G' was the last checkpoint before they began the run-in to the target areas. It was also the point where the two forces would divide, the Ostend ships turning five points to starboard and heading almost due south to rendezvous with Commodore Lynes who'd be coming with small craft from Dunkirk. Lynes commanded the

240

Dunkirk base, under Keyes, and the Ostend operation was being left to him.

Ahead, a shaded light flashed briefly. The Ostend blockships would be putting their helms over now, passing astern of this starboard column and disappearing into the night. Nick was watching *Grebe*, who seemed unable to maintain constant revs.

'Up ten revolutions, Mid.'

'Aye aye, sir.' He heard Bailey shout the order down the tube. Elkington reported, '*Brilliant* and *Sirius* passing astern, sir.'

'Mid, what's the time?'

'Ten-thirty, sir.'

Perfect. And the visibility was still closing in as the drizzle thickened. This was 'X'-hour, and in precisely ninety minutes, at midnight, *Vindictive* should be alongside the Zeebrugge mole with her assault force pouring ashore. She'd been fitted with special hinged gangways all down her length, which would be dropped to rest against the top edge of that massive stone barrier.

Elkington said, 'Wind seems to be holding, sir.'

'Yes. Touch wood.'

A change of wind from north to south had forced Keyes to cancel the operation and turn the force back to England when they sailed the first time, on April 11th. A northerly wind was an essential weather condition: the smoke-screens, vital to the whole business, had to be carried shoreward, not dissipated or blown back seaward. There'd been a second attempt on the 13th, but that had been abandoned too; wind and sea had risen to such an extent that a landing on the mole would have been impossible.

Third time, and third time lucky, Nick thought. This was the last chance they'd get, with high water falling in the right period of darkness; and if it had to be cancelled for a third time the Admiralty wouldn't let Keyes try again. There was the matter of security, for one thing; you couldn't go on for ever putting to sea and turning back again, and holding an assault force locked up in their ships in the Thames estuary, without some knowledge of it finally leaking to the enemy.

It could have happened already. Even now, the Germans could be waiting for them.

Nick asked Elkington, 'Is McAllister all set up, aft?'

'It's a daunting sight, sir. You wouldn't recognize your cabin.'

He'd got McAllister, who'd been *Mackerel*'s doctor, appointed to *Bravo*. She'd had no doctor, and Andy McAllister had proved his worth after that Christmas Eve action. He'd stayed in Dover when *Mackerel* had left for the London dockyard, and Nick on a visit to the hospital yacht to see *Mackerel*'s wounded had found him there still looking after them and hoping for a new destroyer job.

However well matters turned out in the next few hours, no hospital yacht would be much use. Whole wards of big hospitals in London and elsewhere were being held ready; special trains had been ordered, staffed by doctors. Even with total success, they'd all be needed.

The ruse of that letter from Admiral Wemyss to Keyes about a possible evacuation of Calais and Dunkirk, and perhaps having to block those two ports, had worked splendidly. Right up to the final briefings, everyone had believed it. And the German land offensive which Ludendorff had launched a month ago – with alarming success – had seemed to justify and support the fears

242

of having to pull out. Now, with the German army still attacking and gaining ground, determined to make the most of their numerical superiority before enough American troops arrived to tilt the balance, this attack from the sea would be a timely diversion as well as a naval necessity.

Nick glanced round his bridge, at new steel plating that had been welded to its rails. There were splinter-mattresses outside that shielding steel. The guns – six-pounders – on the upper deck, and the torpedo tubes, had been given extra protection too. *Bravo* and *Grebe* were to be inside the mole, backing up the CMBs and MLs who'd be inshore to lay smoke and to rescue blockships' crews. Things were likely to be fairly brisk, inside that mole.

'There they go.'

Warwick – Keyes's flagship – with *Phoebe* and *North Star* astern of her, and with *Whirlwind* and *Myngs* on their port beam, were all putting on speed, drawing ahead to act as vanguard and deal with any enemy patrols that might be encountered between here and Zeebrugge. Everything was happening exactly as planned and scheduled in the orders; and as each stage was reached there was a degree of relief in moving forward to the next.

Elkington said, his voice echoing Nick's unspoken thoughts, 'Be glad when we get to grips with it.'

What must it be like, Nick wondered, for the men in the landing parties, cooped up over there in *Vindictive, Iris* and *Daffodil*. For them, this raid would be something like Russian roulette – with five of the six chambers loaded.

He lowered his binoculars, and answered Elkington:

'Better than sitting over that damn minefield, isn't it?'

'Mind you roast 'em, eh?'

Edward Wyatt, in *Vindictive*, nodded to Brock, the RNAS Wing-Commander whose smoke, smoke-floats, flame-throwers and other pyrotechnical products were to be much in evidence during the coming battle. Brock was planning to land on the mole with the storming parties, too, to try to find some new sound-ranging apparatus which the Germans were believed to have installed there. He'd smiled at Wyatt's proposal: Wyatt added to it.

'Or boil 'em in oil, while you're at it?'

Brock was making adjustments to the after flame-thrower. Wyatt left him in the steel shelter they'd built for it, went down the ladder and over to the starboard side of the upper deck. There was plenty of time in hand, and he could still have been down in the old cruiser's wardroom, where coffee and sandwiches were available; but it was difficult, he'd found, to sit about, doing nothing. Tension, expectancy: it stretched the nerves, made you want to move, crack jokes, flex your muscles! Plenty of other men were doing the same thing: prowling to and fro, joking, laughing: or alone, silent and deep in thought. He walked for'ard along the starboard side; there was open deckspace here, room to move – unlike the port side, which was a mass of fittings and equipment for the mole boarding operation.

Destroyers' shapes were visible to starboard, and the white curls of their bow-waves. He stopped, leant with a shoulder against the cutter's after davit, and stared across a jumping, loppy sea at the attacking force's

244

starboard column. Those two destroyers' silhouettes were unmistakable, dark or no dark: they were thirty-knotters. For inshore work, he guessed – expendable. stern of them, just abaft *Vindictive's* beam, were two much more modern boats – *Trident* and *Mansfield* – towing the submarines. Narrowing his eyes, he peered at them through the darkness. He could make out the destroyers well enough, but only one submarine. The leading one was there, in tow of *Trident*; but the other seemed to have disappeared.

The harder you looked, the less you saw. One needed binoculars to make sense of it. They must both be there. Otherwise surely both destroyers wouldn't be.

He pushed himself off the damp, grey-painted steel, and strolled on for'ard. Hardly any motion on the ship: but plenty of squeaks and rattles. Well, she'd seen a bit of service in her time, had *Vindictive*.

Nothing to what she'd see in the next hour or two!

Up on the level of the false deck, on his left, loomed one of the 7.5-inch howitzers that had been installed to bombard gun positions on the mole after the ship was secured alongside. She'd be below the level of the parapet, so howitzers were the obvious things, for their high trajectory. There was an 11-inch one on the quarterdeck, and another of these 7.5s on the foc'sl.

It was going to be hellish noisy, alongside that mole.

A false deck had been built on the skid-beams – the supports on which seaboats normally rested – all down the port side from foc'sl to quarterdeck. Wide ramps from this starboard side sloped up to it: three of them, providing ample and easy access to that higher level, which would be almost as high as the mole's parapet. Not quite, though; and there'd be a wide gap to be bridged as well, so there were eighteen gangways hinged to the false deck and triced up. Released, they'd crash down on to the parapet. The false deck provided cover, too; while they were waiting to be ordered up the ramps and over the gangways, the storming parties could take shelter under it.

Wyatt's palm stroked the butt of the revolver at his side. He'd like to be moving *now*: leading his company of fifty sailors with their grenades and rifles and machine-guns in a swift, wild charge on to the mole and over that shed's roof to the guns. Speed was the thing: speed and ruthlessness and the hell with what might be coming at you. *Attack*: and think of nothing else. Like a rugger dash, in a way; and as one who'd played rugger for the Navy, Edward Wyatt knew all about that.

Not quite as gentlemanly as rugger. Bullets and cold steel and high explosives and no handshakes either before or after. The training at Chatham had been rigorous and intensive: the men were hard as nails and they wouldn't be looking for prisoners.

He saw Harrington Edwards strolling aft with Peshall, the padre. They were coming this way, and he didn't feel like joining their conversation, so he turned away quickly and went up the nearest of the ramps to the false deck. Padre Peshall would be going ashore with the storming parties: he'd played rugger for England and he was unlikely to confine his activities to saving souls. Edwards, a bearded and one-eyed RNVR lieutenant-commander, had been all through the Gallipoli campaign and had since been wounded in France; it was odd, Wyatt thought, that a naval officer should be in a position to claim three years of trench fighting experience. But he was a good fellow.

They all were: fighting-cocks, handpicked; it was just that he didn't feel in the mood, at the moment, for chatting.

At each end of this false deck a ladder led up to a flame-thrower hut. And all along it were the brows, gangways with hand-rails and transverse ladder-grips for footholds; they were upright on their hinges, angled slightly outboard and held there by topping-lifts which were secured to eyebolts in the midships superstructure. The mole would be something like six feet higher than this raised deck, and the brows would lead upwards to it across a gap of twenty or thirty feet. As well as the *flammenwerfers* and howitzers, there were three pom-poms, ten Lewis guns and sixteen Stokes mortars on this side of the ship; and in the foretop, which of course would be high above the parapet of the mole, were three more pom-poms and another six Lewis guns to fire downwards and sweep the mole's surface clear of Germans as the men rushed ashore.

Vindictive's port side had been lined with huge fenders to protect her as she bumped alongside; and the mainmast had been lifted out of her, and laid horizontally across the quarterdeck with its heel embedded in concrete and its end projecting over the port quarter. It would fend the stern off and keep the port propeller clear of the mole's underwater projection.

Wyatt heard someone coming up the ramp behind him. Glancing round, he saw that it was Cross, his second-in-command in E Company.

He frowned. 'Looking for me, Cross?'

'Not really, sir.' Jimmy Cross smiled. He was one of the contingent lent to the operation from the Grand Fleet in Scapa. Beatty had called on Flag Officers commanding the battlefleet's squadrons to provide selected volunteers from their ships; they were to be 'stout-hearted men, active and keen, who could be depended upon in emergency; and having regard to the hazardous nature of the enterprise, wherever possible, unmarried or without dependants.' Officers were to be those whose powers of initiative and leadership were known to be high. Flag Officers were to select officers, and Captains the petty officers and men. And one of those selected under this edict had been Cross, who was a gunnery officer and a fleet boxing champion. He stopped at Wyatt's side.

'Just it's getting a bit stuffy below, sir.' He stared up at the tracery of wires, jackstays and topping-lifts above their heads. Black parallels against a background of night clouds that were faintly lighter because they had a full moon behind them. He said, 'The Germans won't believe we'd be such idiots as to attack with a moon that could show through at any time it feels like it, d'you think?'

Wyatt didn't like that much. It sounded like a criticism of Keyes. He grunted, stared across a couple of hundred yards of sea at a whole pack of MLs keeping station on the beam. There was another horde of them, smoke-screen boats, further astern. Cross was looking aft, at the huge grappling-iron suspended from its derrick; there was another for'ard. He murmured, 'They've done a pretty thorough job of disfiguring this poor old hooker, sir.'

Wyatt growled, 'Dare say the Huns'll add their tanner's worth.'

'Anyway –' the younger man sighed – 'not long to wait for it, now ... The men seem to be in good heart, sir.'

'Why shouldn't they be, for God almighty's sake!'

Explosive . . . You never knew, with Edward Wyatt. It was so easy to say the wrong thing, rub him up the wrong way. Crusty swine: worth his weight – which wasn't inconsiderable – of course, but – Cross shrugged it off. There was a touch of nervous tension in them all, just now. Wyatt added, as if he wanted to justify that outburst, 'They've all asked to be here, haven't they?'

Every man in the storming parties, whether marines or sailors, had expressed a personal wish to take part in what had been described only as a 'hazardous enterprise'. Then early this month Admiral Keyes had visited the ships at their anchorage in the Swin, the Thames estuary, described the operation in detail and told them that any of them who were married, or had other reasons to wish to withdraw, could do so without being thought the worse of. Not one man had expressed any such wish.

'I'm off for a word with Halahan.' Wyatt turned away. 'Join you down there presently.'

'Aye aye, sir.'

Not *much* later, Cross thought. It was past eleven o'clock. In less than an hour, they'd be leading their men up those gangways.

He turned his back on them, and went down to see if any of E Company might have last-minute queries. On the way down the ramp he glanced up at the clouds again. If they blew away, and the attack had to be carried out under a full moon, bright as day: *phew* . . . There'd be the smoke-screens, of course, and they were necessary in any case because of starshell and searchlights; but with the whole area lit up by a moon, old Brocky's smoke would need to be five times as thick as smoke had ever been. *And* the wind

249

must hold . . . A story had gone round, leaked by one of Keyes's junior staff officers, that after the first two attempts to launch the operation had been abandoned the Admiralty had been about to call off the whole thing, pay off the ships and disband the marine battalion, send the Grand Fleet detachments back to Scapa. Keyes had pleaded with Sir Rosslyn Wemyss, the First Sea Lord, for his support in allowing a third sortie. Wemyss had said, 'But you wanted a moonless night, as well as a high tide at midnight!'

'No, sir.' Keyes had told him, 'I wanted a full moon. Couldn't wait for it, that was all.'

Wemyss had stared at him incredulously. Then he'd grinned.

'Roger, what a damned liar you are!'

Wyatt found Captain Halahan with Colonel Elliot of the Marines and Carpenter, who was commanding *Vindictive* but not her landing forces, in the cruiser's chartroom just abaft the bridge.

Halahan was in command of the naval landing force. Until he'd volunteered for this job he'd had the siege guns on the Belgian coast. He and Elliot had worked closely together and with Keyes, in the last three months, planning the mole attack; Elliot's Royal Marines had trained at Deal, and Halahan's bluejackets at Chatham. At Deal they'd built a mock-up of the mole, and stormed it day after day, putting the story out that it was a replica of some position in France which in due course they'd be attacking.

Carpenter, although he was now *Vindictive*'s captain, was primarily a navigator and staff officer who'd been with Keyes in the Plans Division in London and since then had been the prime mover and chief coordinator of all the planning.

There was concern now in his bony, sharp-featured face as he looked up, saw Wyatt, glanced back at Halahan. Wyatt asked Elliot, 'Something wrong?'

'Monitors haven't opened fire. They should have several minutes ago.'

Erebus and *Terror*, to the north-east of Zeebrugge, should have started their bombardment forty minutes after 'X'-hour. And when they did start, those big guns would be audible. Wyatt said, 'I saw three CMBs go tearing off, just as I came up here.'

'Units A and B.' Carpenter nodded. 'Laying smoke ahead of us as we approach. Three waves of it.' Halahan murmured, 'Oh, what a fount of knowledge.' He glanced at Wyatt. 'Problems?'

'None at all, sir.'

'Good. It's too late for problems.'

Carpenter had gone out on to the bridge. Lieutenant-Commander Rosoman, his first lieutenant, was at the binnacle, and Wyatt heard Rosoman's shout of laughter ring out at some remark his captain made. A happy, lively fellow, Rosoman. And keen as mustard, another of Keyes's personal selections. He'd had the responsibility of *Vindictive*'s fitting out, since Carpenter had been occupied with all the planning.

Osborne, the ship's gunnery commander, walked in.

'Shouldn't the monitors be doing something by this time?'

Halahan glanced up, nodded, returned to his quiet conference with Elliot. They were studying a plan of the mole, checking over the details of which company would do what, and when. Osborne looked at Wyatt, raised his eyebrows, and stalked out again. Wyatt looked over Elliot's shoulder at the mole plan.

The most vital objective was the capture or destruction of the guns on the end of it, where the blockships would have to pass. But there were other guns here and there, and a garrison with its living-quarters and other buildings on it; plus a seaplane base with four hangars, a railway station and two large goods sheds, and an overhanging submarine shelter. The mole itself was a massive stone construction just over one mile long, connected to the shore causeway by a 300-yard viaduct, a lattice-work construction of steel girders under which the tides raced and which carried a double railway line and a roadway to the mole. It was this viaduct that the submarines were intended to blow up, so that the Germans wouldn't be able to rush reinforcements over it.

The mole was eighty yards wide. On its outer side where the assault ships would berth it had an outer wall twenty feet high; on top of this was a ten-foot roadway protected by a three-foot parapet. So the attackers would have to get over that little wall on to the roadway, then down the sixteen-foot drop to the broad surface that was concreted, dotted here and there with guns, buildings and so on.

Near the end of the mole a long building had been erected fairly recently, and its flat roof seemed to be more or less level with the raised roadway. This had been chosen as the place for the attack. The landing parties could rush over the flat roof and get close to the mole-end guns, thus avoiding the alternative of a painful advance up the mole itself against barbed wire and well-sited machine-guns. (There seemed to be trenches on the mole, too, with stone embankments

252

protecting them.) The guns at the end, and on the extension – after the mole's full width came to its end, the ten-foot roadway alone was carried on for another 360 yards to a lighthouse on its tip – those guns were in an extremely exposed situation, and once over the long building's flat roof the landing force should be well placed to rush them.

The guns were thought to be 4.7-inch. Once they were taken, there was to be an advance westward down the mole, marines covering a demolition party of specially trained bluejackets whose orders were to do as much harm as possible to cranes, guns, the seaplane station and any ships or dredgers alongside. Sandford, Keyes's staff officer who'd planned the submarine attack and was now in the rescue picket-boat, had also planned the demolition work – in such detail that he'd borrowed wicker baskets on wheels, from the Post Office in London, for the explosive charges to be wheeled along in.

Thunder, suddenly, in the north-east . . .

Elliot and Halahan looked up, and smiled. Halahan murmured, 'Better late than never.'

Elliot ran a forefinger along his little clipped moustache: 'Thank God for it, anyway!'

The monitors had opened fire fifteen minutes late. Captain Carpenter pushed in through the doorway from the bridge. 'Hear that?'

'Late.' Halahan nodded. 'Rotten staff-work.' Carpenter opened his mouth to answer: but an aeroplane-like roar close by made speech impossible for the moment, drowned out the rumble of the cruiser's engines and the multiple rattlings of her fabric. As the noise lessened Colonel Elliot asked, 'What was that?'

'CMBs.' Carpenter had knitted this whole thing

253

together, he knew each move, minute by minute. 'Units C, D and E, to be precise.' Halahan interrupted, teasing him again: 'You're showing off, Alfred.' Carpenter's deepset eyes smiled: he went on, 'C lays a smoke-float off Blankenberg and renews it with another every twenty minutes. D goes flat-out to the mole and lays smoke-floats in the western section, and patrols that line until he's relieved by Unit I—'

'Oh, for heaven's sake—'

'—which consists of eight MLs. And E does precisely the same thing in the eastern section.' He bowed to Halahan. 'Now if you'll excuse me—'

'Who wouldn't.' Halahan turned to the others. 'But –' he glanced at the clock on the bulkhead – 'we'd better go down. Fun starts in half an hour.'

Tim Rogerson stopped beside Petty Officer Harner. Harner was on the stool behind C3's wheel, in the dimly-lit control room, although he wasn't doing anything about steering. Rogerson said, 'Permission for me to go up, please, cox'n.'

Harner leant sideways to the voicepipe.

'Lieutenant Rogerson on the bridge, sir, please?'

'Wait a minute!'

Baldy Sandford's voice. John Howell-Price, the submarine's first lieutenant, was doing the steering from the bridge; down here, Harner was only standing by a disconnected wheel. In the engine-room, ERA Roxburgh and Stoker Bindall had just started the boat's petrol engine; the rush of air through the control room, sucking down through the hatch and aft to the engine, was fierce.

Sandford called down, 'In engine-clutch, half ahead!'

Rogerson moved to the telegraph on the after

254

bulkhead, passed the order through to the ERA. He heard Dick Sandford's voice in the tube again: 'Cox'n – what's the time now?'

'Eleven twenty-six, sir!'

'Very good.'

Rogerson wondered what was happening up top. They'd slipped the tow: that was obvious, from the fact that they were moving now under their own power. Altering to starboard, by the feel of her, the slight heel. They were supposed to wait, once they were clear of the main assault force, for C1 and the picket-boat to join them when they'd slipped *their* tows.

'Stop engine!'

Harner repeated the order as Tim whirled the handle of the telegraph. Stopping now to wait for the others, he thought. And then, *I make a first-rate telegraphman* ... He was spare, really. If anything happened to Howell-Price he'd step into his place; or if Sandford was hit, and Howell-Price took over the command ... But C1 had only two officers, and Rogerson wondered whether Sandford hadn't issued him with the invitation to this party before he'd known he had Howell-Price with him anyway.

She was stopped now, wallowing, rolling like a tub. An ancient craft. Built in 1906, the Cs were almost replicas of the earlier Bs. Single-screw, 200 horsepower out of a 16-cylinder petrol motor, 135 feet long and displacing 300 tons. Entirely fit, he thought, for this conversion to floating bomb.

One was acutely aware of that Amatol up for'ard. Of what might happen, for instance, if a shell hit it, on their way inshore. But it was easier when one turned one's mind elsewhere, and there were problems enough to come without considering the possibility of accidents, pure bad luck. Such misfortunes were insured against by having two submarines instead of only one; one would be enough to do the job, but the second was the back-up, making sure of it. Only one thing was sure, he thought: that within a very short time all this would be ripped apart, blown to shreds. He looked round the cramped, cave-like control-room. The two periscopes were down and housed; the single brass hydroplane-control wheel gleamed like dull gold. It was handy that in these old Cs and Bs there were no fore 'planes; it would have been necessary to have removed them, so as not to impede the boat's penetration of the viaduct.

The idea was that her forepart would drive in between the girders, and explode right in the middle of it.

'Time, cox'n?'

'Eleven-thirty and a half, sir!'

A moment's pause: a muttered exchange up there on the bridge. Then: 'Half ahead. And tell Lieutenant Rogerson he can come up.'

'Aye aye, sir!'

Leading Seaman Cleaver's seaboots came into sight at that moment, clumping down the ladder. Stepping off it, meeting the coxswain's enquiring stare, he announced, 'We're on our tod. No sight o' C1 and no bleedin' picket-boat neither. *I* dunno.' He shook sea off his oilskins. He'd been down on the fore casing, casting off the tow. Rogerson went behind him and stepped on to the ladder, hauled himself up through the lower hatch and then the dark, salt-smelling tube of the conning-tower and up from there into the rocking bridge.

Sandford, leaning in the front curve of the bridge beside Howell-Price, turned and nodded to him.

'All well, below?'

'No problems, sir.'

'Well, we have one up here, old lad. The others 've gone the wrong way, or something. Silly cusses!'

A rumble of gunfire from astern somewhere. Turning, he saw flashes lighting a clouded horizon some miles off on the port quarter. Sandford murmured, '*Erebus* and *Terror* stirring the Hun up ready for us.' He laughed. 'But they're used to it, they won't think it's anything special. The idea's to make him keep his head down for a bit.'

Damp night air: drizzle and the stickiness of sea-salt. Swish of sea rushing aft over the saddle-tanks and washing through below this free-flood bridge. Racket of the engine, its exhaust drowned in the white-foaming wash. Rogerson thought, *So we're alone. All up to us.*

How long now?

It hit him suddenly, the reality of it. This wasn't something in the mind, a plan, something rather thrilling that one was thankful to have been let in on. It was *now!*

At least, in about twenty minutes . . .

In the circumstances, the need to make sure of it because the whole thing was in their hands alone, he didn't think Baldy would use the gyro-steering device. Both submarines had been fitted with it. When they were a hundred yards or so from the viaduct they could, if they wished, take to the dinghies and leave the submarine to steer herself on the pre-set course.

He didn't think Sandford would have used it anyway. Nobody had ever discussed doing so. And it would be frightful to get that close and then leave everything to a gadget that might let them down.

'Uncle Baldy' said, 'Lovely weather for a continental visit. Eh, you chaps?'

'Beautiful.' Howell-Price was still concentrating on the steering, and looking at the white wake astern you could see that the boat's track was ruler-straight. 'This sort of drizzle makes a man feel he's never left home.'

Sandford began to warble the Eton boating song. Rogerson wondered what the devil could have happened to the others. Might the picket-boat have been swamped? She'd very little freeboard. The people in C1 were pals, former shipmates and messmates. They'd be thoroughly fed up, to find themselves out of it. Engine-trouble, probably. It was sensible enough to use old scrap-iron ships for throw-away jobs, but there was that disadvantage, the element of unreliability.

He wondered how Nick Everard was getting on, in his old oily-wad. That was a throw-away job if there ever was one! And thinking of Nick, his mind turned to his own sister, Eleanor, who was – or *thought* she was – in love with him. Nick somehow held back: you could see he was attracted to Eleanor and that they got on well together, even got a bit spoony sometimes; but he was – oh, sort of detached, he acted like a man in love with someone else, or married, even . . . Strange fellow, in some ways. And mad keen – one might almost say a raving lunatic – these days about the Navy.

Howell-Price said suddenly, 'I can smell Brockish vapour.'

'Just as well.' Sandford had stopped singing, which was kind of him. He said, 'We're going to need that smoke of his. Unless they don't spot us at all, of course. And that *could* happen, don't you know?'

Howell-Price nodded, watching his course. He muttered, 'And pigs could fly.' Rogerson thought of something: 'Aren't the birdmen supposed to be plastering 'em with bombs, by this time?'

'So they are.' Sandford removed his cap, and scratched his head. Even in this darkness, you could see how he'd acquired his nickname. 'Weather, probably. Wets their feathers, or something. Shouldn't think it'd make much odds.' He stooped to the voicepipe: 'Cox'n – time now?'

'Fourteen to the hour, sir!'

'Thanks.'

Smoke: they were running into the edges of it. Pungent, foul-smelling. It would be worse in a minute: you could see, ahead, a sort of bank of extra-thick darkness. A CMB had done that to it, pouring some chemical from its exhaust and depriving all the old ladies back home of their favourite sugar-substitute. *Vindictive* would be approaching the smoke-barrier too, Rogerson thought. The other side of it, they'd find the mole. Smoke – *thick* smoke – surrounded C3 now. Howell-Price called suddenly, 'Hey! I say . . . D'you *feel* that?'

'What?' Sandford stopped, leaning to put an ear to whatever his first lieutenant had to say. 'What's that, John?'

'Wind. Breeze. I'd swear it's – *off-shore!*'

'Oh, surely not . . .'

Rogerson felt it too. And realized what it meant. All the smoke the CMBs and MLs were laying to shroud the advance and the assault would be wafted out to sea: which meant total exposure to the German gunners on the shore and on the mole . . . But the shift in wind direction might not be permanent: it could be a fluke, a false alarm. Sandford called into the voicepipe, 'Cox'n – send Cleaver up, please.'

Harner's voice was thin in the copper tube: 'Leading Seaman Cleaver on the bridge!'

He was there almost instantaneously, a dark figure hoisting itself out of the hatch. 'Sir?' Rogerson edged sideways and aft, squeezing round the after periscope-standard, to make room for him. Sandford said, 'Go down on the fore casing, Cleaver, and turn on the smoke-canisters. Wait there and see how it drifts.'

'Aye aye, sir.' The killick cocked a leg over the side of the bridge, swung over, clambered down the rungs welded to the outside of it. Sandford began, addressing Howell-Price, 'If our own smoke could be persuaded to blow along *with* us—'

Westward, heavy guns crashed, flamed. Smoke made it confused, difficult to pinpoint them: but it was savage, continuous firing breaking suddenly out of silence, as if it had been held back, pent up and now suddenly released. Wreathing, eddying smoke watered the flashes still: but there were explosions of shells striking as well as the sharper spurts of gunfire: the roar of it spread, increased, thickened. A splitting crash, like close and vicious thunder, made them all look up; overhead, above the enshrouding smoke, a starshell burst into a source of brilliance that lit the clouds like daylight. The smoke was blowing past them faster than they were moving across the sea. Rogerson was sure of it. The wind *had* shifted: he thought of *Vindictive* suddenly exposed as she approached the mole at point-blank range. Sandford was shouting over the front of the bridge, 'Pack it in, Cleaver!' He raised his arms, fore-arms crossed, the visual signal meaning 'belay'. Cleaver waved acknowledgement, bent to the canister to turn it off; its smoke had been streaming seawards, useless. Sandford was at the voicepipe now: 'Cox'n?'

'Sir!'

Gunfire to port was tremendous. *Vindictive* must be getting hell. But whoever was being shot at, it wasn't C3. Not yet. Sandford shouted to the coxswain, 'Come up, all of you!'

'Aye aye, sir!'

Cleaver's head appeared over the rim of the bridge. Sandford ordered, 'After casing, old lad. Shelter behind the bridge. After we strike, take charge of the port dinghy's for'ard fall.'

'Port dinghy's gone, sir.'

'*Gone?*'

A great leaping flash to port: like a sheet of lightning. One could hear, between the thunder of big guns, the chattering of machine-guns and the steady thump-thump-thump of pom-poms. Sandford told Cleaver, 'Starboard dinghy, then.' Cleaver vanished, down on to the catwalk and aft round the conning-tower to the casing behind it. Stoker Bindall shot up out of the hatch, with Roxburgh the artificer behind him; Sandford told Rogerson, with glasses at his eyes and searching for the viaduct, 'Send them down to the after casing and then join 'em there yourself, there's a good chap.' Suddenly it was light. Starshell breaking overhead, hanging, flooding the whole area with their harsh magnesium brilliance, and the smoke drawing off them, pulling aft, shredding away and leaving them naked to German eyes: the sea leapt, shell-spouts springing up right ahead of the submarine as she clawed in landwards, floodlit, an easy target for gunners on the mole, on the viaduct itself when they chose to open fire.

261

Gun-flashes in a ripple of bright spurts to the westward of where the mole must be: where the mole *was*, by God! You could see it, the great black bulk of it – and the viaduct too – as clearly as if this was midday, not mid*night*, and Howell-Price was altering course by about five degrees, aiming her to strike it in the centre and at right-angles. More shells fell – abeam, this time, to starboard – grey spouts jumping, hanging, collapsing back into black rings on the sea, and the rush of others ripping overhead. Now a searchlight beam sprang out – from the viaduct – swung to them and fastened. A second one joined it: C3 was speared on their points, held between them as if she was a piece of chicken and the beams two chopsticks. Sandford shouted in Howell-Price's ear, 'Hold hard now, John! Smack in the centre now, old lad!' Another shell plumped into the sea to starboard: and then the searchlights, to everyone's astonishment and relief, switched off. Gunfire to port was rising to a crescendo, a continuous and rising roar. Sandford grabbed Tim's arm: 'Damn it, I told you to go *down*!'

'Sorry!'

Not only had the searchlights switched off – which could have resulted from a power-failure, that was the most likely explanation – but that western gun battery had ceased fire. No easy explanation covered *that*. C3 had the viaduct right ahead of her, she was cutting a dead-straight white track across the sea towards it: and a flare burst suddenly to hang over the harbour on the other side of it, silhouetting its struts and girders and the high roadway it carried: a vast, looming, criss-cross structure – and men moving about on top of it: still no shots aimed this way. What did they think – that she was harmless, mistaking the viaduct for a gap she hoped

262

to pass through, so she'd get stuck there and be easy meat? Rogerson, climbing over the side of the bridge, saw that towering lattice-work of steel etched black against the brilliance of the flare, growing, expanding across the sky as it towered towards them, and men running about on the roadway like upright ants, and he thought brutally *It'll be* German *meat . . .*

C3 plugged doggedly in towards it, her petrol engine hammering away: the Germans looked down, watched her come, did nothing at all to stop her. She had about a hundred yards to go.

Wyatt shouted back to Cross, 'Tell 'em to wait there till we send for 'em! There's no way up yet!' He was on the false deck: he'd been there all the time, and although it was littered with bodies and slippery with blood it was safer now, protected by the sheer wall of the mole. *Vindictive* still rang with the noise of her own guns and the crashes of German shells ripping into her and exploding, showering her decks with steel splinters which in turn drummed on steel, screeched away in ricochets, but for the same reason – the mole's protection – it was only in her upperworks now. The stone wall was a solid shield to her vitals – which, God knew, had suffered enough as she'd forged across the last few hundred yards of sea through a hail of shells. Now she was flinging herself about as if in agony, rising and falling and seesawing against the wall, rocking close to it and then away again, still nothing like close enough alongside. She'd come in at full speed and the surge had come in with her, her own following wash and the thrust of water from the bottom forcing up between herself and the mole: a maelstrom of her own making, and there was no escaping it. Half the gangways had

263

been smashed against the wall: three-quarters of the others had been shot to matchwood before she'd got that close, during that last murderous three hundred yards. When they'd burst out of the smoke they'd been too far east: Carpenter had swung the wheel over and increased to full speed, to save the ship and the men in her more punishment than they needed to suffer: in the process, conning her from the port flame-thrower hut, he'd overshot the mark – engines were going full astern now, Wyatt noticed, and they were adding to the turbulence and motion – overshot by nearly four hundred yards: she was that distance from where she should have been. It wasn't going to be at all easy to reach the guns at the mole's end: they were a quarter of a mile away, there'd be a quarter-mile of exposed, shot-torn concrete to cover . . . Well, they'd do it, somehow, E Company'd do it – for the simple reason that it had to be done, it was what they'd come here for. And the first thing was to *get ashore* . . . Another shell had just burst in the bridge: but the guns from the foretop were still blazing, and the howitzers were in it now. (Not the for'ard one. The *foc'sl* howitzer had had two complete crews wiped out, and then the gun itself.) Wyatt, staring upwards as the ship rocked away from the mole again, realised that the derricks carrying the grappling-hooks weren't tall enough: the hook on this for'ard one wouldn't – *couldn't* – be dropped to grab the parapet, which was what it was designed to do. If it could be got over, the ship could be secured – with the after one as well, of course: and the only way to effect it would be to *put* it there: to get up there and damn well *do* it! He pushed past Cross, dodged round a hurrying stretcher-party – below, the doctors were already inundated with work – reached the

264

derrick and began to climb it. The ship's superstructure was in ribbons, torn and shattered, sieve-like, and she was ringing like a gong – a *cracked* gong – from the ceaseless pounding she was getting. Bedlam: a screaming slaughterhouse. It would be all right, he told himself, deliberately steadying himself with the thought, once they could get ashore and sort things out a bit: this was just the awkward interval, the sort of thing you had to expect, should have expected, really. A sailor hurrying down the ladder-way from the *flammenwerfer* hut suddenly sprang off it, crashed down, bounced once, hit the deck below it and lay still in a spreading pool of blood. The higher you were, the more exposed, of course. He was getting to the derrick's curve, and this was the tricky part. He was no lightweight, no monkey, damn it. But it would be all right, everything would work out: a couple of the gangways were still intact and serviceable and several of the others could probably be repaired; when she was properly secured there'd be cover enough to do that, under the mole's wall. A cracking sound and a sting on the back of his neck was a splinter or a bullet passing. They'd been in against the wall and trying to get secured for – how long, two minutes? Three? It had been much worse before she'd got in close. The bridge had been hit for the first time within seconds of the Huns opening fire; Elliot of the Marines and his second-in-command, Cordner, had both been killed by that shell. Less than a minute later Captain Halahan had been cut down. Wyatt had been standing within feet of him at the time, on the false deck. Most of the senior men, company commanders and others, had been waiting there ready to lead their men ashore the minute there was a gangway to get over. Halahan had gone down, and Edwards had been shot through both legs; Harrison, who by that time had inherited command of the naval landing force, had been shot in the jaw. He was below now, unconscious. Wyatt inched out along the derrick: it was an unpleasant thought that if he was hit he'd drop between the ship's side and the mole and be squashed. The foretop must have been hit a few times but the chaps up there were still blazing away with their pom-poms and Lewis guns and, please God, killing Germans. He was in semi-darkness here, shadowed as the lower part of the ship was by the mole, but a few feet above his head her upperworks were lit by the glare of German searchlights and shells were bursting on and in her several times a minute, machine-gun and small-arms fire continuous. The sharply-etched dividing line between lower shadow and upper brilliance was the margin between life and death, and as he dragged himself out along the derrick and the ship rocked on the piling sea he was sometimes within inches of it. He had his legs behind him with their ankles crossed over the derrick's curve while his arms took most of the strain of hauling his own weight out towards the wires with the hook dangling on them; suddenly there was a crash that had nothing to do with gunfire, and an almighty lurch: the ship rocked, and he and the derrick rocked too, over towards the parapet: at the same time she was shooting upwards, lifting on the surge: he'd thought he was about to be flung off but in the next second he saw his chance and grabbed it, swung and swivelled, launching his body out to hang by his arms and swing with his feet and legs extended towards the grappling-hook: and he'd *got it* . . . On deck they cast the wire loose as he forced the hook across: it dropped – over the parapet, and he was blinded, in the searchlight glare, hearing the slap-slap-slap of machine-gun bullets streaming past his ear: he didn't wait for the gunner to adjust his aim, but slid down the derrick head-first, ended in a thumping somersault on the deck. Cross began trying to haul him up, grabbing at his shoulders and stuttering congratulations or something of the sort; Wyatt shook the idiot off, snarled at him to go down and see what casualties they'd had. There'd been plenty, he knew, on the way in; if any company was up to half strength by this time, it was lucky. So many shells had penetrated and burst in crowded spaces. He could see what had happened to cause that sudden lurch: *Daffodil* had arrived, at last, put her great rounded, heavily-fendered bow against *Vindictive*'s side and pushed her bodily against the mole. That hook was holding her, at this for'ard end. There was a tinny, rattling sound, what would have been a roar except for the bedlam of sound drowning it, as Carpenter let go his port anchor. And *Daffodil* was staying where she was, holding the cruiser hard against the wall. Plenty of movement still, though, on both ships. Where the hell was *Iris*? Those two brows crashed down: Wyatt heard a cheer, drowned in gunfire; he saw Bryan Adams – commander of A Company, and now after Halahan's death and Harrison's wounding Adams was in command of the whole bluejacket landing force – leading his men up and on to the mole. Running, cheering: Wyatt whipped round to tell Cross to get the men up, but Cross had already gone: reappearing, now, with Wheeler and about twenty men behind him.

'All we have left, sir.' Two dozen at most, out of fifty. Royal Marines were pouring up the second of the two surviving brows. Wyatt roared, 'Forward!', drew his revolver, and flung himself up in the middle of them:

it wasn't a time for 'after you's'. As he reached the top, Adams was leading one bunch of men straight down the roadway while others climbed down to the surface of the lower, broader mole; Brock was with the roadway lot. The guns in the ship's foretop were jabbering and thudding, firing fast to cover the rush of men on to the mole and down it; then a shell came from heaven knew where and burst right in the foretop, a gush of flame and objects whirring, trailing smoke, and now no covering fire. The flame-throwers would have been the thing: and Brock had even sworn that if *Vindictive* had been berthed in the right place – which everyone had assumed she would be – those *flammenwerfers* of his would even have wiped out the crews of the guns on the mole-end, without any other help from guns or landing-parties. In fact the oil-supply lines to both of them had been cut by German gunfire minutes before the ship had crunched against the wall. So there were no flame-throwers. The main body of the Marines was going westward: they had to ensure that no Huns could push up this way from the viaduct end and take control of the mole close to where *Vindictive* lay; if they did, the landing-parties would have been cut off. Adams had stopped to help Rosoman, the cruiser's first lieutenant, settle the after grappling-hook across the parapet; they weren't having much success. But the rush was slowing, bogging down, with mortars bursting here and there and machine-guns from the buildings farther up raking across the concrete. A, B, D and E companies were all earmarked to rush the mole-end guns, but 350 yards of open, flat concrete, enfiladed by machine-gun and mortar fire from half a dozen different places and directions – mostly at the moment from No. 3 shed, on the mole's inner side,

268

and from actually *behind* the advancing bluejacket companies – *remnants* of companies – from where two Hun destroyers were berthed on the mole's inner curve almost opposite *Vindictive* – Wyatt admitted to himself, *It isn't going to be all plain sailing.* Noise indescribable. Adams going forward now, to a small blockhouse on the raised roadway: Wyatt decided to go for No. 3 shed, to try to knock out those machine-guns. The mortar-fire might be coming from somewhere close behind it, too. If E Company could deal with that lot, others – A Company of the Marines, for instance, who were moving up in support of Adams – could push on through, eastward. There was one of the iron ladders just level with him now, leading down to the mole proper: stone chips were flying from the wall near it and from the parapet. He turned, looked back, saw Cross clasp both hands across his belly, sink down and double over in an attitude of prayer: Wyatt waved his revolver and screamed, 'E Company, *with* me!' and ducked down on to the ladder, half climbed down it and half fell, hit the concrete at its foot and started running, zigzagging towards No. 3 shed. It was about ninety yards long and he was aiming roughly for the centre of it. Behind him, Lieutenant Wheeler was limping as he ran, grasping the region of his hip with both hands and shouting to the men behind him. Shrapnel screamed from two successive mortar-bursts: Wyatt was halfway over, telling himself, *They can't hit everyone, the more of us there are the better the chance that some of us will get there.* Poor old Cross: wasn't a bad fellow, bit slow-witted sometimes but – nearly there: and an open window or embrasure right ahead of him with the barrel of a machine-gun spitting fire towards a group of Marines with Adams's crowd; the Marines were setting up a mortar behind that little blockhouse on the higher level – well, they *had* been, the German gunner was scattering them now, he'd dropped two of them and the other three had dived for cover: Wyatt bent double as he ran and stopped zigzagging, aimed straight for the gun and pulled a grenade off its clip on his webbing: he tugged the pin out with his teeth, a sideways jerk of the head – and he was *there*, throwing himself flat then rising again to lob the grenade in the window. He'd dropped flat, heard it explode and a yell of pain of fear, sent another in after it to make sure. This was dead ground; he flattened himself against the wall while blue smoke eddied from the open window. Wheeler was still limping over, lumbering this way and that; there was a petty officer by the name of Shrewsbury with him, half a dozen E Company men and a mixed bag of others, including a Marine with a machine-gun. Wyatt grinned, waved his pistol, beckoning them to join him. *The more the merrier*, he thought. *We'll pull it off! By God we will!* On an impulse he hoisted himself up, right up with his head and shoulders in that window: it was a sort of bunkhouse, and he could see two dead men sprawled against the far wall: below him, a German groaned, called something in his own brand of Hun-talk: Wyatt leaned right in, saw him, a boy of about sixteen, fair and pink-faced, scared stiff: he shot him in the head, and slid down again, turned to meet Wheeler who was only a dozen yards away: and it was at that moment that he saw it. Westward – a mile or so away – the biggest sheet of flame he'd ever seen in his life before. The place was bright with starshell anyway, but that great tongue of fire dimmed everything with its own fierce brightness. Now as it dimmed, smoke poured upwards: black, pluming up and the plumes bending, carried northwards on the wind. But no sound came, and none had; there was so much noise close-to and everywhere else as well that nothing had been audible in any separate way – and yet it must have been a bang like the crack of doom. Wyatt roared with pleasure, exultation: there was only one thing it could have been, and that was the viaduct, the submarines had pulled it off, God bless them! He was bellowing, as Wheeler reached his side and sank down at the end of a trail of blood he'd left across the concrete, 'Well done, by God, well *done!*'

Shrewsbury said, 'Goin' to be tricky gettin' off this wall, sir.'

'What?'

The petty officer pointed. Two of Adam's party had just tried to rush across and join them there, carrying a mortar between them. They were both down: one lay still, sprawled on his face, and the other was trying to crawl in that way, dragging the mortar and using only his elbows for propulsion, his legs trailing and blood pouring from a black gash in his neck. Then as they watched the machine-gun found him again and the stream of its next burst of bullets bent him round in a sort of knot, eel-like: it stopped, moved on, leaving him to unwind slowly like a broken spring in a spreading, scarlet stain. Other men were joining Wyatt here against the wall, dodging as they ran, scrambling for the cover and diving, flopping into it. Over on the other side, the high-level roadway, a mortar-bomb landed and burst on the roof of the blockhouse behind which Adams's bluejackets were gathering. Wyatt saw them crouching, trying to make more of its cover than it was capable of giving them: and Adams was sending a runner back, either for reinforcements or for covering fire. If Osborn could use his stern howitzer, Wyatt thought, to drop a few shells on the mole just here to the east of them: that, or if they could bring up some of the Marines with mortars? He scowled, staring round: it wasn't in his nature to sit here and wait. They were wasting time: they hadn't been trained for months on end and then brought here just to *sit* . . . He stared at Wheeler.

'You fit? Eh?'

'Only a scratch, sir.'

Wheeler was blood from the waist down. Wyatt nodded. 'Good man.' He looked round at the others. 'We'll make another move now. We've got to get to those damn trenches, that's the first thing. All we've got to do is move *fast*, surprise 'em, rout 'em out like winkles . . .'

Nick, on *Bravo*'s bridge, saw the leap of flame as the viaduct went up. He put his glasses on it: and that – what he was seeing now – had to be some sort of mirage . . . Men on bicycles, in mid-air. Then, as they whirled like leaves in a high wind and fell like stones into the rising gush of smoke, he realized what he'd seen: a German army bicycle platoon, hurrying to reinforce the mole defenders, had pedalled to a sudden, devastating doom. It was all smoke there now, under the glare of starshells bursting intermittently. He looked at Garfield. 'Starboard twenty.'

'Starboard twenty, sir!'

Garfield was built like a GPO pillar-box. If you painted one navy blue and stuck a cap aslant on top of it, you'd have Horace Garfield, near enough. To knock him down you'd need to tie something like that charge of Amatol to his shortish, tree-trunk legs. Nick had wondered briefly about Rogerson: now his attention, only a part of which had in fact been diverted, was concentrated entirely on *Bravo*'s current manoeuvrings, on the smoke off the mole's tip, that gun battery on the extension which *Bravo* and *Grebe* had already engaged in passing – before they'd come across the moored barge with the gun on it, and sunk that . . . 'Midships!'

'Midships, sir.' Cap tilted left, eyebrow cocked, flinging the wheel over. *Bravo* slewing to port still, leaving the floating net obstruction on her starboard beam, turning her stern to it now as she swung on. At any moment *Thetis*, the first of the three blockships, should emerge from that smoke which Welman's and Annesley's CMBs had laid. The CMBs were everywhere, racing in and out of their own and the MLs' screens, replacing smoke-floats as they fizzled out or Hun gunners sank them; the screens had to be constantly renewed, since the wind had changed and was working in the enemy's favour.

Grebe was inshore, three or four cables' lengths to the south of *Bravo*, engaging and being shot at by the Goeben battery. Shell-spouts were round her almost constantly. Her own guns were toys compared to the battery's, but she was a small target for them – and she was under constant helm, circling and zigzagging, darting in and out, no doubt driving the Hun gunners berserk with fury. Foolhardy, Nick thought, much *too* close: Hatton-Jones was a poker player, and he was playing this like a game of chance too. But, at the same time, serving an undoubted purpose. The whole of this operation, everything, was aimed at one objective, namely getting the blockships into the canal mouth: and if guns that might interfere with that purpose could be kept busy, particularly now that the crucial phase was due to start at any second . . . Shell-spouts leapt close to *Bravo*'s stern: Nick told Garfield, 'Port fifteen'. He shouted to Elkington, 'Where did those come from?'

'End of the mole, I think!'

'Midships.'

'Midships, sir.'

Steering northwards, roughly. Mole-end fifty degrees on the port bow and about half a mile away. Smoke drifting clear of it: flaming onions – German flares – bursting brilliant above the smoke where it was thick offshore. Not brilliant enough to penetrate Brock's smoke, though. He saw the flashes of the guns, and then *Vindictive*'s howitzer shells exploding like black, red-edged mushrooms. It was *Vindictive*'s rocket-barrage – rockets designed by Brock and fired almost horizontally from her stern ports to light the end of the mole extension, where the blockship would have to turn – making *that* firework display. Really very clever: to show them where to turn, and at the same time provide them with thick smoke-cover within yards of the same spot. Nick told Garfield, 'Steady as you go . . . Number One – hold your fire!'

Thetis, plunging out of the smoke. He had his glasses on her. This was what really mattered, what the whole thing was *for*. A CMB raced in between *Thetis* and the mole extension, smoke belching from its stern. Brock-type smoke: what the hell would anyone be doing without Brock? He had no way of knowing, at this moment, that Brock was dead, killed on the mole. The mole-end guns were all flaming, and *Thetis* was shooting back at them. That CMB's captain – either Welman of Annesley, it must be – was a brave man. Welman, only two years Nick's senior, was commander of all the CMBs. *Thetis* had rounded the point: now she was swinging to port, either to avoid the barge

274

boom or hit suddenly by the eastward-running tide. Nick wondered if her captain, Sneyd, knew there was a barrage of net obstructions just off his bow.

'Starboard fifteen.'

'Starboard fifteen, sir!'

Shell-splashes on the quarter, forty yards away. From the Goeben battery, probably. Elkington shouted, '*Grebe*'s been hit, sir!'

'Midships.'

'Midships, sir!'

'Steady on north twenty west.' He wanted to get closer to the end of the mole. Not *much* closer, but ... He told Elkington, 'When *Thetis* has cleared the range, try a few shots at the mole guns.'

'Aye aye, sir.'

Elkington was trying to look impassive. It wasn't easy for him; he had the sort of pale-skinned, fine-boned face that tends to show its owner's state of mind. *Grebe*, inshore there, had a haze of smoke – or was it steam? – hanging over her amidships, and she'd slowed. It could have been a hit in one of her two boiler-rooms. If that was steam, it *had* been. But she was moving again, picking up speed, and her guns were still busy.

'Tremlett!'

'Yes, sir?'

'Make to *Grebe. Are you all right?*'

'Aye aye, sir.'

Shells falling all round *Thetis* now. Some – too many – hitting her. And she was still swinging to port. At any moment she'd be in that net. The mole-end guns were firing at her about as fast as guns could be fired and re-loaded. By this time the landing parties should have captured them. He focused his glasses on *Thetis*. She *was* in the net! Carrying it away with her. Fine

275

for the two who'd be following her in – but if she
got it round her screws . . . He saw that one of the
two German destroyers alongside the mole was firing
at her now, and he shouted to Elkington: 'Number
One!' The first lieutenant turned, with a hand cupped
to his ear: he'd been watching the mole-end and *Thetis*,
waiting for a chance to get the four-pounder into action.
Thetis herself was fairly well clear now but there was
an ML there with her now, trailing her; her attendant
rescue craft. Nick told Elkington, pointing at the Hun
destroyer, 'Try a torpedo shot!'

'Aye aye, sir!'

Leading Signalman Tremlett reported, 'From *Grebe*,
sir: *Thank you, but we Grebes are tough chickens*.'

'Right . . . Number One. Hold your fire till *Thetis*
has gone by. I'll go in closer and we'll fire to starboard.'
Elkington went to the torpedo-control voicepipe and
began shouting orders down to Raikes, the gunner
(T). Nick had intended to save *Bravo*'s two torpedoes
in case of attack from outside, German ships coming
from other bases, and also because the CMBs were
supposed to be taking care of any destroyers inside
the mole. But if those Huns were going to shoot
at the blockships as they steamed in past them, it
seemed a good use for torpedoes here and now. He
told Garfield, 'Starboard twenty.' *Thetis* was passing
now, about halfway from the mole-end to the canal
mouth; she'd been hit hard, mostly by the guns on the
mole extension; she'd developed a list to starboard and
she seemed to be slowing. Garfield reported, 'Twenty
o' starboard wheel on, sir!' Nick took a quick look
at *Grebe*: he thought she'd been hit again, for'ard
this time. Hatton-Jones might think of himself as a
tough chicken, but he was a damn sight too close to

that *Goeben* battery. On the other hand, if they were shooting at him they couldn't also be shooting at poor old *Thetis*.

'Midships! Stand by, Number One!'

Elkington was at the voicepipe, in touch with Raikes. They had a static target over there; it only needed a properly aimed torpedo that would run straight. You couldn't *shoot* at those destroyers, because you might hit British sailors and Marines on the mole behind them. *Thetis* was past, heading directly for the canal, listing harder and moving rather slowly and still being hit: Nick saw gunflashes in a new location, suddenly – a little way back from the foreshore but to the west of the *Goeben* battery and quite near the eastern arm of the canal entrance. It would obviously be more than just a good idea to knock *that* lot out.

'Steady!'

'Steady, sir – south ten west, sir—' Reversing the wheel . . . Nick heard Elkington yell, 'Fire!' Looking aft, he saw the splash of the torpedo's entry. He told Garfield, 'Steer that.'

Just off the mole extension, *Intrepid* burst out of the smoke.

Back at the binnacle, Nick beckoned to Elkington. He pointed out the position of that new battery: they were firing at *Thetis* now and the flashes were easy to see. *Thetis* was almost in the canal, just short of the two breakwater arms that made the approach to it funnel-shaped: he was thinking that it was a miracle she was still afloat when he saw that she was swinging off to starboard. He told Elkington, 'Hit those guns. See if you can't knock one or two of 'em—'

He'd seen a bloom of fire and a blossom of black smoke on *Grebe*. If she stayed where she was much longer, she'd be a *cooked* chicken. Elkington had rushed for'ard to the gun. It would have been nice, Nick thought, to have had *Mackerel*'s four-inch instead of these pea-shooters. *Intrepid* had cleared the barge boom – a string of barges linked by chains and probably with nets slung under them – and there was no net boom there now to impede her, since *Thetis* had towed it in. He looked back at *Thetis*: she'd stopped, aground, on the starboard side of the fairway, well short of the canal entrance. *One down, two to play!* That battery was raising spouts all round her. *Bravo*'s twelve-pounder fired: a surprisingly loud and penetrating *crack* for so small a calibre.

'Captain, sir!'

Tremlett was pointing out to starboard.

Against the mole: a great gout of smoke and spray, debris flying. That German destroyer: *Bravo*'s torpedo had struck her right amidships, under her second funnel. Men were cheering – on the bridge and gundeck. Nick shouted, 'Well done, Number One!' The four-pounder fired again, recoiled: shell-splashes sprang up close to the ship's port side almost simultaneously. The battery was answering their attack: and that was to the good, it might even give *Intrepid* a clear run in.

'*Grebe*'s hit again, sir.'

Garfield said it; but his eyes were on the compass-card again now. They'd hit *Grebe* amidships again, as if they knew where it would hurt most and struck always at the same spot, like a cruel boxer inflicting a maximum of punishment.

'Tremlett – make to him, *Are you still all right?*'

'She's calling *us*, sir!' Tremlett jumped to the searchlight and gave them an answering flash. The four-pounder fired again. Garfield said, 'We're 'itting them guns, sir. Saw the muck fly, that last time.'

278

'From *Grebe*, sir: *Have been winged. A tow would help.*'

'Number One!' He yelled into the engine-room voicepipe, 'Full ahead together!' Elkington came aft quickly. Nick shouted in his ear as the gun fired again, 'Stand by to take *Grebe* in tow. Have to look slippy because we'll be damn close to the battery. See that the other guns engage it as soon as they bear. Starboard ten, cox'n.'

Intrepid was more than halfway to the canal mouth. Intact, going strong, hardly touched. *Thetis* had two cutters in the water, packed with men, and two MLs were closing-in on them, Elkington had gone down. Nick told Garfield, 'Steer for *Grebe*'s stern.'

'Aye aye, sir.'

Grebe shouldn't be there at all, he thought, let alone in an immobilized condition, which presumably was what Hatton-Jones meant by 'winged'. She was right opposite that battery, no more than half a mile from it, and only a little more than that from the Goeben guns. She was being hit repeatedly and the sea all around her was a mass of leaping shell-spouts. Hatton-Jones, who in civilian life was some kind of art expert and an international yachtsman, and was now an RNVR lieutenant-commander, could reasonably be granted a third description – that of bloody fool. It wasn't only *his* chicken's neck he'd put on the butcher's block.

'Aim in towards her quarter now, cox'n.'

'Aye aye, sir!'

'I'm afraid we may get knocked about a bit, in a minute.'

'I wouldn't bet against it, sir.'

*   *   *

C3 had hit the viaduct at nine and a half knots, right in the centre of a section between two rows of piers. Only her captain had been in the bridge by the time they'd struck it; he'd had all the others on the other casing, behind the bridge.

Striking, she'd ridden up out of water, on one of the submerged horizontal girders, smashed through the cross-braces and penetrated as far as the leading edge of the bridge. That had been the really solid point of impact, when the front of the bridge had slammed up against the lattice-work of steel and stopped her. So the Amatol charge had been thrust deep inside the structure of the viaduct, right in the centre of it and under the centre of the roadway overhead. When the bow had hit the underwater girder she'd jumped and jarred: on the casing they'd hung on, hearing the rush and scrape as steel struts snapped and ripped: then the final stop had knocked them off their feet, grabbing for fresh supports: above them in the darkness there'd been German shouts, yelled orders, then lights of torches, rifle-shots, bullets clanging and whirring off the casing. Tim Rogerson recalled a sense of confusion, of hardly knowing what had happened or was happening.

Sandford's voice cut through it.

'Get the dinghy in the water! Fast, now!'

Cleaver was at the for'ard fall. Rogerson cast off the after one, and the boat came down with a rush, its stern bouncing off the curve of No. 3 main ballast tank; the small, frail craft slid into the water almost on its beam-ends, then righted itself and floated.

'Get aboard, all hands!'

There was a lot of shooting now from directly above their heads. Now a searchlight blazed down, and the shots came faster. Scrambling into the little rocking dinghy: six aboard, and Roxburgh trying to start its engine. Sandford came down the side of the bridge like a trapeze artiste; he swung, landed on his feet on the tank-top where the sea washed over it: the submarine was stuck fast but the tide still moved her, grinding her against the girders that held her and supported her explosive bow. They were more than conscious of that five-ton charge now, because Sandford had lit the fuse before he'd left the bridge. He was climbing into the boat, shouting 'Come on, shove off!' The searchlight was blinding, petrifying, and a machine-gun opened up and fired one long burst that sent bullets screaming, rattling and ricocheting through the girders. The sea leapt all around the boat and splinters, large ones, flew from its port side. Rogerson heard himself say, 'She's holed. There's a great—'

The engine started. The machine-gun hadn't fired again but the riflemen were hard at it, bullets singing through the struts and beams, clanging off C3's tanks and sides and smashing into the boat's planks. The engine whirred, screamed unnaturally, jarring oddly on the transom. Roxburgh shut it off.

'Screw's damaged.' He shouted to Sandford, 'Bloody propeller, sir. It's no bloody good.' Rogerson, feeling water round his ankles, asked the ERA 'Where are the bilge pumps, can we—' A whole section of the gunnel flew away. Sandford yelled over the noise of a fresh fusillade of shots, 'Get the oars out! Tim—' Rogerson's ears were singing from the rifle-fire. He was already groping for the oars, bent over and trying to get his boots out of the way, tugging at the loom of one of them. He pushed at someone else's legs that were in the light, got hold of the oar and dragged it up, and his own right forearm seemed to explode in

281

front of his face. It felt as if it had been hit very hard with a hammer, but the skin and flesh had opened, tendons and bone flown out rather like the spines of a smashed umbrella: he was staring at it and thinking vaguely *dumdums, then*, almost impersonally as if it wasn't his own arm he was looking at. Cleaver had snatched the oar and shipped it in the port-side crutch, and Harner had the other one out to starboard; Harner was pushing at C3's black, wave-washed side with the blade of his, trying to shove off; there was a lot of water in the dinghy now, from the bullet-holes riddling her planks, but Roxburgh had just got the second of the two special bilge-pumps going and it didn't seem to be getting any deeper at the moment. The boat was slewing, coming clear, both oarsmen trying to get her moving out against the flood of tide: at any time it would have been hard work. Harner grunted, let go of his oar and rolled sideways: he was covered in blood and Rogerson suspected he was dead. He tried to take his place, seeing no reason he couldn't row with one good arm, but Bindall got it and slid into the coxswain's place on the thwart. The boat began to move away from the viaduct, shots whistling round, ricochets whining, water leaping, more holes in the boat's sides. Bindall cursed, fell backwards, letting go his oar: Roxburgh grabbed its loom just before it vanished, sliding away out of the crutch – there were no spare oars, oddly enough, and there was a five-ton pack of Amatol a few yards away with a fuse burning steadily towards it and only a few minutes left: Roxburgh and Cleaver knew it, and they pulled like fleet champions at a regatta. Howell-Price was dragging the wounded or dead men clear of the thwarts and Sandford was at the tiller. Rogerson felt two quick hammer-blows, one into the top of his left shoulder and the other lower, in his ribs on the same side: he remembered afterwards thinking at that moment, not actually feeling pain but knowing he'd been shot twice more and that it was against any sort of odds for any of them to live through this, *Well, that's it, we did know the chances weren't too bright* . . . The boat was being forced out against the tide, half full of water, both oarsmen straining, grunting with the effort of moving her and her water-ballast and seven men's weight: another searchlight joined the first, and the machine-gun opened up again, and most of the stem and the starboard gunnel flew away like chips off a high-speed lathe: Howell-Price was taking over one of the oars, Sandford at the tiller had been hit, and a second machine-gun joined in. Sandford shouted, 'Keep it up just another half minute, boys, and the swine'll be blown to—' He'd been hit again. He was all blood and he couldn't finish his sentence but he was keeping the boat on course with his teeth gritted and his eyes shut: what made him open them was the Amatol exploding. It was as if the air, the whole night round them, were inflammable and someone had put a match to it: they were part of it, a deafening roar and an engulfing wall of flame. Rogerson, stupefied but vaguely aware that he was cheering, saw a lot of men on bicycles falling into space: some of them appeared to catch fire as they tumbled over. He thought he might be dead, or delirious, or mad. No searchlights now: the power cables to them had been blown apart, of course. Things were dropping everywhere, heavy things and small things, splashing down all round them: a wave came against the tide, lifted the dinghy and rolled it on its way. No shooting any more. Just one small foundering boat with dead or near-dead men in it. Sandford croaked, 'We've done it! *Look!*'

283

There was a hundred-foot gap in the viaduct. The mole was isolated from the shore. Howell-Price grinned sideways at ERA Roxburgh: 'Come on, *pull!*' Roxburgh complained, 'I'm no *sailor*, sir . . .' Howell-Price, Sandford, Rogerson, Roxburgh and Cleaver were all laughing, or making sounds that passed for it; Sandford told the rowers, 'Save your breath, you loonies. Pull.' There was starshell-light now, and flaming onions from this end of the mole, but nothing close or bright enough to show up details here in the boat. Just as well, Rogerson thought. We'd scare each other silly if we could see each other. We should all be dead. From the time they'd been dazzled in the beams of those filthy searchlights he had imprinted memories of what the others looked like. Sandford particularly, who'd been hit and hit again and still incredibly held the tiller and held it straight: Sandford, Uncle Baldy, should have a VC, he thought, and when he wore it he'd wear it for them all. His own numbness was wearing off and he was beginning to feel, to hurt: if it got much worse it might be difficult to keep quiet. But there was also a feeling of great tiredness, and in opposition to that a certainty that one should not give way to it, that it was imperative to stay awake. It was quite rough, out here, and he wondered where they were going; the little boat was sluggish with all the weight in her, and she must have sunk lower in the water because waves were lopping over the bow behind him.

'Boat *ahoy!*'

A light trained on them, its beam dancing on the water. He thought, *I'm delirious . . .* On the picket-boat the elder Sandford shouted to his stoker, 'Stop her! Slow astern!' He hurried for'ard, beside himself with excitement and relief, and tossed a line across the dinghy. Roxburgh caught it. Howell-Price shouted, 'We've several men quite badly hurt. Skipper needs attention urgently. So does—'

'He'll get it, don't you worry.' The skipper's elder brother knelt, grabbed the dinghy's gunnel; there were sailors behind him ready to get over and lift the wounded into the larger boat. Dick Sandford said in a surprisingly strong voice, 'See to the others first. Cox'n's worse than I am.'

'All right, old chap. Here – easy, now . . .'

'What happened to *you*?'

'Tow broke. Damn near capsized first. Miles back, right out at sea . . . Never mind, we're here now. We'll get you fellows to a destroyer with a doctor. My God, what a *splendid* job you've—'

'What about C1?'

'Broke her tow, too. She's all right, though. Fed up, I've no doubt, at missing it. Anyway, who cares, you did it! You *did* it, Dick!'

'Tow's fast, sir!'

Nick bent to the voicepipe as shells came whirring through thinning smoke and their splashes sprang up to port. 'Slow ahead together.' The twelve-pounder let off another round: target the Goeben battery. *Vindictive*'s howitzers were blasting at that battery too; without their help things might have been a great deal worse.

'Slow ahead together, sir!'

'Keep the helm amidships, cox'n.'

'Aye aye, sir.'

Another salvo hurtled over: splashes all ahead, then one shell came late and short, burst on *Bravo*'s foc'sl: the capstan went up vertically, spinning like a huge top, splashed down a few feet clear of the bow as

Bravo struggled to forge ahead with *Grebe*'s dead weight dragging at her stern. *Bravo* had lost her mainmast and the quarterdeck six-pounder; the superstructure that the after gundeck was built on, which was also the wardroom access door, had been smashed in and set alight, but the fire was out now and Elkington had reported that there was no internal damage. Just as well – and lucky: McAllister had a lot of wounded below there in the wardroom. Looking aft over the stern as the wire came taut again, Nick saw *Intrepid*, lit by starshell, settling inside the canal entrance; two cutters and a smaller boat – skiff, probably – were pulling away from her, out into the harbour. There was a lot of machine-gun fire from the shore, and shell-splashes that must be coming either from the mole's inshore end or from that shore battery. An ML was laying smoke in there, and two others were heading to meet the blockship's boats. *Thetis* had been abandoned, but they'd left a green light burning as a guide to help the other two past. *Iphigenia* had rounded the end of the mole, and was halfway across towards *Thetis*: she seemed to be getting in unmolested.

The wire was taut and straining. Two shells dropped short of *Grebe*'s starboard bow, throwing a heavy rain of foul-smelling water across both ships. A starshell burst right overhead: with the smoke gone, they'd be punished again now; the Goeben gunners would want to make up for lost time and they wouldn't be pleased to see their prey escaping. The wire quivered, bar-taut, and *Grebe*'s bow hadn't moved yet.

'Starboard five.'

'Starboard five, sir!'

Turning to port – or trying to – so as to head out at an angle and drag *Grebe*'s bow round, get her pointing out the way they had to go. *Bravo*'s engines were only at slow ahead, but to put on more power at this stage would be to risk parting the tow. Then they'd have to start from scratch again.

'Damn . . .'

He'd whispered it, to himself, as a searchlight fastened on them. *Grebe*'s middle funnel exploded in a shower of steel. That damned light . . . But she was moving, just a little, and it was the start that counted. Once there was some way on her, the inertia overcome, you could put on more revs. It was a sudden strain on the wire that one had to guard against.

'Bosun's mate!'

Clark jumped forward. 'Sir?'

'Tell Maynard to shoot at that light until he hits it.'

'Aye aye, sir!'

Maynard, leading seaman, was the layer of the twelve-pounder. 'Midships.'

'Midships, sir.'

'One-five-oh revolutions.'

Flat out, for an oily wad, was about three-fifty. One-fifty would give her eight or ten knots on her own. Four or five perhaps with *Grebe* in tow. Straightening from the voicepipe he flinched as *Grebe* was hit again right aft. Smoke welled up from her quarterdeck. The twelve-pounder fired – going for the searchlight. Smoke was what they needed: not *that* sort, though. Stinking, blinding stuff, drifting seaward. *Iphigenia* was passing *Thetis*, and she was being hit: by the Goeben guns, probably, which would account for a slackening of the bombardment here. That was another hit on *Iphigenia*: the Huns had been getting too much practice, in the past hour, they were beginning to get the hang of it,

God damn them! They'd cut a steam-pipe or something like that, in *Iphigenia*, you could see it pouring up, white in a searchlight's beam. *Grebe* was coming round nicely now.

'Starboard five, cox'n!'

'Starboard five . . . Five o' starboard wheel on, sir!'

Inching her round. Increasing the strain by degrees, getting her on the move, in the process turning her so she'd present a smaller target to the shore guns. The searchlight left them: swept across the harbour, lighting patches of drifting smoke – an abandoned ship's boat – sweeping on: fastening on an ML that was coming out stern-first from the canal entrance with tracer streaming at her from all directions and towing a cutter from her bow. Cutter and launch were both black with men. *Iphigenia* was inside the canal mouth: from this angle she and *Intrepid* were one solid black mass against the light of flares.

'Midships.'

'Midships, sir.'

Elkington climbed into the bridge.

'So far so good, sir.'

'What?'

He shouted, 'Tow's holding, sir, so far!'

'You've done damn well.' It was no more than fact. Elkington had got the line over, then the grass and the heavy wire, in half the time it might have taken. Under heavy fire that wasn't as easy as the Manual of Seamanship Vol. I made it sound.

'What about casualties?'

'Rotten, sir. Nine dead and –' he hesitated – 'about sixteen wounded.'

Almost half the ship's company. And nowhere near out of this hole yet.

The guns in the waist were silent now. *Grebe* was in their way, and there were no targets they could bear on. The twelve-pounder sent one last shell crashing into the darkness: then that one was out of it too, blanked-off from its enemies by the smoking, smouldering ship astern.

'Steer north-east, cox'n.'

'Steer north-east, sir . . .'

That would take them wide of the mole's extremity, towards *Phoebe*'s and *North Star*'s patrol line to the east and north-east of it. Nick put his glasses up to see if either of them might be in sight, or even perhaps the flashes of their guns. He caught his breath: no more than four hundred yards off the lighthouse, one of them – impossible to see which – was stationary, and as he watched a sweeping searchlight gripped her, held her: shells burst all over her and all round her, for a moment she was hidden by their splashes and he thought, *She's done for* . . . How the hell she's got trapped in that position – she must have got lost in smoke perhaps, or – now he saw her partner, sister-ship, moving in at speed, laying a screen of smoke to hide her from that searchlight and the guns on the mole extension: he'd been stooping to the voicepipe while he watched it, all in the space of about four seconds: that smoke *might* save her, if she wasn't already finished . . . He called down to the engine-room, 'Two hundred revolutions.'

'Two 'undred revs, sir!'

'Number One, I think we'll—'

A flight of shells came screaming down and burst across *Bravo*'s stern. She seemed to convulse – to flinch and shudder, recoiling from the blows: flames leapt, died back, smoke expanded and came flying for'ard on the wind. Elkington shouted, 'The wire's gone, sir!'

Something like a brick had hit his right shoulder. It had knocked him back, throwing him against the binnacle, and Garfield had reached out one arm to steady him. He heard himself order, 'Starboard fifteen!' He'd been about to say it when the thing had hit him.

'Starboard fifteen, sir . . .' Garfield spun the wheel round. 'You all right, sir?'

'Yes . . . Stop port. Number One –' he couldn't feel his right arm, or move it – 'I'm going to lay smoke inshore of *Grebe* again, then go alongside, port side to his starboard side, and we'll lash him to us. Stand by on the upper deck, please.'

'Aye aye, sir!'

'And I want a report on how things are below . . . Half ahead port, two-five-oh revolutions both engines . . .' *Bloody* searchlight back again! He heard Garfield asking him, 'Are you *sure* you're all right, sir?'

'Midships . . . Cox'n, don't chatter at me.'

'Midships. Sorry, sir.'

The twelve-pounder was back in action. Shooting at the searchlight, Nick hoped. He actually hated it, that light, quite personally and viciously. He bent over the voicepipe: 'Engine-room – make smoke!'

'Make smoke, sir!'

Bravo was on fire aft. But she still wasn't as badly off as *Grebe*. Nick had to use his left hand to raise his binoculars. The right-hand side of his body was all wet: he could feel it running down. He told himself, pulling his thoughts together in order to clarify his intentions, his sense of direction and priorities, *The*

290

blockships are in, our job's done, in this state we can't be of any practical use to the MLs in there, so the thing is simply to get out of it – with Grebe . . . The searchlight left them, swung to *Grebe*: there was a pom-pom firing at her from the beach. A starshell burst high over the middle of the mole: he saw a cutter pulling seaward, two MLs heading the same way, another stopped with a skiff alongside her and men being hauled up. He let his glasses drop on their strap and told Garfield, 'Starboard ten.' Black smoke had begun to flood out of both funnels. The top of the after one was shattered, and in the smoke you could see the glow from the furnace down below. For an old coal-burning oily wad there was nothing new in making smoke: only usually it wasn't deliberate, it made senior officers curse and send offensive signals. All *Bravo*'s surviving guns were firing as she swung inshore. He thought, *Better lay two lines of it, one parallel to the other* . . . That way, it might last.

'Midships.'

'Midships, sir.'

He felt ill, suddenly. A sickly weakness spreading from the gut. If one could have been sick it might have helped. The racket of the guns was bewildering, deadening to the senses: something in his head told him *Time to go round, lay smoke behind that lot* . . . 'Port fifteen.'

'Port fifteen, sir.'

Garfield was very steady, very calm. *Bravo* was lucky in her coxswain, Nick thought. Russell was a good hand too. Not as good a chief buffer as Swan had been, but—

There'd been no mention of Swan in the list of ship's company awards for *Mackerel*. Not that it would have

291

made the slightest difference to Swan himself; but for his parents' sake, his people: they should have been allowed some sign, some acknowledgement of the man's quality. Too late now: and it all seemed so long ago. Shells screeched overhead; there were flames on Grebe's iron deck. Her casualties must be terrible, much worse than *Bravo*'s. Now she'd vanished: the first line of smoke lay between them. It should be just as blinding to the Hun gunners. Nick thought he was falling: he held on with his left arm around the binnacle, bent his knees, slid down until the soft-iron correcting-sphere on this side was under his armpit. He let it take his weight, leaning towards it, resting for a moment with his eyes shut. It was amazing how the sick feeling drained away. Garfield boomed, 'Captain, sir!'

'Yes?'

Opening his eyes, and hoisting himself up.

'We've fifteen o' port wheel on still, sir!'

'Midships!' He checked the compass-card quickly. 'Meet her!'

'Meet her, sir . . .'

Gun-flashes ashore now. *Bravo* was inside her own smoke; it drifted seaward as it poured like black treacle from her funnels. And probably they'd made enough of it now: the next thing was to locate *Grebe* again.

'Port ten.'

'Port ten, sir.' Garfield seemed to be watching him all the time, and Nick found it irritating. He took the chance of another rest as he leant against the voicepipe. 'Slow together!'

'Slow together, sir . . .' The smell of the voicepipe increased the feeling of nausea. *Bravo* was turning to starboard into her own black, suffocating smoke. Elkington should have the wires and fenders ready down there by now. When they got through the smoke it should be easy enough to find *Grebe*, particularly if she was still on fire. He heard shells passing overhead, that cloth-ripping noise big ones made when they were passing mast-head-high or higher. They must have been firing blind.

'Midships.'

'Midships, sir.'

'Bosun's mate.' Clark moved towards him. 'Go down and tell the first lieutenant to stand by.'

'Aye aye, sir!'

'Wheel's amidships, sir.'

Able Seaman Clark had only got as far as the head of the ladder; he was coming back. Sub-lieutenant York was with him.

'First lieutenant says he's ready and standing by, sir.'

'Good.' He glanced round the bridge. 'Where's our snotty?'

'Aft, sir. Shell-splinter in his back.' York was goggling at Nick's arm and shoulder; Nick scowled at him, and turned away. It was a peculiar and very unpleasant sensation, to have feeling in only about half one's body and no control over one arm and hand. The limb just dangled. *Bravo* broke out suddenly into clear night air: starshells were drifting over the harbour and a flaming onion soared over the canal mouth. There were shells bursting on the mole extension and he thought those must be *Vindictive*'s howitzers still at it.

'Forty on the bow, sir!'

Garfield was pointing. *Grebe* looked like a wreck, burnt out. Nick shouted, 'Tremlett!' The coxswain said, 'He was hit just now, sir, he's been took down.' It was like a dream one had had before: hadn't Wyatt

293

shouted at a dead yeoman? But he, Nick, hadn't known anything about Tremlett.

'Killed?'

'I don't think so, sir.'

That wasn't so bad, then. Signalman Jowitt asked him, 'Sir?'

'Make to *Grebe, Please stand by to take my wires on your starboard side.*'

'Aye aye, sir.'

'Sub, go down and assist the first lieutenant . . . Bosun's mate!'

'Yessir?'

'Go down to the chartroom and bring me up a stool.' He moved to the port side of the bridge, hooked his left elbow over the new protective plating – dented and scorched in places, it looked less new now: half the splinter-mattresses had been ripped or scorched away – and leant his weight on it. He called to Garfield, 'Port fifteen. Stop starboard.' Behind him he heard the clatter of the searchlight as his message was flashed to *Grebe*. He was glad he'd started it with the word 'please': Hatton-Jones was a touchy sort of man, he'd have objected to a signal from a junior that read like an order. Nick's head jerked towards the mole: that was a new sound altogether – the high shriek of a ship's siren.

The recall?

Vindictive's signal to the landing force. The order to start falling back to the ship. It meant the blocking had been completed, that the withdrawal would be starting now.

And consequently, that the howitzer plastering of the Goeben battery would be ceasing. *Damn!*

'Ease to five. Stop port.'

He watched carefully as the gap between the two ships closed. 'Midships.'

'Midships, sir!' Garfield unruffled, stoic.

Staring at *Grebe*'s battered, lacerated hulk, Nick thought *Have we pulled it off, then? Really?* But it was a detached, rather academic consideration. The smoke was already wafting out, surrounding them; *Grebe* was half hidden in it. All right, so there was another bank to drift up behind it, but that gave – what, five or ten minutes? To get two ships lashed together and under way, creep out of range?

Wyatt croaked, 'Hold on, damn you . . .' Crawling, sliding himself along with the Marine corporal on his back. This one seemed to have been shot in the lungs. His own wounds, Wyatt thought, were mostly superficial. His left leg was smashed from ankle to kneecap – *that* was bad enough . . . Whenever the pain of it reached his brain he had to stop, lie flat, press his face against the concrete and – he'd passed out, two or three times. It came in spasms, and when it ebbed – he said aloud, 'The *hell* with it!' His shoulder – no way of knowing whether that had been shrapnel or a bullet: and a bayonet-stab in the neck. Flesh-wounds, those. Bled a lot, but – nothing. He'd been stabbed when he'd led a rush of bluejackets over some wire – they'd thrown planks on it and dashed over them – and cleared out one end of the first lot of trenches. Huns back there now, damn them! A long time ago, that felt like, but it couldn't have been, they'd only been on the mole an hour. He told the man on his back, 'Don't worry, you'll live to have another crack at 'em! So'll I, by God!' Talking helped, now and then. One's own voice reassured one. Almost as much as seeing Keyes's flag had, just now:

over the smoke out there, within a stone's throw of the mole, he'd seen *Warwick*'s masthead go by with that great banner of a vice-admiral's flag streaming from it – big because it had been made to fly from a dreadnought battleship, Keyes's squadron flagship up in Scapa – the St George's Cross and the single red ball in its upper canton: it had passed by floating above the smoke although the destroyer under it was hidden. Men had cheered to see it, there'd been a shout of 'Here comes Roger!' A few minutes before the recall signal, that had been; and now by unspoken agreement, without any order being given, they were bringing back the wounded and the dead. Wherever they could be got at: some, you couldn't reach. Wyatt had passed Padre Peshall half a dozen times: Peshall, not even scratched so far – perhaps the Lord looked after his own lieutenants? – had an odd way of running in a crouched, bear-like shamble with a man across his shoulders. He kept delivering them and going back for more. Wyatt was doing the same, a lot of chaps were, but he couldn't move as fast as the padre, with this damn leg. He'd saved three: this one would make four. It wouldn't be fitting, to leave the dead for Huns to deal with; and the wounded, of course, *had* to be brought out. In the last hour, Wyatt thought he'd seen everything fine that there could be to see, he'd come to realize there was no standard to which the British sailor or Marine could not measure. Harrison, for instance, who'd been laid out half-dead by that shot in the jaw: he'd come-to, and immediately rushed ashore and taken over command from Adams. By that time Adams, who'd led an assault on the wire and trenches beyond No. 3 shed, had been hit several times himself and lost three-quarters of his men. He'd reinforced them with some of B Company,

296

whose officers had all been killed, and led another rush along the parapet, but a machine-gun had pinned them down and another one from a destroyer moored on the inside of the mole had caught them in a cross-fire. They'd had to retire again, leaving a lot of men dead out in front. Harrison, taking over, had sent Adams back to ask for Marine reinforcements, and Major Weller, the senior surviving leatherneck – the Marines by this time had cleared two hundred yards of mole to the westward of the ship and were holding out down there in the face of particularly fierce attacks – sent up a platoon. Meanwhile Harrison, who couldn't speak because of his smashed jaw, had led another dash along the roadway. He and every single man with him was either killed or wounded. Wyatt, who'd been flat at the time, temporarily knocked out by the shock of his leg-wound, had seen it, and helped some of them to crawl back. The half-dead leading the three-quarter dead. Able Seaman Eaves had tried to carry back Harrison's body, but Eaves was knocked out himself while he was doing it. Another sailor, McKenzie, a machine-gunner, had gone on working his gun long after he'd been badly wounded: he'd caught a group of Germans running from a blockhouse to the destroyer – which had shortly afterwards blown up, hit by a torpedo from God knew where – and he'd polished them all off, like a row of skittles, one behind the other. Wyatt asked the man on his back, 'Know your Captain Bamford, do you, eh?' The corporal didn't answer. Couldn't: couldn't hear, quite likely. Wyatt told him, not caring too much about being heard or not, 'Man's incredible. Never seen anything like it. Doesn't know bullets kill a man – or doesn't give a brass—'

'Hello there, Edward!' The padre crouched down

297

beside him, staring at him anxiously. Probably thought he'd been talking to himself, gone off his head or something. He smiled. 'Give you a hand with this fellow?'

'No. You fetch your own.' Wyatt thought that was funny. He said it again, because Peshall hadn't laughed. The padre said, 'Ought to pack it in now, Edward. Let 'em take you aboard this time. The recall's sounded, did you hear it?'

Wyatt crabbed on towards the ship. A Royal Marine platoon was holding a small perimeter and providing covering fire, and there were scaling-ladders up to the higher roadway. Bluejackets were hauling the dead and wounded up as they were brought back from all directions, and carrying them across and lowering them down the brows. Four brows in commission now. Wyatt had one more chap he was determined to fetch: he had to, he'd actually told him he'd come back for him. He'd seen him sprawled in a half-sitting position in the doorway of a wrecked blockhouse or store near the Hun wire that started beyond No. 3 shed. There were some railway trucks lined up there, and they'd provide enough cover for a man on his own to crawl up under them and drag him away. The Germans were damn close by, since they'd reoccupied that trench: but if one was quiet, and as quick as this damned leg would allow . . . Wyatt had been almost within touching distance of the wounded man already: he'd put the Marine corporal down, crept under the trucks and inspected him from not more than ten feet away. An able seaman with three good-conduct badges. Badly hit – his face all black on one side with crusting blood. Wyatt had called to him, 'Hold hard – I'll come back for you!' The recall wasn't an order to be obeyed promptly, it only gave

298

notice of withdrawal. You couldn't just draw stumps and walk away. He lay flat while a machine-gun flamed and clattered from the left: there'd been too much light, one of their blasted flaming onions. *God*, he thought, *How I hate the bloody Huns!* There was quite a bunch of men in the shelter of No. 3 shed now. A young Marine sergeant was controlling them, sending them across the open mole in small groups between bursts of enemy machine-gun fire. On one's own, keeping to the shadows and moving this slowly, as slowly as was necessitated by this damn-fool condition he was in, you had a certain advantage over men in groups legging it about. He grinned, muttered, *Marvellous chaps. Thank God I'm an Englishman!* Better cross over now. He'd been lucky with that parapet hook, he thought. That lift of the ship, just as *Daffodil* shoved her in, had done it. Wouldn't have, otherwise. Bargained for a tide three or four feet higher than tonight's. *Last* night's. One minute after midnight, *Vindictive* had bumped alongside. Young Claud Hawkins of D Company hadn't been so lucky, when they'd been struggling to get *Iris* tied-up alongside: Hawkins had used a scaling-ladder, got right up on the parapet to manhandle the hook over; he'd been on it when they opened up on him, and he'd started firing back at them with his revolver, and they'd killed him with the hook still not in place. Then George Bradford, Hawkins's company commander, had tried going up the derrick, and a machine-gun firing across the mole had cut him off the top of it: he'd fallen – his body had fallen – between the mole and the old ferry-boat, and one of his petty officers had gone down after it and that had been *his* end, too. The hook tore away in any case, as soon as the weight of the steamer came on it. But you felt so damn *proud*, to have had such friends . . .

Nearly there now. The shade under those trucks was deep: once he got under there, he'd be – Flattening, as a mortar thumped down somewhere behind him. Shrapnel lashed the trucks, splintering wood and striking sparks off metal, sang away into the flaming dark. Last trip, this. The ships wouldn't be alongside much longer. He was dragging himself forward again. Never mind about it hurting, you milksop, doctors'll fix all that up. What they're for. Had enough practice by this time to know how to set about it, too. That recall wasn't sounded on *Vindictive*'s siren, but on *Daffodil*'s. Reason: poor old *Vindictive*'s had her whistle shot off. She'd been shot to bits, above the level of the parapet she was a smashed-up scarecrow of a ship. God bless her! And Carpenter, Rosoman, Osborn, Bramble – what a crowd! Hilton Young with an arm half off: Walker waving without a hand: Keyes knows how to pick men, all right. Any man Roger Keyes picks for a job of work is fit to know. Under the second truck now . . . Putting his face right down on the cold concrete between the lines he could see light – radiance of distant starshell and closer flares, constantly changing but always there to some extent – and the black outline of the wrecked building where his three-badger would be waiting for him. *Told you I'd be back, my friend, eh?* Movement: scrape of a boot on concrete, and then a metallic click. Something bounced, skittered towards him under the truck. It touched his face. In the half-second that was left to him he realized it was a grenade.

Grebe was on fire again, and all her guns had been knocked out. He could see just one man moving on her after-part. The stern itself was shattered, funnels split and torn, her bridge was a charred heap of scrap-iron

300

on which Hatton-Jones, recognizable by a bandage round his head, had a helmsman and a snotty with him. The fires aft provided enough illumination for the occasional starshell to be superfluous, from the shore gunners' point of view. *Grebe* was a dead weight to *Bravo*: it was probably only the fact that she was well down by the bow with her stern consequently raised high in the water that she hadn't flooded aft and foundered.

Bravo's twelve-pounder had been knocked to bits by a direct hit which had also killed all its crew; it was a miracle that shell hadn't killed everyone on the bridge as well. At least with the gun finished one wasn't obliged to go on bringing up more men to man it in the place of those already killed: stuck out there in front of the bridge, and with its protective screening shot away, it was about as exposed a position as one could imagine. Every shot that hit the foc'sl sent splinters screaming over it. More shells ripped overhead: Nick was tensed for new flame, blast, destruction, death: it hadn't come. Not this time. They'd *all* gone over. *The bastards have to miss sometimes* . . . *Bravo*'s worst wound had been a hit in her for'ard boiler-room. Chief ERA Joseph had shut it off now: so long as the feed-water held out they could manage on the after boilers. She could make a few knots through the water; and while she could move, and float, and *Grebe* could float and move with her, there were lives in both ships that one could try to save.

'Port five, cox'n.'

'Port five, sir . . .'

To keep the for'ard wires taut. When they were slack, the sea's movement drove the two ships together – thumping, scraping . . . He saw flashes from the Goeben battery: he'd had his glasses on it, holding them in his left hand with his elbow on the top edge of the port side plating, looking aft over *Grebe*'s smashed stern. With nothing shooting at those shore guns now – *Vindictive* and the others had left the mole some time ago – they were using the two old thirty-knotters for target-practice.

Wreaking some vengeance, perhaps, for the indignity their side had suffered, the rape of their stronghold.

Perhaps I'm being stupid? Perhaps there's no point in this now?

No alternative, though. Badly wounded men drowned, when a ship sank. *Bravo* and *Grebe* had more dead and wounded now than they had fit and living. Less than half *Bravo*'s crew of sixty were on their feet.

Salvo scorching in now. He met Garfield's impassive stare. Behind the coxswain, young York. York had taken over from Elkington, who was dead. There wasn't anything one could do, except struggle on. At what – two knots? The only miracle that he could think of that anyone could have prayed for was the Goeben guns to run out of ammunition. It wasn't really likely. Nick said, 'One thing – they'll have to give us a new ship, after this.'

Garfield's raised eyebrow managed to climb another centimetre, then dropped back. He muttered, 'Don't make 'em like this no more, sir.'

'You think that's *bad*?'

Jowitt laughed. The shells came down in a hoarse rush ending in leaping fountains of black sea and a streak of flame across both ships, clap of thunder under your feet and inside your skull, stink of explosive and fried metal: on the starboard side abaft the bridge yellow flames danced, crackling and spurting, leaping to throw the foremast into silhouette. The yard had gone and most

302

of the rigging with it, the rest hanging in a tangle of steel-wire rope, halyards and aerial wires, but the mast still stood. Nick realized that the yellow burning was a cordite fire; bits of it were springing in the air, landing elsewhere and continuing to burn. Ready-use cartridges at the starboard for'ard six-pounder. He called to York, 'Sub – go round the guns and dump all the ready-use. Cartridges specially. Over the side.'

'Aye aye, sir!'

'*Bravo, ahoy!*'

Hatton-Jones was bawling through a megaphone as the shell-stink blew clear. Nick found his down by his feet. Moving was a strange business: you forced your limbs to travel in a desired direction, but when it started it felt like floating, lacking support or contact with the surroundings. He was up again, with the megaphone.

'Everard here. You all right?'

Hatton-Jones shouted, 'You'd better leave me. Cast off and get out of it.'

'What about your wounded?'

Shouting hurt him. He looked aft. 'Sub, wait here!' York came back from the ladder; there was a considerable gap in the bridge screening there at its head. He asked Hatton-Jones, 'Can you send them over to us?'

Garfield shouted, 'Captain, sir!'

Nick turned, looked at him. The coxswain was pointing out to port, across *Grebe*'s smoking, shattered waist. Nick saw, by starshell light, a streak of white. Broken sea, some sort of—

'CMB, sir!'

He let the megaphone drop and put his glasses up. Left arm doing all the work. It *was* a CMB. One's mind was slow-moving, sluggish; one had to drive

303

it, prod it. What could – well, take off some of the
wounded, or—

Smoke!

Streaming from that racing, leaping boat's exhaust:
lovely, heavy, Brock-type smoke! Jowitt cheered suddenly, a cowboyish whoop of joy. Garfield snarled,
'Quiet, you silly—'

'Sub.' Nick told York, 'Go down and empty all the
shot-ready racks. Then see to the wires, see if anything
needs adjusting or doubling-up. Look for fraying, and
see the fenders are still in place. All right?'

Flashes of clarity. York was grinning as he turned
away, looking at the CMB as she passed astern, rocketing
by to spread her blessed smoke between these destroyers
and the shore. Well inshore, plenty of room for it to
drift out astern of them as they dragged themselves
away like crippled animals. The CMB might even hang
around, be at hand to lay another streak if that lot
blew away.

It was all they'd needed. There'd been no hope of
getting it, and the MLs had all been fully occupied
getting the blockships' crews away. The launches had
been packed to capacity, and it was obvious that a
lot of the blockships' passage-crew stokers *had* defied
orders and stayed on board . . . Shell-splashes sprang
up way off on the quarter: the Hun gunners were trying
to knock out the CMB now.

'*Grebe*, ahoy!'

'Yes, Everard?'

'Shall we proceed now, sir?'

Waiting for the answer, he leant against the plating
and shut his eyes, whispered in his brain, *Thank you,
God* . . .

*　　*　　*

304

More motion on them now, as the linked ships struggled seawards in a stiffening breeze. Crashing together, lurching, scraping ... 'Like two junk-yards 'aving a go', Garfield had rumbled. York had nearly split his sides. York said now, with binoculars at his eyes, 'Looks like *Warwick* coming back in, sir. The admiral.'

Nick was on the stool. They'd lashed it to the binnacle for him. He slid off it, moved to the side of the bridge and got his glasses up. He wasn't certain, but he felt as if he might have been asleep. Perhaps only for a second? Otherwise he'd surely have toppled off the stool.

It was *Warwick*, all right. Garfield said approvingly, 'Come to round us strays up, sir. Gath'ring 'is flock.'

Nick was remembering how a month or so ago, when he'd been getting to know his new coxswain and to like him, he'd asked him one day, 'What year did you join the Navy?' Garfield had told him, 'Nineteen-oh-three, sir.' Nick had thought, *When I was seven* ... He'd asked another question: 'Why did you? What made you join?' The coxswain had glanced down at his boots, frowned, looked up again. He'd answered with one word: ' 'unger, sir.'

The Navy was made of men like Garfield.

Warwick passing close ... Daylight coming rapidly: the Belgian coast was a low black line with a haze of mauve-tinted dawn behind it. Nick had come back to the binnacle, but the stool seemed about twelve feet high. He let himself slide down, sat on the step and leant back against the binnacle's round solidity. He shut his eyes. Garfield said quietly, 'Sub-lieutenant, sir ...'

Warwick had flashed, *I am ordering Moloch to stand by you. What is your situation?* Jowitt was using a hand-lamp; the twenty-inch had been blown overboard a long time ago. Raikes, the gunner (T), was crouching beside Nick. 'You all right, sir?' York looked down at him: 'Get McAllister and a stretcher, gunner, would you?' He turned to Jowitt, and told him, 'Make to Warwick: Bravo *towing* Grebe. Believe can make Dover if weather holds. Very heavy casualties. Captain has just succumbed to wounds. Sub-lieutenant York assuming command.

Jowitt wanted to know how to spell 'succumbed'.

Sarah had said in her letter, *There is something I must tell you, because I must share it with someone and I believe that you, my dearest Nick, will at least try to understand. Please? You may remember that I introduced an old friend to you – Alastair Kinloch-Stuart, a major in one of the Highland regiments, here some months ago. Since then he has visited several times in this neighbourhood, and I cannot pretend otherwise than that his purpose has been to be close to me. I have not, I admit it and beg you to understand the circumstances, been as firm as I know I should have been in preventing this. He was such a very old friend, my family and his were on almost cousinly terms when he and I were only children. But – Nick, my dear, I should like to be speaking to you about this, not struggling to describe it so inadequately in a letter – he fell in love with me, and I have always had a high and warm regard for him; he was a good and honourable person and had no despicable intentions, indeed it was in some ways an agony for us both, and all the worse, that is to say more difficult for me at least to – oh, Nick, I am only saying what you know so well, that your father and I have not made the great thing of our marriage that I had hoped we should and intended. I must not ramble on, although I could scribble and scribble and still not tell you half of what I have in my heart and in my brain, of*

306

my feelings and deep sadness. But I did nothing wrong, Nick, ever. I promise you. And now poor Alastair has been killed in action. It was on March 22nd when the enemy broke through south of the Somme. Alastair had written a letter addressed to me, and it was brought to me here by his sister, to whom he had entrusted it. Now I have wept again. Nick, you are the one person on whose sympathy and love I place reliance: please come as soon as you can – please, Nick dear?

McAllister was crouching beside him. Two sailors were opening the folding stretcher, placing it where they could lift him on to it.

Garfield asked without moving his eyes from the lubber's line, 'Will he be all right, sir?'

The surgeon-probationer looked up. He gestured to the stretcher-bearers. Rising to his feet, he answered slowly, emphatically, 'If he does *not* become "all right", cox'n, you may shoot me.'

The coxswain looked at him, and nodded.

'You said that, sir. There's some might 'old you to it.'

Nick murmured, 'Sarah. Oh, Sarah.'

McAllister and York exchanged glances. Nick spoke again; he'd been away somewhere, but for the moment he was back.

'Sub.'

'Yes, sir?'

'We're supposed to rendezvous at Thornton Roads. North-west for fifteen miles. Don't forget the tide. Transfer the tow when you get a chance.'

'Aye aye, sir.' They were lifting the stretcher, with Nick on it. York added, 'But now you – take it *easy*, sir, don't—'

Garfield laughed. Sudden, explosive. Then he was

himself again – stolid, not even smiling. McAllister and York were staring at him, wondering what had caused that uncharacteristic bark of mirth. He wasn't bothering to explain.

INTO THE FIRE

Alexander Fullerton

Summer 1943, and Rosie Ewing is leaving on her second mission to German-occupied France. She's a Special Operations Executive agent and a 'pianist' – Resistance slang for a radio operator – and with pianists' average life in the field currently six weeks, it's hardly surprising she's shaking.

Her brief is to set up a new network in Rouen, where the one agent still at large is suspected of having betrayed his colleagues. She's to be landed from a gunboat in a remote cove on the Brittany coast, then to get to Paris by train, carrying forged papers, a radio transceiver and more than a million francs in cash. Terrifyingly vulnerable, she knows the dangers of a second's carelessness or treachery, and the consequences of crumbling under the force of Gestapo torture . . .

RETURN TO THE FIELD

Alexander Fullerton

Spring of 1944, and Rosie Ewing, a 'pianist' (radio operator) in Special Operations Executive, is returning to German-occupied France. By air, this time.

She's carrying a radio, half a million francs, a pistol and two cyanide capsules, to Finistere in north-west Brittany. With D-Day looming, and the Maquis still dangerously under-armed, part of her brief is to organise immediate paradrops of weaponry, while there's also a chateau used as a rest-home for U-boat crews, where naval top brass periodically foregather; Bomber Command needs only a date and a few days' notice.

Rosie knows, though, that the man who'll be meeting her on the ground tonight may be a traitor, that a frighteningly large number of agents have been arrested recently, and that the likely end of the road for female agents is Ravensbruck – or l'enfer des femmes, as the Resistance calls it . . .

THE BLOODING OF THE GUNS

Alexander Fullerton

At 2.28 pm on the last day of May 1916, in the grey windswept North Sea off the coast of Jutland, the fire-gongs ring.

The champions: Sir John Jellicoe with his battle squadrons out of Scapa and Cromarty, and Sir David Beatty with his battlecruisers from Rosyth: one hundred and fifty ships, and sixty thousand men. Six thousand of them are to die.

The challengers: Admirals von Scheer and Hipper, with the Kaiser's High Seas Fleet. A hundred ships, and forty-five thousand men.

The Blooding of the Guns is the first title in Alexander Fullerton's acclaimed Nicholas Everard series of novels. It is also an extremely dramatic and meticulously researched novel of a uniquely fascinating sea battle. The reader shares the excitement, fear and anxiety of those who fought at Jutland: this is how it felt to be in a tiny destroyer racing to launch torpedoes into a line of dreadnoughts' blazing guns: this is how men fought inside a battleship's fifteen-inch turret: or on the bridge of a cruiser under pulverising bombardment. This *is* battle at sea.